AFTER ...
Barbara's Story

Leslie Johnson

AFTER … Barbara's Story

PUBLISHED BY:

Leslie Johnson

Ebook ISBN 978-1-0693588-3-7
Paperback ISBN 978-1-0693588-6-8
Hardcover ISBN 978-1-0696989-0-2

AFTER ... Barbara's Story
Copyright © 2025 by Leslie Johnson

DEDICATION

To my writing family, The River Bottom Writers, who have been invaluable in assisting me in bringing my stories to life. You are my best champions.

AFTER ... Barbara's Story

ACKNOWLEDGMENTS

The publishing of AFTER … Barbara's Story has been a long journey. Barbara's Story was more fun to write than my first novel. She is a very different character, and I loved putting her into situations that forced her to look at her choices and her behavior. The words I chose to shape the lovely Barbara were an adventure of their own.

I want to thank the writing pals from my writing group who joined me on weekend mornings to work on their projects while I wrote this book. Brock and Shannon, I still miss those days. The adventures we had as we worked on our projects, the people we saw every week, and those who became friends were times I remember fondly.

My writing group was also valuable to the process as well. They listened to my chapters and provided vital feedback. Weekly, I edited and shared my chapters, and you always listened and provided your wisdom and construction comments.

Thanks to Cindy Roberts who read an early version and provided me with her thoughts and feedback.

Finally, I would like to thank my editor, Jonas Saul, for reading and editing my words to strengthen them and make them more powerful. You have helped me bring my childhood dream to fruition. You have been encouraging and helpful with your insight into the writing process and you feedback. Thank you, thank you, thank you.

CHAPTER ONE

Sweat beaded my brow as I stepped off the treadmill, grabbed my towel, and mopped my face before heading to the changing room. I spent my workout thinking about Bobby's proposal and still hadn't decided. There was much at stake.

Several women were in the changing room, putting me on edge. I never knew how to be around women. Men, though, I knew how to handle.

Bobby was all man. I'd known about him most of my life. Everyone knew the Grahams, one of the founding families of our small city of Crawford. I learned more about him when I was working at the Skylight Lounge. We danced the dance for a long time before he ever made a move on me. I had thought he wasn't interested and was nothing but a flirt. He treated me like a lady, never undressing me with his eyes, which men do when looking to conquer a woman. However, when he acted on his desires, I discovered he was well worth the wait.

We'd been together for a little less than a year. I thoroughly enjoyed his company. He was funny and witty and very attentive in the bedroom. I almost envied his wife, Thelma, the permanent place in his bed, but I pulled myself back from going there. I didn't need that sort of entanglement again. After my last fiasco, I vowed never to live with another man. It wasn't worth the headache.

Three nights ago, after a rambunctious couple of hours together, he had offered me a suite at the Ivory Towers in exchange for exclusive rights. The Ivory Towers was the latest project for Graham Ventures, a pretentious condo development next to the golf course. He wasn't promising the penthouse suite but an apartment with a view. The offer dumbfounded me, even though I should have expected it. He'd grown more and more possessive in the last few months. Not that he was acting jealous, but he was vocal about not wanting to share.

I pulled my purse from the locker. As a force of habit, I checked my cell phone to see if I had any messages. I hoped that one day, my daughter, Andrea, would send me a text message or call me to meet for coffee. I wanted to reestablish a relationship with her, but she rebuffed my suggestions, claiming she was too busy to meet.

Kevin, Andrea's father, told me she was dating someone. I hadn't met the young man yet and hoped our first introduction would not be at their wedding. That level of callousness would crush me, even though I might deserve it.

The red circle by the phone icon showed I had missed ten calls, but there were no voicemails. Looking at the call log, it was Kevin's number. That was highly unusual. Kevin was adamant about leaving messages, but he hadn't this time. As I scrolled down the call log, I noticed that Kevin was the only caller during the last fifty minutes. My heart sped up, and I found it hard to breathe.

I sat on the bench across from my locker, my head swimming and my hands shaking as I pushed the telephone icon next to his name. The call went to voicemail. Dammit. I ended the call and dialed again. Voicemail. I continued to do this, the sense of foreboding building in my core. Anger and annoyance strengthened me.

I left the changing room when I couldn't stand the suspense a moment longer. Moving quickly, I pulled the door open with fury. A young girl entering stumbled and righted herself.

"Oh!" she exclaimed. "I'm so sorry, so very sorry."

I looked at her, confused. What was she apologizing for? My mind was elsewhere, tripping through hazardous thoughts. I walked across the gym, dialing Kevin's number again. This time, he answered.

"Hello, Barbara. Where are you?"

"I'm at the gym. Why? What's going on?"

"I would like you to come over."

"Why? What's going on?" I asked again. My nerves were about to explode.

"Just come over."

"No, tell me what's going on." My voice was shrill. "It's Andrea, isn't it? She's been in a car accident. Oh my God. Shouldn't I go to the hospital?"

"Barbara!" Kevin shouted, trying to gain my full attention.

My mind spiraled again. My legs stopped working as my knees weakened. I looked around for a place to sit. I stood near the recumbent bicycles, so I sat on a vacant one, turning my back on the woman, pedaling furiously on the one next to it. Trying to control my galloping emotions, I bent over, taking deep, slow breaths. Something was dreadfully wrong. I knew it. I felt it.

"Kevin, please just tell me what's going on."

Sighing deeply, he spoke, but his voice caught in his throat. He stopped, took a labored breath, and cleared his throat. "Andrea …" His voice cracked again. He choked on a sob, and I knew what he was going to say. Now, I didn't want him to say it. I wanted to plug my ears so I wouldn't have to hear the words.

I looked around wildly. Everyone stared at me. They were whispering, too. I averted my gaze and focused on the floor at my feet. Kevin was still trying to control his emotions. "She's dead, isn't she?" I whispered.

"Yes!" He howled like a wounded animal. That sound pierced my brain, and all my thoughts exploded. The shrapnel of my hopes and dreams for Andrea shredded the soft tissue of my heart. The pain was immediate and everlasting. Life as I knew it would never be the same. My world tilted, and I slid right off.

My phone fell to the floor. I looked at it, not sure what it was doing there. I recognized it as my phone and bent to pick it up. It seemed a long way off, so I slipped onto my knees as I reached for it. Everything was happening in slow motion as I maneuvered sideways into a sitting position, my phone in my hand. My purse dropped to the floor beside me. I was unaware of my surroundings outside of my phone, which I now held loosely in my hand. I heard Kevin talking faintly from far away. His voice sounded metallic and sharp. I couldn't understand where it came from.

A blurry figure kneeled in front of me. It was Gavin, the owner of the gym. I couldn't see his face—everything was out of focus. His signature white T-shirt and bulging biceps were mesmerizing, like snow drifting in the wind. He waved his hand in front of my face. I watched it, moving my head to follow it from side to side. He reached down and tried to take the phone from my hand. I gripped it more firmly, pulling my hand away.

"Barbie! Barbie!" He snapped his fingers. I jerked back as if he'd snapped me with an elastic. "Barbie!"

I looked at him, blinking furiously to focus. His face appeared from the blur surrounding an aura of black. I kept blinking. "Are you okay?"

I took a breath before looking around. Where was I? Why was I on the floor? My thoughts jumped from idea to idea. I was at the gym. Had I completed my workout? I tried hard to remember. A memory of nearly running into the young girl in the locker room flashed into my mind. Yes, I was leaving. My phone. I was on my phone. Where was my phone?

I glanced down and spotted it in my hand. I pulled it closer. It was still engaged. Displayed on the screen was Kevin's picture and number. Reality flooded back in. I put the phone to my ear. "Kevin?"

"Barbara! Are you okay?"

I nodded. "Yes, I'm okay. I'm on my way." I stood.

Gavin reached over and helped me rise. I wobbled a bit but then pulled myself together. Someone handed me my purse. I took it without thanking them. I dropped my phone into the depths, shouldered the purse, and turned toward the door. Walking with dignity, my head held high, I left the facility and went to my car. I realized once inside that I hadn't thanked Gavin, either.

CHAPTER TWO

I drove to Kevin's on autopilot. I don't remember the drive—visions of Andrea consumed my thoughts. Seeing my daughter as a baby, then a toddler. Watching from outside myself on the day I left home for good. I remember her clinging to me, screaming. Her chubby red cheeks were scarlet with emotion. I shoved her away roughly into the arms of Mrs. Cunningham, our next-door neighbor. Then I turned and walked out the door. Hating myself for leaving her, the loathing I felt as I drove across the city grew with each passing block. I had abandoned my precious, darling girl, and now I would never make that right. It was too late—I had waited too long. Why had I not fought harder to get back into her life? Because she was only nineteen, and I thought I had time.

The roller-coaster picked up speed as I neared Kevin's house. I pulled in, not bothering to park straight but angling my vehicle across the driveway. Once parked, I lurched from the car, careening up the walkway to the front door. I left the car door open—the chime pinging because I hadn't even turned off the engine.

Kevin opened the door before I arrived. I stumbled up the two steps and fell into him. He wrapped his powerful arms around me and pulled me into the house, closing out the world when he slammed the door behind us.

Once inside, feeling safe, I let go of the torrent that threatened to consume me. I didn't know the details, but her loss was acute. Too much to bear alone. When I'd drained the cistern, I pulled back, gulping fresh air. I looked at Kevin—really looked at him for the first time in such a long time. His face was much older. Lifelines creased his once smooth complexion. Gray hair sprinkled his well-groomed stubble, but his blue eyes, though, were just as deep as they had been the first time we'd met. Shame washed over me as I recognized his love for me shining in them. Avoiding his undeserved emotions, I looked away, searching the room for pictures of Andrea.

After rising to get her graduation picture off the mantle, I brought the framed photo back to the couch. My fingers caressed her image as my emotions settled into something manageable. I felt ready to know how my baby had died. I wondered if she had been the driver or the passenger. Had she experienced much pain? Sniffing loudly, I turned back to Kevin. "So, what happened?"

Before he answered, his phone rang. He picked it up off the coffee table, looked at the caller ID, and put it back down.

"You not getting that?"

"No, I will call them back." I nodded and waited expectantly for him to answer.

Kevin looked at me, his blue eyes welling up again. I waited. "It was murder."

"Pardon me?" I shook my head. "Say that again. I don't think I heard you right."

"You heard me right. It was murder." He whispered it, trying to soften the blow.

"Who?" I snapped, my voice shrill and harsh. Kevin flinched.

"That boy she was dating. He took her out into the country and shot her."

Mental pictures whirled across my mind like a fast-moving slide show. "Where is he? Has he …? Can we …? I mean … I want … Could we …?"

Kevin shook his head back and forth slowly. "He's dead too. He killed himself."

The horror of what happened reached into my chest and squeezed hard. I brought my arms up, hugging the portrait to my body. The pain was so sharp—I thought I might die, too. For one moment, I wanted to. I wanted to lie down on the floor and die so I could be with Andrea. "Oh, God!" I murmured. "Oh, my God!" I repeated over and over, my tone getting softer with each utterance. The reality was harsher than I ever imagined.

"Why?" My voice broke. "Why would he do that?"

"I don't know. The police have some theories, but they haven't finished their investigation. They said they'd tell us more if they discovered anything new."

Fresh tears rolled down my cheek. It was surreal and unreal, and I wanted to wake up. I wanted to be in bed, stretching my limbs before fully waking. I went back to a few hours ago, waking in my bed and thinking of Bobby Graham and his offer. I couldn't decide whether that was real—or this was. It was too much to take in. Drowning in this soupy, enigmatic world, I didn't want to be here. If I stayed, I would not survive.

With every ounce of strength I had, I shoved all my emotions down. Struggling with the lid, I soon had all those rogue and unwanted feelings contained. My soul was empty, but I was in control. I was all business, just as I had been all my life. My emotions were too real—locking them away was how I survived.

I sat up straighter. "We need to organize a proper funeral. She deserves something grand and beautiful, something worthy of her. I want it to be memorable and powerful. Her memory needs to be burned into the heart of this city for the sacrifice she made for all women. She is a martyr. Her life needs to be celebrated."

Kevin looked at me like I'd lost my mind. In all the years I'd known him, with all the stunts I pulled, he had never shown his dismay before. "Slow down, Barbara. We have time."

"I know, but there is much to do. I want it to be perfect."

"It will be." He grabbed one of my hands and pulled it toward him. We sat there locked like that, staring at each other. Then Kevin broke away. He stood and crossed the room. "I'm going to go out and park your car and bring you the keys. You left it running with the door open."

I closed my eyes and took a deep breath as Kevin walked out the front door. A few minutes later, he came back inside carrying my purse. "Someone turned off the ignition and closed your door. Thankfully, they didn't lock it, or we would be calling AMA. I put the keys in here." He handed me the purse. I took it and dropped it on the floor at my feet.

The phone rang again. This time, Kevin answered the call, walking out of the room as he whispered. I sat there, staring at nothing. My thoughts were racing. I planned to put all the glamor and glitz I would have wanted at my daughter's wedding into her funeral. She needed enormous flowers, a venue worthy of her, and a choir. I pictured her laid out in a Cinderella gown, wearing a tiara. A white coffin? Yes, I liked it. I grabbed my purse and searched through it for something to write on. Finding an old pay stub envelope, I scrounged for a pen with light purple ink. It would do—I made a list.

Kevin came back, but I didn't look up. I was busy scribbling down details. He sat beside me, trying to get a look at what I was writing. "Barbara, what is this?"

"It's her funeral. I want the best for her. Look!" I handed him the list, pointing halfway down with the pen. "See, we rent the Carver

Theater and put her on the stage. It would be perfect." I looked up at him, expecting to see a smile. Instead, there was sadness in his eyes.

"This is touching, Barbara, very touching, but it will not work."

"Why not?" I snapped.

"Well, for one thing, who's going to pay for it? I certainly don't have the money to pay for this, and I doubt you have a load of cash under your mattress."

"No, but I could sell my jewelry. We could make it work."

He was shaking his head, looking sadder by the minute.

"Barbara—he shot her in the back of the head. They can't put her back together well enough to lay her out like Cinderella. We cannot have an open coffin for her."

"Okay, okay, okay." I snatched the list back and scratched off that line. "We could still have the white coffin, though."

He was shaking his head, and I was losing my temper with his stubbornness. "Come on, Kevin, she was our daughter."

"I know that, and I don't want to argue with you about this, but we will not make this a big splash. Even if we could afford it, it is garish. It's almost like you're planning her wedding, not her funeral. It's …" He didn't finish his thought.

I sat there open-mouthed, staring at him. How could he be so obtuse? Didn't he understand that this was the last thing we were going to do for her? The last thing she needed us to do. "Fine! If you won't help me, I will find someone who will." I jumped off the couch, grabbed my purse, and stormed toward the front door.

"Barbara!" Kevin called as I pulled open the door. I turned back, expecting him to tell me he had changed his mind.

When he stayed silent, I yelled at him, "I am her mother! I know what's best for her."

"Just like you knew what was best sixteen years ago when you walked out?"

Not once in all the years we'd been apart had Kevin ever berated or chastised me for my decision to leave the family. I always thought that he supported my decision one hundred percent. He was the only person in the world who ever seemed to understand me, and now he was using it against me.

"How dare you, Kevin!" I spat those words from across the room. "How dare you throw that back in my face!"

CHAPTER THREE

As Kevin's words rang in my ears, the lid blew off my carefully packed emotions, and a rage burst out of me. I grabbed the door that had swung partway closed and slammed it open with all my might. It hit the wall hard and bounced back. I nearly collided with the edge, stopping myself just in time.

I grabbed that door, and using all my strength, I shoved it back against the wall. Then I pulled it toward me and shoved it back again. And again, and again and again. A low, guttural growl ripped from my throat, rising in pitch with every shove. My screams fueled my anger and gave me strength as I raged out of control.

Part of me, something deep inside, recognized this, but I couldn't stop. I wanted to destroy something, anything. Starting with this door, then the wall behind it, I would rip, tear, and shred until I destroyed this world. I stepped back, feeling the door jamb against my spine. Leaning on it, I kicked the door with my right foot, repeating this until I was exhausted. I slid to the floor, panting. The door swung toward me, seemingly unscathed. Using my foot, I pushed it open and held it there.

Kevin came over. Feeling his stare, I refused to look back. I was gasping for air. I couldn't get enough. Bending over me, Kevin blew in my face. Air rushed into my lungs. Deep sobs racked my body as I cried. Exhausted from my fight with the door, I rolled face-first onto the floor. The chilly October air swept over me, freezing me to the bone. My teeth chattered. Reaching down, Kevin pulled me into a sitting position. With ease, he hoisted me up and over his shoulder.

He took me down to the bathroom, where he sat me on the closed toilet lid while he ran a bath. He grabbed a bottle from under the sink and poured a generous amount into the flow. The aroma of lavender filled the room. I sat there shivering, convulsing with the chill that had filled me. Setting the bottle on the vanity top, he turned to me. He stripped my clothes off, treating me like a toddler. Naked and shivering, he helped him into the hot, foamy water. The heat was offensive as I sank into the tub. My body adjusted, and tension leaked from every pore. As I leaned back, the cold porcelain shocked me for a second. Then I eased deeper under the water and closed my eyes, tears still streaming down my cheeks.

Kevin left and returned with his terry towel bathrobe—the new one I'd given him for Christmas last year. It looked unworn. He left without a word, closing the door behind him. I stayed in the tub for a long time, releasing the cold and replacing it with hotter water from time to time. Finally, with fingers and toes pruned beyond recognition, I emerged and toweled myself dry. Wrapping myself in that large robe, I went to the kitchen.

I smelled something good, and my tummy rumbled. I realized I had eaten nothing since yesterday. There was a pot of soup simmering on the stove's back burner. Kevin stood in front, flipping over a grilled cheese sandwich, done to perfection. He looked at me as I came into the room. "You hungry?"

I nodded.

"Take a seat." I pulled out a stool from the raised eating bar and sat, watching him work. He ladled some soup into an oversized bowl, setting it in front of me. It was a creamy tomato—my favorite. A spoon and a sleeve of crackers appeared. I crumbled some into the bowl, then bent low to sniff the aroma. It smelled homey and delicious. I dug in.

Kevin set a cup of tea, a grilled cheese sandwich, and the ketchup bottle beside me. He stood across from me, dipping his grilled cheese into his bowl of soup. I smiled, grateful for the nourishment.

When I had cleaned my plate and emptied the bowl, he spoke. "You want more?"

I shook my head. "No, this was perfect. Thank you."

We stayed on opposite sides of the counter, each lost in thought.

"Do you think she's in Heaven?" I looked at Kevin expectantly.

"Of course she is. She's one of God's angels now." Tears filled his eyes as I, too, cried again. *One of God's angels. Just like she had been ours when she was born.*

Kevin left the kitchen. I sat there thinking about Andrea and wishing I had one more chance, one more minute, once more anything with her.

Kevin came back in as I finished my tea. "Okay, I've made up the spare room. I'll get you a toothbrush." He left the room and returned with a new toothbrush still in its packaging. "There should be some toothpaste in the medicine cabinet."

I didn't argue. It seemed normal that I would be here tonight. I went into the bathroom, found the toothpaste, and brushed my teeth. Staring at myself in the mirror, I noticed lines that weren't there yesterday. I had aged, but for reasons I couldn't understand—it didn't frighten me. It seemed natural here in this house.

When I exited the bathroom, I crossed the hall to the spare room. It was clinical in its sparseness, devoid of personality. Kevin had turned down the covers on the double bed. I walked over and sat down. I listened to the sounds of Kevin finishing up in the ensuite.

The water was running, the tink, tink, tink as he tapped his toothbrush on the basin's edge. I sat there waiting, staring out into the hallway.

The light in his room went out. I leaned over and shut off the light in my room, too, but I didn't lie down. I sat there watching the empty hall, lit only by the eerie blue glow of the night light in the outlet outside Andrea's room. A minute passed, then another. I rose, walking out of the room, down the hall, and around the corner into Kevin's room, the master bedroom. In the moon's dim light shining through the curtainless window, his shape under the covers was visible. He was on his side, facing away from the door.

I stared for a minute. He must have sensed my presence because he turned over, looking toward me. Then, he flipped back the covers on the other side of the bed. I moved into the room, dropped my robe to the floor, and climbed into bed next to him.

I slipped under the covers and scooted close, unable to describe my need—it was deep and urgent. He repositioned himself as I reached for him, pulling me closer. Kissing me on the lips, he was gentle, almost uncertain. I kissed him back. Sensing my urgency, he kissed me again, deeper this time, with more confidence. I groaned, and Kevin switched positions, moving over me. I let go, and I lost myself in the heat between us. It was as if we'd never been apart. We were lovers again, tasting and touching, moving together until I couldn't take any more. I needed him—I needed to feel like a woman, to feel alive and loved. I shifted to take him in as we danced the dance of a thousand lovers before us, finding our rhythm.

It was natural and perfect, erotic and fulfilling. When I went over the edge, he came with me. The experience was so beautiful, my emotions so fragile, that when it was over, I crumpled into tears.

Transferring to his side, Kevin pulled me close, spooning me. He wrapped his arms around me and let me cry, nuzzling my ear and whispering unintelligible words. The sound, though, was soothing, and soon, I drifted off to sleep.

AFTER … Barbara's Story

CHAPTER FOUR

Disturbing images filled my dreams, but the moment I opened my eyes, they disappeared like smoke in the wind. I sat up. I was alone. The aroma of coffee and bacon made my stomach rumble. Kevin had picked up the robe I had dropped on the floor and laid it across the foot of the bed. I slipped it on.

On my way to the kitchen, I stopped in the bathroom. As I stood at the sink, washing my hands, I took stock as I always did when I faced a mirror. I leaned in across the sink, noticing the wrinkles again. I tugged at my skin, then stopped, thinking I was making them worse.

Sighing, I had to admit I was getting older, but I was holding together well for a thirty-eight-year-old. I smiled at myself, but it was a weak smile. Andrea's death lay heavy on my shoulders.

I headed to the kitchen, still justifying my decision to leave the family all those years ago as the right one for everyone. The unanswered question would haunt me forever—would I have done the same thing had I known I wouldn't have a lifetime to make it up to her?

Kevin heard me coming. He poured me a cup of black coffee and handed it to me as I settled on the same stool I'd occupied last night. "You want any breakfast?" I shook my head. "Didn't think so."

He scraped the pan of fried potatoes and scrambled eggs onto a plate of bacon. He picked up a smaller plate with four strips of bacon on it. This he placed in front of me. "I know from experience that you will steal my bacon if you don't have some of your own. So, this is for you."

Before I responded, he crossed to the fridge and pulled out a ketchup bottle. He squirted a liberal amount on his eggs and potatoes. Then he grabbed a cup of coffee and treated it with sugar and cream before taking the stool next to me.

As I nibbled on my bacon, I watched Kevin dig into his breakfast, reminding me of our years together. He always had an appetite in the morning. He loved to eat and attacked his food with gusto, savoring each bite. I stole another glance at him out of the corner of my eye. Dressed in a white T-shirt and his flannel pajama bottoms, he still cut a handsome figure. He may not have been as firm as twenty years ago, but he'd held together well. His job as a cabinet maker kept him trim with its physicality.

He made a decent living, but he would not die a millionaire. What I admired most, though, was that he was content with it all. He worked on what he wanted to, fiddling with restorations and building beautiful furniture. Items with character. He often smelled like sawdust even after he showered. It was in his blood. A rush of affection warmed me, and I wanted to lean over and wrap my arms around him, lean my head on his chest, and hear his heartbeat, but I couldn't. I was being silly.

Tears burned my eyes as I shoved my emotions down, sipping my tepid coffee. To avoid any more sentimentality, I slipped off my stool and walked around the counter to the coffeepot. Topping off my cup, I turned to Kevin. He held his cup toward me. I took it and added sugar and cream to it before pouring the last of the coffee into his mug. "Should I make more?"

"Not for me, thanks. Two is my limit."

Setting the carafe back on the burner, I turned off the unit before unplugging it. It was Tuesday morning—I was supposed to work tonight. That meant that I would have to get a quick nap this afternoon. Should I go to work? I couldn't imagine hanging around my apartment alone. What was Kevin doing? If he was going to stay home, maybe I should too, but I didn't want to be in his way. I moved back onto my stool.

"We need to talk about the funeral," Kevin said, removing his cleaned plate to the lower level of the counter in front of him. While taking a sip of coffee, he turned toward me, his blue-green eyes searching my face.

I nodded. A good night's sleep had made me see things more clearly. I was ashamed of my actions yesterday. I realized that in my grief—I was trying to make things up to her. But it was too late for that now. Sadness blanketed me. It was too late for anything.

"I was talking with a police constable, and he recommended we contact Penny Franklin at Franklin's Funeral Chapel. He thinks it's going to be a big turnout. Andrea was a popular girl, and the police think there will be a large community presence just based on how she died. People will be curious, and if we advertise, we'll get onlookers. If we don't advertise, people who knew her and want to pay their respects might be missed. It's a double-edged sword." He paused for a moment, gathering his thoughts. "Anyway, apparently, this funeral place has access to this large church next door for larger funerals. There's some connection between the businesses. Hopefully, they can accommodate us."

Tears pricked my eyes again. I didn't know my daughter at all. Did I have any right to plan this? Feeling sorry for myself, I cut off my nose to spite my face. "Whatever you think, Kevin. I really didn't know her well enough to have any valuable input."

Kevin set his jaw. He didn't get angry often. He was the most easygoing man I'd ever met, but I had crossed the line. "This isn't about you, Barbara. This is about our daughter, and as her mother, you have a right to share this."

Ashamed again, I let the tears roll down my cheeks. Kevin reached over and squeezed my shoulder with his hand. "I know, I know." He placated. "We'll do this together."

I leaned into him, and he took me in his arms. I lay there against his chest, breathing in his scent and wishing I hadn't walked away all those years ago. It seemed like the right thing to do back then. Sitting here today, feeling close to Kevin for the first time since I left, I doubted that decision was best for any of us.

I pulled away, and Kevin let me go. He moved off his stool, walked to the far counter, and returned with a box of tissues. I dried my eyes and blew my nose.

He picked up the cordless receiver and, referring to a yellow sticky note, he dialed the phone. The phone at his ear, he kept his eyes on me. "Good morning. This is Kevin Pritchard. My wife." He paused and cleared his throat. "I mean, my ex-wife and I would like to come in and talk to Mrs. Franklin." He looked away, listening to the person on the other end of the phone. "Well, this morning, if we could."

He looked directly at me. "One o'clock?" He lifted his eyebrows at me. I nodded. "Yes, that would work. Thank you."

It was time to go home. I couldn't wear my exercise outfit, which was all I had. As Kevin hung up, I said, "I'm going home to get ready. Do you want to pick me up, or should I just meet you there?"

"I'll come and get you."

"Thank you." I hadn't wanted to go alone to the funeral chapel, but I would have. I appreciated Kevin was making this easy for me.

I found my clothes in the spare room neatly laundered and folded on the bed. When had he done this? My heart burst again. He was making this hard for me. Why couldn't he just be a jerk? Why did he always have to take such good care of me?

I dressed as tears flowed down my cheeks. I wiped my tears, angry that I had allowed Kevin to get to me. Fully dressed, I crossed the hall to the bathroom. I splashed some water on my face, brushed my hair, and pinched my cheeks to add color. When I was ready, I walked to the front door and put on my shoes.

As I tied the laces, Kevin appeared. He watched me, saying nothing. When I stood up, he smiled. "I'll be there at twelve-thirty."

I nodded, pulled open the door, and left. He stood in the doorway for only a second, watching me. As I rounded the corner of the garage, I heard the door close.

I looked back, feeling, for the first time since yesterday, like I was all alone in the world. Alone! Then I remembered that this was how I wanted it. I liked my freedom—I didn't want to be encumbered. Losing my daughter was making me feel melancholy. It was grief attaching itself to Kevin, not genuine feelings. And for his part, he was comforting me—just as I was giving it back to him. I was attaching too much significance to what had happened last night. It was nothing more than taking solace in his arms—in feeling alive. It was not to be confused with love.

I started the engine. As I backed out of the driveway, Bobby Graham's smiling face slid into my mind. That's better, I thought. Bobby Graham will look after me with no strings attached, no encumbrances, no expectations.

Continuing to work at the job I loved, I would live in an elegant apartment overlooking the golf course, where I rubbed shoulders with influential and powerful people. I occasionally had a man to satisfy my physical needs, but not underfoot. Driving across town to my apartment, I made my decision. I was going to take Bobby up on his offer.

Bobby Graham was my future. Kevin Pritchard was my past. He'd been sweet to me but only did it because I was Andrea's mother.

I reminded myself to have no illusions that it was anything more than that.

CHAPTER FIVE

I found it frustrating that Kevin was still on my mind after making my decision. In the shower, I wondered again, as I had over the years, why he had never remarried. I never asked him. Maybe because I didn't want to know the answer. At that moment, I decided I would encourage him to move on. He didn't deserve to be alone. He was a wonderful man, and yes, if I admitted it to myself, I loved him. I always had, and I always would. But I didn't deserve him. He needed someone to put him first, and I had never been that person. I thought of my needs before anyone else's needs. It was selfish, but if I didn't look after me, who would?

I shook off all my reverie. It wasn't healthy to wander down old roads. Look forward. Look to the future. Andrea's beautiful, smiling face flashed before me, and my knees buckled. I reached for the tub's edge and sank to my knees, letting the water pound my back. Tears ran down my cheeks, mixing with the shower water. I closed my eyes and turned my face into the spray. I stayed there for a minute, losing myself in my grief.

As it took me deeper into the pit, I couldn't deal with it—I didn't want to. It was too much to bear. Turning my face down, I gulped in air, but it was humid, unsatisfactory for my needs. I was suffocating.

I turned off the water and crawled out of the tub, wrapping a large fluffy bath towel around me. Then I hurried from the bathroom to the bedroom, where I sat on the bed, taking deep breaths of cooler air until I gained control of my runaway feelings. Even as I gained more control, I took several more breaths, consciously expanding my lungs, sucking my breath deep into my body. Calmer, I hurried to get ready. Kevin was going to be here soon.

I dried and styled my hair and applied fresh makeup. In my closet, I chose a deep red crepe dress for work—one of my favorites, with a fitted bodice and a soft flair to the skirt. I draped classic pearls around my neck with matching earrings. The sleeves reached my mid-forearm, so I chose a slim-band watch. My red heels finished the outfit. I turned and twirled in front of the full-length mirror. It was perfect.

I was switching handbags when Kevin rang the bell a minute later. I pushed the buzzer to let him up, then hurriedly finished my task before walking to the door. Before I selected an appropriate jacket, I pulled it open for Kevin. When he saw me, he smiled. "You look … amazing."

"Thank you. I'm going to work after we see the funeral director."

"You're going to work? Tonight?" He looked hurt but quickly recovered. "Yeah, I guess …"

"You guess what?" Anger rushed up to meet his disappointment. "Nothing."

I goaded him, ready to fight, maybe even needing to fight. "What, Kevin? Am I not supposed to earn a living? Am I supposed to lie in bed and cry that my daughter is gone? There is absolutely nothing I can do to bring her back, so wallowing in self-pity will not make things better."

"I'm sorry." He sounded sorry, too, diffusing my anger.

"Fine! Then let's get this over with." I said it more harshly than I meant, so I smiled at Kevin, touching his arm. "I'm sorry—I'm being bitchy."

He smiled, though his smile didn't quite reach his eyes. "It's okay. I understand. It's hard for me, too."

A rush of affection rose inside me. "Of course it is. She was your life." I stepped to the closet and pulled my long, black wool jacket off the hanger. Kevin stepped forward to help me with it. As he tugged it around my shoulders, I decided this was a good time to broach his status. "Now that she's gone, maybe you should consider finding someone to share your life with."

I turned toward him in time to see his wounded expression. It disappeared in an instant. "Let's just get Andrea taken care of, eh? That's all I can think about at the moment."

Feeling slighted for my thoughtful advice, I bristled. We left the apartment with an immense chasm between us. A raging river of disappointments, anger, confusion, bitterness, and grief rushed to fill the space—like a roiling river, engorged and dangerous. I didn't dare to cross it. I girded myself and took an emotional step back, and the chasm grew.

The ride was silent, and the radio played softly. Kevin kept his attention on the road and the journey while I stared out the side window, watching the houses pass by. I tried not to think about what was coming up or what had just happened, but I purposely considered my earlier decision.

My future awaited.

CHAPTER SIX

We pulled into the empty parking lot. Kevin parked and exited the truck. He walked over to open my door, but I opened it myself and slid to the ground unaided. As I straightened my dress, I thought about how I appreciated Kevin, who had always been a gentleman.

Stop thinking about him in glowing terms, I chastised myself. Remember, you have decided that he is your past.

Kevin took my arm as we walked up the sidewalk together. He pulled open the door and guided me inside. A large, brightly lit foyer welcomed us. It looked modern and expensive, and the expertly arranged décor implied peace and tranquility. Kevin steered me toward the left. We crossed on the soft carpet, our feet sinking into the deep synthetic fibers.

An impeccably dressed, burly man came toward us. His soft peach tie against his crisp white shirt was the only color in his outfit. He reached out his hand to Kevin. "I'm Earl Franklin. It's a pleasure to meet you, Mr. Pritchard." He nodded toward me. "Mrs. Pritchard."

I stiffened. "It's Ms. O'Shea, actually."

Without missing a beat, he smiled. "I'm sorry, Mrs. O'Shea." I took an instant dislike to him. He was sleazy and smooth. Too smooth. He had secrets he kept well hidden behind that phony exterior. I bristled even more. Kevin, sensing my mood, took charge.

"Thank you for seeing us on such short notice."

"Short notice is often how we see people. Very few deaths are planned." He appeared sympathetic, though it seemed insincere. "Please come into my office, and we can make the arrangements."

We moved into a vast open room. A few large prints graced the walls, visions of angels and Heaven in rich pastel tones. They looked out of place against the opulence of the room. A large, ornate oak desk sat at one end of the room. A few papers were sitting on the top, but otherwise, it was clean. Two heavy, black leather padded chairs sat on this side of the desk. Two more were pushed up against the wall to the left of the desk. An even larger black leather chair sat behind. The room, perhaps meant to seem warm and cozy, came across as cold and clinical, with an attitude of superiority.

Mr. Franklin moved around the desk and then gestured to the chairs in front before sitting down.

Kevin waited until I sat before sitting down. We waited as Mr. Franklin shuffled the papers, tapping them into a neat bundle. He picked up a pen, then looked up, raising his eyebrows slightly.

"So, what sort of service were you wanting? Simple, extravagant, the sky's the limit?"

Kevin cleared his throat, looked at me, and said, "Elegant, but not opulent."

Mr. Franklin nodded.

"It can be simple in its elegance," Kevin continued. "I mean, we think it should reflect who she was."

Mr. Franklin glanced my way expectantly. I shivered—unsure this was the venue I wanted for my daughter's last goodbye.

"Okay, let me show you some prices." Just like that, the funeral for our daughter became less about who she was, what we wanted, or what we wanted to share. It became more base. It became about the money. Kevin took the paper that was offered and looked at it. Then he leaned over and shared the form with me. Tears pricked my eyes when I read the least expensive package option was well over fifteen thousand dollars. Neither of us had that kind of money, not right at hand.

Kevin seemed to take it in stride. "Do we have to have it packaged like this? I'd like numbers one and two, but number three doesn't apply."

Mr. Franklin nodded as if he understood. "Certainly. We package things to make it easier. Surprisingly, so many people have not prepared for this day—yet no one gets out of here alive." He chuckled at his own joke. Neither Kevin nor I joined in, so his quip was short-lived.

"Okay then. What do you want? Let me make some notes." He opened a desk drawer and pulled out a yellow-lined notepad. With his pen poised, ready to write, he looked at us, waiting.

"Um, well ... We don't want cremation, and we thought that maybe a white casket?" Kevin checked my response. I smiled, nodding my approval.

"What about the service? Do you have a minister to officiate? Who's doing the eulogy?"

Kevin looked at me, his eyes wide. "We're not religious, so I don't know about a minister. Do we need one?"

"No, we can take care of that for you as part of our service if you like. Do you want us to do the eulogy, too?"

"I don't know. I think I'd like to speak for my daughter. I mean, I would have asked her best friend ..." He didn't finish.

"Oh right, I read that in the paper. Brenda Taylor, wasn't it? She's not being handled here," Mr. Franklin interjected.

I wanted to roll my eyes, get up, and walk out. We needed to go somewhere else. As I prepared to tell Kevin this, a tall, elegant, copper-haired woman entered the room. Her attire was casual but classy, and her classic pantsuit was crisp and feminine. She smiled warmly as I turned to her.

"Good morning. I'm Penelope Franklin. Sorry I didn't meet you when you arrived. Another family needed some attention. I trust Earl has been taking good care of you?" She smiled at Kevin before turning back to me. "Do you want coffee or something?"

With her presence, the atmosphere in the room brightened. The man behind the desk faded into the background. For the first time since we arrived, I relaxed. "I would like a coffee, please, black, no sugar."

"I'll have coffee with both," Kevin added. He looked at me and smiled. I guess he sensed the change in the room, too.

"Earl, please get our guests some coffee. Thank you."

Earl rose with a huff, and she slipped into the chair behind the desk and waited for him to leave the room.

CHAPTER SEVEN

"Now, where were you in organizing the formalities?" Mrs. Franklin said, organizing the papers on the desk.

"Not too far, Mrs. Franklin. I said I thought we wanted a white casket and that I would do the eulogy, but we can't afford this fifteen-thousand-dollar funeral package." Kevin moved the paper back across the desk.

"Please, call me Penny." She took the paper, looked at it, then discarded it under the desk. "You're right. That package is not for you. So, let's unbundle everything." She took the pad of lined paper and made notes. "It's Kevin Pritchard, correct?"

"Um, yes, this is my ex-wife and Andrea's mother, Barbara O'Shea."

Penny smiled and nodded in my direction. "So, Barbara, maybe if you told me a bit about your daughter, I could steer this in the right direction so you get exactly what you need for her."

Kevin looked at me, and I looked back at him, my eyes wide. I didn't know where to start. Kevin reached over and took my hand. I was afraid the world was going to open and swallow me whole. Tears flooded my eyes. I opened my mouth to speak, but the words wouldn't come. Kevin squeezed my hand, and I relaxed as he took over. He told Penny about Andrea, sharing her zest for life, her bright and funny personality, her open and welcoming nature. He was the perfect person to give her eulogy because he brought Andrea to life—to share her with the world.

I sat, tears streaming down my cheeks, listening to this man while my heart wrenched with great affection. Realizing I was going down that path again, I pulled my hand away, sat back in my chair, and took a deep breath. I focused on Andrea, purposely removing my thoughts from those of Kevin. I silently lectured myself. What are you doing? He's your past. You've been there. Going down this road will only lead to heartache. He deserves better than you.

My thoughts hurt, so I was glad that tears wouldn't be suspect. I allowed them to sting my eyes and flow down my cheeks unabated. Penny handed me a large box of tissues. I took a handful and wiped my eyes. I concentrated on my breathing, which allowed me to recenter myself again, and I came back to the conversation.

Earl Franklin came in as Kevin wrapped up. The china rattled on the tray as he labored under his heavy burden. He set the tray down recklessly, spilling coffee from the carafe onto the tray. Penny clucked as she mopped up the mess. Earl looked at her contemptuously, and I shuddered. He didn't appear to be a nice man.

"You must forgive my half-brother. He's not usually so clumsy. It's just one of those days." Penny smiled at us. I might have believed her had I not seen his earlier expression. She was covering for him, and I wondered what pact she had made with the devil that forced her to keep such a man in her employ. Of course, I was presuming she was in charge as Earl obeyed her, though he did it without pleasure.

"You wanted black coffee, Barbara?" Penny arched her eyebrows in my direction. I nodded. She poured the hot liquid into a large mug with the funeral home logo and name on the side. "Cream and sugar?" She looked at Kevin, and he nodded. With flair, she poured a liberal amount of cream, then dropped two sugar cubes into another mug before pouring in the coffee. This one she passed to Kevin, along with a spoon. She poured two more mugs before passing me a plate of cookies and squares. I shook my head.

She smiled and handed the plate to Kevin. He selected a large cookie, and then she set the plate on the desk before resuming her seat. Earl had pulled a chair from the side and was sitting near her. We all sipped our coffee, and no one spoke for a minute; everyone was lost in their own thoughts. Finally, Penny put her cup down, picked up her pen, and made more notes.

"Okay, from our discussion, I think a white coffin is perfect. I think we should go with mostly non-traditional music as this is a celebration of her life. I think, though, that we need to add something like 'Amazing Grace' to the program, perhaps just before the end." She paused, but her pen was still going. "Maybe we open the microphone for a short bit after the eulogy? What do you think?"

Kevin looked at me, nodding. I gave him my acceptance without talking. He looked at Penny. "Yes, that is fine. I think a fair number of people might want to say a word or two."

"Now, what time are you thinking? Morning, afternoon?"

"Morning?" Kevin asked me. I nodded. He turned back to Penny and said, "Yes, morning. Say about eleven?"

"What day are you thinking?"

"Saturday. The police said they would release her body tomorrow at the latest. Is that enough time?"

"Certainly. We will contact them and have the body moved here when it's ready."

The body! That offended me. I bristled, but I bit my tongue.

"Now, about the newspapers, are you going to prepare an obituary, or do you want one of our competent staffers to write it up based on what you told me here today?"

"Um, we're not writers, so maybe you could do that?" I suggested.

"Most certainly," she scribbled something on her notepad. "Of course, nothing would go to print without your consent."

Kevin nodded.

"Okay, last question. How many days do you want the obit to run? Every day starting tomorrow and ending Friday? Or do you want it in Saturday morning's paper as well?"

"Saturday, I think?" Kevin looked at me, and I agreed.

"Good. Now, we'll need a picture. Can you scan one for us or …"

We looked at each other. I didn't have a clue about computers. Kevin smiled. "Yes, I can scan one. If you have an email address, I can send it to you. You'll have it this afternoon."

"Perfect!" Penny made a few notes, then reached across the desk and plucked a business card from a tiered brass holder. She handed the card to Kevin. "This has my email address on it, so just send it along, and I'll attach it to the obituary when I upload it to the newspaper."

Spinning her pad around so we could read her notes, she pointed to the first item with her pen. Kevin and I leaned forward to follow her. "This is the base cost for the funeral. Using our facilities, the cars, the hearse, the transport to the cemetery." I was curious why she didn't say the total out loud. It was like speaking about money where it concerned the dead was uncouth. Even unverbalized, the cost seemed excessive. But neither of us said anything.

"This is for the casket, the white oak one, though it is quite a bit more if you want titanium." Again, the cost was astounding.

"Now, do you have a minister to officiate? Or do you want us to take on that role for you? The minister for the church next door is always willing to assist if you need him, otherwise …"

Kevin interrupted. "I think we'd rather not bother with a minister. As I told Earl, we're not religious."

"Oh, I apologize for going over ground you've already covered." She grinned at us before returning to her paper. "So, have you talked about the reception?"

"Reception?" I asked, not sure why we needed a reception.

"The lunch after the funeral, so people can offer their condolences in person."

"Oh." I sighed. I didn't want to have one at all. I just wanted this day over with, or better yet, to have Andrea back, alive and well. "No, we haven't talked about that."

"Okay, then. For coffee, tea, and a light lunch, the use of the hall …" she continued, pointing to another figure.

"And finally, for the obituary. With a picture, running for four days, this is the cost. The grand total is …"

"Hold on a minute," I interrupted. "About the lunch, is this the cost for having it catered?"

Penny nodded.

"What about catering it ourselves? Can we do that?"

"Of course, many people pay service groups to do this sort of thing. We use the Lions Club, and this is the standard donation they receive for their work."

I looked at Kevin. "I'm sure I can get the Skyview Lounge to put together a light lunch for free."

Penny interjected before Kevin responded. "By all means, if they are willing, we can work with that and reduce the fee accordingly."

"The obituary cost is rather steep, too," Kevin said. "How can we cut that down?"

"You can write the obituary yourself, keep the words to a minimum, and no picture. Pictures are quite expensive, but everyone does pictures nowadays. If you run it for fewer days, maybe have a brief blurb on Wednesday and Thursday with no picture. Then, on

Friday and Saturday, run the full obituary with pictures. That would …" She paused as she scribbled some numbers. "That would cut those costs in half."

"Okay, I think together we can come up with something." Kevin looked at me for assurance. "We can call some of her classmates if need be. She was in a journalism class, after all."

Penny chuckled appreciatively. "Fine, that sounds fine." She pulled her pad back, scribbled away, and then turned the page back with a new price circled at the bottom. I looked at the cost, and it was still too much. Yet, if I were honest with myself, her wedding would have cost more.

Kevin looked at me, and I looked back at him. We communicated silently, reading each other's thoughts. His expression silently pleaded with me to let it go as it was. I was fine with it, too. Paying my share would be a financial hardship, though I figured I could pawn some of my good jewelry to come up with my share.

"Yes, that is acceptable," Kevin said, turning back to Penny. She scooped her pad back, then turned to her computer.

"This will take a moment to complete. While I'm doing that, Earl can take you on a tour of the church next door. It's affiliated with us, and it's where we hold the larger funerals. The hall where the reception will be is downstairs." She looked at Earl, who looked less than impressed with his assignment.

He stood, and we followed him out of the office across the large foyer to a set of honey oak double doors. We went into a wide hallway to another set of doors leading to a large sanctuary that seemed large enough to suit our needs.

After the sanctuary, Earl took us downstairs to the reception hall, which seemed cozy enough for our purposes. Once we were done, we returned to the office, where we resumed our seats across from Penny.

"So, will it suit your needs?"

We both nodded, neither of us speaking.

"Perfect." She handed us a contract detailing what they were offering and our duties, as we had discussed. Kevin signed it, and then she passed it to me for my signature.

"Now, how will you be paying for this?"

"Do we have to pay today?"

"Well, we'd need a deposit of at least fifty percent. The rest is due the day of the funeral."

Kevin leaned over and pulled his wallet from his back pocket. Opening it, he tossed his credit card on the desk. Penny pulled out a machine. "So, you want to do half?"

"Sure, that's fine." She punched some numbers into the machine, slipped the card into the end, and turned it over to Kevin. Kevin took it, punched some keys, waited, and then pulled his card out before returning the unit to her. She noted the deposit on the contract and made a copy for us. She slipped these into a folder and handed them to us.

She stood, signaling to us it was time to leave. "I will see you on Saturday," she said as she walked us out of the office and down the foyer to the front doors. Once there, she extended her hand to Kevin, and they shook. Then she turned to me and did the same. It was brief and formal.

We turned away, leaving her standing there watching us. When we reached the end of the sidewalk, I looked back. She was still standing there watching us. I looked away again, embarrassed at being caught.

Kevin opened my door to the truck, and I climbed in. A great deal of relief flooded over me. I was glad to be away from this place and those people. As beautiful as the building was, as courteous as Penny was, this entire experience was unsettling.

It wasn't even about burying my daughter—it was this place.

I couldn't wait to get this behind me.

CHAPTER EIGHT

Kevin started the truck, and we headed back to my apartment, where I'd get into my car and go to work. I looked at my watch. The day was ticking along, just like any other day. That seemed disconcerting. Why was time marching on when Andrea was no longer here? Why was it going too fast and too slow? The time at the funeral home seemed to have taken a lifetime, yet it registered as a couple of hours. And a couple of hours seemed to be too long.

"I still have an hour before I have to leave for work. Do you want to grab a bite to eat or coffee or something?"

The words were out of my mouth before I realized I was speaking. The moment they were out there, I wanted to take them back. I needed to put space between Kevin and myself. I was feeling things I didn't want to feel, and I didn't like that. Something deep inside me was generating situations to perpetuate this. I prayed he would say no.

Kevin shrugged. "Could do. That cookie certainly wasn't enough. How does Jack's Diner sound to you?"

Damn. "I have never been there. What do they offer?"

"All kinds of things. Sandwiches, soups, baked goods. They make the best cinnamon buns."

My mouth watered. I hadn't had a cinnamon bun in years. What I'd been eating at Kevin's was also food that seldom crossed my lips. Grilled cheese sandwiches, bacon. I would have to work out extra hard tomorrow to compensate for my lack of dietary discretion.

"Are they quick? I only have an hour."

"I don't think you should even go to work. They would understand some leave for compassionate reasons."

Bristling, I replied, "Well, I'm not going to ask. Working will help me keep busy. Too much idle time, and I'll go stir-crazy for thinking too much. Keeping busy will help." I spoke with the compassion of truth. Feeling as fragile as I was, too much time alone would shatter me. "I'm sorry if that offends you."

"It doesn't offend me. I'm just thinking you need time to grieve, is all."

"Well, I have days off for that."

We came to a red light. Kevin stopped the truck and looked at me. "You can't bottle this up and dispense it at will. You need to focus and deal with it—it can't be controlled."

"Maybe you can't control yours, but I will control mine. I will because I have to in order to survive." I looked out the side window. The light turned green. A horn honked impatiently behind us.

Kevin faced forward, put the truck in gear, and we set off. His silence was stony and brooding. He seldom acted like this, so I recognized this was serious. All that distance that was between us loomed. I took a deep breath, satisfied that now I could walk forward with my plans, such as they were.

We arrived at Jack's Diner, went in, and found a table against the wall. The server came over and told us about the specials written on a chalkboard near the counter. I rolled my eyes at the lack of sophistication. This place was a dinky little hole in the wall, the kind of place I would never frequent again. I ordered a bowl of soup with a biscuit and a cappuccino. Kevin ordered an egg salad sandwich and a cinnamon bun. We sat in silence, not making eye contact.

Finally, Kevin broke down. "This is silly. There is too much at stake for us to be at each other's throats at a time like this."

"Fine," I said with more assertiveness than I intended. "Let's just agree to disagree then, shall we."

Setting his jaw, he nodded. "Fine."

Before we got further, our meal arrived. The chicken soup smelled heavenly, and the cinnamon bun looked delicious. Kevin tucked into his sandwich as I broke crackers into my soup. I scooped up a spoonful, and when it hit my mouth, my taste buds danced with joy. This was homemade—the noodles, the chunks of chicken, not broken into strings from excessive stirring or prolonged cooking. The person who made this soup was a connoisseur. I like to think that given enough time in the kitchen—I made a pretty mean soup, but this had flavors I had not imagined before.

I sighed, and Kevin raised his eyebrows at me. "Good, huh?"

"Yes, it's wonderful. I didn't expect much given the location, but honestly, I'm impressed."

Kevin laughed. "You need to try this cinnamon bun."

I looked at the large bun hungrily. "Well, maybe just a taste."

Silence fell between us as Kevin worked on his sandwich, and I ate my bowl of soup. I looked around the room. It wasn't as bad as I imagined. The place was clean. There were stools along the counter. Two servers bustled between it and the room of tables. The place was busy even at this time of day—after lunch and before supper.

Our server came over. "How is everything?" she asked.

I looked at her nametag, which read Beckie.

"Good, everything's good," Kevin said before I spoke.

She nodded and turned to walk away.

"This soup," I added. Beckie stopped to listen. "This soup is truly marvelous. Please tell the cook that I am impressed. This is my first time here, and I am delighted. I will be back."

"Thank you, I will tell him." She smiled brightly and moved to the next table.

Kevin finished his sandwich, and then, using a knife, he sliced off a piece of the cinnamon bun for me. He tucked into his portion, groaning with pleasure as he sank his teeth into the bun. When I finished my soup. I picked up the tiny corner he'd set aside for me. He was right. The flavors perfectly combined—the cinnamon, the syrup, the dough. Everything was in the perfect portion, which left the diner feeling like they'd hit the jackpot.

"Good, huh?" Kevin nodded at me.

"Perfect," I replied.

"Want more?"

I shook my head. "I'd love more, but I mustn't. I work too hard to keep my figure to spoil it with one cinnamon bun."

"One won't hurt you, and you could use a bit of extra padding."

Surprisingly, his comment hurt. I worked hard to keep myself in shape, and I was proud of my angles, my tiny waist, and the pride I felt when I slipped into that perfect dress. My body shape was important to my career and my self-esteem, not to mention my attractiveness to men. I turned heads when I walked by. Kevin might have meant his words as a compliment, but it hurt me deeply that he didn't like my body.

"I didn't hear any complaints last night." I shot back with more venom than necessary.

Kevin sat back like I'd slapped him. I was remorseful, but I said nothing. He finished his bun in silence. When he'd swallowed his last bite, washing it down with the last of his ice water, he stood and walked to the cash register. I sat at the table, feeling terrible about what I'd said but too proud to toss him an apology.

I stood and walked to the door to wait for him. He passed by me, holding the door open for me to walk through. This annoyed me. Why did he have to be so perfect? I straightened my shoulders and walked through the door with attitude and anger. I was itching for a fight and not getting one. At the truck, he opened my door for me, instinctively helping me up.

The ride to my apartment was quiet. Neither of us spoke. I wanted to talk and apologize, but I was too stubborn.

He pulled the truck into the stall next to my car and opened his door.

"Stay put," I said. "I can manage on my own."

He closed his door as I opened mine.

"Thank you for …" I paused. I wanted to say *everything*, but I was second-guessing myself. "For lunch."

"You're welcome," he said with some stiffness.

I slid out of the truck and turned to close the door. He watched me, and I looked deep into his handsome face.

"Call me if you need me," he added.

I nodded, then slammed the door. The sadness that had fallen on my shoulders at the news of my daughter's death slipped like a shroud over me as I opened my car door and climbed in behind the wheel.

I was on my own again, alone with the emptiness that I'd danced with for years. The emptiness, my companion, my soul mate, my comfort zone, no longer seemed easy. Sharp edges and the darkness of despair now lodged in my soul.

Chastising myself for letting all this get to me, I stuffed down my emotions and feelings.

I was stronger than this—I would not succumb to this.

I would rise above.

CHAPTER NINE

I entered the Skyview Lounge to find Sherry setting menus on the podium. Disliking people doing my job, I bristled. "What are you doing here?" I snapped. "You don't normally work on Tuesdays."

She looked like a deer caught in the headlights. "We didn't expect to see you."

"We?"

"Yes, Mr. Martinez called me. He told me what happened. I'm so sorry."

"Yes, it's tragic. But there's nothing I can do about it, so I'm here. Staying home won't bring her back." My tone belied my true feelings.

I marched past Sherry into the back to Raoul's office. I knocked on the closed door but didn't wait for the invitation to enter. He looked up as I stepped in, closing the door behind me. "I'm surprised to see you, Barbie. I didn't expect that you would be here."

"Well, I am here. I would have called if I wasn't coming."

"I'm sorry, but I think you need to take some time off. What happened is horrific. You need time to grieve."

"You sound like my ex-husband. So, I'll tell you what I told him. If I sit at home brooding and grieving, I will go stark-raving mad. I need to be busy—I need to be around people. I need to work. Please do not take this away from me."

He looked at me long and hard. Removing his glasses, he wiped one lens, then the other. He did this often when he was thinking. I waited, ready to plead my case further if his answer didn't suit me.

"Okay," he said as he replaced his glasses. "You can work. I will speak to Sherry."

"Thank you. I have one more request. Would you be able to cater the funeral?"

"Cater? That's not something we do."

"I know, but it would be such a help financially if you found a way. I will pay out of my pay packet each week, and it would be cheaper than those vultures charge."

He hesitated and closed the ledger he was looking at. "So what were you thinking?"

"Sandwiches and squares, nothing fancy. Maybe some fruit or veggie platters. We'd need a few bodies to serve, too, but I hope some of Andrea's friends might do that."

"What about coffee and tea? Juice?"

"Yes, I guess those, too, please."

"And what day would this be?" He was furiously writing notes on a pad of paper.

"Saturday. The funeral is Saturday at eleven, so we'd need it set up by noon or twelve-thirty at the latest." He nodded without looking up. I waited.

"So." He lifted his gaze. "I hope you're taking Saturday off."

I nodded. "Possibly. I can't imagine how long this might take, and I certainly won't be here at four to set up. But I could be here by supper time."

"Barbie, I know you don't want to hear this, and I'm letting you work tonight because you're the best hostess we've ever had, but I don't think you should come to work on Saturday. Take the day to honor your daughter. If not for yourself, then for her."

Tears pricked my eyes. I hadn't been thinking about Andrea. I'd been thinking about me. Taking a deep breath, I shoved down that thought. I couldn't think about her now. I had to work. "Okay, I will take Saturday off. But no more. I will be back here on Tuesday as usual."

"Agreed. Now, I will put some costs together and let you know later tonight how much it will cost and how we will take care of the payment."

I turned to leave. "Thank you, Raoul. I really appreciate this."

"You're welcome. Now send Sherry in here." He hesitated as I opened the door. "But do it nicely, please. She's new, and I think she's going to work out well, so I don't want to tick her off."

I smiled. "I will show my usual tact and decorum." He rolled his eyes and shook his head as he chuckled.

I walked out to the front and told Sherry that Raoul wanted her in the office. She looked thoroughly annoyed—but stomped off into the back. A few minutes later, she left, her coat slung carelessly over her arm and a wide smile on her face. I wondered what Raoul had promised her. I shrugged it off and went back to work. It didn't matter what he'd promised as long as she was out of my way. I had work to do.

The night passed quickly. Many of the regular customers seemed surprised to see me. Some people asked about the news they heard—unsure if Andrea was my daughter. I assured them that, indeed, she was, but that I needed to stay busy or the grief would consume me. Everyone patted my hand and offered condolences. I teared up each time but kept a tight rein on my emotions. When the day was over and the door locked behind the last patron, I sat heavily, exhausted.

Raoul came over and sat down across from me.

I blew out my breath. "Well, you made it. And you did good. I was actually quite concerned to tell you the truth."

"I'm made of tough stuff! But I will admit that I am tired."

"That you are." He paused before going on. "Well, I had a talk with the board chairperson, and he thinks we can cater the funeral for free. He thinks it was the least we could do to help you out."

I smiled. The board chair was Bobby Graham. I sent up a silent thank you because this was precisely what I wanted to happen when I asked. I could have gone to Bobby directly, but I played the game to keep people feeling like they played a part.

"Thank you so much, Raoul. And thank Mr. Graham for me, too, please. I really appreciate this. You wouldn't believe how expensive funerals are."

"No, I can't. But we're happy to help. You've been with us a long while. It's the least we can do." He looked across the table from me. "Why don't you call it a night? I will take care of the little bit of cleanup."

"Thank you, Raoul. I really appreciate that, too."

He took my hand and squeezed it. "You just take care of yourself, okay?"

I left my hand in his for a moment. He always had feelings for me, remembering the night several years back when he'd taken me in his arms in a moment of passion. The kiss was everything a woman looked for: deep, probing but not intrusive—moist but not too wet, and stirred the embers of longing. I wanted to snap the buttons off his shirt and run my fingers across his chest and down his back. We broke apart, panting. He apologized, and I placated him, hoping he didn't notice the sheen on my brow from the heat of passion he'd stirred in me.

Since that time, we'd flirted, but we never repeated the kiss. It was too dangerous because the next time, we wouldn't stop. Neither of us wanted to complicate our friendship. There was too much at stake when things went sideways, and they always went sideways. At least for me.

I squeezed his hand, and he released mine. I stood, collected my coat, and left. On the drive home, I thought about Raoul. I like him a lot. He was a wonderful boss, and we worked well together.

I pulled into the parking lot, turned off the ignition, and sat there for a minute, lost in thought. A tap on my window startled me, and I screamed before realizing that Bobby Graham was standing beside my car. I opened the door, laughing. "You scared the tar out of me!"

He smiled. "Sorry about that. Are you okay?"

"Once my heart goes back to beating regularly, I'll be perfect."

"I'm not talking about scaring you. I'm talking about your daughter."

"Oh!"

"Let's go inside." He put his arm around me and pulled me toward the door. I hurried as fast as my heels would let me. He took my keys, opened the main door, and ushered me inside. The elevator was painstakingly slow. We stood next to each other, neither of us talking, but the heat was building.

Hurrying down the hallway in my high-heeled shoes was something to watch. Wearing them meant sauntering, swinging your hips voluptuously, not running. Halfway there, I hopped on one foot and then the other to remove my shoes on the run. Bobby is grinning at me, my daughter forgotten. I reached the apartment door barefoot. The door opened, and then we were inside and in each other's arms.

Bobby Graham was not a selfish lover—he takes his time. It was a long, delicious stretch before we talked about the reason for this visit—well, one reason for his visit. Bobby rolled to his back and pulled me close to his side in one move. "So, how are you doing?"

His question brought a shadow down over us. "I'm doing okay considering."

"I couldn't believe you were at work!"

"Everybody says the same thing. Kevin, Raoul, you. But I have to work to stay busy. If I stop and think about it, it will overtake me, and I don't know if I can come back from that."

"Sure, you will. You're strong. You can find a way."

"No, I'm not strong and will not take that chance. Raoul has forced me to take all of Saturday off. I'd rather go to work after the ceremony than come home to an empty apartment."

"Sweetie, I understand, but most people don't."

"Why do you understand? What makes you different?"

"I think because you're more like me than I'd like to admit. Normal emotions impede what needs to be done. When I get knocked down, which isn't often, by the way, I don't cry and snivel and fret about things I can't change. I just get back to work."

I snuggled next to him, happy that someone understood my needs. We were quiet for a while.

"So, have you thought about my offer?"

I chuckled. "Yes, I made my decision this morning. I would love to take you up on your offer."

He leaned up on one elbow, looking into my face as I smiled back at him.

He kissed me tenderly and then more deeply, and I discerned his need again.

I reached up and pulled him toward me.

CHAPTER TEN

When I awoke, I was alone. I hated that—hated waking up alone in my bed after a night of passion. Yesterday, was it only yesterday? Kevin was making breakfast. This morning, it would be dry toast and coffee alone.

Feeling low, I rolled over and grabbed one of Andrea's photographs from the drawer. There were several pictures of her in there—they were always there. Of course, some were in frames in the living room, but I didn't like photos of people in my bedroom. Call it silly superstition, but it made me feel better knowing the people in the pictures weren't privy to what went on behind closed doors.

Andrea smiled out at me from her grade nine school photo. She was beautiful, her hair curling around her face, her smile showing perfect white teeth. My heart broke open. Why did she have to die? What was it about her that made fate choose her? I thought of the girls at her high school graduation. She didn't look any different from them. Some of them were from single-family homes. Some of them had multiple parents, their real ones and then step-parents on both sides. What marked her as the one who would die young?

My heart was aching, but my eyes remained dry. I couldn't let go of control. I rolled out of bed, showered, and did my hair. Then I made some calls. I spoke with my landlord and gave him notice for the end of November. Bobby told me the apartment would be ready by mid-November. Then I called several moving companies and planned for them to come and give me an estimate to move. Heaving my meager possessions up or down any stairs was something I refused to do.

Grabbing the brochure Bobby had left me, I stared at the layout. I would have two floors. A main floor for the kitchen, living room, laundry, and a half bathroom. The upstairs had two bedrooms, a full bath, and an ensuite off the master bedroom. It was far more space than I needed. My current home had only one bedroom. I would have to figure out how to use the second room. Maybe a treadmill or some gym equipment? I didn't need to decide today. I loved that I would have a private laundry room. Not that I did a lot of laundry. Towels and sheets and my run-around clothes. My work outfits were all dry-clean only, to maintain shape and color.

I called Cute-icles and made an appointment for a manicure and a pedicure. Caitlin told me she would move things around to make room for me on Friday morning. What a sweet girl she was, so like her mother, who had done my nails for years. Delilah retired a few years ago, and Caitlin took over. I was skeptical at first, but she was far better at her job than her mom had ever been.

With the calls behind me, I made coffee and toast and sat at the table with the morning newspapers. I hadn't read yesterday's, so I looked at it first. The front page regurgitated the story of Andrea's death. There were pictures of her, Brenda, and Caleb, all three smiling at me. The story was succinct, showing neither judgment nor compassion.

I looked hard at Caleb's picture. He was a murderer, but there was no trace of evil in his face. Frozen in place, I tried deciphering what my daughter saw in him. He was nice looking, with a pleasant smile. There was no facial hair making him appear to be innocent and naïve. His eyes were perhaps too small to make him Hollywood gorgeous, but I could see why my daughter might find him attractive. A loathing for him bubbled in my gut. I stared long and hard, my coffee growing cold.

Part of me wanted to wipe the smile off his face, but it was just a picture. My feeling of rage was strong. I grabbed the phone book and searched for their names in Freyden, finding two Bradshaws, a Joseph and a Jonathan. I dialed the number for Joseph, but no one answered. Frustrated, I slammed the phone down. I wanted to vent to his parents—mother, or father. I didn't care. They needed to know how much I hated their son and, by association, I hated them, too. Why didn't they have an answering machine or voicemail or something?

Thwarted by the lack of vengeance, I jumped to my feet and paced the floor, my anger spurring me on. I was cursing these stupid people and God. Funny that I blamed someone I wasn't even sure I believed in. I recognized that my anger was out of control, but I didn't know how to slow it down. The phone rang. I looked at it momentarily, projecting my anger toward the caller who was interrupting me.

What if the Bradshaws were calling back? What if they had call display? Leaping for the phone, I sighed, disappointed that it was Kevin.

"Hello," I said after I answered.

"Good morning, Barbara. I'm just calling to check in. How are you doing?"

"Fine, given the circumstances."

"Did you sleep okay?"

"I slept just fine." He didn't need to know I hadn't been alone.

"Good, I'm glad."

I wanted to ask how he was, but if I did, I would open that door to caring about him. That was a door I was already struggling to keep closed. I hated that I was being selfish. Kevin deserved better, but I was all about self-preservation. I needed to keep my distance.

There was a long pause. I imagined Kevin waiting for me to ask after him, hoping I would. When I said nothing, he spoke. "Do you need anything?"

"No, I'm good. My nail appointment is booked, so I'll have nice nails for the funeral."

He didn't huff, but I sensed it. I detected his judgment of me. The anger I aimed toward the Bradshaws changed direction and I hurled it at Kevin with all my might.

"What is your problem, Kevin? You have looked at me sideways since yesterday, when I wanted to go to work instead of hanging around the house feeling sorry for myself. I'll tell you right now, I will not stand for this. I am not stupid, I know what you think of me, what you've always thought of me. That I'm more interested in my appearance than anything else. But so what? So what? You can back the hell up right now and get off my back. Do you hear me?" I stopped talking, my heart was pounding, my body was shaking, and I was out of breath.

There was silence on the other end of the phone. I wasn't sure he was still there or if, during my rant, he'd hung up the phone. "Hello? Are you still there?"

I heard him blow his breath out, like he'd been holding his breath. "Yes, I'm here, Barbara."

"Well?"

"Well, what?"

"Are you going to apologize?"

"No, Barbara. I won't apologize for what you *think* I might be thinking. I never said anything, and I never even thought anything. I was only calling to make sure you are okay."

His patient response did not diffuse my temper. It fueled it. Maybe I was itching for a fight. Maybe I just wanted to push him away. A flash of caustic bitterness rushed through my veins, but I had no words, so I screamed. Desperate to vent, to pour out the ugly feeling roiling inside me, the urge to break something spiraled through my mind. I visualized smashing the phone over and over on the edge of the counter until it fell apart into tiny pieces in my hand. I wanted to hurl something heavy out the window; to hear glass shattering. I wanted to stare at those shards and match the pieces to my heart.

But I just screamed until I was out of air, then I took a deep breath and screamed again. A primal roar of pain and anguish, of loss, of misery. The screams turned to sobs. I ended the call and threw the phone across the room. It landed with a thud on the carpet by the door, the battery cover separating but otherwise intact. I threw myself on the couch, punching the cushion until I was exhausted. I lay there hiccoughing, exhausted by the rage. The familiar emptiness settled in as my anger dissipated.

Minutes passed. I concentrated on my breathing to keep from feeling the emptiness too deeply. As the calmness drifted through my body, it was time to burn off the residual frustrations. I needed to get to the gym.

CHAPTER ELEVEN

I slipped into my exercise outfit and headed out. The drive was routine, and I don't remember seeing much of the road. Jumbled and unfocused thoughts swirled around me as I entered the gym and went right to work. I ran on the treadmill, away from my thoughts, feelings, and myself. Eventually, my legs turned to jelly, so I ran harder. Sweat dripped down my face. I didn't wipe it away, not even when it dripped into my eyes. The stinging was a welcome penance. I grabbed the handles and continued to run, punishing my body.

When I couldn't run anymore, I stepped off, moving to the stair climber. I did only a few reps when my muscles refused to take any more. Stepping off, I retreated to the change room. Inside, I splashed cold water on my face. Then I grabbed my purse out of the locker and headed out.

Gavin was at the front counter when I stopped to buy a sports drink. Handing the bottle to me, he asked, "How are you doing, Barbie? I'm sorry to hear about your daughter. Tough break that."

"I'm fine, Gavin. Thanks." I handed him a five-dollar bill.

Waving his hand back and forth, he refused my money. "It's on the house today. You just take care of yourself."

I nodded, gave him a weak smile, and headed out the door. In my car, I popped the top on the beverage and drank half of it before starting the engine. Feeling marginally better, I drove home. While eating a quick lunch—a salad with green onions, chunks of red pepper, feta cheese, and a boiled egg for protein—I read the rest of yesterday's newspaper. Then I went for a shower.

I dressed with care, arriving at work at my usual time feeling like the morning had been a bad dream, best left forgotten. I set out the menus and tidied the dishes and other things left from last night. It didn't take long to have the place whipped into shape.

Raoul appeared a moment before I unlocked the door. "How are you, Barbie?"

"I'm doing okay." I smiled at him. He looked so serious.

"You sure?"

"Of course, I'm sure," I snapped. "Gawd, why does everybody second guess me? If I say I'm fine, I am fine!"

"But you're obviously not, because you are the most even-tempered person I've ever met. You don't fly off the handle at minute provocations. You don't let the peevishness of others bother you. And yet, here you are snapping at me for asking if you're okay."

"I'm sorry. I guess I've been struggling today. Reading the news article about the murder this morning made me so angry at that stupid boy ..."

"That's understandable." He paused a moment, looking into my face, holding my attention. "Well, I need to know you will not take this out on the customers. You know how some of them can be. I cannot risk having my customers upset because you have a hate on for this boy."

Chastised and angry at Raoul for questioning my professionalism, I nodded. "I understand. I will be a model of temperance."

He reached over and squeezed my shoulder. "There is no harm in admitting you need help or can't cope. You have an awful lot on your plate and none of it is palatable at the moment. If you need to go home, just come and get me. If you need some time off, just ask. Whatever you need, I will do my best to ensure you get it."

"Thank you, Raoul. You are too kind. I appreciate it, and I will ask. Tonight though, I am working and I will not let you down."

He left me then, and I walked to the front door and unlocked the bolts. Then, I retreated to my station to wait. I didn't have long. The place gradually filled up. Everyone again offered condolences, and I was glad no one asked me why I wasn't at home. Either they understood, or they didn't care.

Either way, I was happy to resume business as usual.

At eight o'clock, Bobby came in with Thelma in tow. Thelma didn't greet me. I was beneath her. I often wondered if she even knew I was there. She never made eye contact and spoke to me like I was nothing more than "the help," there to serve her and nothing more. I'd never met anyone like her before. Most of the women who came in with their husbands were at least polite. Thelma was different, and I appreciated why Bobby looked for affection elsewhere. I couldn't imagine her letting anything or anyone muss with her perfect hair or her professionally applied makeup. Getting sweaty between the sheets seemed a far fetch given her personality.

Though I had to admit, they had two kids. A boy and a girl, so obviously she had to have allowed Bobby to defile her at least twice. I snorted at the thought. Bobby deserved someone who would offer him a warm place to lie, a welcoming spot in her bed. That's where I came in. I didn't believe for one minute that he would divorce Thelma and marry me, and I wasn't interested in marriage. I'd been married too many times already. Marriage put restrictions on me I didn't want.

But I was glad to be the one who gave Bobby what he needed.

CHAPTER TWELVE

The night passed. Bobby and Thelma didn't stay long. He never did when she was along. The night ended, and I left, exhausted. It had been a long one, and I was looking forward to my bed. My message light was blinking when I entered my dark apartment. I looked at my call display. It was my mother's number. I nearly dropped the phone. I hadn't spoken with her in years. We still lived in the same city, but I made sure I never frequented places she would. That's part of the reason I shopped at high-end stores. She couldn't afford to breathe the air in stores like that.

I debated listening to the message. I wasn't sure I wanted to hear anything she had to say. She had never met my daughter and was no longer part of my life. Did I want to let her in?

It's not that my mother is a bad person. She isn't. But she is an enabler, and that is why I shut her out of my life. She allowed my father … NO! I couldn't go there. I didn't want to go there. Why was this happening now? I had too much on my plate already. Damn.

I replaced the handset and went to my bedroom. I stripped out of my work clothes, putting the dress in the plastic bag that I dropped at the dry cleaners every other Monday. There were enough dresses and outfits in my closet that I never wore the same one in a month. I hadn't changed sizes in years, so it was easy to build upon. If I grew tired of one, I sent it to the secondhand shop and replaced it with something new or new to me. I guess I selected something new at least six or eight times a year.

As I slipped my nightgown over my head, my thoughts circled that flashing red light and the voice behind it. Once in bed, I tried to sleep but couldn't. That flashing red light bothered me. Finally, I reached for the bedside phone and dialed the number to retrieve my voicemail. The mechanical voice said I had one new message. I pressed the keys to listen.

My mother's voice trickled out into my ear. It was older and weaker than the last time I heard it. That made me sad. Sad that I had missed all those years with her. Then anger rippled through me because it wasn't my fault. It was hers. If she'd had the courage to leave my father, we could have had those years. We could have ... I stopped myself.

"Barbie, this is your mother. I read the newspaper today and saw Andrea was ... well, she has passed away. Your brothers send their condolences and if you don't mind, we'd like to come to the funeral on Saturday. Don't worry, we will sit in the back, and we won't cross any lines. Your dad won't make it. He'll be having dialysis on Saturday and he's never very well afterward. He's not a well man, your dad. I know you say you don't care, but just in case you do. Well, that's all I have to say. Goodbye Barbie. I love you."

I pushed the button to listen to the voice again. My heart constricted and my eyes burned with rancid memories; the ones I had stuffed away. Those neglected memories I didn't want to deal with. They had rotted and putrefied, and now they were vile and disgusting. Tears flowed down my cheeks as I pressed that button again and again. I listened to her voice eight or ten times and then instead of erasing the message—I saved it. It seemed surreal, and I wondered if I was being irrational.

I had been so strong—I'd kept her away by sheer force of will, and now things were changing. A part of me wanted to phone her, to feel her arms around me—to remind me, as she always did, that life wasn't always hard. She would tell me that there were seasons for everything, and I should rejoice in the sunny ones, for they would keep me warm during the long, cold ones.

As a little girl, terrified during and after one of my father's rampages, she was my rock. In my teens, I wanted her to stand up to him, to tell him that his behavior was wrong. But she never did. She placated him and enabled him to keep up his tantrums. She became part of the problem and not someone with a solution. Anger and hatred directed toward my father arced off in her direction. She was someone I vented at, spewing my fear and frustration in her direction.

My brothers Patrick and Dennis were already drinking by high school. They were the leaders of the party crowd, seeking solace and relief in the bottom of a bottle. Patrick scraped through high school and Dennis dropped out. By the time Dennis was twenty, he was in jail for drug-related offences. I turned my back on him.

Patrick and I stayed in touch after I left home. He'd realized he was on the wrong path when the cops busted Dennis. He turned his life around, working hard and putting himself through school. I was very proud of him. Once he became a social worker who worked with troubled youth, he turned into a sanctimonious Pollyanna. It was impossible to listen to his lectures. When I left Kevin, he became outraged. He couldn't understand why I would leave a doting husband, and leaving my daughter behind was reprehensible. He argued with me incessantly, and one day, he crossed that uncrossable line, which was the last straw. After that, I refused to talk to him.

Keeping him out of my life was much easier when I started

working at the Skyview Lounge. It was members only, and he didn't qualify. There were no more sudden appearances at my workplace or embarrassing arguments in the parking lot. Eventually, he faded into the background of my life and my memories.

I hadn't spoken to either brother for years. I heard through Kevin that Dennis had turned his life around after prison. He'd learned a trade, married a wonderful woman and was a decent family man. He must be doing well if he could afford the expensive china cabinet he'd commissioned from Kevin for his wife's fiftieth birthday last year.

I climbed back under the covers, my mind swirling with conflicting emotions about the impending reunion. I desperately wanted them to feel like I wasn't all alone in the world. But a part of me still wanted to keep them as far away as possible. The memories they stirred were volatile. Keeping them buried was all that kept me sane. I was afraid that seeing my family again would pull the corner off the lid and my childhood traumas would leak into my future. Having too much to lose, I needed to be vigilant to ensure that didn't happen.

My dreams were fragmented scraps, unsettling yet out of focus. I woke exhausted, like I hadn't slept at all. It was going to be a long day.

CHAPTER THIRTEEN

Bobby came over again on Thursday night. When I arrived home, he was waiting in the parking lot. I met him at the door, and we hurried upstairs. He brought a bottle of red wine, which he uncorked when we were inside my apartment. He poured two glasses and then handed one to me. This habit of his annoyed me. He always poured me a drink, even knowing my family history and my fear that if I took one drink, I might end up like my father.

The first time he poured me a glass, I was incredulous at his lack of sensitivity. I ran out of the room and locked myself in the bathroom, crying hysterically. He didn't come after me. He never apologized. Eventually, I decided it was easier to placate him by pretending to go along with it.

"Let's toast to your new home." He held his glass toward me. I stepped closer, linked my arm through his, and he drank while I merely tipped the glass upward. He set his glass on the counter and leaned toward me. His lips were cool and bitterly sweet with wine as he captured mine. I groaned and stepped closer, pressing my body to his. His hands found my zipper, and soon, my dress was a fabric pool at my feet.

After he eased off the straps of my slip from my shoulders, he quickly tugged it and it joined my dress on the floor. His lips never left mine as he removed my bra. His thumbs caressed my nipples to attention. I groaned again. Since I was wearing my usual garter belt and stockings, he undid the snaps before slipping the belt and my panties to the floor. The stockings—he left in place.

Then he lifted me onto the counter. I lost myself in his affection and his attention, drifting down the stream of sexual passion. The soft strokes of calm waters, each stroke building tension as I hurled toward the rapids; swirling, rushing, deafening feelings until I could hardly catch my breath. I was urgently seeking release, heading toward the waterfall, my heart pounding and my blood rushing until my passions swept me over in one exhilarating moment. I fell against Bobby as my emotions exploded with my body.

Bobby caressed my back, and as my sobs subsided, he lifted me into his arms and carried me to the bedroom. Once he set me on the bed, he removed his clothes. For the next hour, he made me forget everyone and everything except him and what we were doing in this room. Afterward, I nestled under his arm, content and at peace with my choice. I imagined this would be my life once I moved into my new home—more nights like this.

Bobby stroked my arm, absently.

I craned my neck to look at him. His eyes were closed. "What are you thinking?"

"Hmm." He smiled. "I was thinking that you truly are a remarkable woman."

"Were you now?" I smiled.

"Yes, I was." He didn't elaborate.

"Well, you're pretty remarkable yourself you know."

"Am I now? In what way?"

Oh, how I hated these games. "Well, you're tall and handsome. You have beautiful blue eyes."

"But those are attributes I cannot control. How am I remarkable?"

"Well, you make me happy and that is something, believe me!"

"Okay." He smiled. "I'll settle for that."

My answer disappointed him, but it was so hard to tell him, or anyone else, for that matter, what they meant to me. My feelings were inscrutable, and words always failed.

"I am much better at showing you ..." I shifted positions and showed him how remarkable I thought he was.

Afterward, I lay in the bed listening to him in the shower. I fell asleep before he was done.

CHAPTER FOURTEEN

Although I was better rested in the morning, my dreams unsettled me. I tried to remember them when I awoke, but they were elusive, scattering like leaves in fall as I reached to retrieve them.

A quick breakfast and I was off to the nail salon. Cute-icles was in the basement of a former chain store. When they closed forever—the owners subdivided the building into several smaller stores, basement salons and upstairs professional offices. It was truly a magnificent location in the heart of downtown Crawford. I loved the wide-open feel of the place, with its black-and-white marble floors, high ceilings and the wide staircase leading to the upper level.

I often thought I would be good at running a high-end dress shop. When I daydreamed of that venture, I envisioned setting it up right here in this building. My stomach contracted pleasantly when I took myself along this path. I was excited about what my life could be.

Maybe that was something I should talk to Bobby about. I had never thought to ask for anything before, but he was a shrewd business owner, and I'm sure he would see the value of this. That thought alone made me feel lighter. I skipped down the steps and into the well-lit salon. Caitlin was waiting for me behind the desk. She rose when she saw me.

"Good morning, Barbie. How are you this morning?" She smiled as she came around to hug me. It wasn't normal for her to hug me, but she was thinking about Andrea and my loss, so I allowed the brief exchange. When she released me, we walked to her table and sat across from each other.

As she worked, she talked. After a while, I stopped listening to her and thought about my shop. I had the perfect name too— "Sincerely." I would bring in designer clothes that women longed for, dreamed of, and desired above all others. My shop would scream elegance. I pictured the racks of Dior, Louis Vuitton, Yves Saint Laurent and Chanel. High end outfits meant to showcase a woman's figure, making her feel as beautiful as she looked. I would sell silk stockings, not pantyhose. Even the lingerie and undergarments would be a finery fit for any queen. My stomach was squiggling with delight.

"Barbie … uh … Barbie?" I came back to the nail salon. "Gosh, you were miles away there. I need to know what color you want."

I had thought about this since I made the appointment. "Black and white, please, on an angle, black at the bottom."

"Absolutely." Efficiently, she coated my nails. I rested one hand under the lights while she did the other. When she was done, I held my hand up, looking with pride at my hands. I loved my long fingers, and the nails added to the beauty. My rings set off the entire picture. I was pleased.

"Thank you, Caitlin. This is perfect." I walked to the front counter.

"There's no charge today, Barbie. I am so sorry for your loss. It's the least I can do."

Surprised at her generosity, my eyes filled with tears. I hadn't thought of Andrea beyond the cursory reason behind this unscheduled visit. Yet, here was this young girl, thinking about her and about me. More tears fell, not because of my loss, but because I was still a selfish person, making this all about me.

"Thank you, Caitlin." I tossed a ten-dollar bill on the counter. "This is your tip today."

She left the bill languishing there, smiling sadly. "Thank you, Barbie. I am so very sorry. I didn't know Andrea, but I know that what happened was a tragedy."

Trying to smile, my lips quivered dangerously, so I turned and walked out. My return trip up the stairs was heavier—my thoughts on my daughter. I stepped out into the frosty morning. We still had not seen snow, but the temperature belied that. It had the feel of a winter morning. I climbed into my car, shivering from the short walk. Not dressed for the weather, I reminded myself to dig out my winter jacket.

That's another thing I would add to my shop. Nice coats. I hated the trend toward short winter jackets. The bombers, the shiny, brightly colored, down-filled or fiber-filled disgraces that passed as winter attire. They were sporty, perhaps meant for the ski hill, but they showed no class. How often had I seen women rushing down the street in a dress, wearing that fashion abomination? I hated to think.

I preferred my winter coats to be long, hanging just below the knee. Coats should be classy and functional. Those short jackets did nothing to protect the buttocks or the legs, leaving them exposed to the elements. Even if a person wore jeans or heavy slacks, the brutal winter winds easily pierced them.

A long, wool coat kept a body warm from head to toe, especially with high boots. I imagined influencing local fashion by seeing short jackets disappear in place of long coats. Young women wearing jaunty tams and scarves, coordinated to dress up the outfit.

I would make the city pay attention to fashion and dress for beauty again.

It was something that would give me a great deal of pleasure.

CHAPTER FIFTEEN

When I returned home, I stripped the bed and replaced the sheets with fresh linen. I then started a load of laundry and checked my phone. Two messages were there. The first one was from someone at a monument company trying to sell me a headstone. I erased it because I wasn't ready for that challenge.

The other was from Kevin.

"Good morning, Barbara. I'm just checking in. How are you doing? Are you holding up? I was also wondering about tomorrow morning. The funeral is at eleven, so I thought maybe you could come over early so we can ride to the funeral together. Barry and Agnes have hired a car for us, so we don't have to drive. But if you'd rather come over tonight, there is room. Doug and Valerie arrived last night. I've put them in the guest room. You can sleep in Andrea's room. Anyway, get back to me and let me know."

I pushed to erase the message. Barry and Agnes were so sweet. They were perhaps the best next-door neighbors anyone could ask for. Every time I was there, they treated me like a long-lost daughter.

They never asked questions; they just took our situation at face value. Best of all, the elderly couple doted on Andrea like she was their own grandchild. It didn't surprise me that they would do something this generous.

Valerie was Kevin's sister. I wasn't sure I'd get a warm welcome from her. I hadn't spoken with her since before I left Kevin. Back in high school, we were never close. I think she looked down on me and my group of friends. Truth be told, so did I, but they were all I deserved. We received no encouragement from her when Kevin and I married, but then again, she never gave me any grief, either. Perhaps that was just her way. I hadn't seen Val in many years. Occasionally I would see her from a distance before she and her husband Doug moved to BC. I wasn't sure what to expect if I went over.

Did it really matter? By the time I finished work tonight, it would be two o'clock in the morning. Surely, she would be in bed long before that. I paced the floor, uncertain. Finally, I bit the bullet. Even if I arrived in the morning, I'd have to see her and talk to her. I would not go to the funeral home on my own. I didn't think myself capable of that level of bravado. So, meeting Val over coffee at the breakfast table, or meeting her an hour later at the front door, would not change the outcome if she was intent on tearing a strip off my hide.

Having decided, I called Kevin. "Hi, Kevin. I heard your message."

"Good. How are you?"

"I'm doing okay. You?"

"Well, it's been easier with Val here. My parents should arrive late tonight. I told them they shouldn't have come, but they insisted they could go back to Europe anytime, but they'd only bury their granddaughter once." His voice broke. I wanted to leap through the phone and wrap my arms around him. What was I doing? He needed me and I was way over here. I was about to tell him I'd be right there when I heard her in the background.

"It's okay, Kevin. Just let it out."

I imagined her rubbing her hand across his shoulders. Her interruption of our private conversation seemed like a betrayal, and anger stirred in my belly.

Kevin put his hand over the receiver, so I didn't hear what he said, but it sounded like a rebuke. I smiled, glad that she was being pushed back.

"Sorry about that," Kevin said, returning to the conversation. "Anyway, it's been a long couple of days."

The light came on. I understood it. I was so busy working to keep my feelings at bay that I had forgotten that Kevin was also going through similar feelings and was all alone. Even if he went into work, he'd still be alone with his thoughts. A rope tightened around my chest as guilt swept in. I was not giving him my support, though by giving it to him, it would reel me back in his life with no way out. He was too good for the likes of me.

"I'm sorry, Kevin." I let that hang between us for a heartbeat before I continued. "Anyway, about your offer, I thought I would come over after I finish up tonight. But it will be late, say two-thirty-ish."

"Sure, that's fine. I'll wait up."

"No, please don't. You need your rest. Tomorrow is going to be a long day."

"I haven't been sleeping much, but we'll see. I'll probably hear you come in."

"Would you rather I not come?" I said this softly to cover my fear.

"No, I need you to come. Please." He whispered this back to me, trying to keep big ears from hearing.

"Okay. I'll try to get off early."

"It would be better if you didn't go in."

For one moment, I wondered if I should call Raoul and take the night off. He wouldn't mind, he might even be relieved. Friday nights were busy, and the tips were more than generous. I'd lose a night's wages plus nearly three hundred dollars in tips. A portion of the tips that the girls earned came to me. I also received cash, which was slipped to me surreptitiously—a handshake with a bill left in my palm. A side hug, and a bill slipped up my sleeve. These tips were mine, from my guys giving me something for no other reason than because of who I was. Could I afford to miss this?

"I think I should go in for a little while at least. I can't drop Raoul in it on a Friday night without notice. But I will try to get off early. Do you want me to call?"

"No, just come over when you're done. I'll see you later then." He paused. "Thanks Barbara."

I hadn't given him an inch, and yet he was generous enough to thank me for it. My selfishness confirmed that I didn't deserve him.

"Okay, I'll see you then."

"Goodbye." He hung up.

"Goodbye, sweetheart." My heart constricted painfully, and a lump formed in my throat. How would I get through this without breaking that man's heart again? He deserved someone who would put him first. He was still in love with me. I chastised myself for letting my feelings take over the night I'd heard about Andrea. Sleeping with him had only given him hope I was still his. And I was. Deep in my heart, I would always be his. I didn't deserve him, though, and I would do my utmost to ensure he moved on after this. He needed to be loved and cherished.

I was moving on. In a month, I would live in a condo on the golf course and, hopefully, work on sprucing up that empty suite in the old chain store building for my new dress shop.

I was taking control of my future.

Kevin needed to do the same.

CHAPTER SIXTEEN

I left work half an hour early. As I slipped into my jacket, it was one-thirty. Raoul had promised he would look after any cleanup. We went over the menu for the funeral catering. The company would pay for the ingredients, and Craig, the chef, had agreed to do the work without pay. Also, Lena, my current co-worker, and Beverly, who left a few weeks ago, had agreed to help without being paid.

Their generosity overwhelmed me. I promised I would get them something, not money, because money was cheap. I would have to get each of them something special. Once I was living in the condo and had no rent, I could afford a nice, unique gift.

As I climbed into my car, the heaviness I had kept at bay for a long time settled on my shoulders. Unlike an old friend, these feelings were not welcome. I had hoped to never feel this again. Looking around the parking lot, I wondered if this world was real. Was I real? Or was I merely a player on some stage, a character in a book? When I first left Kevin, I experienced this feeling often. When I talked to my doctor about it, he put me on some drug for several months, an antidepressant. I couldn't figure out why I would slide back there again.

Sure, Andrea was gone. That would warrant a trip to the dark side, but I also had so much to look forward to. A new home—a new beginning. A man who would take care of me. Before this became serious, I needed to get a grip and shake this off. I would allow myself to be sad about Andrea, but I would not get down into the pits again. I could not let that happen.

Arriving at Kevin's, I saw a burgundy Lincoln Town Car parked in the driveway with BC plates. I parked on the street. Wondering if his parents were also staying, I checked the neighborhood for another foreign car. I didn't see one.

A small light burned behind the curtains, perhaps the stove light. I grabbed my train case and the plastic carrier with my clothes inside and headed toward the house. The outside light popped on as I stepped up to the door. Kevin swung the door open. He looked old, like he had aged ten years since I'd seen him only a few days ago.

Neither of us spoke. He reached out and took my suitcase and the dress carrier, taking them into the house and down the hall to Andrea's room. He returned as I was hanging up my coat. I turned to him, assessing his mood. Without a word, he pulled me into his arms and embraced me. Wanting to keep my distance, in this awkward situation, I stiffened. Kevin sighed, and I relaxed into his arms. He tightened his grip. I sighed. We stayed like that for a moment or two, neither of us willing to be the first to let go.

When we separated, an awkward silence fell over the room. I realized where Kevin wanted to go. Part of me was willing; part of me was afraid that if I did, I'd never leave. I had too much to lose by giving in. Even though I wasn't tired, I feigned a yawn. "We have a big day tomorrow. Let's get some sleep, eh?"

"Okay." He let me lead the way down the hall, passing the closed guest room door. At the end of the hallway, I stopped in front of

Andrea's door. My suitcase sat by the bed, the clothes bag lying across the bed. I paused and looked at Kevin.

"Good night, Kevin. Sleep well. I'll see you in the morning."

"Good night, Barbara." He leaned in to kiss me. I turned slightly, letting the kiss land on my cheek. He pulled back, his expression sadder than when I arrived. I wanted to throw my arms around him, pull him close, and whisper my love into his ear. I wanted to let go. But the harness I kept on my emotions was strong. I pulled myself back, reined myself in, and stepped backward into the room, grabbing the door with my left hand.

"See you in the morning." I closed the door, leaning against it. Bracing against the longing in Kevin's face, I steeled myself to be strong and resist it. I battled my longing as well. It would be so easy to just open the door, walk into his bedroom, and resume my old life. At that moment, there was nothing I would have liked better, but I resisted for Kevin's sake. He didn't need me. I was just going to screw up his life like I screwed up everything else.

I leaned against the door, concentrating on my breathing for several minutes. When it seemed safe to let go, I moved into the room toward the bed. I looked around, taking in the ambience of this space because this was Andrea's room. Her sanctuary from the world. I wandered to the dresser, looking at the trinkets she had left behind when she left home. Those things she couldn't yet part with but which were too juvenile to take into her new life.

Nothing was familiar. There was nothing I'd ever given her displayed on the top. Had she taken the stuff I'd given her or tossed it? I dared to hope it was the first thought. I pulled open the top left dresser drawer. It was empty except for one short sock, its mate obviously missing. This orphaned piece of clothing lay alone in the dark.

The right dresser drawer was also empty. The long middle drawer held some long-forgotten T-shirts and sweatpants. They looked shabby and perhaps a few were ready for the bin. A task she'd never undertaken.

In the bottom drawer, I discovered a plethora of items that seemed familiar. Picking through them, I noticed each one was a gift I'd given her. All of them were in original packaging. She'd never even taken them out of the packaging. The earrings, the necklaces, the gloves, the music discs. Everything I'd given her since I left. There were a few Barbie dolls near the bottom, a Polly Pocket, and even the My Little Pony that I thought she'd love. All of it stuffed into this big drawer and left behind. Just like I'd left her behind.

My heart was on fire. It scorched my chest, charring my lungs until I couldn't breathe. I never understood that she resented me this much. She was standoffish, and I put that down to being hurt. It was a fence I intended to mend when she was old enough to understand, but try as I might, she wouldn't let me in. I hated to think she left this world with all that resentment hanging around her neck.

I closed the dresser drawer, cursing myself for snooping. Why had I looked? Why had I invaded her privacy? Moving to the bed, I sat down heavily on it. I wanted to sprint to the door, run to Kevin, and have him assuage my guilt, but this wasn't his problem.

Having brought this on myself, I understood this was mine alone to bear. I deserved everything I was feeling and more. After all, it wasn't as if I was loveable.

The pain of my thoughts pierced my soul and all the light inside me drained out, leaving nothing but the darkness of my thoughts. They swirled angrily in my belly, making me nauseous. I lay on the bed, curling into a ball as my mind wandered down the dark alleys of despair. Tears flowed with abandon. Rolling over into the pillow, I poured out my sorrow in great heaving sobs. Not wanting to disturb Kevin or Valerie, I tried to keep the sounds low. The last thing I needed was someone to come in and offer me comfort when all I wanted to do was die.

The sobs subsided, and I drifted off. Later, I woke up shivering. I rose to my feet, stripped off my dress, then climbed under the covers in my underwear.

Snuggling under the warm covers, I was soon asleep again.

CHAPTER SEVENTEEN

The next time I awoke, it was to the sounds of plates and cutlery and the smell of coffee and bacon. I lay curled under the covers for a few moments, the darkness that had invaded my soul a familiar comfort. Eventually, I climbed out of bed, slipped on a robe, and padded down the hall to the bathroom.

I looked like death warmed over. My eyes were puffy, my complexion marred by the lines of my pillow. I scrubbed my face, brushed my hair, and tied it into a ponytail. Then I walked down to the kitchen to face the day.

As I entered the kitchen, Val turned to greet me. She wasn't smiling. My breath caught as I waited for her to lash out in anger. She wore a pink fluffy robe—looking much older than her years. Once upon a time, I envied her. She was a classy young woman against my unrefined youth. Now she looked frumpy and timeworn. Her blond hair was lifeless, her complexion sallow, her figure an hourglass with too much sand in all the wrong places. I wondered how I ever wanted to be her.

"Good morning. Did you sleep well?"

"After a time, yes, thank you."

We stood eyeing each other warily. "Come here you!" She approached and wrapped me in a hug. "So sorry, so, so sorry," she whispered into my ear. I held on to her, waiting for her to release me. Eventually, she did, stepping back to look at me. "You look good, though. Still as skinny as a teenager. How do you manage that?"

I smiled, but I didn't answer. I didn't think she really wanted to know.

"Breakfast is nearly ready. You want a coffee?" She rattled a few cups out of the cabinet, setting them onto the counter.

"Doug!" Valerie shouts. "You ready for coffee?"

Doug stumbled into the room, wearing pajama bottoms and a dingy white tank top. Tufts of gray hair poked out above the neckline, which was the only hair visible. His once long, curly locks had disappeared, leaving a pink bald dome in its place. The T-shirt stretched tightly over his ample belly. Clearly, he and Val did little to fight the inevitable.

"Hey, Barbie." He growled when he noticed me. He came over to give me a cursory squeeze. I noticed the stubble on his cleft chin was decidedly gray. He'd aged too. I guess we all had. I just hated to give in, and I did my best to stall the process.

Kevin came in, his hair wet from the shower. He looked rather dapper, dressed in suit pants and a baby blue shirt hanging open to expose a bright white T-shirt. He kissed Val on the top of her head as he helped himself to a coffee. "Thanks for making breakfast, Val."

"I'm here to help." She smiled at him. "If the bathroom is free, I think I'll make myself presentable. The bacon is in the oven, the scrambled eggs are on the stove and here is the toast." She handed him a small plate stacked high. "I've eaten, so go crazy."

Kevin looked at his watch. "Okay. I'll grab a quick bite. Mom and Dad will be here soon and we need to leave in a little over an hour."

Sipping my coffee, I felt pressure to get busy. Kevin opened the oven and set the hot plate of bacon on the counter. I grabbed a piece of toast, laid several strips of bacon on half of it, and folded the toast in half. Butter dripped down my chin as I bit into the sandwich. I never bought bacon for myself, considering it too fatty for my diet. Yet here I was, for the second time in a week, enjoying every single bite.

"You want any eggs with that?" Kevin smiled at me.

I shook my head. "No, this is perfect. Thanks."

"Okay, Doug, it looks like it's just you and me. He divided the eggs onto two large plates. Doug scooped half the remaining bacon onto his plate and dropped four pieces of toast on top. Then he took the plate to the eating bar, setting it down with a thud. He sat down heavily, digging into his breakfast like a man who hadn't eaten in a long time. I couldn't watch. I turned my back, taking another bite of my bacon sandwich as I leaned against the counter. Kevin took half the bacon in the pan and one piece of toast, then settled back against the other counter, facing the door. He ate his breakfast, standing near me. I finished my sandwich.

"Is your bathroom free?"

"Sure, go ahead."

I scooted down the hallway into his room. The bathroom was still damp from his shower. I closed the door, turned on the fan and then stripped. As soon as the water was hot, I stepped under the spray. I washed my hair and lathered away the darkness of my night thoughts.

When I had finished my shower, I opened the door to the bedroom, letting the steam out and the cooler air in. I brushed my teeth, applied my makeup and styled my hair into a French roll. When I was done, I slipped across the hall to Andrea's room and closed the door.

I dressed in black—black bra and panties, a black garter and black hose. The dress I donned was a classic little black dress. There were a few of these in my closet. This one was demure in its style. The sleeveless bodice was plain, and the skirt was ornate—embroidered with thin black ropes that swirled, curled, and looped around. They gave the dress an elegance that the material on its own could not. The skirt came to my knees. I seldom wore this dress. Although beautiful, it was too subtle for my position. I preferred louder outfits; ones that spoke with class and style; ones that made me visible and approachable. I slipped on the short, lined, lace jacket, the long sleeves tapered just above the wrist.

I was ready with a string of pearls around my neck and pearl earrings on each lobe. Turning this way and that, I admired myself in the mirror. Low black pumps finished the outfit—high heels seemed inappropriate for a day like today. I was ready.

I walked down the hallway to the living room. Kevin's parents had arrived. My stomach contracted. Again, the fear of reprisals flashed through my core. Karl and Mildred were in their late sixties. They looked much younger. Mildred was standing, looking out the picture window. A glossy, wide black belt cinched her dowdy black dress to her slender frame. She wore no jewelry. Karl, in a dark brown suit with a pale yellow shirt, looked wearily at the floor. He had brushed his curly gray hair into obedience. He stood up as I entered.

Mildred turned, and the three of us stood eyeing each other nervously. I wanted to run back down the hallway, but I held my breath and stood my ground.

"Oh my dear, this is so awful. Such a tragedy." Mildred gushed as she came across the room toward me. "Andrea, my little Andrea is gone. I cannot believe it." She wrapped her thin arms around me and squeezed me briefly.

Karl moved in for a quick side hug, but he said nothing. His eyes were moist and red-rimmed.

A memory of Karl playing with Andrea came into my mind. It was so clear—it was like I was watching it happen all over again. It was a few months before I left—Andrea was across the street, playing with Cathy Morrison. While the two of them were jumping on the bed, Cathy had fallen off and broken her arm. Unable to contact me, forced her to take Andrea to the emergency room with them.

Andrea had become fixated on doctors for a while after that. All her dollies wore fabric casts and bandages instead of clothes. Karl enjoyed playing with her, and he was an excellent doctor. A memory of them playing in the living room came to mind, both cross-legged on the floor. Andrea would chatter and point at spots on the doll that hurt. Karl would carefully take the doll from her, then listen with the toy stethoscope to the place that was being discussed. The arm, the leg, the abdomen, the head. Then he would tut gently, and place another Band-Aid on the solid plastic form. He had used up an entire box of Band-Aids that afternoon, and I had never experienced a happier moment.

I was grateful that she had a man like this in her life, and I was still grateful. Tears filled my eyes. I looked more closely at him. His complexion wasn't good. He was almost gray. Mildred, too, looked fragile on closer examination. I wanted to wrap them in cotton—they had always been so good to me. Why did life have to be so hard? It was unthinkable that parents and grandparents had to bury their children. This wasn't normal and not how life was supposed to go. My anger bubbled up, sweeping away all my tender feelings for Karl and Mildred and the moment we were in.

I took a deep breath and pulled back into myself again. I couldn't deal with all this "happy family" stuff. Why wasn't anyone lashing out? Why was Kevin's family treating me like I deserved sympathy? I expected a cold shoulder and hurtful words, not this kindness. This was wrong, so wrong. I wanted to shake them and demand that they treat me as I deserved. Inside, I demanded their contempt. I was about to speak out when Kevin walked into the room.

He brushed past me, moving to the center of the room. Val and Doug followed. Val was wearing a flowing black pantsuit with a red collarless tank top underneath. Transformed from the frumpy woman an hour ago—she had energized her hair into a fluffy mane that curled and tumbled to frame her face. She still had style. She quickly hugged her parents. Doug merely shook hands with Karl before kissing Mildred lightly on the cheek.

The group of us stood like chessmen on the board, waiting for someone to move.

Kevin caught my eye and held my gaze for longer than necessary. I looked away, the words I wanted to speak dying on my lips. He understood what I was thinking and told me now was not the time. I took a deep breath, stuffing my anger deep into my soul. I was good at this practice: stuffing things away, out of sight, out of mind.

Having removed the threat of a family breakdown, Kevin spoke. "Okay, the limousine is here. Do we have everything we need?" No one responded verbally. We all nodded. "It's time to say goodbye to our angel." His voice cracked again.

Both Mildred and Val rushed to his side. I caught Kevin's eye. He squeezed Val's hand, hugged his mom, and then extricated himself from their clutches. "I'm okay you two." He took his mom's hands. "Mom, Dad needs you." He turned to Val. "And Val, you're a brilliant sister. I'm going to be okay. I have a hard day ahead, but so does Barbara. She needs me, and we will get through this together."

Val nodded, moving back to Doug's side.

Kevin walked over to me and took my hand. "Okay," he said, addressing everybody. "We won't need our coats until the cemetery, so don't put them on now. We can leave them in the car and be warm enough on the drive." He paused. No one had moved. "Here we go."

Kevin led me to the front door. He opened it and let everyone exit ahead of us. Before we left, he asked, "Are you okay?"

I nodded. Neither of us was okay with what was in front of us, but I was handling things as well as possible.

I squeezed his hand.

We walked to the car together.

CHAPTER EIGHTEEN

The car pulled up under the awning at the funeral chapel, parking behind the hearse that would take our child to the cemetery after the ceremony. I noticed a steady stream of young people going through the doors. The parking lot looked full, and cars lined the street beside the funeral home.

The young chauffeur opened the left door first, then the right.

Kevin climbed out and reached back to help me. As I stood up, Doug and Valerie came around the back of the car. Kevin reached back and helped his dad first, and then his mom exited the car. Then, he took my elbow and led the way into the chapel.

Everyone looked at us. My eyes darted from person to person. I didn't recognize anyone, perhaps because I couldn't focus on them. I wanted to fall through a hole or become invisible. Instead, I concentrated on my steps, reminding myself to move one foot, then the other.

Penny Franklin appeared beside us as if by magic. "The place is packed," she said. "I've had to open the balcony, and people are still streaming in. If this keeps up, I will have to put them downstairs with the monitors. From the looks of the delivered food, I don't think we'll have enough for everyone. This is insane. I haven't seen this many people at a funeral in my entire career."

I flashed back to the funeral I had initially thought I wanted. My cheeks flamed, and I wanted to weep—not for Andrea, but for myself—my shame. The itchiness was back as panic filled me. I wanted to turn around and run out the door. This was a spectacle, not a funeral. There was no way that all these people knew our daughter.

Kevin stopped walking. He turned toward Penny. "Well, there isn't a whole lot we can do, is there? People have come and we have to deal with it. I think many of them will leave when we go to the cemetery. If we don't announce a reception until then, maybe we won't have anything to worry about."

Penny shook her head. "It's in the memorial pamphlet. We've run out of them, but Earl is doing what he can to make more and ensure the ushers are getting them distributed. We also recruited a few college students to help with that, recommended of course, by the ones you had already chosen."

The rest of the family had crowded up, listening to what was being said. Valerie spoke up. "Why is this our problem? Surely as a funeral director, this is something you should deal with. My brother has enough on his plate without having to solve your problems."

I couldn't breathe. I wobbled a little.

Kevin looked at me with alarm. "It's okay, Val, it will be what it is." He turned to Penny. "Please do your best for our girl." He patted my hand. "Now, let's get seated."

We moved into the sanctuary, walking down the long aisle to the front pew, where the reserved sign hung. In my peripheral vision, a sea of dark colors was on both sides. I kept my focus on the destination, the front pew. When we arrived, Kevin and I stepped aside, letting his sister and parents move in ahead of us. We sat then, and he leaned back and blew out a long breath.

I looked over at him. Tears glistened in his eyes. I looked away. That's when I noticed it. The coffin. The white casket that held our girl sat off to the left of a podium near to where I sat. Red roses and white carnations adorned the top. Why hadn't I seen it before? This was why we were here.

Of course, I thought. I was so worried about me—I wasn't thinking of her. Typical Barbara! Selfish to the end.

Those words echoed inside, cutting deeply into my soul. Every fiber of my being was screaming. Knowing I couldn't get past Kevin, I was unsure what to do. I sat stiffly as the panic escalated until I was panting for air. When Kevin noticed, he put his arm around my shoulders, forcing me to bend forward. He leaned over me, whispering in my ear. The first sob caught in my throat.

I coughed. Gently, he rubbed my shoulder, whispering words of comfort. "It's okay, it'll be okay. You'll be okay. Hang in there. You're stronger than this. I'm right here. Breathe deeply, darling. Breathe in through your nose and out through your mouth. Long slow breaths. I'm still here."

I heard the term of endearment, and for once—it didn't frighten me. Like a life preserver on a stormy sea, I clung to it. Kevin was all I needed at that moment. My shattered heart beat a little as I took a long breath. It was like this in the early days of our marriage, when I was first pregnant with Andrea. Panic attacks threatened to destroy me, yet Kevin was always there like a beacon on shore, calling me home. At that moment, I couldn't remember why I'd left him.

The music stopped, and the crowd hushed. Though I was still gathering myself together, I drew on my inner strength to sit up. Two young people stood at the podium. I recognized the girl. It was the girl from across the street. "Good morning," she said. "I'm Cathy Morrison Dempsey."

"And I'm Leo Dempsey," the young man said as he stepped

forward. "Cathy and I were friends with Andrea throughout school. Cathy and Andrea lived across the street from one another. I lived only a few blocks over. Our hearts are heavy with sorrow for losing our friend, and we feel privileged to be here today to commemorate Andrea's life. Andrea was someone who lived life to the fullest. She wasn't reckless, she was exuberant. Challenging convention, she walked with purpose. She recognized what she wanted out of life and was working toward that when her life ended abruptly."

Cathy stepped up to the microphone again. "Andrea loved music. She often said that music ignited the soul, soothed the savage beast or lifted the spirits. She listened to all genres. Here to sing us one of Andrea's favorite songs, a song that she often said she could have written herself, is another classmate, Sara Nichols." Leo and Cathy moved back from the microphones and sat in the two chairs on the right side of the platform.

A tall, thin woman with long, straight black hair hanging down to her waist stepped to the front. She was wearing a hands-free microphone over her ear. A strumming guitar lifted the melody into the room, a tune I recognized from the radio. A few people shuffled around, but the crowd was mostly quiet.

A low, soft hum filled the room as her voice built the melody. Then, she poured out the lyrics with her clear and smooth vocals, easily carrying the song. I followed along for a moment before letting my mind wander.

Andrea was three when I left her for the last time. She shrieked her grief at me, reaching her chubby little arms toward me as if she could catch me, stop me from leaving. I can still see her tear-filled brown eyes. A pang of guilt tugged at my heart as it did every time this image came to mind. I usually pushed it away, though. Today, I allowed it to hang there as I let go for the first time since Monday night. Tears streamed down my face, dropping unceremoniously from my chin. I didn't wipe them—I just cried.

The song ended, and the two hosts stepped back up to the microphone. They introduced Kevin. The moment he left, the icy breeze of abandonment hit me as he ambled toward the podium. He spoke to Leo and Cathy, hugging them both briefly before turning to the microphone. Extracting some white cards from an inside pocket, he set them on the podium. Then he raised the microphone slightly.

The crowd shuffled nervously as he stood there without speaking. He wasn't smiling. He was staring. I worried he had stage fright and didn't know if I should go up there to help. Val was hissing the same thought to Doug when Kevin spoke.

"First off, I would like to thank you all for coming out today. Andrea's mother and I are at a loss ... well, frankly ... we're entirely overwhelmed." He ran a hand across his brow and down his face, covering his mouth.

He cleared his throat. "Andrea was a precocious child. She could be willful, but not stubborn. She knew what she wanted, and she worked with great determination to achieve her goals. Her grades in school allowed her to go to the university of her choice. She received a bursary to pay the tuition for her first year. With many friends, clear by the crowd here today, she didn't discriminate—everyone was her friend. Laughing, dancing and having fun was her nature."

Kevin paused and looked around the room.

"Above all, Andrea loved words and telling stories. She wanted to write for a living. She worked on the school newspaper, writing a human-interest column. I think one of those columns would tell you more about who she was, far better than I ever could, so I will read that to you now. She read this at the funeral of our neighbor, the woman in this story. These are Andrea's words."

Her name was Rachel Horowitz. At eighty-seven, she was perhaps the oldest person I knew. Her laughing brown eyes inside a round wrinkled face were always welcoming whenever I stopped by for tea. I would watch her putter around her antiquated kitchen, pulling out homemade cookies and warming her tea pot as I pretended she was my grandmother.

I loved watching her tuck loose strands of steel gray hair back into the bun she always wore. She was meticulous in her appearance, though she seemed homey and welcoming, not stiff and perfect. Rachel was a powerhouse, giving and working until the day she went to bed for the last time. The street mourned her like they had lost a part of themselves. Yellow ribbons and wreaths with yellow flowers adorned each door on the block, and few can say that about any neighbor before or since who has made that kind of impact on so many people.

As a young girl, I spent time with Mrs. Horowitz whenever my father had to work overtime. Usually, he worked his schedule around mine, but sometimes he needed to see clients or work later than normal, and, on those occasions, I went down the street to stay with Mrs. Horowitz. I spent time with her in my teens because she was always encouraging, comforting, and inspiring. If I had a problem or a concern, she always made me feel better. She never told me what to do but pointed me in the right direction.

If I had good news, she was the person I wanted to share it with. She would cluck excitedly when I won an award or made the team. I never left her house feeling empty. She always spun the air and made it lighter, even when the sun was shining and life couldn't seem to get better.

My curiosity drove me to discover her secrets. I

wanted to know why she always saw the good in people, searched for silver linings, and was never angry or frustrated with life. Had she lived a charmed life? Had she never experienced the traumas, chaos, and turbulence of life? I had so many questions, so I went to the source.

In the afternoon, I sat with her in her tiny house, which was filled with trinkets and treasures from the children whose lives she had touched, including my meager offerings. She told me the story of her life. It would be our last conversation. Four days later, she died.

Rachel Goldstein was born in Germany when the Jewish people lived in great duress. Her father helped his family out of Germany before the atrocities started. The little family suffered many hardships and setbacks on their way to freedom. Once in Canada, her father suffered a heart attack and died, leaving her mother alone with four children under ten. Mrs. Goldstein found work and kept the family together, even helping three of her children attend university.

Interested in helping people, Rachel studied nursing and was in her first year at Crawford Memorial Hospital when she met and married Albert Horowitz. She dreamed of having several babies, even picking out names and recording them in her journals. But babies were not in their future. Albert had suffered an acute case of scarlet fever as a young boy, and he could not give Rachel what she most desired. Rather than becoming bitter and angry, Rachel returned to work at the hospital. She took extra training until she learned the specifics of working in the preemie nursery, or what today we would call a neonatal care unit.

She excelled. Here she lived out her dream of having many babies, though these were only in her care for a short time. Some she nursed for a few months, some for a few weeks, and the unfortunate ones who lasted only a few days. She treated each one with love and care, going the extra mile to make sure that these new tiny bundles were nurtured and felt loved.

Fragile and precious, these tiny, premature and struggling babies did more than survive. If you spoke with anyone in that department—doctors, nurses, parents—they all said that Rachel Horowitz performed miracles. Statistically, that fact was borne out by the numbers of babies who survived and the short time it took them to be released from care. Rachel Horowitz is a local hero.

Albert died, and Rachel continued working. When the hospital forced her to retire at age sixty-five, she continued to go to the hospital daily, sitting with the little ones and giving them her extra attention and care. She gave of herself because she couldn't imagine doing anything else. At age eighty, she stopped going daily, and at age eighty-five, she stopped going at all. She said she no longer trusted her arms to hold such fragile blessings.

She died two years later, three weeks before her eighty-eighth birthday.

I will remember Mrs. Horowitz for her laugh, smile, and the joy on her face every time she looked at me. She made me feel like the most precious thing that had ever graced her doorstep. When I spoke with the other neighborhood kids, they all said exactly the same thing.

I can't pretend to know why God didn't bless Rachel Horowitz with her own children, but if I had to hazard a guess, I would say that in his infinite wisdom, he identified that someone with such a capacity for love would serve the greater good in the place where he led her to be. A place where hundreds, if not thousands, of tiny souls experienced a special brand of kindness and love. A place where, in the most delicate moments of life, miracles were born.

CHAPTER NINETEEN

Kevin paused after reading Andrea's words, tears glistening in his eyes. I wanted to rush up and throw my arms around him. But I sat there, my own eyes watering.

A deep breath and in a cracking voice, he spoke again. "Andrea was my miracle. She brought me so much joy through the years. That spark inside her, put a bounce into everything she did. Unique, she didn't go through the moody teenage years, testing the boundaries and fighting every rule. She was always respectful to others, treating people with kindness. She gave more thought to the feelings of others than she did her own."

All around me, I heard people breaking down—sobs being stifled, noses being cleared, whispers of comfort and consolation being offered. Doug was holding Val in his arms, both faces wet with tears. Karl and Mildred looked truly shattered, neither shedding the tears that rested behind wounded expressions. Their hands linked so tightly that their knuckles were white.

I sat there, apart from everyone, alone and frightened, holding my emotions tightly. Unwilling to become a spectacle, fodder for the supper tables and water coolers, I needed Kevin to shield me. I wanted to scream with the pain inside my heart, to shout at someone to stop this. Why didn't Andrea come in and say it was all a joke?

As Kevin spoke, the longing to break down the barrier between Andrea and me grew. If only I had asked her for forgiveness and shared with her why I had left. Would she comprehend my heart, though I didn't understand it myself? I was learning who my daughter was, who she had been. I was jealous and angry that Rachel Horowitz knew my daughter and that I would never learn about Andrea firsthand. It was unconscionable that I hadn't taken the time to really talk with her. It had been too easy to put it off to tomorrow, thinking I had years to make amends.

Lost in thought, I wandered down roads not only untraveled, but not built. Celebrating her wedding, joyously welcoming her babies into the world. I silently promised I would be a better grandmother if only by some miracle, Andrea would come back. Hadn't I been punished enough? I was making deals with the devil, but he wasn't listening.

I looked at Kevin. He was mopping his tears with a large white handkerchief. He cleared his throat. "I'm sorry. This has not been easy." A wistful smile flashed across his face as he continued.

"Andrea's heart was bigger than most. She understood people, loved them beyond their frailties and forgave them without question. Surrounded by friends, she was the life of the party."

I stopped listening, my mind snagged on a piece of driftwood on the stream of consciousness.

"She forgave without question ... she forgave without question ... she forgave without question." Those words repeated until I thought I would come out of my skin. She hadn't forgiven me. How could he say that about her? Staring at him, standing up there all pious and self-assured, proclaiming truths that weren't true, I wanted to hit him. I wanted to hit him hard. I wanted to keep hitting him until he realized how cruel and unfair he was being. Preparing for battle, I sat up straight.

Part of me acknowledged I was being unreasonable. Most of me, though, believed I was justified in my anger. I was preparing to stand up when the music began. Kevin's part was over. He hugged Leo and Cathy again as the soloist approached the platform's edge.

"Please stand and join me in singing, 'Amazing Grace.' The words are on the back of your pamphlets." The quiet room erupted with the sounds of people shuffling and rustling to their feet. Coughs and whispers rolled across the expanse, echoing inside my head. I wasn't ready for this. Caught in an eddy of emotions, I did not want to play nice.

Kevin left the stage, trudging toward me. I glared at him, and he smiled sadly back. I stiffened. He slipped into the row beside me, turning over the program to the words as the soloist sang.

I didn't sing. I listened to the words, trying to calm my anger. Why had he said that about Andrea when he knew it wasn't true? He knew she was stiff and formal with me, perfunctory in her conversations with me, like I didn't matter. If she had forgiven me, we would have had a relationship. I would have had a daughter to dote on, not a stranger that I tried to pry words from.

This wasn't the place for that discussion, so I did my best to stuff it away. Kevin sang quietly, almost mouthing the words rather than singing his booming baritone. A wave of compassion rolled over me. I could have caught it, but I let it go. I didn't want to feel compassion for him right now.

The song ended. The crowd sat, and Leo and Cathy were at the podium. Kevin reached for my hand. I pulled away. He looked at me quizzically. I ignored him. He stiffened.

Cathy and Leo each spoke about Andrea. They recalled stories of Girl Guide camps, school dances, and graduation. The crowd laughed appropriately as their words brought Andrea to life. Then they opened the microphone to the crowd, asking for special memories. A few people came down and shared stories, but mostly we sat in uncomfortable silence.

Then it was over. Leo spoke to the crowd for the last time. "On behalf of the family, thank you all for coming. We invite close family and friends to stay for a light lunch in the reception hall following the interment at St. Paul's Cemetery." The background music lifted through the air again as we all stood.

Six young men walked to the front. Three to a side, they heaved the casket up onto their shoulders. Then they made their way down the ramp. They crossed to the middle before turning down the aisle beside us. Once they had gone past, Kevin stepped out and allowed me to join him before following them up the aisle. People reached toward us, wanting to shake hands and offer condolences. Shrinking back, I wanted these strangers to stop attacking me with their kindness, their need to express their sorrow when mine was already too much to bear.

Kevin reached out, nodding and thanking people as we made our way out.

Penny met us in the foyer, guiding us to the front doors and into the waiting car. After Val, Doug, Karl, and Mildred were inside, the driver closed the doors.

We waited behind the hearse and as it moved forward—we followed.

CHAPTER TWENTY

It was a short drive to the cemetery. My nerves—frayed and stretched beyond capacity, caused me to feel shattered. If someone had even looked at me, I might have fallen apart. Knowing I had to get through this, I focused on my breathing.

My pain was self-inflicted. It was my choice to abandon Andrea, and looking back, I wondered if it was better in the long run. If I stayed, would she have learned to hate me not because I left her but because she couldn't approve of my lifestyle? She would have judged me six ways from Sunday and wouldn't have been wrong to do that. She never had the chance to reject me because I assumed her feelings were like my own. In the beginning, I hated what I was doing until it became my life, until it was all I knew.

The car stopped, and I emerged from my dark thoughts. No one was speaking. Val and Doug huddled across from Kevin and me. Mildred and Karl looked truly destroyed, their eyes red-rimmed and puffy with emotion. Kevin wiped his palms down the front of his slacks several times, then took several deep breaths. I was so involved in my misery that I was oblivious to the suffering around me.

Kevin vacated his seat when the door opened, then reached his hand back to assist me again—always the gentleman. The rest of the family followed.

A slow winter breeze rushed past—the day was cold and clear. Kevin pulled our coats out, wrapping mine around me before shrugging into his. I stuffed my hands inside the pockets and pulled out my gloves. I noticed we were all doing the same, standing beside the car preparing for the elements we would be subjected to.

None of the six pallbearers wore coats, but they all wore black gloves. The back door of the hearse opened, and Penny stepped forward to lead the way. She presented an imposing figure as she walked ahead of the casket, and we followed behind. There was a crowd of mourners behind us, too. I recognized a few from the neighborhood. Leo and Cathy were striding along in the middle of a pack of young people. I turned back, but not before I spotted my mother and my two brothers. My heart beat a little faster.

The pallbearers settled the casket on the green straps, then stepped away, their job complete. Earl took a moment to lay the large bouquet back on top of it. When it was in place, he stepped away and Penny moved to the head of the grave, a prayer book open before her. She encouraged everyone to step closer. A moment of hesitation ensued before people shuffled forward. The wind picked up, and I shivered, huddling into myself. Kevin put his arm around me, and I nestled into him for warmth, grateful for it.

I stared at the white box until my eyes burned. Avoiding the crowd, I studied the pewter handles and the red and white floral display. The last thing I wanted was for my mother or brothers to catch my eye. I also didn't want to focus on why I was there. Knowing my daughter was inside—was already too much. If I imagined her lying in there—I would lose my mind. She should be at home in her room. I wanted her to stroll up and ask what we were doing. It wasn't right that we were standing here without her. It was surreal to be here. Part of me was unsure I wasn't dreaming, part of me stood on the truth and wished it weren't so.

Penny spoke in a powerful voice. I think she offered a prayer for Andrea's safe ascension, but I couldn't grasp her words. I was following my own thoughts. Earl appeared with a bucket of flowers. On cue, he moved over to us. We each took a flower. He moved around the group. I watched as many people with wet faces and red-rimmed eyes took an offered flower, wondering who they were to Andrea. Close friend? Co-worker? Fellow student? Most of the faces were strangers to me. My family didn't come forward. Perhaps they were too far back in the crowd.

After distributing all the flowers, Earl moved away from the crowd. I noticed he had something in his hand and, with the push of a button, the casket descended into the ground. My heart lurched, my breath caught in my throat, and I let out a strangled cry.

Kevin sniffled loudly. I looked up into his face. His cheeks were wet. He'd been crying, maybe this whole time. Wrapped up in my own thoughts, I hadn't even bothered to check.

The casket stopped when the top was about one foot below the ground.

Penny stepped forward. "Ashes to ashes, dust to dust." She tossed her flower onto the lowered casket. Then she glanced at Kevin. He understood her look, moved forward, and tossed his flower. I followed, stepping close to the grave as Kevin stepped back. I didn't throw my flower and, after a moment's hesitation, Val and Doug stepped up together and tossed theirs, followed by Mildred and Karl.

The other mourners with flowers all moved forward and took turns, but I stood there, my flower clutched to my chest. I watched the others, helpless to let go. If I threw that flower in, it was over, so

I stood my ground. I waited as stem after stem landed on the coffin, bouncing recklessly before settling in place. Red and white carnations, red and white roses underneath—red and white, red and white.

My breathing changed, and I felt faint. Yet I stood there, head bowed, watching. When there were no more flowers, when the ceremony was over, Kevin stepped up beside me. He looked into my face, but I ignored him. If I looked back, I would lose it for good. I would jump into that grave with Andrea and demand they throw the dirt on me.

The crowd grew restless, everyone waiting expectantly. Taking a firm grip on my emotions, I let down my guard. I whispered, "Goodbye Andrea." Then I tossed my flower in. The moment the flower landed, the coffin descended farther into the ground, like the weight of that one flower was more than it could handle. I sank to my knees.

"Noooooo!" I howled. "Noooooo!" I couldn't take the pain. It was more than I could bear at that moment.

Kevin kneeled beside me, whispering words I couldn't hear. The only sound audible was the hissing of the wind. I sobbed loudly then. It was all too real. I would never see her again. She was gone forever. The only good thing I'd ever done in my life, the only unselfish thing.

This wasn't how life was supposed to go.

CHAPTER TWENTY-ONE

I had never been one to look back. I had always done things without fully contemplating the ramifications or consequences, believing that if it were meant to be, it would be. At that moment, I wanted to rewind the clock to that year when I lost control of the wolves at the door and fed them instead. This time I would figure out how to live with them until I had mastery over their snapping jaws and their enormous appetite for destruction. I would stay with Andrea and this day would never come because our lives would have taken a different path.

Why wasn't it possible to go back? Life had always been hard, but this was more than I could manage on my own. How would I live in this world, knowing she was no longer here?

Kevin lifted me to my feet, and I let him. I took gulps of cold air and then turned my face away, pulling tight against Kevin's body.

The ceremony was over. People turned away. Some came over offering condolences, but many would be returning to the funeral chapel. I let Kevin lead me away, back along the short path to the car.

I was shivering now. My teeth chattering loudly.

The six of us sat in the car, each in our own thoughts. The driver handed us blankets before closing the door. Kevin took one and placed it across my lap. My shivering slowed as some warmth returned.

Moments later, we were pulling up to the funeral chapel. Several clusters of people stood deep in conversation, watching us curiously.

Once more, we were climbing back out of the car. I needed the washroom, so once inside, I excused myself and slipped away. The room wasn't empty. A tall, thin girl stood at the sink. I hurried past her into a stall, slamming the door shut.

Minutes later, I was at the sink, taking stock. My eyes were bloodshot and puffy. My complexion was blotchy, and my hair was wind-blown. I looked like hell.

Val came in as I was fixing my hair. "How you doing? You need anything?"

For a moment, I didn't respond. I wanted to shout at her—I needed my daughter to not be dead. Glancing sideways, as she stood at the sink next to mine, patting her hair, it was obvious she was there to check up on me.

"Sarah Jean and Sam called my cell when we were at the cemetery. They wish they could be here, but their commitments … you know." She shrugged.

Sarah Jean and Sam were Val and Doug's children. They were fraternal twins born a year before Andrea. After university, they both chose to go to Japan to teach English and left in August. Their commitments to their jobs meant they could not come home for this.

I nodded at Val, not daring to speak. Val, however, had no compunction to keep her mouth shut. "It was a lovely service. Andrea would have liked it."

I closed my eyes and bit my tongue. Then I took a deep breath and finished my hair.

"You seem a little tense, are you okay?"

"A little tense? A little tense? Sure, I'm a little tense. I just buried my daughter." My anger raged through my veins. I wanted to tear her hair out, to take my frustrations out on her, if for no other reason than she was here.

When the door opened, two young girls came in. I grabbed my purse and took the opportunity to leave, rushing past them before the door closed. I went into the hall. Inside, a sea of people sat at tables, talking among themselves. The noise was deafening—inane chatter spilled from lips.

Kevin stood on the far side of the room with a cup of coffee. He was talking to some people I didn't know.

I turned and raced up the stairs, looking for a hiding place. The upper level was quiet. A few people exited the main doors, but there were no clusters of people hanging out and chatting. I looked left, then right, frantic for air. My coat was in the car, so I couldn't be outside long before the temperature forced me back in. I noticed the small chapel and hurried over, hoping the door was unlocked.

It was.

I slipped inside.

CHAPTER TWENTY-TWO

The room oozed calmness. The glow diffused through the high stained glass windows, leaving more darkness than light. Slipping into a pew, I leaned back, closed my eyes, and exhaled loudly. Emptying my mind as best I could, I focused on my breathing. In. Out. In. Out.

I heard the door open. Damn, I hoped it wasn't Earl. He gave me the creeps. I didn't want him to tell me I should not be in here. I sat rigidly, keeping my eyes closed.

"Hello, Barbara." I sat up straight, swinging around toward the voice. My mother stood meekly at the end of the pew. "May I sit?"

I wanted to shout at her to get out. She was stealing my peace—I needed this peace. I stared hard, hoping she would get the message. She took my silence for permission and sat down next to me, settling her purse on her lap.

Needing distance, I scooted a little farther away from her.

"I watched for you downstairs and when you left, I followed you. I'm sorry for your loss, Barbara. No mother should have to bear such a burden."

It was funny—as much as I thought I despised this woman, those words cut right through the years and I was five years old, standing in the backyard with a shoe box and a dead cat. Baby Gray wasn't an old cat, but she wasn't a kitten either. A car had run over her and it devastated me. My mother had scooped that cat up, and laid her into a large shoe box along with her favorite toys. Before Dad came home from work, she had dug a hole in the backyard and we'd given Baby Gray a funeral. Patrick and Dennis and I had held hands while mom said a prayer for her soul. It was the first funeral I'd ever been to.

"Patrick and Dennis are downstairs. I didn't want to overwhelm you, but I wanted to talk to you."

"Why? What is there to say?" I spat those words at her. She flinched, and I felt elated for a second because I'd hit the target. Then I dropped my eyes, as shame for having attacked her for no reason hit me in the face. "I'm sorry," I muttered, unable to look her in the face.

"Look, Barbie, I don't want to fight with you. There are many miles between us and many hurt feelings. But I loved Andrea, and I love you, too. I just wanted you to know I am here if you need me."

My dander was up. She was here now. Where was she all those years ago when I needed her? It was too late. We had too much unresolved. I would not make this easy for her just because she wanted it that way.

"Well, I don't need you. Not anymore. So, you can take your patronizing attitude and your platitudes and get the hell away from me."

"Don't you speak to your mother that way!"

Patrick stood at the end of the pew. Bristling and angry, he looked ready for a fight. I was being ambushed. How dare they do this to me on this day? I stood, my heart pounding so loudly it was all I heard. It was fight-or-flight time, and there were two of them. In a very unladylike manner, I stepped onto the pew and leaped to the one behind me.

Patrick moved to cut me off.

I stopped, panting with fear. "Let me pass, Patrick."

"No! It's time we settled this once and for all."

"This is neither the time nor the place. You will not bully me!"

"I am not bullying you. I am trying to get you to see sense."

"If you understood anything about me, you'd know that letting me go makes sense."

"This family has been fractured long enough. It's time to find common ground."

"So you think it's the right time to ambush me on the day my daughter is buried?"

"It's not the best time, but you make talking to you hard work."

"I am not doing this now. I am not doing this ever."

"Grow up, Barbie. This isn't about what you want."

"Enough!" My mother interrupted our sparring.

"But Mom ..." Patrick whined.

"Let her go. She has made up her mind."

Patrick stepped aside, his expression hard and angry. For a moment, I wondered why there was a sudden rush to resolve this today. But my way was clear, and I wanted to get out of there. I ran from the room as fast as my high heels would go. Once in the large foyer, I took a deep breath, tears pricking my eyes. I wanted to go home, to be alone with my thoughts and my grief.

I grabbed my phone and scrolled through my contacts. I found Bobby's name and pushed send. The phone rang several times before he answered.

"Hello?"

"Hi, it's me. Can you come and get me?"

"Um, not right now."

His refusal slapped me back, and I floundered. "Please, I'm

dying here."

"Okay. I'll be fifteen minutes."

I sighed, the weight of the day dropping away. Out of the corner of my eye, I noticed Dennis coming up the stairs. Running for the main door, I spotted the limousine parked just where we'd left it. I scrambled inside. The driver jerked up, surprised. "Hey! Oh, it's you."

"I'm sorry. I just need some space. Someone is coming to get me. Can I just sit here until they arrive?"

"No skin off my nose." He turned around, slouched back down, and pulled his cap over his eyes.

Alone, I texted Kevin, telling him I was on my way home and would talk to him later.

There was no reply. Maybe his phone was turned off, or maybe he didn't even bring it. Unlike most people, he wasn't attached to it.

True to his word, Bobby pulled up. I opened the door to the limo. "Tell Kevin that I went home," I said as I grabbed my coat and exited the vehicle.

"Yes, ma'am." He replied, though he stayed in his relaxed position.

I quickly stepped into Bobby's car. "Please take me to Kevin's so I can get my car." He nodded and put the car in gear. As we pulled away, the tension inside me drained away. The relief was so intense that I cried. Bobby reached over and patted my hand.

I cried all the way to Kevin's house. Bobby pulled up behind my car. I looked over at him, grateful for his help. "Do you want to follow me home?"

"I can't, love. I left Thelma and the kids in the lurch. I told them there was an emergency on the site, and I'd be there in half an hour. Sorry."

I was both relieved and annoyed. It would be easy to lose myself in his arms, so I didn't have to think, but I also needed to be alone to sort out what happened. "Okay. Thanks for rescuing me." I opened the door and stepped out.

"Anytime." I walked to my car, and before I was inside, Bobby was speeding past. I drove home. The quiet of the apartment surrounded me. I tossed my purse on the couch, kicked my shoes into the bottom of the closet, and walked into the kitchen to make a pot of tea. After I filled the kettle, I went into the bedroom and changed into jeans and a T-shirt. Barefoot, I padded back to the kitchen and made the tea before settling in the cozy armchair.

I thought about turning on some music, but right now.

I wanted to just think about things.

CHAPTER TWENTY-THREE

The first thing I thought about was my mother. I hadn't seen her in years. Was it ten or twelve years? It had been an accidental meeting that time. We were both Christmas shopping at the mall. I had been so absorbed in getting something nice for Andrea that I wasn't paying much attention to the surrounding throng. I nearly jumped out of my skin when she came up behind me and said, "Hello Barbie."

We chatted about Christmas plans. She was hosting a family dinner and wanted to know if I would come. I politely declined, and she nodded as if that was the expected answer. I was gracious and offered to buy her a cup of coffee at the food court. It was awkward, and neither of us knew how to talk to the other. She told me about Patrick and Dennis and their kids. I nodded and said the right things.

Just before I left, she placed her hand over mine and said, "It was so good seeing you today, Barbie. I don't need anything else for Christmas, now that I've seen my girl."

I remember being pleased and annoyed. If she had just stood up to Dad, even once, we would have been a family. I walked away, a great lump of sorrow burrowing in my heart.

Today, she had once again caught me off guard. She had promised in her phone message that she would behave, so why had she ambushed me? I thought about that now. She was thinner. Not that she'd ever been truly fat, but she had always been round. Today she looked angular. I guess looking after dad was hard. Well, that was her choice. She should have left the bastard years ago. Now she was paying the piper. Was her weight loss intentional or because of the tensions in her life? Was she ill? That thought sent a chill down my spine.

Why hadn't I just listened to her? I chastised myself for being a coward and for running. I don't think I would have if Patrick hadn't shown up and jumped into the fray, though. If we had been alone long enough, despite the hissing and the spitting, we would have talked.

Thinking of my mother, I realized we had many parallels in our lives. There were also chasms of differences. She did what she thought was right, at least what was right for her. So, it would seem, did I. She had gone from school to marriage. The only career she had was being a homemaker. I had done the same until I took up a career as a server/hostess, a job from which I derived a lot of satisfaction. She needed to be needed and took pride in looking after her family. I didn't want to be needed—it was a burden that weighed on me. Her role as a mother and a wife was paramount to anything else. My role as a wife and mother ended the day I walked out on Andrea.

I think I loved her somewhere, under all the resentments and anger. I just didn't know how to be with her without being reminded of what life had been like back then. Back when Dad had changed lovers, from Mom to whisky, life took on an ominous air. Before that, we were, or so it seemed to me, a happy family unit. We went on quick trips to the mountains and camped in a tent.

Then whisky became more important to Dad. The dark clouds of shame and embarrassment crowded out the sunshine. We all walked on eggshells, expectant and fearful. Anger bubbled under the surface. Anger that we'd lost the joy of living. I didn't see it as a sickness or a weakness. It was a selfish choice. My dad chose that amber liquid over his family every time he tipped that bottle to his lips.

In those early days, Mom pretended that things were fine. I remember coming home from school, excited that I had won the grade three spelling bee. She hushed me and told me my father was ill. I was so concerned that I went to my room and made him a get-well card. When I had completed it, I walked down the hall to his room. The door was closed. I hesitated momentarily. I would be quiet and slip the card on the bedside table and leave without waking him.

When I opened the door, the smell overwhelmed me and I gagged, hesitating to go farther into the room. Wanting to leave my gift, though, I put one hand over my nose and tiptoed into the room. Dad was lying on the bed in his underwear. He had messed his pants. A stream of vomit ran down the edge of the bed; the pool of vomit lay drying on the floor. I gagged again and stepped back.

My dad rolled over, half sitting up as he took in my presence. There was no warm affection in his eyes, no smile on his face. Instead, his eyes peer menacingly at me from a red and angry face.

I stepped back as fear gripped my heart. Then he roared—the words lost to me today. I dropped the card on the floor and ran to my room, slamming my door behind me. Inside, I looked for some place to hide, some place safe where he couldn't reach me. I opened the closet but rejected it. Too much stuff on the floor. I ran to the bed, dropped to my knees, and scooted underneath, worming my way to the farthest corner and curling into a tiny ball. I heard my father's roars echoing through the house over the pounding of my heart.

Terror and self-preservation prevented me from relaxing. I didn't know how that monster had taken over my father's body, but

I certainly didn't want that to happen to me. Afraid the monster would hear me; I choked back my tears. It seemed like an eternity as I lay tucked under that bed, my breath shallow and thin, before the door to my room opened. Shrinking back against the wall, I held my breath.

Someone padded around the room, and then a hand pulled up the bedspread, and a face appeared.

Patrick. I sobbed.

"Come here you. It's okay." He placated.

I shook my head. "No, I don't want it to get me."

"Nothing is going to get you."

After shaking my head again, he let the bedspread drop, and I heard him leave the room.

A few minutes later, he was back. "She won't come out, she's under there."

"Barbie, please come out," my mother called softly.

I hesitated, then I crawled out.

She was standing in the middle of the room, her eyes wet with tears. "Barbie ..."

I scrambled to my feet and slammed into her, wrapping my arms around her waist. She hugged me, cooing softly. Then she moved us over, enabling her to sit on my bed. When she sat, she pulled me onto her lap. Continuing to soothe me, she rubbed my back in circular motions, all the while shushing my sobs and whispering platitudes.

"What happened to Daddy? How did that monster get inside of him?"

"Oh, honey, it's not a monster." She squeezed me briefly. "I told you that Daddy was sick. He ate something terrible. If I had known you would make him a card, I would have told you to wait to give it to him. Or to let me take it in."

"What did he eat?" Whatever it was, I wanted to make sure I never ate it.

"He didn't eat nothing, you stupid girl. He drank an entire bottle of whisky!" Patrick shouted from the door.

"Patrick!" my mother shouted as she stood, placing me on the bed. "That will be enough of that!"

He looked chastised but defiant. He stood his ground, waiting for her to contradict him.

She didn't. She looked back at me. "Now, I need you to be very quiet and not disturb him again. He will be better tomorrow." She left the room, and I sat there knowing in my little eight-year-old heart that life as I'd known it would differ from then on.

And it was. We had good days and bad days for years. There were times of frivolity followed by months of insanity. The carefree days of childhood melted into the background as the years passed, and Dad's affair with the bottle grew into full-blown alcoholism. I dreaded coming home from school—I stopped inviting friends over. I learned to despise my father, the rage in my belly eating away at me, at who I was, as surely as he changed. We became a family of survivors, each day a battle, sleep, the only reprieve from the war.

CHAPTER TWENTY-FOUR

My tea had grown cold as I sifted through the memories of bygone days. I had forgotten that today I'd buried my daughter. I picked scabs and peered underneath, reminding myself why I avoided my family. My lukewarm tea sloshed onto my jeans when the buzzer interrupted my reverie.

"Dammit!" I jumped to my feet.

The buzzer pealed again, urgently. For a moment, I wondered if it was Patrick. Had he come to finish what he started? Well, he'd not get any further. I picked up the receiver. "Hello?"

"So, you are home!" It was Kevin, and he didn't sound too pleased.

"Yes, I'm home. I sent you a text."

"I left my phone at home, so I didn't know. Can I come up?"

"Not if you're going to pick a fight with me, you can't."

"Well, I can't promise it will be pleasant, but we must talk."

I hesitated. The last thing I needed was to fight with Kevin, but then I remembered he didn't fight. He was about the only person in the world I had never fought with. Even during our marriage, I would go crazy at his level-headed calmness. I'd tell him that sometimes a fight clears the air. He never took the bait.

"Fine." I buzzed him in.

A few minutes later, he was tapping at the door. I had already changed out of my wet jeans when I opened the door.

Kevin brushed past me and moved into the living room before turning around. "I can't believe you would leave Andrea's funeral without saying goodbye. I spent all my time looking for you, watching the door and you didn't have the courtesy to show up." He stared at me.

I stared back.

"Val said you were in the bathroom, and she thought you were on your way into the reception when you left her."

"I was."

"Well, what happened? I really needed some support. Not to mention so many people wanted to pass along their condolences."

For one brief second, I was going to play fair. I thought about apologizing for being weak, for being scared. But something rose in me and that beast wiped away all the kindness inside. "Yeah, like so many people care about me," I shouted.

Kevin's eyes widened at my verbal assault. Then sadness replaced his surprise. "That's right, Barbara, no one cares about you. Same old story, same old song. Your record never changes, does it?"

Tears pricked my eyes. In all the years we'd known each other, Kevin was the one person who never took me to task. He cajoled, he comforted, he encouraged. He never reprimanded me or my behavior.

I didn't let the sadness of that realization stop me, though. I steeled myself for the fight and dove back in.

"That's right Kevin, my record never changes because it's the song of my life. It's my *theme* song! People have been mistreating me my whole life. But I take their crap and put a smile on my face, and I keep walking."

"Never have truer words been spoken. You walk all right. You walk away when the going gets tough. Whenever you might have to give something back. I'm sick of it. I needed you today, but you weren't there. AGAIN!"

He looked like he was going to cry. Part of me wanted to wrap my arms around him and part of me wanted to drop kick him. I waffled.

"Well, at least I'm consistent."

He smiled sadly then, the fight draining from his face. He really wasn't a fighter, so if he came this far, he must be close to the edge. I softened, too, though disappointment surged that we weren't going to really get into things.

"Well, if you must know, I was going to come in. I spotted you standing there talking with some people I didn't know, and I just needed a little time to get my head together. So, I went up to the chapel. I wasn't there long, but my mom showed up, and then Patrick came in. It was about to kick off, and if I had stayed any longer, it would have. So, I just left."

Immediately, Kevin was concerned. "I'm sorry. Are you okay?"

"Yeah, I'm fine. Mom promised to be on her best behavior, so I'm annoyed she would trap me like she did."

Kevin said nothing. He knows the story and the history of my family dynamics.

I stepped closer. "I'm sorry I wasn't there for you. It's been a bitch of a day all around. I still can't believe she's gone—you know."

"I do." He nodded. "All week, I kept expecting her to come bouncing through the door. Then I'd remember that she would never come home again." His voice broke, and a sob escaped. I touched his arm compassionately. He struggled to get his composure. I moved closer. He stepped closer. I put my arms around him and he wrapped me in his embrace.

Standing there in my living room, he let go and sobbed against my shoulder as I patted his back and placated him with hushes and tender words. Tears rolled down my face as well. My heart ached. It was a desperate feeling. I was glad he was there. We had lost something precious, something magical we had created together, and we'd never get that back. It was devastating, and at that moment—I think for the first time—I realized just what I had missed out on.

We didn't take our sorrow to the bedroom this time. It seemed important that we focus on Andrea, not on our needs. We moved to the couch and sat side by side as he regaled me with stories as they came to him. Instead of making me feel better, his stories made me feel worse. The life I had left had never haunted me before, but with Andrea's death, the ghost of all those lost opportunities, missed memories and time wasted rose and stirred my heart to despair.

I smiled, though, not letting him know how shredded my heart was.

My pain was my doing.

It was my choice to go, and in doing so, I missed the most important thing in the world.

CHAPTER TWENTY-FIVE

When Kevin left, I went to the bedroom and fell into bed exhausted. I thought sleep would come easily, but it eluded me as my mind whirled through the stories I'd heard today. As my breathing slowed and I fell into a restless sleep, I found myself on the road home, walking up the sidewalk to the house I grew up in. My heart pumped rapidly. My breath was quick and shallow. The house looked weathered and unloved. There were no pretty flowers outside. Next to the steps, trash clung to the shrubs. The windows were dirty, and the siding needed a coat of paint.

As I drew closer to the door, it swung open. The dark interior called to me as I walked up the steps. I was screaming on the inside but unable to stop. I couldn't see anything as my eyes adjusted to the house's darkness. The door slammed behind me, and I screamed. Standing motionless, my heart pounding in my ears, the room came into focus. It wasn't the living room as it should have been. It was Andrea's bedroom. The posters on the wall, the half girl, half woman décor. Someone was standing in the corner. A man.

I waited, willing the man to turn around. When he did, I sighed. It was Kevin. I was relieved until I watched his expression change. He sneered, his lips curled back against his teeth. Although his lips never moved, his voice filled the space between us.

"You know, Barbie, it's too bad you left when you did. A man has needs, you know, and there was no one here but my little Andrea. She was quite the girl. She helped her daddy all the time. Helped him in every way he needed her to."

My stomach roiled against his ugly words. "No, no, no."

"Oh yes, your sweet baby girl was an excellent substitute for her delinquent mother. She kept my bed warm, and we were happy together."

Anger spewed forth. "You bastard!" I rushed to close the space between us. I raised my hand and slapped him hard across the face. He threw back his head and laughed. When he stopped laughing, he looked at me again, his eyes hard and hateful. Only it wasn't Kevin anymore. It was my father.

"Oh, Barbie, you always had such a temper. A good old Irish lass weren't you. So much spirit compared to your poor pathetic mother. Is it any wonder I watched you, wanted you, and finally took you?"

I turned to run, needing to put space between us. He grabbed my arm. I tried to wrench it free, but his grip was tight. I struggled against him. He laughed. "All this fight, Barbie, is making me want you more."

I stopped.

He pulled me close, his rancid breath inches from my face. "Oh, Barbie, I've waited so long to have you in my arms."

Screaming, I sat up straight as the sound echoed around my room. I burst into tears. I hadn't had that dream in years. Seeing my mother and brother must have shaken all the boulders loose—the ones stacked on top of that memory. It was time to bury it again. I never wanted to remember what had happened when I was a girl. I didn't want to go back.

Instead of going back to the days when that house was my prison, I went back to the last time I'd been home. Once I'd married Kevin, I rarely went to my parents' home. I would meet my mother at the mall or a restaurant for lunch. After Andrea came along, I was even more resolved to stay away. I vowed, even while I was pregnant, that I would never expose her to my father.

I went back once a few years after I'd left Kevin. Not by choice, mind you. Patrick told me that Mom had tripped over the ottoman and broken her arm. I didn't believe it for one minute. Dad was drinking again, which meant he was abusing her—again! I went, hoping to talk some sense into her, hoping she would leave him for good.

As I walked up the sidewalk, the dilapidated state of the yard and the exterior of the house saddened me, but didn't surprise me. All the money would feed his habit, and he certainly didn't have the time or the desire to look after his home.

It was a wasted trip. Mom listened to my pleas, but in the end, she was not interested.

Dad was there, in his tank top undershirt that no longer covered his girth. His bare belly hung repulsively over the waistband of his stained pants. He stormed into the kitchen, shouting at me to get out of his house. The verbal abuse he hurled at me went over my head. I didn't care about his opinion of me or my life. My mother pleaded with me to leave before things escalated. I stood, glad to put distance between us. But before I left, I walked right up to him and through clenched teeth, I hissed that if he ever touched her again, I'd kill him. Then I left, and I'd never gone back. I held a level of sympathy for my mom, but it was her life and her choice. I just didn't want any part of it.

Having replayed that memory, I realized that finding sleep again wouldn't be easy. Wrapping myself in a warm terry robe, I moved to the living room. Searching through my music collection, I found my Brahms lullaby CD. After turning on the stereo, I curled under a blanket on the couch. I sat there, letting the music soothe me. I loved classical music, but secretly. No one would understand this about me. They regarded me as a pop music fan. Don't get me wrong. There is nothing wrong with pop music. Much of it is delightful, but if I wanted to connect with my core, classical music worked for me. No lyrics, just powerful melodies that tantalized and mesmerized the senses.

I fell asleep on the couch and woke stiff and sore. The music was still playing softly. I rose and turned it off. It was early November, and I was moving in less than a month. It was time to purge and clean in preparation. I made coffee and started in the kitchen. I pulled out the contents of each cabinet and made two piles. One for things to send to the charity shops, one for things to be packed and moved. I used the dining room table for the stuff I wasn't keeping. I put the other stuff back into the cabinets after I cleaned them.

It was a slow process. Things weren't too dirty, but it's tedious work. I came across a set of salt and pepper shakers that Andrea had given me for Christmas one year. They were ugly little things, a Santa and Mrs. Claus with tiny holes in their ceramic heads. Santa was pepper, Mrs. Claus was salt. I always wondered about that. I would have thought it would have been the other way around.

Remembering the drawer of unused gifts, I put the salt shakers on the dining room table and went back to work. I was purging—getting rid of things I would never use. I finished the cabinets and moved to the pantry. My mind wandered through a myriad of thoughts, from my parents to my brothers to Kevin and then Andrea.

Having finished the kitchen, I moved toward the living room. I passed the table of charity shop items, noting the contents; rose bowls, flower vases, wicker baskets, and those shakers. Moving into the living room, I purged my music collection and ornaments. I pulled all the CDs out and put them on the floor. I sorted them into piles of music or artists I still listened to, those I stopped listening to, and ones that I had stopped listening to but still wanted to keep in my collection.

I popped in a CD I hadn't heard in a long time, trying to decide whether to keep it. When the music played, it took me back to yesterday. Was it only yesterday? The song playing was the one the soloist had sung. My mind whipped back to the church, the white casket languishing on the platform as this tall woman lifted her voice in song. I remember Kevin's arm resting protectively around my shoulders. I closed my eyes and let the music wash over me. Tears spilled down my cheeks.

When the song ended, I stood and put the Santa shakers in a box. Regardless of their uselessness, they were from Andrea and, therefore, precious because there would never be another one.

CHAPTER TWENTY-SIX

I took a break from my sorting and cleaning and went to the gym. Back home, I looked at the mess I'd left behind. Stacks of CDs sat in three piles on the living room floor. The contents of the two end tables lay outside their open doors. The thought of digging through any more today was too much. I wanted to sit down and relax, maybe watch a little television.

But first, I needed a shower and something to eat. After a hot shower, I donned sweatpants and a sleeveless T-shirt. In the kitchen, I made an omelet with finely chopped tomato, onion, green pepper, and cheese. Junk cluttered my table, so I sat in my messy living room. I found the remote and turned on the television just as the newscast detailed Andrea's death. The film clip showed her white casket being carried from the church.

I was too stunned to hear the words spoken by the anchor person—I watched the tragic part of my life playing on my television set.

I called Kevin. He placated me as best he could, but his words couldn't take away the distaste for what I'd seen. I had no desire to be part of the conversations around the city. People took pity on me or justified it by saying that this was what the world was coming to. Everyone had an opinion. Is it the lack of morals or the removal of God from our schools and workplaces? Is it because people pursue their own selfish ambitions ahead of the good of their neighborhood, city, or country? Are we, as a society, on the road to Hell, but don't want to admit it? I shuddered to think about what people were saying about us. About Andrea. About me.

Was this the reason the church filled up beyond capacity? Was it the news coverage that brought our story to their doorsteps and then brought them into my world? It was a huge invasion of privacy. I wanted to call the station and complain, but Kevin said it would die down now that Andrea was buried. The boy was dead. There was no more story. My hope was he was right.

Having lost interest, I turned off the television. I didn't have girlfriends for many reasons, but I wished I could call a friend and go for coffee. The weather was too cold for a walk. There was no snow yet, but it was coming. Everything about my life was unsettled. I was restless.

How had I come to this? Why was I in this place where my life was devoid of people? Kevin had been great this past while, but normally we seldom talked or visited each other. I'd seen and talked more with Kevin in the last week than I'd done since Andrea's high school graduation, when we'd planned a celebratory party together.

I'd been on my own again since I'd kicked Greg Simmons out last Christmas. Greg was the last in a string of failures—I wasn't good at permanent relationships. Some men I'd married; some I hadn't. I vowed to never get into another permanent one. I would live alone and get my needs met through other means.

That's why Bobby was perfect. He was married, which meant he wasn't looking for permanence. I enjoyed having my space, my place, and my schedule. I didn't have to look after anyone, do their laundry, make their meals, or entertain them regularly. Until this moment, this past year had seemed perfect.

I could turn to Kevin. Good old reliable Kevin would be there for me—he'd even said as much. But since I couldn't give him what he wanted, taking advantage of his kindness seemed wrong. He deserved someone who would be faithful. I wasn't that girl—I never had been. I loved the excitement of being with someone new. Someone who didn't need me any more than I needed him.

But in this moment of despair, living the life I'd chosen was deafening in its silence. I needed someone to talk to. Someone to hold me, pat me on the back. I didn't know where to turn as panic gripped my chest. I would have a full-blown attack if I didn't do something fast.

It was not an option to call Bobby again. He could be with his family. Two calls in two days might raise suspicions, or it would infuriate Bobby. The one thing that made this work so well for us is that it was entirely up to him to come to me. I was free—he had encumbrances. He came when he chose to.

My thoughts were not calming me. I was getting more agitated as I stewed about the news report. The clutter and boxes scattered around my apartment added to my restlessness. All the serenity I'd gained by going to the gym was about to be lost. I paced the floor, chewing on my lip, longing to go to work. To take my mind off my situation, I needed to distract myself.

I thought about my mother and how she wanted to talk to me. If Patrick hadn't barged in, despite all the hissing I was doing, she would have been able to say her peace, eventually. I wondered if I should call her. That thought should have caused my stomach to flutter in fear. Instead, a great deal of calm came over me.

Before I allowed myself to wonder any further, the memory of that drawer of unopened gifts flashed to mind. I was doing to my mom what Andrea had done to me. I wanted a relationship with Andrea, but she wouldn't let me in. My mom wanted one with me, and though my reasons seemed justified in keeping her out, the result would be the same. One day, one of us would be on the other side of the earth, and there would be no more chances to make things right.

I looked at the clock. It was seven-thirty. Lots of time.

The phone rang several times before my mother's voice came on. She sounded tired. I hesitated, wondering if this was a recording—it sounded so lifeless. "Mom."

"Oh, Barbie! I didn't expect to hear from you."

"I know. I just ... um ... well ... I just thought maybe we could talk, you know."

"You didn't seem interested in hearing what I had to say yesterday. Why the change?"

That's what I hated most about my family—judgments! They always judged me—my thoughts, actions, and choices. If they weren't judging, they weren't talking. "I called, didn't I?" I snapped, then remorse pricked my tongue. "I'm sorry. Do you want to talk, or did I waste my time calling you?"

"I want to talk," she whispered.

"I won't come to the house. I could meet you somewhere."

"Maybe at that coffee shop, Jake's Diner or Café, or whatever it's called. Do you know it?"

"Yes, I know it. Half an hour then or do you need more time?"

"I'm sure Patrick can get me there by then."

"No Patrick! I don't need him wading in with his two cents."

"Well, I don't know how I can meet you then. I don't drive anymore since my eyesight isn't so good. The bus will take too long, and I can't afford a taxi."

"Is it just night driving? Or don't you drive at all?"

"I don't drive at all. I have glaucoma and my eyesight is failing because it went unchecked for years. Eventually, I will go blind. If I live that long."

I did not know that my mother's health had changed. I seldom thought of her, but when I did, I remembered her as she was when I was growing up.

"Anyway, we sold the car. It was useless to either of us, and we needed a new furnace more than we needed a car."

Wham. There was the guilt again. "Okay, I will pick you up in twenty minutes. Is that okay?"

"Twenty minutes is fine."

"Watch for me, because I will not come to the door."

"I will do my best. I'm not totally blind. Yet."

Her words slapped my face. I hung up feeling angry, frustrated, and sad. Why do things have to change? Why do things have to stay the same?

CHAPTER TWENTY-SEVEN

Half an hour later, I pulled up in front of the house. It looked a little tidier than the last time I'd been here. The dilapidated picket fence was gone. Besides, it was a thing of the past to have a white picket fence surrounding the little cottage of your dreams.

The front door opened, and my mother descended the stairs, clinging to the railing. She trudged down the sidewalk, taking care with every step. I hadn't noticed her slow movements on the day she surprised me in the church. Watching her now, I realized how she snuck up on me—she moved so slowly she wouldn't have made a sound. I sucked in a deep breath as another laceration ripped at my wounded heart.

She climbed into the passenger seat. I had the car in gear heading down the street as she fussed with the seat belt. When I stopped at the first stop sign, I took the end from her and snapped it firmly into the buckle.

"Thank you."

"You're welcome." I looked at her. She was closer to me than she'd been at the funeral that day. Dull eyes looked out from her worn face. She had attempted to doll herself up by applying lipstick and a little rouge. Both were a shade too garish for her skin tone. Still, my heart flipped over at the sight of her. All those years I had spent keeping her at arm's length seemed to be a waste of time. I hated myself for doing what Andrea had done to me.

"No, I mean, thank you for calling."

I turned my attention back to driving as I wrestled with my emotions. Imprisoned inside me, I really didn't understand them most of the time. At this moment, I wanted to laugh, cry, and scream as my heart spun in circles. Not liking how I was feeling, I wondered if it was possible to get things under control again. Detachment was my preferred conduct, dealing with anything clinically—without emotion. Now everything I did turned my heart inside out. It had to stop or I would go insane. I grabbed hold of my feelings and manually stuffed them down.

By the time we arrived at the coffee shop, a modicum of peace had settled over me. I waited at the front of the car for my mother. Together, we proceeded inside. The place was nearly empty, so we had our choice of tables. I chose one in the nearest corner. As we sat, a server arrived with a menu and a pot of coffee. I turned my cup over. She poured. My mother asked for tea.

"Do you want menus?"

"I don't think so. Mom?"

"May I have a slice of carrot cake?"

I wasn't really paying attention. I expected the server to leave, but she didn't move. She stared at me as I looked back at her. I couldn't understand why until I looked at my mother. Then I understood. She hadn't asked the server if she could have some carrot cake—she had asked me. I was humbled and annoyed.

"Of course you can." My tone was harsher than I wanted it to be.

The server moved away. I watched her go, imagining she judged me for my rude behavior, but I didn't care.

We sat quietly waiting for Mom's tea and treat. Neither of us spoke. After her food arrived and the server was gone, I asked, "So, what did you want to talk to me about?"

I sipped my coffee as I watched her slice off a piece from the large square of cake. She rested her fork on the plate before she spoke. "I wanted to tell you about my eyes but more importantly, you need to know that your father is dying." She lifted the fork and ate the bite, watching me intently.

I stared at her. I thought I would be glad to hear he was dying. He was an evil man—a monster who had betrayed himself, his role as a parent, and his family with his actions. Whenever I'd thought of this moment over the years, I envisioned myself dancing on his grave. Yet, here it was. My fantasy was nearly a reality, and I didn't feel like dancing. I wasn't sure how I felt.

I didn't know how to react. Was I supposed to offer condolences? Was I supposed to tut and say how sad this was? Did she expect me to crow? I sipped my coffee, staring at her, tension building inside me.

Damn! Another burden for me to bear. Why was this happening to me? Finally, knowing she would say nothing to ease my tension, I asked, "Is he in the hospital?"

"Not yet. He's at home for now, but it won't be long. The dialysis isn't working as effectively anymore. I can see him failing every day. Maybe no one else can see it, I don't know."

She took another bite of cake. Neither of us spoke. We sat there in companionable silence, each lost in her own thoughts.

"He wants to see you."

There it was. The other shoe. Of course, this was her mission all along. She was a crafty old woman. She knew that if she told me that first, I'd have been off like a shot. By putting him at death's door, she lulled me into a false sense of security. Then she laid out the real reason for contact.

"He does, does he? Well he can whistle in the dark, because I will not see him."

My response didn't surprise her. She acted like that was exactly what she expected me to say. That annoyed me. I scanned the room to avoid her stares and my own feelings. A few tables away sat two couples. They were young. Maybe the same age as Andrea and foolish in their behavior. Holding hands, kissing in public, touching each other like new lovers do.

I looked away. Had I ever been that young? Was I ever that in love with life that public displays of affection were normal—that I drew attention to myself in such a lewd fashion? I flashed back to the days before Kevin, those lost high school days, when I lived with the monster impersonating my father. Yes, in those heady days of youth and stupidity, I thought I was living life by my rules. I wasn't adhering to the laws of conventional society. I did what I wanted because it was the best way to get at my parents. I wanted to show them that they may have brought me into the world, but I was the one who decided how to live in it.

Looking back at my mother, she sat there, perfectly at peace. She had delivered her message and whatever the answer was going to be—she wasn't stupid enough to believe she controlled it. She had to tell the story and let me come to it on my own. I realized she had been doing this her whole life. This was her method. She never forced me to do anything. She just posed the question and let me stew and chew until I came to my decision.

This had served her well, and I think it also helped her live with the consequences of my lack of contact. She allowed me to choose without forcing me to make the right decision. She permitted me to live with my choices. I couldn't have been prouder of her at that moment. New admiration came as I understood for the first time the level of patience she bore inside that thin frame.

For a moment, I wished I had a little of what she had. I wasn't patient. I lived with Andrea's separateness, not because I was patient enough to know she'd come back, but because of the guilt I bore for causing it. Taking responsibility for Andrea's choice made it impossible to separate myself from it.

The server came by and topped up my coffee. I sat back, watching the steam rise from my cup. I lifted my gaze to my mother. She stared back at me, her face filled with a mother's love. I reached across the table and took her hand. It was dry and papery. She had aged so much since I'd last spent time with her.

Her blue eyes were watery with unshed tears. I smiled at her. "I don't know if I can see him."

She squeezed my hand. "I know. I know," she whispered.

Then she released my hand and sat back. "I have delivered the message. I knew you wouldn't want to see him, but I told him I would tell you. Now I have done what he asked. But I will tell you this, Barbie. I don't blame you for hating him. He was not an easy man to love. When the drink took over his life, he changed from the man I married to the man he is today. But I still saw the man he was, trapped inside someone else's skin. That's why I stayed. That man needed me."

I sat there staring at her, taking in her confession.

"And I'll tell you one more thing and then you can take me home. I can't leave your father with Mrs. Lutz for too long. I think you need to know, Barbie, that seeing him is not for his benefit, it's for your own good. If you don't say your peace and your goodbyes, it will be a regret you will bear for the rest of your days. This must end someday, and for your sake, I hope it ends with some absolution rather than death."

She gathered her coat around her shoulders and pushed her arms into the sleeves. After wrapping her scarf around her neck, she stood. She was waiting for me by the door as I paid the bill. I wanted to hug her and to take her home to my house, not back to the jail cell she lived in, the one with a life sentence of servitude to a monster.

Neither of us spoke as I navigated the streets. The radio played quietly, covering the silence like a small bandage on an amputation. I wanted to say something to her, but everything that crossed my mind seemed trite in the wake of her last words. *For my own good.* Those words rolled around my brain like a steel ball in a pinball machine. Ping, ping, ping.

I pulled up in front of the house. Mom released her seat belt, opened her door to get out, and then stopped to look back at me. "Thank you, Barbie. This was nice." She climbed out of the car, closed the door, and made her way up the sidewalk to the house. I watched her, hesitant to drive away until she was safely inside. As I watched her make her way toward the house, my chest swelled with so much love. Before I stopped myself, I exited the car. "Mom!"

She turned toward me. I ran up the walk toward her. I threw my arms around her neck and hugged her. She hesitated for a second, surprised by my show of affection, then she hugged me back. Tears pricked my eyes as I held her, wishing that life didn't have to be so hard. The curtain in the front room moved aside. I flinched and released her, stepping away from her quickly. The curtain dropped and the outside light came on. "Good night, Mom. I love you," I whispered—as I turned and hurried back to the car.

As I climbed inside, I observed the front door open and an old woman, heavyset with black hair in tight curls, stepped out on the porch. They were speaking, but I couldn't make out the words over the pounding in my chest.

I watched my mother make her way up the steps, and the two women disappeared inside the house. I let out my breath. That was too close. The fear that my father would be at the window and then at the door had triggered a rush of adrenaline.

My hands shook as I put the car in gear and drove home.

What was I going to do about my father?
I did not know.

CHAPTER TWENTY-EIGHT

I had one more day at home before returning to work, but the isolation stretched before me like a year on a deserted island. Andrea's death and coffee with my mother were disruptions to my solitary routine. Adding to the unsettled feelings was the disarray of my apartment as I packed my belongings and removed those things I no longer needed.

I had collected some boxes and was busy packing and sorting for most of Monday. A small part of me longed for Bobby to pop over. I was tense and needed some attention. The thoughts of my father's request and my mother's words bounced around my mind on and off throughout the day.

I came across a few mementos of Andrea. Inside a cardboard frame was a picture of her with her dance troupe. She was perhaps six or seven and was taking dance lessons, which she didn't continue much beyond when this photo was taken. She took up diving and was quite competitive for a few years. Her love of reading and writing took her in another direction. To continue to compete in diving, she needed to practice long hours. She just didn't care enough about it. She wanted a different path, and so she dropped out.

For a moment, I thought, what if she had stayed with diving instead of taking courses to become a journalist? What if she had never met this Caleb person? What if she was an Olympian instead of being dead? What if …

My mind wandered through a magnitude of scenarios, all of which put Andrea out of danger and into another place where she was safe. It was a silly game, but it helped me to think of her as alive and well instead of where she was. In a wooden box, deep in the cold ground at the cemetery. That thought put me on my knees.

I went to the gym again and worked out. Gavin was there. He met me as I came off the treadmill.

"How are you doing, Barbie?"

"Good." I nodded.

"I'm sorry for … well … you know. That things turned out like they did."

I touched his bulging biceps. "I know you are. Thank you."

"If you need anything, you let me know. Okay?"

"I will. Thanks." I moved away. The heat coming from him was combustible. I would not allow our friendship to move in that direction again. Thirteen years ago, I joined this gym when I left Lenny, my second husband. I met Gavin, who was fit and available, and he filled a void in my life for a time. It was a brief fling. His lovemaking was unsatisfactory, and no amount of coaching on my part seemed to help him. I wondered if the intervening years had taught him anything in the bedroom department, but I wasn't desperate enough to find out.

Back at home, I showered. Feeling refreshed, I made supper. In a T-shirt and boxer shorts, I whipped together a salad. As I chopped the lettuce, peppers, and tomatoes, my mind wandered to Mom's words. *Your father is dying.*

When I let that thought flit through my mind, I didn't react at first. As it swirled back again and again, gritty emotions pinwheeled until I didn't know what I was feeling. I was relieved, sad, angry, and scared, all mixing into a lethal cocktail of pain and sorrow. I became confused. Confusion made me feel helpless, and helplessness made me feel things I would rather not.

Wounded and numb, I sat on the couch in front of the TV with my salad resting on the coffee table in front of me. I hoped to find a movie to take my mind off my feelings. Searching through the guide, I chose a movie that sounded interesting. Within the first ten minutes, I realized that this was a movie I shouldn't be watching. I don't know why I didn't turn it off or change the channel, but I didn't. I sat there, eyes glued to the set, my salad uneaten as the female character on the screen went through the brutality of life.

I identified with her. She annoyed me. I wanted to climb into the television and give her a few home truths. My heart rallied toward a happy ending. As the credits rolled, the camera pulled away from the characters, leaving the image of reconciliation, of happily ever after. My stomach churned, and my heart tightened inside my chest. The hardness splintered as gigantic cracks in the façade of my life opened before me. Fearing that the ordinary act of breathing would cause me to self-destruct, I hung onto this life by a thread as below me sat a vat of boiling oil. I had nowhere to go, nowhere to jump. One false move, and it would all be over.

In bed, I tried to sleep, to escape the roiling inside. It took a while, but I fell into a troubled sleep. I dreamed I was with my parents and my brothers. We were camping beside a river. There was a fire blazing, and Mom was cooking hot dogs. Dad was chopping wood, and the boys were playing not far off. I was sitting on an old stump. Beside me were several purses. The images blurred, and when they cleared, I was inside a white van, searching for my belongings. Dad was in the driver's seat. Mom beside him. I was busy pulling all my purses onto the seat beside me, unaware that Dad was driving the van into the river.

The van hit the water with a splash. I panicked, screaming at Dad that he was trying to kill us all. He didn't respond. The van floated along, moving across the river to the other side, the wheels somehow providing momentum. The van lurched onto the bank on the other side of the river, and everyone bailed out. Wanting to be safe, I left my purses behind. I watched as the van slid back into the river and floated away. I screamed at my father that he hadn't set the brake. He assured me he had, claiming the temperature of the water prevented the brake from catching. Helplessly, I stared as the van floated down the river, taking my purses with it. How was I going to get them back?

I awoke, ready to cry. What did it mean? Was the dream a premonition of what was to come? Was seeing my father again going to be disastrous for me? Or maybe it was nothing more than an interpretation of what transpired in our lives. My father had deliberately driven his family across a raging river the moment he took a drink. Every minute after that decision, we were all in danger of being destroyed. Even though we arrived safely on the other side, we were stranded far away from where we should be. The hardships that followed were his fault because he wasn't even sorry that he had put us in jeopardy. He shrugged it off as insignificant, but it disturbed me.

A feeling of uncertainty settled down into my heart. Trying to mitigate the dream's importance, I decided I needed to clarify my feelings about seeing my father before I dismissed it.

I did not want to do that, yet.

CHAPTER TWENTY-NINE

My first night back at work was uneventful. Raoul hovered over me at first, but I soon took him back to his office, where he belonged. The customers offered condolences, for which I graciously thanked them. The only time I was close to choking up was when Bobby squeezed my hand. It took me a moment to catch my breath.

Eventually, the night was over and Raoul locked the door. After a quick tea and a recap of the night, I left the restaurant and headed home.

Pulling into the parking lot at my apartment building, I looked for Bobby's car. It wasn't there. Disappointment and relief washed over me. I hadn't seen him since before the funeral, and I missed that connection. But I was thinking about something Raoul said and didn't want to be derailed from sorting out my thoughts.

I turned on the light inside my apartment—the disarray of my belongings assaulted me. I hated this part of moving. Less than three weeks before I'd be in my new home, with plenty of space to shove unpacked boxes out of sight. In this tiny one-bedroom, there wasn't any room to hide a red penny.

I walked into the bedroom and changed into sweatpants and a T-shirt. This was the worst part of working late. You couldn't go shopping after work or have coffee with a friend. The only place a person could go was home. Most nights, I fell right into bed. My routine was to get up late in the morning, and go shopping before I went to work, or more often on my days off.

But there were some nights when I came home overstimulated and unable to settle. This was one of those nights. Going to bed now would find me twisting the covers around. Tension made me jittery. I wanted to relieve it—I needed Bobby. Instead, I sat on the couch and forced myself to think about my father. I opened the door to my memories—the portal I had sealed shut because I didn't want to think about him. I pulled out an early recollection.

The three of us—Patrick, Dennis, and I—were marching behind our father. He played "Turkey in The Straw" on the harmonica as he wound his way through the house. We marched around the room, into the dining area, around the table, into the kitchen. Mom was standing at the stove, stirring a pot of stew. Dad grabbed her around the waist and twirled her around the room. She laughed, her head thrown back in delight. We clapped and laughed. It was great fun.

Where did that man go? He was a great dad in those days, so much fun. We had a happy home. Why did things have to change? Why did he love alcohol more than he loved us? I hated him for being weak and for making the choice he made.

It didn't slip my mind that I worked in a business where alcohol featured prominently. Bars and lounges were an easy way to make my living because the tips were better than in restaurants. *A fool and his money, as the saying goes*. I also didn't drink. In all my years of rebellion, I may have hung around with drunks and druggies, but I never used myself. I dressed the part, but I witnessed the monster emerge from the belly of my father enough to know that I didn't want to see that monster in my mirror at night.

When I left the memory, that happy childhood day, my heart lay open to the emotions evoked. Grabbing a nearby cushion, I curled around it and wept. I wept for the little girl I had been—the one who adored her father. I wept for the lost years and because I wanted to go back and see that man again. Who would I find if I visited him now? Part of me recognized I had to try. I had to go if only to tell him that what he did to me was reprehensible and unforgivable.

Somehow, I would have to find the courage to face him; to find the strength to do what I needed to do—for me—not for him. I prayed for enough compassion to forgive. The hardest part was the need to tell him I loved the man he once was, to remind him that as a young girl, he was my world and that his choices took that away from us. I didn't know if that was cruel, but if he wanted to see me, he surely had to be prepared to hear some horrible truths.

When the tears subsided, I went into the bathroom and splashed cold water on my face. My skin was pale, my eyes puffy and washed out. I looked awful. I tried to smile at my reflection but didn't seem to have the energy. It had been a long week.

In the bedroom, I pulled back the covers and slipped out of my clothes. Sliding between the sheets, I rolled onto my side. Laying there in the dark, staring at the emptiness, I turned over onto my other side. Most nights, it didn't bother me to be alone. To me, it was a choice I'd made. Tonight was not one of those nights. It wasn't just the sex either—it was the comfort of having someone in my life.

I thought about the men who'd come and gone. Each had been important to me for a while, but their relationships ended bitterly. Life was imperfect, and our relationships were complicated. I stopped when I came to Greg Simmons, the man I was with last year. We were only living together. I had been married three times before meeting him and did not want to do it again. Cohabiting seemed easier.

We were at Kevin's on Christmas day, where I gave Andrea her gift. It was a perfect day until I noticed Greg's behavior. He was lusting after my daughter, making a play for her attention. Even thinking about it now makes my stomach turn. As we drove away, I brought up his actions.

"What is wrong with you?"

"What are you talking 'bout, babe?"

"You know perfectly well what I'm talking about—Andrea."

"What about her?"

"You were practically drooling, sitting there with your mouth hanging open."

"No, I wasn't." He laughed, trying to lessen his culpability. He wasn't fooling me. I saw through the charade. His laugh was an acrid admission of his guilt. "So, what if I was? Ain't no harm in looking is there?" He reached over and squeezed my knee.

I shivered, repulsed by his confession. "You were doing more than looking. If she had encouraged you, you'd have forgotten all about me."

"It wasn't like that, babe."

"Bullshit!"

"Fine! You're right. She's fitter than you, younger than you, prettier than you, and sure it crossed my mind. I'm a guy, that's what we do. Shoot me for being human!"

"You disgust me!" I shouted at him. "You're a filthy pig."

He laughed derisively. "And you're the queen of Sheba. You're so perfect that you've been married three times and slept with how many men? Ten? Twenty? Thirty?"

"Stop the car! Stop the car right now!" I screamed.

He swung wildly to the curb. I gathered my purse, then turned to him. "Give me your key?"

"What?"

"Your key." I spoke softly but with authority.

He looked at me, hatred burning in his eyes. He turned off the car, twisting the key off his key ring.

I held my hand out.

Ignoring me, he started the car again. Then he lowered my window and tossed the key out into the snow.

"You jerk," I shouted.

"Get out of my car. I'd rather be alone than with a washed-out trollop like you anyway." Stunned by his ugly words, I sat there, stunned. "I said, *get out*," he shouted.

I moved to get out, but before I did, I swung back at him. Not being left-handed, I hadn't expected to do much damage, but I struck his nose. I don't know if I broke it, but there was enough blood to give me the satisfaction that I had. I scrambled out before he retaliated. He swore, clutching his face.

"Tell Jerry he can come and get your crap. I don't want to see you, ever again." I shouted this at him as I slammed the car door shut. He put the car in gear and sped away, leaving a bit of rubber on the road. I turned toward the yard to see where the key might have landed. The snow was pristine, so I found the key easily.

It was a treacherous walk home. I was wearing high heels, and snow covered some sidewalks. I also wasn't wearing a warm jacket. Since we were driving, I had dressed for style, not functionality. Chilled to the bone by the time I arrived at the apartment, I took a hot bath. It warmed me up, though my mood didn't improve. I was angry with myself for leaping into a relationship so quickly following the end of my third marriage.

When we met, Greg was staying with friends, sleeping on their couch. He was charming, and I was feeling rather low. I remember the night he came home with me for the first time. He was attentive and took his time, and we both enjoyed the experience. The next day, he stayed, and he never left. When I went to work, he was making himself a bite to eat. It just seemed natural that he was there when I entered the apartment after work. It was simple, and I didn't argue.

But it wasn't love from my side and as I look back, I think he viewed me as his rescuer, more than his lover. I gave him what he didn't have—a home, a place to sleep.

I packed up his meager belongings and set them by the door. Jerry came three days later to collect them.

I never saw Greg again, although I heard he'd moved out of town.

I didn't care, as long as he was far from Andrea and me.

CHAPTER THIRTY

The next day, I awoke feeling lower than I had in a long time. It was like I was alone against the world. A vulnerability racing through my veins threatened to explode if one more thing landed on my plate. I had reached maximum capacity, my emotions were tight.

As I had since the funeral, I made my cursory call to Kevin. We had agreed to keep in touch for a little while to ensure we were coping. It was my distinct impression that Kevin wasn't managing as well as I was, but I also seemed unable to find the strength to give him more than that one call. I shook off all feelings of inadequacy though—I had too much going on, without adding Kevin to my list of projects.

I called my mother, too, to let her know I would see my father, though I wasn't ready to do it this month. The upheaval of moving into my new home was enough—I would not add a potentially disastrous reunion to my load.

We agreed I would meet with him on a day when he wasn't undergoing dialysis at the hospital and I didn't have work scheduled.

That meant the best day to meet would be a Monday. I looked at my calendar, and we set the date for the earliest Monday I had free. By then, I would be semi-settled in my new apartment for a week.

Even though I spoke confidently, my heart fluttered wildly in my chest. *Maybe I wasn't ready for this? Maybe I should wait.* But delaying it any further wasn't the answer. I needed to do this before it was too late. It wasn't like I would make a habit of this—it was a one-off. One visit, one chance for me to say what needed to be said, to find grace where none existed.

The rest of the day followed in a blur of routine. Chores around the house, trip to the gym, a brief stop at the drugstore on my way home to get some new hair accessories. Then home to get ready for work. As I surveyed the clutter of boxes, I decided I was feeling pretty good about the move. I had purged a lot of useless stuff. Everything left was the things I wanted. The lack of possessions made me feel lighter.

As I was applying my makeup, I thought of Andrea, and how pretty she was. She had the natural beauty of youth but also carried herself well. She was confident in her body, moved like a dancer, gracefully, like liquid being poured from a pitcher. Closing my eyes, I tried to bring her into focus. I managed a snippet of her laughing at something Kevin had said at Christmas. I was just coming into the living room and she was sitting on the arm of the couch, her head thrown back.

"What's so funny?" I smiled, hoping to be included.

"You had to be there." She whispered it like she was trying not to hurt me, but her expression contradicted the tone. She had meant to hurt me, not because I wasn't there, but because I was never there. Making her point, she punished me again for my choice. It took great effort to smile, shrug it off with a laugh, and move on.

That memory pierced my heart anew. Putting my eyeliner pencil down, I sat on the edge of the bathtub and wept. For a long time, I hoped she would set aside her disappointments and talk to me about her wounds. She didn't understand what was going on inside me, and I desperately wanted to explain myself. I wanted a chance, though I feared I had left it too long. She was living with scar tissue on the inside; scars that would never heal properly. Shaped by my actions, I wondered if she would ever be.

When I left, all those years ago, no one could have told me how devastating it would be for all of us. Many people thought I was selfish by leaving—they judged me and misunderstood my actions. Until this moment, I would have defended myself to the end, knowing that what I did was selfless. I had left for her and Kevin. I was living a lie and it would have destroyed us.

No one understood my emptiness, a pit of blackness that was never sated. It drove me to do things, to seek pleasures and excitement. If one fling were enough to fix me, it would have been done, but it was never enough. I needed something I couldn't find in my marriage to Kevin. It wasn't Andrea's fault, though she bore the burden. I wish I knew how to feel normal, how to go back to being the girl I was before that night.

"No!" I jumped up from the tub. I refused to go back there. I would not open the door and let that beast loose. That would fix nothing. It was dead and buried—done. Taking one deep breath, then another, I pushed all the memories back into the box. I purposely focused on what I needed to do in the next two weeks to prepare for my move.

I found the brochure that Bobby had given me. It showed pictures of the show suite for the development where I would be moving. My new home had the same layout as this one. I stared at the kitchen and imagined being there. Bobby stood at the counter, opening a bottle of wine. I flipped to the living room picture and imagined a gathering; a small dinner party having drinks before the meal, sitting around casually, enjoying the company. I turned to the bedroom and visualized myself coming out of the ensuite, dressed in a slinky nightie. Bobby waiting on the bed …

Okay, enough of that, too! Get to work! I sure hoped Bobby would come to me tonight. It had been too long.

After setting the brochure down next to the coffeemaker, I returned to the bathroom. I washed my face with a cool cloth before applying makeup. Fluffing my hair, I took a critical look before heading to the bedroom to dress.

The crowd was lively, and the night passed quickly. I found a moment with Raoul to let him know I would see my father. He squeezed my arm. "How are you feeling?"

"Well, I'm nervous for sure. But I think I have to do this. Not for him, he doesn't deserve it, but for me."

Raoul nodded. We parted, and the night was soon over. I was home for less than five minutes when the buzzer went. "Hello?"

"It's me."

I pushed the button to allow him entry. A few minutes later, I opened the door to him. He stepped in, swept me into his arms, and kissed my neck. "Mmmm. I have been missing you."

I felt his need and mine burst into flame. "Me too. You feel so good."

His grip tightened. Every pore on my body was alert, my senses heightened. The air caressed me. My senses sprang to life. With swift hands, Bobby undressed me, and I returned the favor. We made our way down the hall to the bedroom. Kissing, touching, holding, shuffling as the need to have contact with one another was important.

Our coupling was fast, furious, and satisfying. We lay together afterward, enjoying the peace that comes after sex. I explored his body, letting my fingers touch and tease him to arousal again. This time, it was slower and sweeter. We are so good together.

Later, we lay curled together, my back against his front. Bobby's arm draped lightly around me, his fingers resting on my stomach. I sighed. He kissed my ear. "You are so beautiful." He whispered before settling back down against me.

I smiled, closed my eyes, and let his words ease me into total relaxation. I drifted off, happy he'd come and glad he loved me. I drifted into soft dreams of a life without turmoil and strife, a life where heartaches didn't exist and feelings were marshmallows, soft and sweet. It was a happy place.

When I awoke, I was alone.

It was long before I needed to get up, so I curled into myself and let the waves of dreamland sweep me back to sleep.

CHAPTER THIRTY-ONE

The rest of the week passed in much the same way, though it was busier. Work, home, work, home. Short phone calls to Kevin every morning and another night with Bobby. Sunday arrived on schedule. I was exhausted. To prepare for my departure, I cleaned the apartment—scrubbing walls, shampooing carpets, cleaning cabinets, and washing floors. I purchased a couple of crates to move my clothes, as well as reinforced boxes with rods to hang them from.

It was my day off, and I intended to use it to regroup. Until mid-afternoon, when I met Bobby at my new place for a walk-through, I had nothing on my agenda. So, I relaxed on the couch with my book and music. I was so wrapped up in my plans that I forgot to call Kevin.

At two-thirty, I showered before dressing in a navy and white cable-knit sweater and navy slacks. I slipped into my dress boots, grabbed my purse, and headed out to the new apartment. Bobby was already there. I didn't bother to knock—I opened the door and stepped inside.

I slipped off my boots and padded into the living room. "Hello?" I called.

Bobby appeared in the doorway to the kitchen. I stopped. Dressed in his customary white shirt and dark suit, he looked impressive. Everything about his attire was perfect: dark eyelashes over sea-blue eyes, a complexion that may have freckled as a child.

He smiled, and my heart turned over. "Well, hello there handsome." I growled.

His smile widened. "Come here you."

I crossed the hardwood floor, not noticing the room's size or layout. My entire focus was on Bobby. I stepped into his arms, leaning up for a kiss. His lips met mine, warm and welcoming. He unbuttoned my coat and slipped it off my shoulders onto the floor before slipping his hands under my sweater. My hands were busy, too.

"I didn't lock the door," I whispered, not wanting to break the mood, but worried that anyone seeing his car might come in.

He didn't seem to hear me, so I let it go. I lost myself in the wonders of his lips and hands. There was no furniture, so we dropped to the floor, the tile cold against my bare skin. It added to the stimulus as we found pleasure in each other. *We are good together, he and I.* Secure in what we had together, life was going to be bright and new living here.

We didn't cuddle when it was over. Bobby tossed me my clothes as he slipped into his pants. He was buttoning his shirt as I turned my sweater right-side out. For the first time, I felt cheap. I ducked my head to avoid looking at him as I pushed my thoughts and feelings away.

Dressed once again, he gave me the tour. It was very business-like; cold and impersonal. At the door, I slipped into my boots as Bobby leaned against the wall, watching me.

I slid my purse onto my shoulder and turned to kiss him. He

ducked his head and kissed me on the cheek.

As I pulled away, disappointed and unsettled, he leaned back and whispered, "We have christened the kitchen. I look forward to doing that with you in every room." His hand brushed across my right breast, then he stood back.

I smiled at him, trying to recapture our magic.

Then I opened the door and walked out into the dusk.

CHAPTER THIRTY-TWO

Back home, I noticed my phone was blinking. There was a message. I didn't want to talk to anyone. I was still reeling from what had happened at my new home. Bobby had never made me feel like a whore in all the months we'd been together until today. Today, it was like he was letting me know my place in his life. I would never be more to him than a bit on the side.

I was angry, not at Bobby, but at myself. Bobby had never deceived me. I did that myself by applying more meaning to our relationship—by elevating myself from what I was. In my mind, I had built a fantasy where we would entertain his clients and I would be his super hostess, the one everyone loved to be around. Though I didn't want to be his wife, I wanted to be more than his fancy woman.

Wandering through the apartment, my stomach was tied in knots, knowing I couldn't return now. The apartment manager had advised me he wouldn't need to show my apartment again as someone had rented it. Regardless of what the future was going to be like, I would have to go forward. All I needed to do was figure out how to claw back my expectations. *Damn! Why does life have to be so hard?*

I was working myself into an agitated state as I paced back and forth through the confines of my apartment. I needed to get out of the house. But where would I go? The gym was closed. The mall was closed. It was a wintry Sunday night, and everyone huddled indoors, warm and cozy. Maybe I should go for a walk or a drive? When no answer came, I circled back to the same question—where would I go?

Rifling through the box of footwear, I found my winter boots. I was going to toss them out since I never wore them anymore. When Ron and I were married, he bought them for me to go snowmobiling with him. I hadn't gone more than a few times. I never understood why anyone would want to wear two tons of clothes to ride across snow-covered fields on a noisy machine. The boots, though, were warm.

I changed into jeans, added a blouse under my sweater, and dug out my down-filled coat. Then, I wrestled my feet into my boots. I grabbed a hat, scarf, and mittens and headed out for a walk in the nearby park. I arrived at the foyer and observed a familiar figure standing with his back to the doors. I opened the door, and he turned.

Kevin looked at me, his eyes filled with pain. "Thank God you're okay."

Then I remembered I hadn't called him. "Oh, Kevin, I'm sorry. I totally forgot to call you. It's been one of those days." I thought I saw a flash of anger cross his face, but it was so fast, I couldn't be sure.

"That's okay. I'm just glad you're okay. I was thinking the worst. When you hadn't called, I called you but there was no answer. I left a message, but you never called back."

I stood there, ashamed of myself. The blinking light was a message from Kevin.

"So, I drove over here and your car was in the parking lot but you didn't answer your buzzer."

"I must have been on my way down." Taking his hand, I continued, "I'm sorry, Kevin. I never meant to upset you."

He shrugged, pulling his hand away. "Well, I was thinking the worst."

"As you can see, I'm fine."

We stood there awkwardly for a few seconds. "Where are you off to?"

"I'm going for a walk."

"Oh. I'll let you get on with it then." He turned and walked back to his truck.

Watching him, sympathy for him, washed over me. Andrea's death was easier for me. She wasn't part of my everyday life. That didn't mean her death didn't grieve me—it did. But I'd also grieved for her for the last sixteen years. Kevin was just beginning the journey. He had a long way to go.

"Do you want to walk with me?" I called as he was about to climb into his truck.

He looked over, closed the door, and came back toward me. "You sure?"

"I wouldn't have asked if I wasn't sure."

"Okay. Thanks. I wasn't looking forward to going home just yet. Sundays are the worst …" His voice cracked, and he stopped talking.

I reached over and took his hand. "Let's go."

When we reached the sidewalk on the far side of the parking lot, I let go of his hand. I turned right and Kevin followed. A few blocks down, we came to a small park. It had a walking path around the perimeter, an expanse of green grass dotted with trees and benches. In the summer, it was an active place for picnics and wedding photos. In the winter, it was serene, and the city did its best to keep the path clear.

We walked together in silence. I was thinking about Bobby and the deal I made with the devil. Somewhere along the way, I decided I differed from all the girls who had gone before me. I would be the one Bobby would elevate to a pinnacle place in his world. Once I was living in his apartment, he would show me off to his people, to his world.

Even as I thought about what happened today, I couldn't even pinpoint the moment that things changed. Maybe it wasn't Bobby who had changed, but me. Maybe I was the one whose eyes were opened. I was in a horrible situation, or was I?

Then I thought about the money I'd save by living in Bobby's condo. It was rent-free. That meant that I would save a significant amount of money every month. In a year, I would have enough for a swanky holiday, or if I saved for longer, I could buy a condo of my own. I was a fool to let go of such a wonderful opportunity just because I realized Bobby viewed me differently than I wanted him to. Nope, it wasn't ideal. I would have to let go of the dream, but this wasn't the worst thing. At least by dropping the romanticism I'd constructed, living my life would be easier.

"You're quiet."

"Oh, sorry," I said, shaking out of my reverie. "I was just thinking about my move."

"You're moving?"

"Yes, into one of those condos on the golf course. The new ones."

"Wow. Aren't they expensive? How can you afford that?"

"I'm getting a good deal. The owner is the president of the board at work. He's giving me a fantastic deal."

"Oh."

"What—oh?" His tone told me what he was thinking.

"Nothing. Just oh."

"You meant something, so spit it out." I stopped walking.

Kevin took a few steps and then turned to face me. "Well, people rarely do things without expecting something back."

"Really? You never do anything without expecting something back?" I was angry at Kevin for seeing through the thin veil of normalcy I'd tossed over my story. How dare he judge me and what I was doing? "Are you calling me a whore?"

"No ... no, of course not. No." He looked at me, tears glistening in his eyes.

All the anger inside me drained out. "I'm sorry. I guess I'm sensitive, thinking everyone will assume the same thing. But it's not like that. I'll be in a place where I can rub elbows with influential people."

"You mean rich people."

My anger sparked again. "Do you want to fight, Kevin?"

He shook his head.

"Well, you're sure trying to pick one."

We stood there staring at each other, neither of us speaking. Then I turned back the way we'd come. "I'm going home." I walked away, expecting Kevin to follow. Listening for his footsteps, I was ready to slow down to let him catch up so we could walk back together. I didn't hear him, so I turned back, expecting to see him standing there.

He was walking the other way.

I made it home, slamming into the apartment. My walk had done little to settle my mind. I was now wrestling with Kevin's judgment. He could protest all he wanted, but he wasn't fooling me. He was too polite to say the words out loud, but I understood the message, which annoyed me. I had enough wars to fight in the world without Kevin joining everyone else.

I turned on some classical music and ran a bath, dumping a load of bubbles into the running water. I stripped down and climbed into the hot water. Leaning back, I let the tears flow. I kept a tight rein on my emotions, only shedding enough tears to relieve the tension in my shoulders. Feeling some relief, I took a wet facecloth, laid it over my face, and concentrated on my breathing.

When the water cooled, I released some water and refilled the tub with hotter water. Finally, hours later, climbing out of the tub, my hands and feet wrinkled and pruned, I felt relaxed.

I turned off the stereo and went to bed. My splintered dreams were not cohesive.

The morning arrived on schedule, but I refused to leave my bed.

I slept on and off, wasting a good portion of my day trying to avoid my life.

CHAPTER THIRTY-THREE

Tuesday began like every other day. The sun rose, the sky turned from black to blue. Clouds formed and changed and morphed as they sailed across the sky. I followed my usual routine. When I came home from the gym, I called a hairdresser in Calgary to make an appointment for the first Monday in December. I would have the money from my damage deposit and unpaid rent to afford to splurge. A new hairstyle, some nice new clothes, and maybe a new pair of shoes.

I was looking forward to getting a few new outfits just in time for the Christmas season. Getting my hair done and buying new clothes always seemed to lift my spirits. My visit with my father and move into my new home would be over. It would be the forward trajectory I would need to spring me into a more positive frame of mind.

The new year was fast approaching, and I was determined to make it the best year ever. I would no longer live in solitude, surrounded by strangers. In my new home, I would get to know my neighbors. Invitations to the best parties would arrive daily. I was ready to rise in the social scene because it was my time to shine.

As I dressed for work, I thought about my wasted day in bed. I was feeling sorry for myself. The world was against me, and I was going to have to fight again. If Kevin thought that my move to this condo had strings attached, then my new neighbors might have that bias as well. I would prove to them I was just as good as they were—maybe better. Holding my own against the tide of prejudice and judgment might not be easy, but I was up for the challenge.

Overwhelmed by this impending battle, I recognized life was nothing more than a series of them. I punched my pillow in frustration that life had to be so hard. I wanted to stay under the covers and hide from the world. Thankfully, it was a momentary crisis. Feeling sorry for myself would change nothing. I had experienced enough knocks in life to know that if you don't get up, no one is there reaching down to help you. You had to pull yourself up by the bootstraps and make the most of what you had. That long ago morning was proof of that.

My mother didn't help me, my brothers were useless. I may not have been wise enough to know how to fix those broken things, but I knew enough to get up and get moving. I am making the most of my life by breaking with things that no longer worked and moving on—leaving the bad and keeping the good. The only exception was Andrea. She wasn't old enough to make the choice, so I made it for her. Leaving her was the hardest thing I had ever done, but it saved her a life of heartache.

A life of heartache? She didn't have much of a life, did she? She was hardly out of the gate when her life ended abruptly. My heart wrenched as I tried to imagine why she made the choices she had. How had she come to be with that young man? Since I had no way of ever knowing, dwelling on it would drive me insane, so I shoved it aside. I couldn't change anything. I couldn't undo what had been done.

Besides, I had a few clouds on my horizon that I needed to watch carefully. Bobby and Kevin. The scene in the kitchen at my new apartment kept flashing through my mind. Each time that moment played, it rekindled my humiliation until my affection shifted. That scared me. This wasn't like before—I couldn't walk out. Leaving a husband behind when you no longer loved them was easy. Legally, I would get my share, even if I had to take it before I left.

My situation with Bobby was different. He was more than my lover—he was my benefactor. I owed him, and until last Sunday, I was happy to be under his wing. Now, I understood I had made a dangerous choice. I was going to see it through, pretending nothing had changed, being open to him, hoping he wouldn't notice the change from spontaneity to rote.

Kevin was another matter. I resented that his opinion mattered to me. I tried to put him into the same box as Ron and Lenny, former husbands who lived in the past, but Kevin had never belonged there. We had Andrea in common, which kept us in the same orbit. Without her, maybe it was time to shove him out of my world for good. Even as I thought those words, I wouldn't survive without him. I didn't understand that, but Kevin would always be a part of my world. Therefore, how he viewed my life mattered. I was going to have to prove him wrong. I would have to show him that my decision was a good thing.

In the shadows of my mind, my own doubts swirled and lingered like fog on a cool fall morning. Kevin's words and judgment hurt because it was the truth, and I'd seen it firsthand from the kitchen floor. His words, as hard as they were to hear, matched my experience. It was this information that stirred me up inside.

I didn't know what the future would bring me, but I was readying myself for the other shoe to drop; for the balloon to burst with a loud bang and send my world into turmoil.

With this deeply entrenched in my belly, I set off for work.

CHAPTER THIRTY-FOUR

It didn't take long to get the restaurant set up for the night. Ready for the onslaught of customers, I had enough time to spare to sit and have tea with Raoul. I didn't explain what was happening, but he recognized that something was off.

I told him about my argument with Kevin in the park. He listened intently and then asked, "Are you and Kevin getting back together?"

"Oh God, no," I replied.

"Well, that's unfortunate."

Anger formed a knot in my throat. "Why would you say something like *that*?"

"Calm down. I only meant that he's a good guy and you deserve to be with a good guy—that's all. You could do worse, you know. You could be the wife of Bobby Graham. That man gets around."

"Really?" My stomach fell into the basement. Nauseousness threatened to choke me. "What have you heard?"

He leaned close, even though we were the only two in his office. "Supposedly, he's moving some tart into his condo development on the golf course. A tender bit for recreational purposes, if you know what I mean."

"That is disgusting, Raoul!" His words terrified me. That rumor would shape my future, branding me before I even unpacked.

"I know, but there's more. He already has one living in his condo project at the lake, and another in that downtown high-rise. He's a busy boy."

Feeling nauseous, his words surprised me. I thought I knew everything—that I was the only one. I remember in the beginning, asking if there was anyone else. He had assured me I was the only one he wanted. In retrospect, I realized that he never answered my question. What he said to me wasn't an answer. It was words to placate a gullible woman who thought she had found paradise.

Needing to escape this conversation, I looked at my watch. "Time to open."

Raoul stood, and we moved to the front of the club. He unlocked the door as I stood at my post. I grabbed a handful of menus and banged them together, straightening them and forcefully shifting my mind from what Raoul had said.

It didn't work. My blood jelling in my veins. I was such a fool. Who did I think I was? I wasn't "special." I was a joke and an idiot for believing life would serve me a bright future. Soft words and passionate touches had lured me down a garden path—I had been fooling myself all along. I berated myself under my breath. *Idiot, idiot, idiot.*

Raoul turned back to me. "You ready?"

I put a smile on my face and nodded.

With one last twist, he unlatched the door.

Within a few minutes, customers drifted in. Tuesday night regulars coming for dinner and drinks. As usual, the majority were men, though one or two women were in attendance. I went through the motions, said the right things, laughed at the right moments, and was pleasant and accommodating. I acted like nothing was wrong, like life was exactly as it should be. Every time the door opened, I braced, expecting Bobby. Wanting him to come and hoping he wouldn't. Part of me wanted to see if he looked different, now that I realized who he really was.

I scoffed at myself when I remembered feeling sorry for him. Bobby and his frigid wife Thelma, who didn't want sex, so he needed to find it outside the marriage. Bobby, who was funny, gregarious, and adorable, shouldn't be with someone who would not walk beside him through life. He needed a woman like me, who carried herself well through any social situation, making him the envy of his peers.

Raoul came out at seven, insisting I take my break. Tuesday nights were slow, so I worked alone. Bobby arrived while I was on my break. When I returned to my station, I saw him sitting alone at a booth. My heart palpitated wildly. It was hard to breathe. *Oh God, how was I going to manage this?*

Raoul dropped some menus onto the podium. "I'll get the drinks for the Hendersons at table twelve before I go. I managed everything else. The Grahams have menus—Thelma is in the washroom and the food for Stan and Maggie should be out soon. Hal and Georgia have their bill and everyone else is working on their meals."

Nodding, I did my best to avoid looking in Bobby's direction. During my break, I had mulled over the past months. I tried to find anything that hinted to me that things differed from how they appeared. Had I deliberately ignored the warning signs? Was I so stubborn that I refused to see the obvious? Of course, he was married, but the world knew it wasn't a joyous marriage. Or was it? Did it suit them both? I didn't believe that Thelma was a stupid woman. She must know that her husband was a serial philanderer. Had I known that? I was aware he played away, but I didn't realize he housed them. I thought I was the first, that I was special.

My biggest worry was how Bobby would react when he found

out I had decided not to move into the condo. He was president of the Skyview Lounge's board of directors, and if he wanted to be vindictive, he might remove me from my job. Not wanting to lose my job, I lamented my foolish behavior. I should have known better. I should have kept my distance.

Timing would be everything. I couldn't talk to him tonight. Not with Thelma here. Snapping out of my thoughts, I moved around the room, greeting those who had come in while I was on my break, asking if they needed anything. I was only a few tables away when Thelma returned from the washroom, sauntering across the floor in her spiky heels. I had to admit that other than her weak chin that made her nose hawkish—she wasn't a bad-looking woman. She had nice curves and long legs and she always dressed well. I don't think I've ever seen her in anything dowdy or plain. She wore expensive clothes, finely tailored. I realized with a start that she dressed like me.

I gave her a few minutes to review the menu before approaching the table. Bobby glanced up, smiling. Every fear I had manufactured since our tussle on the kitchen floor disappeared. He was gorgeous, and he was smiling at me. I silently berated myself for doubting him. He wouldn't smile like that if he didn't have caring feelings for me, would he?

"Good evening, Mr. Graham. Mrs. Graham." I nodded at Thelma. She looked up at me. Her blue eyes challenged my politeness. *Did she know? What did she know?* My stomach constricted.

"You sure took your sweet time getting here. I'm ready to order." She slapped the menu on the table.

I smiled, though I would have preferred to slap her. "I'm sorry. What can I get you this evening?" I picked up her menu, hugging it to my chest as if it shielded me from the angry vibes she was emanating.

"I would like the rack of lamb with mint jelly, rosemary roasted potatoes, and asparagus in Hollandaise sauce."

"Very good ma'am. And for you, sir?" I looked at Bobby.

"Sure. I'll have the ten-ounce New York strip, with baked potato and ... vegetable of the day."

"How would you like your steak done?" I picked up his menu and added it to the one I was already holding.

"Rare."

"Any starters or salads for either of you."

"Sure, we'll have mushroom caps and some of those frogs' legs." Bobby grinned. He knew I hated that we had frog legs on the menu.

Thelma made a face. "I don't like either of those, Bobby, and you know it." She looked at me, her eyes hard as steel. "I would like a Caesar salad, without the anchovies, dressing on the side. And I want it immediately, I don't want to still be eating it when my meal comes. Do you understand me?"

"Of course, Mrs. Graham." The need to curtsey struck me, but I stopped myself. "Will there be anything else?"

"Yes, I'd like another cranberry martini." She tipped her glass up, drained it, and then handed me the empty glass.

"Yes ma'am." I took the glass before I looked at Bobby. There was merriment in his eyes. Was he enjoying how his wife treated me, or just amused at how ridiculous she was acting and hoping I was in on the joke? "Anything else for you, sir?"

"A glass of red wine, the house Malbec with my meal, and I suppose I'll have another whisky and soda when you come back with Thelma's martini. Thank you."

Dismissed, I hurried away from their table. I really liked my job most of the time. I think in all the years I worked here, I only waited on Thelma once before. She never came on Tuesdays; she had some knitting thing she went to. So why was she here this Tuesday? I had no answers, but I wasn't pleased. She treated everyone with such disrespect, which angered me. I counseled many staff over the years to let her snide remarks and subtle insults go. *She wasn't worth losing your job over.* Yet here I was—I'd only taken her order, and I already wanted to pick up the menu and smack it down on her head.

I placed the order in the kitchen, telling Craig that the salad needed to be ready for the patron to consume before the meal was out. He laughed. "For Mrs. Graham, I presume."

I chuckled. "Yes, sir. You know your customers."

I delivered the drinks and then made my rounds, dropping off bills and taking payments. Thankfully, we had a busboy to clear and reset tables. I hated looking at untidy tables when I was too busy to clear them, so the room was always tidy.

I stopped by to collect Thelma's salad plate and see if she needed another martini, as her glass was empty. I picked up the plate before asking, "Can I get you anything else, Mrs. Graham?"

"Sure. You can get me another cranberry martini. This one has been dead for a while. You're not very good at your job, are you? Usually, I don't have to be asked, they just bring me another."

Burning with humiliation and rage, I said, "I'm sorry. I'll try and do better."

I looked up. Bobby was smirking. My temper soared. I wanted to reach over and slap that half-smile right off his face. How dare he find his wife's treatment of me amusing.

I stormed away from the table, placing the salad plate into the dishwasher tray in the kitchen with great care. I really just wanted to hurl it across the floor and hear it shatter into a million pieces. Instead, I walked through the kitchen to the back door. A blast of cold air hit me as I pushed the door open. I stepped out, gulping frigid air into my lungs.

Craig hollered from the kitchen, "Hey! Close that door!"

I came back inside, slamming the door shut. "Sorry, Craig. I just needed some air."

"Oh, if I'd known it was you, I wouldn't have said anything. I thought it was Brandon. Sorry."

"No big deal."

He returned to his duties, and I took a martini to Thelma. She frowned as I set it down on the cocktail napkin. Watching her expression, it took every ounce of my fiber to not throw it in her face. "That took you long enough. Look, you idiot. You forgot the onion."

I shook, embarrassed that in my haste I'd forgotten her instructions and angry that she was so critical. "I'm sorry, I'll get you another, and you can have this one on the house." Hurrying away before she objected, I made her another martini and added two onions. As I passed the window in the kitchen, I noticed their meals were being set on the serving platform. I grabbed the plates, thinking that at least I would make one less trip to that table.

I asked Brandon to help me. He grabbed a folded napkin, picked up one plate, and grabbed the fixings for baked potatoes in the other. I took the other, and together, we headed to Graham's table. I set the martini down to the right of Thelma before setting her meal down. Turning to Brandon, I relieved him of the plate. Once that was on the table, I took the cruet from him, letting him head back to the kitchen.

"What would you like on your potato, sir?"

"The works please."

I generously dolloped sour cream, real bacon bits, and chives onto the potato. He smiled and nodded. I turned back to Thelma. "Can I get you anything else?"

"Are you new here?"

"No, I've been here for quite some time actually."

"Can you tell me how you have kept your job? Did you sleep your way into it? You are seriously inept."

"Excuse me?" My blood pounded in my ears. I had heard what she said, but I couldn't believe she said something so hurtful.

"Well, all I can say is that it's no wonder your daughter is dead. If your skills as a server are any sign of your abilities as a mother, then that poor girl never stood a chance."

Her words slammed into me like a semi going through a roadblock. Chunks of my heart and mind flew into the air and all I saw was her smug face in front of me.

I dropped the cruet and lunged at her. She was unprepared for my attack. Her chair tipped backward, sending the two of us to the floor. Chairs and tables toppled over as we wrestled one another.

Primal screams filled the room. We were both shrieking like monkeys at the zoo. I was yanking her by her hair—she was clawing at my face and kicking her matchstick legs. I heard fabric tearing, but didn't know if it was my dress or hers. Thinking I had the upper hand, it surprised me when she flipped me over and I was under her. I grabbed her ears and using my legs, I catapulted her over my head.

Scrambling onto my knees, I was screaming obscenities as I crawled toward her. She lay winded—on her back with her eyes closed. I was panting and part of me thought I should get up and walk away. But a larger part of me wanted blood. Never had I wanted to kill someone, but this dark force inside me would settle for nothing less. I wanted to beat her to a pulp, to wipe that smug smile off her face. I wanted to hurt her, not just because of what she said, but because she had opened the floodgates of my rage. All that pent-up frustration of my life, every single disappointment since birth, had filled my soul with a putrid cesspool of anger that wouldn't be satisfied until she was no longer breathing.

I had nearly reached her when arms circled my waist and lifted me to my feet. Struggling to get free, I blindly hit and kicked at the person preventing me from my mission. I opened my eyes to see Raoul helping Thelma to her feet. He whispered apologies and patted her hand as he led her to a nearby chair. She sat there, pretending to cry.

As I stopped struggling, the surrounding arms loosened. I pulled away with a jerk, looking back into the amused face of Bobby Graham.

"Hold on there, tiger," he muttered.

"I want her fired!" Thelma shrieked amid fake sobs. "She attacked me for no reason. I think she's insane. If she isn't fired, I will press charges. I will sue this place for damages, and I have lots of witnesses." She pointed her bony finger at the crowd gathering around us.

I stood there, stunned. Nearly every patron was on their feet, watching and listening. There were smirks and smiles amid looks of horror and disgust. I was remorseful, but too prideful to admit it.

Raoul walked over to me. He took me by the arm and whisked me away, down the hallway to his office.

CHAPTER THIRTY-FIVE

Inside his office, Raoul shoved me into the chair. "I can't believe you, Barbie. What the hell were you thinking?" He paced the floor, running his hands through his hair.

I shrugged. I couldn't tell him what I was thinking, not all of it.

"Not good enough. You realize she will have your head and mine. She is not a person you mess with."

"I'm sorry. It won't happen again."

"I know it won't because you won't be working here." He sat down heavily in his chair, his face ashen; filled with anguish. "Bobby Graham sits on the board of directors. Even if he wanted to let this go, Thelma won't let him. They may not be happily married, but what Thelma wants, Thelma gets. She is vindictive. He will not get a moment of peace until you are history. I'm sorry, but you can clean out your things and go."

Terror filled my soul. Had I lost everything in one moment of madness? Why me? I wouldn't take responsibility for what happened tonight. It wasn't my fault. Thelma deserved what I had given her, and more. She goaded me, insulted me, and treated me like I was of less value than the rug beneath her feet. No one should be at the receiving end of her abuse. Surely Raoul was aware of that. It never crossed my mind that I would lose my job. What was I going to do? I loved my job.

"Raoul, please. I didn't mean for this to happen—it was an accident. I just lost my mind for a moment. Please."

"There isn't much I can do. My hands are tied." He shook his head sadly. "I'm sorry, Barbie, I really am."

I sat there in stunned silence, while Raoul looked at the far wall. Then, there was a knock on the door. Before anyone responded, the door opened, and Bobby Graham came in.

"Raoul, people want to clear out. Maybe you could manage the till while I talk to Ms. O'Shea."

Raoul stood, straightened his jacket, and left without another word. Bobby closed the door quietly.

I stared at him, waiting for him to apologize and tell me he wouldn't let Thelma win.

"Well, Barbie, it looks like this is the end of the road."

As if he had punched me in the stomach, I couldn't catch my breath. "What do you mean?" It came out in a whisper.

"Well, darlin', it means that I can't allow you to move into that condo. You made quite a spectacle of yourself tonight. Many of the folks here would have been your neighbors. How can I let you live there, knowing that they will gossip about the night you attacked my wife? They won't see it as anything more than a jealous rage. It would be scandalous, and I can't abide that."

I had nothing to say. Sitting there, staring at him, I expected and hoped he would say he was joking. I had been experiencing mixed feelings about this move, but having it taken away made me realize I was looking forward to it. I wanted it. "You can't do that, Bobby, not over something like this."

"I'm afraid I can, and I have. Do you have the keys?"

"Not here, they are back at my place."

"Well, how about, I stop by for one last hurrah? I can get the keys then."

I lunged at him. "You bastard, you fucking bastard."

He grabbed my hands before I scratched his face. "Careful, tiger. You don't want to mess with me." Then he threw me back into the chair with such force that it tipped recklessly, forcing me to struggle to maintain my balance. Bobby made no move to stabilize the chair. He stood there waiting for things to settle before continuing.

"I trust Raoul told you that you are fired?"

I said nothing, I just sat there panting, my anger ready to burst the banks again.

"Well, if he didn't, then let me assure you that your services are no longer required." He pulled the door open but didn't leave. Staring at me, he said, "It was a lot of fun while it lasted, Barbie. You were one of the best."

"I wish I could say the same for you." I spat. He looked back over his shoulder and laughed. Then he closed the door and left me alone in Raoul's office.

I sat there, in shock. The night's events played over and over in my head, meshing with one another. It was a kaleidoscope of memories, fleeting images twisting into one another. Nothing made any sense. When the tears came, they burst from behind the dam and spewed down my cheeks. Sobs racked my body, forcing me to bend forward. I wept for all I had lost—the job I loved and the future I had expected. The tears were not enough to wash away my rage. I tucked a huge helping of resentment deep into my heart. I needed the fuel of anger to force me forward or I would sit right here and die.

Sometime later Raoul came back in. I didn't look up. I heard him moving around his office. He tucked some tissues into my hand before settling into his chair. He said nothing. He just sat there waiting for me to gain some composure.

I didn't know if I would ever come to terms with the insanity of this night, but I would have to. Looking into the future, I had no home, no job, and at the moment, no prospects. I didn't know what I was going to do or how I was going to manage.

I would try to get an apartment tomorrow, but without a job, I doubted they would rent to me. They didn't like to rent to people who might not pay their rent.

I looked up at Raoul. "What am I going to do, Raoul?"

He shrugged. "I don't know. Bobby is running this show. He told me to make sure your record of employment stated 'fired' and that I wasn't to doctor it to allow you to get employment insurance. I've heard rumors of his ruthlessness but never seen it. He is out to get you."

New tears sprang to my eyes at his words. "I can't believe I thought I loved him," I whispered.

"What did you say?"

"Nothing."

"Oh yes, it was something. You just said that you thought you loved him." Then his eyes lit up with discovery. "Oh, my God! It's you. You are the one who's moving into his new condo project."

"Was, Raoul. Not is. I was the one, but he told me tonight that it's over. He chose that vile creature over me." My anger rose at his easy dismissal as my tears subsided. "Thelma Graham is a buzzard, who picks the flesh off the bones of others because she's bitter that they're prettier, smarter, and happier than she'll ever be. I can't believe anyone would be willing to be with her."

"I know. She's a piece of work, isn't she? However, she has a father with money, and Bobby needed it to finance some of his early projects. He was competitive and aggressive, wanting to springboard his way to the top. Bobby stood in the shadow of two powerful men—his father and grandfather. He wanted to make a name for himself outside of being the son of the formidable Grahams. Enter Thelma's dad, who had a daughter, who was so above herself, so snide and condescending that no boy in his right mind ever took her on a second date. When Bobby approached him for financing, they struck a deal. If he married Thelma and stayed married to her, he would finance his projects until he could financially make it on his own. No repayment required."

"How do you know this?"

"I'm in a place where I hear things, things that aren't for public consumption. Bobby will never leave Thelma because if he did, she would take half of everything. So, their marriage made in hell will go on and anyone who challenges that, will be on the short end of a long bus ride to nowhere."

I pondered his words, thinking that, indeed, life wasn't fair. Cold, bitter bile stirred in the pit of my being. I had lost everything, and Thelma would continue to live her life on her terms.

"Feel sorry for them, though," Raoul continued. "They are not cheerful people. It's a deal with the devil and neither of them is living the life they want. Thelma can't be happy knowing that Bobby is with her because her dad basically sold her to him. And Bobby must live with a bitter and nasty wife. She allegedly shut him out of her bedroom once she gave him his boy and his girl, and that is why she does nothing to deter his extramarital escapades. She's no fool."

In the months we'd been together and all the talks we had shared after sex, he mentioned none of this to me. He was tight-lipped and secretive, telling me only what he thought I wanted to hear. I was a fool for believing a word from his lying mouth. I was gullible and naïve—once again, thinking I was special.

We sat there together, silently contemplating our conversation. Raoul was leaning back in his chair, lost in thought. He sat up suddenly. "Bobby says I am not to give you a reference. I can't write one down, in case he gets his hands on a copy. My job would be done.

But if any prospective employer were to call …"

"Thank you, Raoul. Raoul, I'm sorry I pulled you into my drama."

"I have to tell you this also. Bobby Graham is going to talk to every restaurant owner in the city. He's going to make sure you won't find a job. So, if you're going to find work, you will have to move out of the service industry. He's making an example of you, which I take to mean, he felt invested in you somehow. You don't destroy things that mean nothing to you. I don't know if that brings comfort or not." He stood and moved around his desk.

Standing too, I said, "I guess I'd better get my stuff."

"I'll help, but go into the bathroom and wash your face, first. You look a mess."

I left his office and went into the washroom down the hall. I stared at my reflection. My dress was torn beyond repair. Dark circles of mascara rimmed my eyes, my hair was tousled and messy. *My hair.* There was no way I was going to afford a trip to Calgary to get it done now. I was going to have to cancel my appointment. Damn, Thelma Graham. Damn her to hell and back.

Raoul stood at the front, waiting to let me out. The room was a mess. Someone had set the table back on their legs and put the chairs back into place, but they had not cleared the tables. Dirty empty plates sat uncollected at many tables. "I should help clear this before I go."

"No, thanks Barbie. I'll get Sherri in early to clear and set up tomorrow."

Sherri! Of course, now she will be promoted to my coveted job. She's going to love that. Bitter rage percolated. Why Sherri? "Fine." I said it in such a way that he knew I wasn't fine.

"Come here." He opened his arms.

It took a second for me to decide, then I walked past him and out the door. I didn't look back. This place, my precious job, the one I'd worked toward all my life, was gone.

Andrea was gone.

Life as I knew it was over.

Where do I go from here?

CHAPTER THIRTY-SIX

Once home, I crawled into bed, turning off the alarm as I did. Pulling up the covers over my head, I lay there feeling numb. It took a long time to fall asleep. My mind was racing through the events of the night, over and over. I tried to turn it off, but nothing seemed to work for more than a minute before I was back reliving the barbs, the fight, Bobby's words and Raoul's lack of compassion.

Tossing and turning, I fought my mind until finally—I slipped into dreamland. My dreams comprising shattered pieces of glass—images that appeared and disappeared. I observed my father come into my room and the terror of his touch revolted me. I woke, my scream dying on my lips as my room appeared and the dream faded. Curling into myself, I wept and for the first time in a long time, contemplating that this world would be better off without me and I would be better off gone.

Those murky thoughts I'd left behind all those years ago rose to swallow me whole. The familiar darkness was comfortable as I sank into the abyss, feeling sorry for myself and for what I'd been through.

My life hadn't been a glory walk. I fought every step of the way, and just when things seemed to go my way, someone tossed a heaping spoonful of adversity into my world to remind me not to rise above my lot. Who did I think I was, anyway?

Unable to fall asleep, I arose. The sun had yet to rise, but the eerie glow of a winter morning peeped through the crack in the curtains. Pulling aside the living room drapes, I watched the snow fall. I loved watching it snow. I wasn't a fan of the cold, but the snow was beautiful. When Andrea was five, I remember one sunny winter day taking her to the park. I showed her how to make a perfect snow angel, just like my father had taught me.

She squealed with delight as we stood side by side, looking at the two angels—the big one and the little one with wings unfurled. I remembered telling her that the angels would always be with her, that she should watch for them and be thankful for their existence because they would protect her.

I dropped the curtain. The angels hadn't protected either of us in the end. It was a fairy tale to believe that anything or anyone was looking after us. When Andrea was murdered, where were her angels? Where were my angels when someone verbally attacked me, and I lost everything in one night? What a stupid thing to believe in. The only sure things in life were death and taxes.

I dropped the curtains, my mood sufficiently darkened. I walked into the kitchen, flipping on the light. The boxes in the dining room assaulted me, reminding me that in less than a week, I would be homeless unless I found a place to live before then. I would check with the building manager to see if there was another suite here. It might be the only answer because I wouldn't have to provide the name of my employer.

I opened the fridge. The shelves were almost bare. A half-bottle of ketchup, a small jar of pickle brine with one lone pickle inside, and a cup of yogurt. I pulled open the crisper. There was a head of lettuce, a couple of tomatoes, a few celery sticks, and a green pepper. There was no comfort food here.

I opened the freezer. A small box of Belgian chocolates sparkled before me. I kept them in there to prevent eating them all at once, and I loved how they melted in my mouth. I opened the box and took stock. The top layer was nearly full. I removed one chocolate shell and popped it into my mouth. As it settled against the warmth of my tongue, the frozen treat melted, oozing across my palate. I moaned with delight. There was nothing better than chocolate. I replaced the lid, closed the door, and walked away. Before getting too far, I returned for another and eventually took the box to the living room. I sat on the couch, turned on the television and stared at the screen while popping frozen chocolates into my mouth.

It didn't take long to empty the box. I tried to savor each piece, but the void inside my core was demanding to be filled. It had been silent, or at least I had kept it contained for so long that now unleashed it was out of control. I dumped the empty box in the trash and looked into the freezer again. A half box of frozen yogurt. I stood at the sink, spooning the creamy decadence into my mouth. When it was gone, I opened and closed every cabinet. They were mostly empty—the contents packed into boxes.

Were there cookies, and if so, which box? I tried to remember. I rarely ate sweets, but occasionally, I needed something. Cookies were easy, as they didn't spoil too quickly.

The boxes were sealed, ready to move. I debated. It might be easier to go to the store.

I looked at the clock. Five o'clock. Too early for grocery stores, but the convenience store at the gas station would be open for business.

CHAPTER THIRTY-SEVEN

I didn't bother to dress. I pulled on my winter gear, slipped into my boots, and headed out. The store was three blocks away, and I debated on the way down to the ground floor whether to drive or walk. When I stepped outside, I realized I would be halfway to the store before I cleaned all the snow off my car, so I just kept moving. I tugged my scarf tighter as I turned into the wind. Lowering my head, I walked on, enjoying the early morning silence.

I was cold when I reached the store. Wandering the aisle, I pulled junk food off the shelves as I passed. I had a can of salted nuts, three bags of chips, two kinds of cookies, two cartons of ice cream, several chocolate bars, a box of sugary cereal, a large carton of whipping cream, bags of licorice, jellybeans, a loaf of white bread, butter, a jar of strawberry jam and a few boxes of assorted candy. The clerk rang through my purchases, not once commenting on my choices as he placed my items into flimsy plastic bags. A shock wave rocketed through me when he told me what I owed. I passed over my debit card to complete my purchase.

While trudging home, lugging my confections, I regretted not bringing my car. The bags were heavy, and I was cold because I had not removed or loosened my coat while I shopped. I put one foot in front of the other, and soon, the apartment appeared. My mouth watered, just thinking that in a few minutes, I would savor the treats I had purchased.

I kicked off my boots and rushed into the kitchen. After putting the ice cream in the freezer, I found a bowl and poured in a helping of cereal. I ripped open one of the chocolate bars while I searched the bags for the whipping cream and took a huge bite. I closed my eyes as I hummed with satisfaction. Then I went back to looking for the cream. Finding it, I poured it over my cereal. I took a spoonful and nearly gagged. It was too rich. But I persevered. I emptied the cereal and refilled the bowl until no cream was left. By this time, I was no longer revolted by the thickness of the cream. My stomach was churning with dissatisfaction.

I didn't care. Pushing on, I opened the potato chips, the sun chips, and the taco chips and consumed them. My taste buds were exploding with the flavor. I savored each morsel, keeping it on my tongue until it had lost its consistency. My stomach swelled until I looked six months pregnant. Physically, my body stuffed beyond capacity squirmed in agony, even as the emptiness at the center of my being remained hollow. I pushed on.

Moving to the living room, I took the bags of licorice. I turned on the television and found some children's programming. I sat there watching the cartoon characters bounce on the screen as I stuffed strings of licorice into my mouth. When I couldn't take another bite, I laid back on the cushions and rubbed my complaining belly. Tears flowed as I realized for the first time what I had just done. I rushed to the bathroom and vomited. When I had emptied my stomach, I crawled into the dry bathtub, curled into a ball, and cried myself to sleep.

I woke up a short time later, shivering. I was so cold. After crawling out of the tub, I went to my bed and tucked the covers under my chin. I lay there shaking and shuddering until the warmth overtook me, and I fell asleep. It was early afternoon before I woke up. My stomach rumbled, but this time, my mind couldn't deal with food. I stayed in bed, eventually falling back to sleep.

This was the pattern for the next two days. I remained in my pajamas, either on the couch or in bed. Once a day, I gorged myself, but not to the capacity I'd done on my initial binge. I was getting the hang of this. I ate one box of ice cream with cookies, and then nuts with the second box. I ate candies, laid on the couch, and watched daytime soap operas. In one sitting, I ate the whole loaf of bread; half the slices I squished in my hand, the other half I ate with butter and jam. In the evening, I ordered delivery.

I reminisced that if all had gone according to plan, I'd be settling into my new home. Whenever I passed a mirror, I stopped to remind myself what a loser I was; useless, stupid, and unwanted. Finding a new apartment never crossed my mind, and I didn't look for a new job. I couldn't get myself to care about either. For the first time in my life, I gave myself over to those evil thoughts. They won as I gave up trying.

Early in the afternoon of the third day, I had less than a handful of days left before I would have to be out of my apartment. I don't know why I cared less about this than whether I had junk food in the house. Because I wanted to go to the store for more food, I showered first. I slipped into my jeans and found that I couldn't button them. In three days? I stared at myself in the mirror. My face was puffy, my skin sallow. I cried again. I removed the jeans and slipped back into my sweatpants.

Moving into the kitchen, I wailed like a lost child. I looked at the surrounding chaos. Wrappers and empty boxes lay on the counter, on the floor, and in the sink. I didn't have the energy to change that. I wandered back to the living room. It was just as cluttered. Blankets and pillows spilled from the couch onto the floor. A pizza box from the night before lay open on the coffee table. An empty plastic soda bottle lay beside the lone crust I hadn't finished. I picked it up and ate it.

Then, in frustration and anger, I threw myself onto the couch.

CHAPTER THIRTY-EIGHT

I curled into a ball, pulling the covers from the floor on top of me. More than anything else, I wanted to die. How could I get this world to stop long enough to let me off? I didn't know what to do or where to turn. No one had called me since I arrived home late Tuesday night—I didn't even know what day of the week this was. I was nearly asleep when the phone rang. I jumped, startled by the loud trill. Then I relaxed, letting it ring. It stopped and then started again. I let it ring. It stopped and started again. I grew angry.

I grabbed the phone and threw it against the far wall. It dented the drywall and fell to the floor in pieces, and the sound died. I reached over and tried to yank the cord from the wall. When it failed to dislodge, I picked up the base and unplugged the phone line. Then, I threw it across the room as well.

Energized at my destruction. I looked around the room. Most of my belongings were packed away—there wasn't much I could destroy, but the urge to smash everything grew stronger. I opened the first box. Inside were the crystal figurines I had collected. I couldn't bring myself to throw them. I moved into the dining room. In the first box, I found tumblers. I tossed one hard on the floor. It broke, but it wasn't satisfying. I dug deeper, finding the delicate wine goblets I purchased for Bobby to use. The first one I tossed against the dining room wall. It shattered. The sound was exhilarating.

Moving the box into the living room, I was unaware that I walked over broken glass to get there. In my bare feet, I don't know how I missed all those shards. The sound of breaking glass was the only thing I was thinking of. The box rocked slightly when I set it on the coffee table. I moved it back to the corner and balanced it with my knees as I picked up the soda bottle and hurled it across the room. It hit the wall with a thud, then bounced back toward me. After settling the carton in the middle of the table, I unwrapped another wine glass.

I took my time, savoring each strike. I laughed. Someone knocked on my door. I ignored them, too. The buzzer went a few minutes later.

"Go away!" I yelled at the top of my lungs before I hurled another glass at the wall. There was more knocking, more buzzing. I went to the door receiver and tried to figure out how to shut it off. The knocking became more insistent.

"Go away!" I yelled at it. The buzzing stopped. Moving back to the couch, I walked through more broken glass, leaving bloody footprints across the carpet. I didn't feel it—I didn't care.

I heard the door open, and then the thud as it hit the end of the security chain. "Barbara?"

It was Kevin. What was he doing here? I ignored him.

"Barbie, please open the door." The building manager called out.

"Go away!"

"No, we can't go away. I will break down the door if I have to, but I'd prefer it if you'd open it."

I unwrapped another glass and hurled it against the wall, laughing with delight as it shattered.

"Barbara Anne! Open this door immediately." Kevin sounded angry.

Ignoring him, I unwrapped the last wine glass. I heard whispering but couldn't make out what they were saying. I held the last glass up before me, admiring the smooth curves and lines of the delicate glass. Then I hurled it with all my might against the wall. As it flew across the room, I heard a thump and then a tinkle as someone snipped the chain in two.

Kevin and Bud entered the room as the glass exploded beside them.

They stared at the debris on the floor before turning to me. The apartment was a mess, and I was a mess. Looking away, I hid my face in the back of the couch, pulling the blanket over me. I hoped to successfully hide myself from their view.

Kevin came over to the couch and tugged the blanket back. It started as a hiccough and as Kevin wrapped his arms around me—I sobbed. The sorrow—so entrenched in my being rocketed from my toes to the top of my head. I vibrated and rocked as it forced itself out through the very pores of my skin. Everything hurt like I was being torn apart.

I don't know how long we sat there, Kevin holding me, rocking me, hushing me. As the sobs slowed and the tears dried up, my body overheated. It was too hot to be so close to another warm body. The surrounding air was suffocating, stifling me, burying me alive. When I struggled to free myself, Kevin released me easily. I turned away from him, then leaned back against him. He wrapped his arm around me. I settled into his arms, feeling like I'd come home.

"So, what's going on?" he whispered.

Tears sprang to my bloodshot eyes. I squeezed them shut and took a deep breath, trying to calm myself. "Everything," I said.

He sighed against my ear, and I wondered why I'd ever left him. He was always so good to me, and I'd repaid him by being unfaithful, unkind, and unloving. Yet here he was, holding me and caring about what I was going through. Then I remembered. I'd left him because he was too good for me. I didn't deserve him. He deserved someone who would love and cherish him. I extricated myself from him, chastising myself for falling into his spell again.

Kevin was so easy to love. He gave everything and expected nothing. I don't think I'd ever met anyone like him. When we first met, he took all my abuse and never once threw it back in my face. He was like a big lovable dog, eager to please but not in a needy way, and I was the hissing, spitting kitten with claws. The more he loped into my life and didn't run away when the claws came out, the more I trusted him. My trust turned to respect and my respect to love.

"So, you ready to talk?"

I sighed. "I guess."

"Okay, let me make us some tea and then you can tell me what's going on." He removed himself. The coolness of the apartment stole in where his warm body had been. I shivered. He pulled the blanket off the floor, draped it around me, and then moved to the kitchen. I heard him rummaging around, but he didn't call for help.

He came back with two mugs of tea. He set them both on the coffee table before sitting across from me.

I picked up the mug closest to me and took a sip. It was hot, but I blew across the top and took a second sip before starting my story. My shame kept me from looking at him, and once I started, I couldn't stop. Tears flowed randomly as I spoke of my affair with Bobby, his offer of a new place to live, and my dreams of being in a place where I would rub shoulders with influential people. I didn't tell him how Bobby made me feel the day I went to my new home for the first time. The shame of that morning was still raw. I went on to the night Thelma Graham came in and how she had accused me of being a terrible mother.

"I know I failed Andrea," I cried. My heart wrenched tightly as I spoke aloud those hurtful words. "She deserved better than me, she really did. But I wouldn't have hurt her for the world, she meant so much to me." My throat was tight—the emotions and the memories of her—struggling to find freedom. Kevin stayed silent, waiting for me to get my thoughts out.

"Oh God. I know Thelma was right. Andrea would still be alive if I'd been a proper mother. She didn't deserve to die." I slipped the mantle of guilt onto my shoulders. It seemed cumbersome, but it was mine to bear. "It's one thing to take on the responsibility, you know?" I looked at Kevin for the first time, needing his reassurance and understanding. He looked at me, his face blank and unreadable. I kept going, needing to make him understand now. "I didn't like that she pointed out my flaws. She was so condescending, so vile. I just wanted to hurt her back—you know?"

Kevin didn't respond, so I continued.

"So, when she said what she did, I came unglued. I jumped on her, knocking her onto the floor, and then we were rolling around kicking and screaming, biting and scratching. All the customers were out of their seats to get a good view of it."

I glanced at Kevin. He was smirking. Something in me shifted, but I continued. "I took a good handful of her hair before someone pulled me off her. She ripped my dress, and I have a nice bruise on my thigh and one on my left arm. I also broke two nails. But Raoul whisked me away to his office before I assessed the damage I did in return."

Kevin guffawed. I sat back, staring at him. The mirth in his gaze and the slight crinkle around his eyes set me off, and I snickered. "We must have looked quite a sight."

That was all it took. We both broke out laughing. Letting go of the trauma I experienced since that night was cathartic. Thanks to Kevin, I laughed at how insane we must have looked. Thelma's shocked face flashed before me, and I laughed even harder.

I was catching a wave of hysteria when Kevin stopped laughing and I brought myself back under control.

CHAPTER THIRTY-NINE

We sat in companionable silence for a few seconds. Then Kevin looked around the room. "So, when do you move?"

"Well, that's the kicker, isn't it? Bobby Graham sits on the board of directors at the Skyview Lounge. He rescinded his offer to move into his condo development after what happened. Without a job, I can't get a new place to live, and the new tenants arrive on Friday. I'll have to live in my car because I have nowhere else to go." My voice wobbled, and I burst into tears again.

"You have another option you haven't considered." Kevin smiled. "You could come and live with me."

A tremor of fear ran through me. Not that I was afraid of Kevin—because I wasn't. Being near him every day might be difficult. I didn't want him to get his hopes up, to put faith and stock into our relationship being restored. I was confused enough already.

Kevin must have sensed my hesitation. "You'd be doing me a huge favor. I've been rattling around that house all month. It's been too quiet, and Christmas is coming. You being there would help. You can have the guest room." He paused. "Please consider it."

Weighing my options, it didn't take long to realize I didn't have any. Staring out the window at the falling snow, sleeping in my car was not something I wanted to experience. It would prove to be more than my pampered self could handle. With no friends to speak of, and having been solely with Bobby for too long, I could think of no one who would open their doors to me on short notice.

"Okay." I agreed. "I will live at your house until I get another job and qualify for my own place. Deal?"

"Deal." We shook hands. "So, when are we going to do this?"

"I don't know. I don't really have a lot to move. A lot of these boxes are for the charity shops." That reminded me. "What day is it?"

"It's Saturday."

"The charity shop was supposed to pick these up on Thursday. I wonder what happened." Then I remembered I had left to get more food. They must have come while I was away. Now they wouldn't come back. They hadn't even called. Or had they? I purposely ignored the flashing message light on the phone. I looked across the room at the shattered phone lying amid the broken glass. "Oh brother."

"What."

"I think I missed them. They were supposed to be here Thursday, but I went out."

"No biggie—you can arrange for them to come again."

"I hope so. They might feel like I've jerked them around."

"There are three or four separate charity shops in the city. Try another one."

"Right. Thank you. I'll call another one tomorrow."

"On Monday. They won't be open tomorrow, it's Sunday."

"Right."

"So, do you want to come tonight?"

"No, I think I'll stay here and work on getting this place in order again. How about Monday?"

"Okay, that works. Maybe I'll grab a few boxes now and come by for a few more tomorrow. I'll even patch that wall for you if you want."

I looked at the wall where I'd thrown my phone. It would need a touch up. "Thank you."

"No, wait."

"What."

"I can't come Monday."

"Why not?"

"I've agreed to see my dad on Monday."

"Wow. Really?"

"Yeah. Mom and I had coffee a week ago and she told me he's dying and that he wants to see me before he does. I'm not sure I want to see him, but I think I'd regret it if I didn't get to tell him what I've wanted to tell him all these years."

"And then you'll come back here to an empty apartment. I'm no psychologist, but I think you'd be better off being with people afterward."

Maybe Kevin was right. "Well ... maybe."

Kevin stood there patiently, waiting. I fidgeted, unsure of what to do. Part of my hesitation was the fear of being close to him and needing him and of his being there for me when I needed him to be. I didn't want to give him any false hope that this was a permanent move.

"Think about it. There is no need to decide right now. I'll arrange for Matt to help me move the couch and other large pieces later in the week. You won't need them at the house anyway. We'll put them in the storeroom at the shop for now. In the meantime, I can move the boxes in batches, and you come with your clothes when you're ready, and then I'll come and get the bed. Does that work?"

"Yes, that works." Relief flooded in because he wasn't pressuring me to decide immediately.

"So, mark the boxes you need at the house and the ones you don't need, I'll take those to the shop, too." He moved toward the boxes. "How about these?"

I looked at the stack he was standing beside. "These are charity shop boxes."

"And these?" He moved farther into the dining room. "Those are ..." I moved around to the other side to see what I'd written. "Those are bathroom necessities. They go to the house."

"Okay." He lifted two boxes easily and moved them to the door, doing his best to avoid the broken glass. "I'll help you clean this up before I go. You stay there, the glass is everywhere. Just find me the vacuum."

Watching my step, I eased down the hall and pulled the vacuum out of the closet across from the bathroom. I moved it to the entry, where Kevin had piled the broken phone and the larger pieces of broken glass on top of the boxes he'd set nearby. I plugged the vacuum in, and soon, the snap and crackle of shattered glass flying up the hose filled the air.

CHAPTER FORTY

As Kevin worked, I scooted down the hall and slipped into a pair of shoes before coming back to help. I retrieved the garbage can from the kitchen and picked up the trash on the floor. Boxes, wrappers, and other assorted garbage, as well as the phone and the glass Kevin had stacked earlier, went into the bin. In a matter of minutes, the room looked better.

The vacuum sighed as Kevin turned off the power. He opened the collection canister and dumped the contents into the garbage can. Then he pulled the bag free and tied it closed. "Do you have a garbage chute?"

"Yes, out the door and to your left. It's on your right near the end of the hall."

He pulled open the door, fiddled with the lock to ensure it was unlocked, and left. The door swung closed behind him and suddenly the room felt empty. A flutter of panic stirred in my stomach—the air in the apartment closed in on me. I took a deep breath. A few seconds later, Kevin opened the door, and the air yielded to his presence.

"Okay, are you sure you're going to be okay?"

I thought about what I had just experienced and didn't want to be here on my own again. "No, I'm not. I've changed my mind. Can you give me a second to pack some things?"

A flash of surprise crossed his face. "Sure. Take all the time you need."

I scooted down the hall and threw a nightgown and some of my loose clothes into a small tote. In the bathroom, I grabbed my toothbrush, toothpaste, hair products, and appliances. It took me about five minutes, and I was a bit out of breath when I returned to the living room. Part of my breathlessness was excitement and nerves. I wasn't sure I was doing the right thing, but I was doing it.

Kevin picked up the boxes as I found my keys. We moved into the hall. Looking back into the apartment before I closed the door was like closing the book on this chapter of my life. I suppose I was. I was moving on, though I had nothing concrete in front of me.

Once I had completed my move to Kevin's, the first order of business was to get a job and then begin the arduous task of rebuilding.

I turned off the light, closed the door, and followed Kevin to the elevator.

CHAPTER FORTY-ONE

In the parking lot, Kevin handed me the key to the house. He was going to drop some boxes at the shop first. "No sense moving them twice," he said. I took the key and headed in the opposite direction.

There was a light burning in the living room when I pulled up. Leaving the driveway for Kevin, I parked on the street. Feeling like an intruder, I slipped the key into the lock and opened the door. I stepped inside and almost turned around again. What was I doing? This was madness. I pushed the door closed with my body, still holding my suitcase in my hand.

The phone rang, and I shrieked. Then I laughed. I was being silly. Should I answer the phone? No, it wasn't mine to answer. I let it ring.

After removing my boots, I walked down the hall and into the guest room. Then I unpacked. By the time Kevin appeared, I was ready for bed. Earlier, I had slipped under the covers before the feeling of cowardice reminded me I owed Kevin so much. I'd climbed out of bed and waited up to say goodnight.

He stomped into the house, knocking the snow off his boots. "It's really piling up out there," he said as he shook the snow off his jacket before hanging it in the closet.

"First proper snow of the season, eh?"

"Yep."

He came fully into the room. "You ready for bed?"

"Yes. I was just waiting to say goodnight."

A look of disappointment crossed his face before he smiled. "Oh, okay. Well ... goodnight then. Sleep well. I'll see you in the morning."

Dismissed, I slipped down the hall to my room and closed the door. Guilt assailed me. It was obvious Kevin wanted more. I'd made a huge mistake coming here. *Dang, dang, dang.*

As tired as I was, it took me a long time to fall asleep—strange room, strange bed, strange sounds. When I slept, my dreams were uneasy. I woke up several times, only to fall back into the same dream, the same turmoil. The fleeting images dissipated when I sat up. I tried to remember them, but the visions were elusive and then they were gone.

The smell of coffee. What a pleasant thing to wake up to—the aroma of brewing coffee. Kevin must have heard me coming. He set a cup of coffee on the eating bar as I entered the kitchen. Climbing onto the stool, I was grateful for the small mercies.

"I didn't cook breakfast since I wasn't sure what you had planned today. I'm going to work this morning, if you want to come."

"No, I think I'll go over to the apartment and haul back some of my clothes. Are you planning to come and haul away anything to storage today?"

"No, I'm going to go to shift some of my storage around to make room for your stuff. I'll also talk to Matt today and figure out when we can move your stuff. It will only take one evening if we both have our trucks. I'll see if we can recruit a few more to make the job that much easier."

"Okay." I took a sip of coffee.

Kevin moved to the stove and cracked a few eggs into the pan. "Do you want any breakfast?"

"I think I'll just have some yogurt, if you have any."

"Not sure." He moved to the fridge, rummaging inside. Pulling out a little tub of plain yogurt, he checked the best before date and pronounced it good before handing it to me. Then he handed me a bowl and a spoon before returning to his eggs.

"Are there any berries or something to put in this yogurt?" I asked, coming down off the stool to look for them myself.

"I have some frozen berries in the freezer. Andrea loved them in yogurt." He stumbled a bit, his voice wobbling. "Ah, ahem, there might be some of her granola left. It would be in the pantry, top shelf."

"Top shelf?" I opened the pantry door and stared up at the top shelf. "Like I can reach the top shelf."

"Okay, give me a minute." He put his eggs on a plate where four slices of toast and several strips of bacon sat. Then he reached above me, pulling down a half-full box of granola with almonds.

I mixed the granola into the yogurt as Kevin settled on the other stool. We sat in companionable silence, each lost in our own thoughts.

I finished eating before him, so I poured more coffee for us. My thoughts wandered toward the future and finding a job. "Can I use your computer, Kevin?"

"Sure. Why?"

"I think I'd better get a résumé together. I think I'll go to the Workplace Training Center tomorrow to get help making it professional. But if I get a start on it, then I'll be further ahead. I don't even know where to start. I've worked toward getting a job at the Skyview Lounge my whole life …" My emotions threatened to run away with me, so I stopped talking.

"Well, what do you want to do, Barbara? Why not try something new?"

"Like what? I'm not trained to do anything."

"Well, that place you're going to tomorrow, can't they help you? I don't know anything about them, but they have training in their title."

"I just can't imagine sitting behind a desk all day. Maybe I should work at a bank."

"Well, it's worth a shot." Kevin slipped off his stool. "I'd better get ready for work."

Left alone in the kitchen, I mulled over the thought that I should do something new. What would I like to do? All I'd ever done was serve or be a hostess. I didn't want to work in sandwich shops or greasy spoons. High-class restaurants would suit, and lounges would be even better.

I scrounged through the drawer of the kitchen desk for the phone book. I made a list of the places I would like to work from the yellow pages. None of them measured up to the Skyview Lounge, but that was lost to me. I needed a job quickly because I couldn't get my own place until I did.

After Kevin left, I showered, dressed, and returned to my apartment. I hauled my clothes down to the car—it took eight trips—laying them in the back seat. Back at Kevin's, I found the lack of closet space annoying, and I wondered if he would mind if I put some clothes into Andrea's room. I wandered down the hall to her room.

I expected to see the room pretty much as it had been the night I'd stayed here earlier this month. But inside the room were perhaps a dozen boxes of varying sizes. I opened the closet. Some of her clothes were hanging there. Recognizing the blouse she'd been wearing last Christmas, I reached out and touched it. I remembered her moving around the living room; the tree glistening behind her.

She was talking on the phone to Kevin's parents, who were vacationing in Arizona. She threw her head back and laughed at something, and her "Oh Grandpa!" comment echoed inside my head.

For one moment, she was alive and vibrant, and I longed to wrap my arms around her. As I came back to the present, I experienced the loss of her again. It was so much easier not being here. In my world, my job, my apartment, my life, Andrea was a peripheral player. She avoided spending time with me, and I had grown used to not having her as part of my life. But here, in this house, she was in every nook, cranny, and memory of being.

This house where I had lived for such a short time—this house where I became the visitor—this house filled with memories of her. I never visited unless she was here. Her birthday parties, Christmases, and the odd summer barbecue at the end of the school year. Andrea running in and out of the back door, sitting on the couch opening presents, seated at the head of the dining room table, and blowing out the candles on her birthday cake. Andrea was everywhere. How did Kevin get through the days? If she haunted me for the smattering of times I was here with her over the years—how much more the everyday memories must torment him?

I couldn't imagine.

I returned the dresses to the guest room and tossed them on the bed. When Kevin showed up, I'd see if he had space in a closet somewhere for my clothes.

Downstairs or in his room, but Andrea's room was off limits to me.

CHAPTER FORTY-TWO

Monday morning, I took my meager résumé to Workplace Training, where I endured a lecture on making an appointment. After she finished, she had me sit in the waiting room. Time ticked by, and it was nearly an hour of waiting. I still hadn't seen a counselor. Being thoroughly chastised for wasting time, I got twitchy when a tall, curvy redhead sauntered into the room. Her clothes were expensive, and her makeup was perfect. She set me further on edge before she even spoke.

"Barbara?"

I stood. "Yes, I'm Barbara."

"I'm Michelle. Pleased to meet you. Come with me." She turned and walked down a long hallway. I followed behind, passing many open doors. Every person sitting behind the desk looked up to watch me walk by. I wondered why I had to wait if no one was busy. My attitude was turning and not for the better. By the time we arrived at her office, I had worked myself into quite a stew.

"So, how can I help you, Barbara?"

"Well, I recently became unemployed and need to improve my résumé." I handed her the copy I had printed.

"Oh, I see." She nodded as she read the page, flipping it over to see if there was anything on the back. "Yes, I see. This needs work." Her tone rankled me even more. It took a great deal of effort to not rip the paper from her hands and stomp out of the office.

She took out her pen. "So, the first thing you need to define is your objective."

My objective? What is my objective? To get a job—isn't that everyone's objective when putting together a résumé? "I don't know what you mean exactly. Isn't it to get a job?"

"Yes, that's part of it, but what kind of job?"

"The one I'm applying for?"

She laughed. "Well, of course, but in the objective, you're putting down what you want for that job. For example, you want a job where you can use your skills to your advantage and theirs."

This was so strange to me. I had always talked with an owner or manager and walked into a new job. When I went to the Skyview Lounge, I had worked for months on making connections and insinuating myself into the world of a few women working there. Through them, I met Raoul and made an impression. When the hostess job opened, he called me.

Ron, my husband at the time, didn't want me to work. He wanted me at home looking after the house and his every need. In the beginning, I was okay with that. I struck up friendships with the other women in the neighborhood, shopped relentlessly, and mostly, my life was happy. One afternoon, I went across the street to Holly's house, invited to join the ladies for mimosas by the pool. Feeling like a queen, I crossed the street in my high heel mules and swimwear coverup. I remember thinking that I had arrived.

As I came into the yard, I stopped short when I heard them mention my name. I listened intently as they referred to me as a plastic barbie doll. Holly laughed before shushing them, cautioning the group that anyone could overhear them. Another voice broke in, saying surely—no one would be gauche enough to come through the yard. Surely, a guest would ring the front doorbell like any person with class would.

I backed away, retreating to my home, where I changed my clothes. Then I drove to a bar. For the first time since I met Ron, I spent the afternoon in a seedy motel with another man, a stranger. I never knew his name. He was a disappointment; inadequate to the task I needed him to undertake and therefore not at all memorable.

When Raoul called two days later, I jumped at the offer for a part-time job. Today, I had no connections. Being secure in my position at the Skyview Lounge, I hadn't worked on the next rung of the ladder. I thought I had arrived. I wasn't even sure any of the business owners who frequented the place would offer me work. Not if they heard what I'd done to Thelma.

But I was desperate. I needed the tools to get myself into a new job and out of Kevin's house. I didn't have time to waste. Every minute I was at Kevin's, I was in danger of breaking his heart again.

Coming back to her question, I struggled to put words together. "Okay, so my objective is to get the job where I can … what? Make the customer feel appreciated?" I did not know if I was even getting it.

"That's not bad. How about: To get a job where my pleasing personality, natural warmth and beauty can make your customers feel like they are the most important person in the room."

On paper, it didn't seem like a bad way to sum up a person looking for a hostess job, but how she said it made me feel trashy and I bristled at her tone. "Are you deliberately trying to provoke me?"

She looked startled. "I am trying to help you." Her tone—clipped and tight.

"Well, I am not feeling that. Obviously, your objective isn't to make me feel like I am the most important person."

"I can't help you if you're going to have this attitude." She pushed back from the desk.

I stood and reached across the desk for my résumé. I snatched it off the desk and turned to go. When I reached the door, I spun around, tears stinging my eyes. "Thank you for nothing, Michelle."

"You're welcome, Barbara." She smiled. "And by the way, Bobby sends his love."

"What?" It came out as a whisper. I stood by the door, staring at her.

She walked around the desk. "That's right. Bobby Graham sends his love. When he stopped by our house the other night, he told me you might stop by. I own this place, thanks to him. He's been very good to me over the years and when he needs a favor, I am always willing to help him out."

"Why? I've lost my job. Why is he trying to prevent me from working?"

"Thelma is a miserable beast. She's not easy on the eyes and she certainly isn't easy on the ears. She has been raising holy hell since you tossed her on the floor and she's making Bobby's life miserable. Maybe he doesn't need her money anymore, but if he were to divorce her, he'd lose half of everything, and he's not prepared to lose anything. Therefore, he's miserable and he's going to make sure you are, too."

"Oh my god. He can't do that."

"He can and he is. His influence is far reaching. I'm sure that eventually, you'll find someone who isn't afraid of him or maybe he'll tire of punishing you." She shrugged. "But in the meantime, you might be best looking for a job in another city. Good luck, Barbara." She reached around me and opened the door. As I walked out the door, she grabbed my arm. "I sure wish I'd seen you knock seven bells out of old Thelma. I don't think there's a woman around who deserved it more."

She released me, and I walked down the hallway. All the doors were still open and this time, the attention I received was even more unwelcome. They weren't gawking at a potential new client—they had front row tickets to the sideshow of Bobby Graham's ex-lover. Keeping my head down as shame rose to color my cheeks, I hurried out to the waiting area, where I grabbed my coat. Slinging it over my shoulders, I shifted into it on the fly. I couldn't wait to put distance between myself and this place.

I tip-toed quickly across the parking lot to my car, watching for icy sections. Inside the safety of my vehicle, I let the tears come. Humiliation washed over me. *How could I have been so wrong about Bobby?* All those months, all those times we were together, I never suspected he wasn't sincere in his admiration of me. I let down my guard and shared my hopes and dreams with him, not to mention my body.

Thinking back, I sifted through my memories. I realized that Bobby never actually said anything bad about Thelma. He never complained about her, never accused her of anything. I was rather relieved that he wasn't dragging his baggage into our world.

What I didn't realize was that he was—in his own sick and twisted way—honoring her in his silence.

I had been such a fool.

CHAPTER FORTY-THREE

Not wanting to be alone with the ghosts at the house, I went to a coffee shop. I thought about Jake's Place. My recent foray into the dark side of eating put me in the mood for a cinnamon bun with cream cheese icing. I promised myself that after this, I would go to the gym and work it off.

The café was cozy and bustling with patrons. I wound through a few tables to one near the back wall. The same server who'd waited on Kevin and me came over with a pot of coffee. I turned over the clean mug and nodded.

She poured. "Anything else for you?"

"Yes, can I have one of your cinnamon buns?"

"Absolutely. Do you want that warmed up?"

"Hmm?" I thought for a few seconds. "No, I think it will be fine as it is."

She nodded and left. A few minutes later, she returned with the massive bun. Unwinding it from the outside, I sipped my heavily creamed coffee and devoured my treat. It was gooey, spicy, and sweet. I relished every delectable bite, knowing that starting tomorrow, I would have to go back to salads and dry toast. I would no longer push the limits until I lost the ten pounds I'd added. I hated tight clothes.

The server came by with more coffee and took away my empty plate.

"I enjoyed that. Please give my compliments to the baker."

"I will. She's new, but her talent is equal to our beloved Marta, who just retired. She'll be pleased to hear." The server moved away, and I thought about someone getting a new job. I am not superstitious, but something inside me sat up and took notice of those words. New job. I pledged to check for other places to get help with a résumé. Surely in a city the size of Crawford, there wasn't only one. With any luck, the person heading this one wouldn't be sleeping with Bobby Graham.

I left a hefty tip, even though I didn't really have much service. Having been a server, though, I know the pleasure of being rewarded just for doing your job. I headed back to Kevin's and grabbed my gym clothes. It was time to pay the piper. At the thought of Gavin making a fuss over me, I smiled. I wanted to hear how he'd missed me. I wanted him to admonish me for destructive behavior and tell me I needed to work hard.

After parking on the street, I rushed up to the front door, searching for the key in my purse. Unable to find it, I searched the pockets of my coat. The left one was empty, but in the right one, I found the key and a folded-up piece of white paper.

Where did this come from? Who put it here? My heartbeat pulsed in my stomach as I unfolded the paper. The note read:

> I don't agree with what was planned for you this morning, but Michelle is my boss, and I do like my job most of the time. I think vendettas and revenge are unwarranted actions and if

people were less retaliatory and more compassionate, the world would be a much better place. Having said that, I think you would be wise to see Stella Nicas at Fashion Sense. She is fearless and isn't beholden to the Grahams. She is looking for someone to train in a management capacity, so she can expand. I don't know a lot about you, but I think, given your history, you're a clever girl. I hope it works out for you.

The typed note wasn't signed. There would be no way to determine who wrote it. Did it matter? I had a lead on a job. My hands shook as I folded the note and stuffed it into my purse. I wondered which person I observed sitting at those desks was the one who had written the note, though I would never know.

Grabbing my workout clothes, I went to the gym, feeling more positive about my future. Gavin didn't chastise me as I'd expected. Instead, he clucked like a mother hen, helping me adjust my workout so I'd burn more calories. He confessed that he'd heard about my dismissal and was giving me one more week to get back to the gym before he was going to hunt me down. Then he lectured me on eating properly and taking care of myself. I loved him for his compassion and care. He was such a good friend.

As I was home before Kevin, I made supper. My cell phone rang. I looked at my caller ID before I answered. My mother. "Hello."

With no pleasantries, she jumped to the reason for her call. "Your dad is very disappointed. How could you do that to him?"

Then I remembered. Today was Monday, and I was supposed to visit my father this afternoon. "Oh shit."

"Yeah, oh shit is right."

"I'm sorry, Mom. I totally forgot."

"You forgot? Your dad was looking forward to this all week. He talked of nothing else."

Remorse washed over me. "I'm sorry I forgot. Things in my

world have been more than a little crazy."

"Well, to a sick man, that means nothing."

"Well, I've been to hell and back, and I am sorry. It totally slipped my mind with everything that's been going on."

"Like what? What was more important than reconciling with your father?"

"First off, no one said anything about reconciliation. Talking to him was all I was going to do. And secondly—you do not know what's been going on so you should just shut up."

"Shut up! You're telling me to shut up?" I had never heard my mother sputter before. I cringed.

"Okay, I'm sorry, Mom. This is out of control right now. I didn't mean to hurt you. I lost my job last week, after I fought with a customer."

Trying to calm herself. I heard her breath coming in quick gasps. "That doesn't sound like you. Why did you fight with a customer?"

"She told me that if I had been a better mother, Andrea wouldn't be dead." I choked those words out, surprised at the depth of pain I still experienced at those words.

"Oh, my girl. That's awful. Why would she say such a thing?"

"I don't know, Mom. She's not a gracious person to start with. And I know I did wrong, but I lost my job and my new apartment and ..." I sobbed.

"Barbie, stop crying. Please stop." Her words were soothing, reminding me of all the times as a young girl when she would sit beside me on the bed or the couch, rubbing my back and telling me it was going to be okay. Somehow, taking me back to that relationship, to that place in time, made me cry harder. I hated that there was so much pain, anger, and negativity in the world. Why did living have to be so hard all the time?

I consciously took the reins of my emotions and pulled hard. The black band settled across my brow. It settled in like an old friend, familiar and comfortable.

There was silence between us for a while. I moved to the stove and turned off the burners.

"So, I'm back at Kevin's …"

"You and Kevin are back together? What happened? I don't understand?"

"No, Kevin and I are not 'back together.' I'm staying with him until I can get a new job and then I'll be able to get my own apartment again. It's a temporary stopgap only."

"Oh. Well, a mother can always hope."

"Well, don't hope too hard. It's not going to happen." I let that hang in the air between us. "Okay, tell Dad it was a mistake, and I'll come tomorrow."

"No, you can't come tomorrow. It's his dialysis day. But Wednesday would work. Same time?"

"Yes, same time. And I am sorry, Mom."

"Well, I will do my best to make him understand. He was looking forward to it."

We hung up, and I checked the chicken.

Supper was almost ready when Kevin walked in. "Smells good." He poked his head into the kitchen. "Are we celebrating? Did you get a job?"

"No, and that's a story. I'll fill you in while we eat."

For one moment, we were like newlyweds again. This scene was one that played almost every night. Supper was almost ready when Kevin appeared. He would wash up and then set the table. The only difference is that back in those days, we were happily married. Today we were … What were we?

"Mmmm. Looks good, Barbara. Thanks for this. It's been a long time since I came home to a meal on the table."

"It's nothing special, just my way of saying thanks."

We dished up, and the conversation died for a few minutes. Then

Kevin reminded me to tell him about my day. When I was done, Kevin sat back in his chair, pondering my tale.

"Well, surely there is someone out there who can help?"

"Yes. Now here's the peculiar part. When I arrived home, I searched my pockets for the key to the house and found this note." I passed it over to Kevin to read.

"Wow! That was a gutsy move for whoever did this. Have you spoken to this Stella Nicas?"

"No, I thought I would dress up and go to her store first thing tomorrow."

"Good plan."

"I also forgot I was supposed to meet with my father today."

Kevin's eyebrows rose. "Oh no. I forgot, too, or I would have reminded you. Have you spoken to your mom?"

"Yeah. We've rescheduled for Wednesday, but she wasn't happy about today."

Tears filled Kevin's eyes. "I'm proud of you for doing this. I think that's a good idea. Make peace with the old guy before it's too late."

Instinctively, I reached for his hand. I don't know how I knew he wasn't talking about me and my dad. He was talking about Andrea and himself, and that broke me.

Our daughter had left this world with unresolved issues with both her parents.

We bore the agony of that on top of the grief of our loss.

CHAPTER FORTY-FOUR

I watched Kevin try to smile. Then he squeezed my hand and went back to his supper. Sitting for a moment, pushing my unfinished meal around, I wondered if I should probe the issue. I decided against it. I was inadequate to the task, unlike Kevin, who jumped into the pot of roiling emotions without fear. Getting up from the table, I cleared the dishes.

"You want the last few potatoes?"

Kevin took the bowl and scooped them onto his plate. I moved away, scraping my plate before stacking it into the dishwasher. Kevin finished and brought his plate in. I was filling the kettle. "Do you want tea?"

"Sure. Thanks."

We puttered around, clearing and wiping. After the tea was made, we moved to the eating bar.

To break the silence, Kevin asked, "You want to watch some television?"

"You know, I don't even know what's on. I usually work, so nighttime TV and I are virtually strangers."

"Me too. I sometimes watch a game here or there, but generally I go back to work myself."

"What are you working on?"

"I have an armoire that came in in terrible shape. It's ash and quite a gorgeous piece. There was water damage, and I have to replace some of the veneer. When I get it finished, it's going to be beautiful."

"Well, if you want to go back, I'm okay here on my own."

"Yeah, I think I might. Matt and I are moving your stuff tomorrow, so I won't be able to work then." He stood.

"Will you still be up when I get home?"

"I don't know. What time are you going to get home?"

"About nine."

"I guess I will be."

"Okay, see you then."

He moved out of the kitchen. A few minutes later, I heard the door close. I set my cup down, put my hands over my face, and wept. This was so hard—trying to pretend we were something when we were not or trying to pretend we were nothing when we were something. I was confused and angry.

I decided to go for a walk. It was cold outside, and I pulled my scarf across my face as I moved down the street. *Brrrr! It sure is freezing out here.* I walked several blocks to the park, did a loop around the picnic area, and then headed back to Kevin's.

Chilled through, I ran myself a hot bath, dropping in a bath bomb. Laying back, I let the water draw the cold out of my bones. When I climbed out of the tub half an hour later—relaxed and warm, I wrapped myself in my fluffy robe and made another cup of tea. Curling up on the couch, I turned on the TV and caught the last half of some mystery movie.

Kevin came back just as the credits rolled. A waft of cold air whipped into the room, and I shivered. Winter. My least favorite time of year. It was already December. Christmas! I didn't even want to think about it.

"So, how was your night?"

"Good. I went for a walk, had a bath, and watched half a movie."

"Nice," he said, but I'm not sure he meant it. It sounded like a forced response.

Stretching, I pulled my legs out from under me. "I think I'll go to bed."

The look of disappointment that crossed his face was reminiscent of last night. "Sure, okay. Well, goodnight then."

I threw him a lifeline. "I don't have to."

He wrestled with my offer before he said, "No, it's okay."

Then it was my turn to wrestle with the elephant in the room. Should I stay and make him talk? Did I want to bear his guilt along with my own? Conflicted—I hesitated. "Do you want some tea? Or hot chocolate?"

"No, I think I'll have a beer actually."

"Okay." I followed him into the kitchen. He pulled a beer from the fridge, opened it and took a long draw. "Ah. That's what I needed."

He moved to the bar and half-sat on the first stool. Standing across the kitchen, I wondered if I should stay or go. As I turned to go, Kevin spoke. I stopped mid-turn and moved toward him.

"When Andrea moved out that first year she was in college, I wasn't happy. I felt she would be better off here. It would be more affordable, you know. But she was determined to prove she was a grown-up capable of handling whatever life threw her way."

He took another sip of beer. Unspoken hopes and dreams, the kind that lay between parents and their children, filled the silence.

"She had worked hard, saved her pennies, and when Rachel Horowitz died, she received a bursary from the estate for school. Rachel paid for her tuition for the first year, which allowed Andrea the financial freedom she needed to move out. We argued about it until I let it go. My arguments would not change her mind, and all the arguing drove a wedge between us."

I leaned on the counter, listening with my heart and my ears. Though the words told the story, what was unsaid told me how deeply he had grieved this.

"So, she moved out and found a nice roommate, and I settled into being alone. She never mentioned that she was moving in with Caleb until it was done. Now, there was an argument she wanted to avoid, and she tried very hard to, but in the end, we had it out." Kevin had drained his beer. He tipped the can back and a few drops fell onto his tongue. He crushed the can and tossed it into the sink.

"She brought Caleb over here one day and the boy was edgy. I didn't like him, although I tried for Andrea's sake. He was too quiet for me. Too, I don't know, too tight? Tight like an over-wound watch. He exuded this energy, that sort of riled me."

I touched his arm. "That, and maybe because he was sleeping with your daughter?"

"Damn! You know how to scrape to the bone."

I laughed to ease the tension.

Kevin sighed. "Yes, I suppose that had something to do with it. He wasn't worthy of her, he really wasn't."

"I know. I get it."

Kevin took my hand, and we sat there for a moment, locked in our own thoughts of Andrea and a life cut short.

"Anyway, she came over here one day and I noticed a bruise on her arm. I asked her about it, and she blew it off, but something was wrong. She had changed in the few months she'd lived with that boy. I won't say she became secretive, but she pulled into herself."

"A week before she was murdered, she came over here in tears. She told me everything. I was so angry. I wanted to go over and teach that boy a few home truths about how to treat women. Andrea begged me to stay out of it. She thought it would make things worse. How much worse could they be?" He laughed, a hard, mirthless bark as fresh tears filled his eyes.

My heart was breaking for him as tears flowed unchecked down my cheeks. I can only imagine the regret he held because he hadn't intervened.

"We fought again because I wanted her to come home, but she wanted to move in with Brenda. She said she was handling the situation." His voice broke. "She was just so ... so damn stubborn and I was furious with her. My last words to her do not comfort me. I am so ashamed that I argued with her and was angry because if she had come home, she'd still be here."

I pulled my hand away and moved around the counter. Wrapping my arms around Kevin, we cried together, letting our sorrow meld into one lump. Aware of Kevin in a way I hadn't been in a long time, I worried that this would lead to something I wasn't ready for—that neither of us was prepared for. I pulled away and the pain of absent dreams dropped into the pit of my being.

Part of me wanted to know his last words to Andrea, yet another part realized they would not be good. I moved into the kitchen and plugged in the kettle. I should be in bed, getting rested for my meeting tomorrow with Stella Nicas, but somehow, all that seemed unimportant compared to what was happening here. "You want another beer?"

"No. Two is my limit."

"You want tea then?"

"Okay."

He sat there watching me putter around making the tea. The silence in the room illuminated the whirring of the fridge, but it wasn't an uncomfortable silence. I focused on how it felt and realized that it seemed natural and normal to be here in this place—like I'd always been here. More than anything, it was like I'd come home from a self-imposed wilderness quest. That stirred something long cold inside me. I didn't squash it—I didn't run from it. I purposely allowed it to stay because it made me feel like I belonged.

Belonging was something I had not experienced often. In my family, I was an outsider. I lived within the same four walls, but my experiences were different. My brothers had never dealt with the things I had, and my mother was immune to it. When I married Kevin, I wanted to belong, but that emptiness inside refused to leave me and overshadowed any peace I had initially. Keeping myself apart at all my jobs, I never mixed with my co-workers. I was friendly with the clientele, but it was part of the act I played. I had no close friends other than men and those were cozy because of what they were—physical relationships demanded a certain level of intimacy.

As we sipped our tea, Kevin stayed quiet, holding his cup between his hands. Glancing sideways, I noticed his clenched jaw, but he remained silent. When he set his cup down, I braced myself to hear what he was going to say. "I was so angry at Andrea—so mad that she had put herself into that situation and hadn't run the first time he exhibited repugnant behavior, I told her I was disappointed ..." He choked, lost in the emotions of those words, reliving that day. "Aaaaghh!"

His scream scared me. He was wounded, far deeper than I imagined. It shook me to my core. Kevin was strong. He'd always been steady, reliable and level-headed. My heart raced. I was going to tell him to stop, to keep the rest of his secrets to himself. I didn't want to know.

Tears were running down his face. I didn't reach out to comfort him this time. Fear of touching him would permit him to divulge more words, I stayed apart. I was equally afraid that by touching him, he would clam up and not reveal the burden weighing on his heart.

"This is so hard. I have always tried to live my life in such a way that I have no regrets. I let people live their lives, even when I don't agree with their decisions. Even when you left, I didn't want to hurt you. I lived with you—and you had moved out long before you actually left. It hurt me that my love wasn't enough, you know." He looked at me, and I regarded the pain in his eyes. A stab of regret pierced my heart, and I gasped as I fell into the vortex of emotions. Pain, regret, love, forgiveness, acceptance, belonging. It was all there, and it was too much. Slipping off my stool, I ran out of the kitchen. I slammed the bathroom door behind me, gasping for air. My stomach heaved, but I choked it back.

Splashing cold water on my face, I took control of myself. I would not go there. Not today, maybe never. We had never talked about that day or our marriage. Kevin had made it easy to just move forward without dissecting our issues. Besides, we were talking about Andrea, not me. I wasn't ready for this.

The knock on the door startled me and I squeaked. "Are you okay?"

"Yes, I'll be out in a minute."

I picked up the hairbrush and stroked my hair. It always soothed me to brush my hair, and tonight was no different. I can't explain why, just that it felt good.

With each stroke, I stuffed back my emotions until they settled enough for me to return to the kitchen. Kevin was cleaning up and putting things away. He turned when I came in.

"I'm sorry," he said.

"Me too." There was stiffness between us again, a formality. "I'm going to go to bed, so goodnight."

"Good night, Barbara."

Like a schoolgirl who needed permission to leave, I slipped down to my room, feeling guilty for not listening to Kevin. I set the alarm, laid back, and tried to sleep. Sleep eluded me for a long time, and eventually, I drifted off into unsettled dreams that left me when I woke.

CHAPTER FORTY-FIVE

The alarm startled me awake. My heartbeat was rapid, and my breathing shallow and quick. I scrambled out of bed, my nerves on edge. As soon as I opened the door, I smelled coffee and padded down the hallway to the kitchen.

Kevin was making himself breakfast. I looked at the clock. It seemed early.

He didn't turn around when I came in. He didn't even offer me a coffee. I pushed past him and helped myself. Taking a stool at the eating bar, I watched him crack eggs into the pan of bacon drippings. Toast popped up, and he buttered all four slices, before scraping bacon grease over his eggs. I shuddered at the amount of fat in that breakfast.

When he removed his eggs, he brought his plate to the counter and sat on the stool next to me. I caught a whiff of his cologne and inhaled deeply. He always smelled good. I also noticed how drawn and haggard he looked. Was he not sleeping?

"Are you okay?"

"Yeah, I'm fine. Just couldn't sleep." His voice was brittle and broken—like he'd burst into tears if I pushed too hard.

"I won't be home for supper tonight. Matt will meet me after work to move your stuff, and then we'll go for a meal afterward."

I had only been here a few days but felt like Kevin was abandoning me. A flick of resentment burst forth, but I squashed it down. "Okay. Well, thanks for that. Do you need me to meet you over there and help or anything?"

"No, I think we can handle it."

"Leave the vacuum cleaner. I'll go back and give it a once-over tomorrow before I meet with my father."

"Okay. Sounds good." He slipped from his stool, placed his plate and coffee cup in the sink, and left the room.

Tears pricked at the back of my eyelids. Last night, we were friends. This morning, there was a wall between us that seemed impenetrable. Living here like this was going to be awkward. I needed to get that job so I could move out.

The front door opened and closed without Kevin saying another word. I sighed, finished my coffee, and went to get ready. After my shower, I sorted through outfits, laying possibles on the bed. I tried each one on, swapping jewelry and shoes before settling on a Chanel I'd picked up at a high-end secondhand shop two years ago. I left it on the bed and went to get some breakfast.

Yogurt and granola and a cup of mint tea. I needed something to soothe the butterflies in my tummy. This was a very important day for me. I wanted to make a good impression. It would be a dream to work in a place like that. Besides running my own place, working at Fashion Sense would be the next best thing.

The store was new to Crawford. It had been open for a little over a year. I had been in it a time or two and had purchased an outfit. What I liked about it, though, was the extensive undergarment section. They had the best selection I'd ever seen in a standalone store. It was high quality, too, not the generic cheap stuff you can purchase at big box stores.

I sat with my cup of tea, lost in thought. The clock crept toward ten o'clock. Half an hour before leaving, I applied my makeup, brushed my hair back off my face, and changed into the outfit I would wear. Because it hadn't snowed, it allowed me to wear my shoes to complete my outfit.

Wanting to show my eagerness but not appear overeager, I arrived at the store fifteen minutes after opening. Taking in the street's ambiance, I liked the look of this block. There were several small storefronts, each unique but symmetrical. This street had recessed doors, which provided big, bowed windows for display. I walked down the street, passing a knitting shop to Fashion Sense. A bell announced my arrival.

The store was quaint, and the clothes were tastefully displayed. I noticed similar colors, along with the complementary black and whites. This season, it was white, so there weren't a lot of cream or soft whites. An older lady with gray hair came from the back room. She was elegant. I took in her style and demeanor. She exuded efficiency and brusque confidence. My stomach fluttered.

"Good morning." She greeted me with a hint of a smile. Her voice was smoky and rich.

I smiled back. "Good morning. My name is Barbara O'Shea." I started off with confidence, but faltered when she changed her expression. "Ahem. I uh ... um ... I heard you were looking for a manager?"

"I am." She looked me up and down. "And you think you're the one?"

"Well, I think I would do a good job."

"What is your experience? Where are you working now?"

"I haven't worked in a dress shop before. I haven't worked in retail. My work history is in the service industry."

"A server?"

"Well, yes. And a hostess."

"I see. Do you have a résumé?"

"Yes." I handed a copy to her. She scanned it without commenting.

"Okay, I will be in touch."

I panicked at the thought of being dismissed. I wanted this job, and I wasn't sure she had given me a chance. "Please, Mrs. Nicas, I know I can do this. I know fashion, I know colors, and I know style."

She smiled at me like a mother smiled at a child begging for sweets. "Well, you see, I need someone with experience. Since I have opened another store in Calgary, I want someone I can trust managing things down here."

"I understand, and if you give me a chance, I will work hard. I'm smart, and I've always wanted to have my own dress shop."

"Then why haven't you been working in one?"

"I guess I was complacent. I had a job, made good money, met people, and I guess I just sort of went with the flow."

"So why now? Why are you willing to change now?"

Here it was. The moment I had been dreading. Did I spill my guts or gloss over the truth? I looked into her face and took a chance. "Well, I lost my daughter a month ago. That shook me a little. Then, in a moment of madness, I attacked a woman who told me that if I had been a better mother, my daughter would still be alive. I lost my job."

"You attacked a customer?" I couldn't tell what she was thinking.

"Yes. Unfortunately. The wife of someone rather influential."

"Please tell me it was Thelma Graham."

I looked at her. "How did you know?" Fear flicked through me. What had she heard? Were she and Thelma friends? I held my breath, bracing for a tongue lashing.

"Well, I heard someone gave her a good rollicking. That was you?"

I nodded, my face crimson.

She looked me over, laughing as she did. "You don't look the worse for it. I heard Thelma has a black eye." She paused momentarily as she stared at me. "I think I've underestimated you. Anyone willing to tangle with Thelma has a lot of chutzpah. And if anyone deserved a good smack down, it's Thelma." I exhaled with relief.

"You know her?"

"Oh yes, I know her. She used to come here when I first opened the store, and she complained about everything. She would purchase and return items like we were a rental place and not a store. I'm certain that she wore the outfits and then returned them for full price. Because of her deceitfulness, I stopped doing cash returns and changed that to in-store credits. Of course, that stopped her in her tracks, and soon, she stopped shopping here. I haven't seen the old dear in years."

Relief flooded through me. She may not like what I did, but she at least understood why.

She continued. "Thelma has more money than God, yet someone will have to chisel it out of her cold, dead hands one day." She chuckled. "Well, thank you Barbara O'Shea for making me laugh."

I smiled—sure she was dismissing me, again. I turned to go.

"So," Stella said. I turned back, ready to hear why she wasn't hiring me. "I know that Thelma and her husband have a lot of influence in this town, more than they should have for the type of people they are. It is for that reason I am going to give you a chance. Standing against them isn't wise, but it is brave, and I like that regardless of what it cost, you did it anyway."

I stood there in disbelief as she continued. "Let's say this is a three-week trial. I expect you to work hard, and there will be lots to learn. It's also Christmas, and many people will come in for party outfits. I expect you to put outfits together for them. I can tell you have good taste, and I will teach you what you need to know on the managerial side. Does that suit you?"

I smiled. "Yes, thank you, Mrs. Nicas. You won't be sorry."

"Please call me Stella. Now, when can you start?"

"I can start right now, but I have an appointment tomorrow afternoon …"

"Well, let's just start on Thursday then. Be here at eight-thirty. There is a car park at the back, just behind the store. It's marked with the store's name. Then ring the bell on the delivery door and I'll let you in. You can meet Jennifer then. She works part time, Thursday nights, Friday, and Saturday. Does that suit?"

"Yes, thank you so much, Mrs.—um, Stella. I will see you on Thursday." I reached out to shake her hand. We shook, and I left the store with a bounce in my step.

Thank you—anonymous note writer.

Thanks to you, I have a new job.

I owe it all to you.

CHAPTER FORTY-SIX

Back at Kevin's, I was at loose ends. He wasn't coming home, and I wanted to celebrate with someone. Anyone. Yet, there was no one. I paced the floor, tried to watch television, and even picked up the phone to call my mother. Nothing helped. Loneliness settled on my shoulders. I thought about calling Kevin, but after last night, his absence made me reticent about reaching out. Thinking back, I realized that I should have pushed through the debris of our life together rather than run from it. My fear had gouged out a huge rift between us.

Part of me wanted to dive into the pool of self-pity that my life was so pathetically empty, but I deliberately turned away. I had been spending too much time in Pity City of late. It was time to turn things around. If I wanted my life to change, I needed to change it. No one was going to come along and make things better.

As I considered the future, I realized Christmas was coming. For the first time in years, I would be with Kevin first thing on Christmas morning. After last night, I needed to figure out how best to navigate the waters so we wouldn't have more drama. Andrea and I may not have been close, but she loved Christmas, and without her, it was going to be a hard day for Kevin.

I wondered if Kevin even wanted to celebrate this year with all that happened. It was inconceivable that a year would pass without some sort of acknowledgment of the day. I wondered if Kevin would get a tree. Maybe I would bring up the subject tonight. If he came home before I went to bed, that is.

I wrestled with myself about moving out now that I had a job. Moving out before Christmas would save me the aggravation of dealing with the emotions of the day. I shook my head. That was cowardly and selfish. If Kevin didn't want to celebrate, then we would have a quiet day. If he wanted to celebrate, I'd be here for that. Whatever we did, it would be a hard day without Andrea.

Besides, I was only on trial at this job. Things might not work out, and then I'd be crawling back here again—that is, if Kevin even offered. As anxious as I was to get away for Kevin's sake, moving now would not be an option. I was going to have to learn to tread carefully.

Even though I settled the argument in my mind, I walked the few blocks to the convenience store before supper and picked up a newspaper. It never hurt to look at what was on offer. At least I would know what the options were when the time came.

I had a quiet supper, sitting alone in the kitchen reading the newspaper. The house seemed too quiet for my liking, so I had the television on for company. It seemed peculiar that I seldom turned my set on when I lived alone in my apartment, yet in this house there was an echo of a missing life without some noise. It must be the ghosts that lived here, making me uncomfortable. The ghosts of my dead marriage and the daughter I never knew.

I drew a bath after I'd cleaned up after supper. Pouring lots of aromatic bath salts into the water, I lay back. My thoughts drifted back through the day, thinking of Stella Nicas and her store. I wondered what to wear. My tummy squiggled with excitement. I hadn't looked forward to anything this much in years. Setting aside my dream of owning my own store for the moment, I decided that learning the ropes from someone successful in business was a significant step for me.

As my mind wandered, I came to the meeting with my father. My skin grew too tight for my body, making me want to run. It was the unexpected that made me nervous. More than anything, I wanted to fire the parting shot, to get the last word in. I didn't want him dying, oblivious to the pain and terror he had inflicted. He knew what he'd done to me, but maybe my absence from his life allowed him to ignore it. I wanted assurance that when he took the boat to hell, he went with my pain resting on his soul.

Climbing out of the tub, my thoughts tumbled and jumbled together. Inside, my five-year-old self loved her daddy. She was in turmoil at my hateful thoughts. The other part of me—the grown-up trying to protect that child from further pain—wanted to annihilate the source. How would I amalgamate the two and come out satisfied and intact? I had no idea. I longed to talk to Kevin. His stability always grounded me when my confliction threatened to dissect my heart. But Kevin wasn't home and after last night, I no longer knew if I could talk to him about my life without creating further intimacy.

I watched a little television, though it was a blur of faces, laugh tracks, commercials, and credits. At ten, I went to bed. Kevin's absence screamed loudly as my thoughts dipped into the recesses of darkness, finding blame. Tears pricked my eyes as the words echoed inside my head.

You are a burden, Barbara Anne O'Shea. In a few short days, you have driven a man out of his home, a place where he should feel comfortable. What is it about you, eh? No one wants to be with you. You are such a loser. You're unlovable and worthless. The sooner you leave and let Kevin get on with his life, the better off he'll be.

I curled into myself, squeezing the second pillow into my body as the tears turned to sobs. I was being hateful, but that record was familiar; it played frequently whenever life grew hard. In the good times, it was silent, but it was there waiting for a weak moment. It was out to destroy me, and nothing seemed to silence it for long. All the poor decisions I'd ever made played out before me as I wept.

It always started with the day the monster came to live at our house, and it rambled through my teen years, through my decision to leave Kevin and Andrea, and it used to end with my breakup with Greg on Christmas Day last year, but this time, it included Bobby Graham. Instead of seeing our relationship in an innocent light, the memory was darker and more sinister. I pictured expressions I missed, sly smiles and the twinkle in his eye wasn't merriment and love but something colder. Ownership and triumph?

Andrea hovered in the back of my mind—her arms folded in disapproval. Her expression broke my heart anew, and I sobbed harder. I had been a fool, hadn't I? In every decision I made, I did what was easiest for me, and I never considered the consequences of my actions on the people I loved. I had driven a wedge between every person I loved and then excused it as their problem. It was time to take ownership and figure out a sufficient punishment.

I didn't deserve to be here in a warm bed, especially here in this house—a house I'd left of my own volition. Kevin was just too decent. If he'd been stronger, he would have closed the door on me years ago. Instead of allowing me to turn to him for moral support every time life threw me under the bus—he'd have remarried and moved on. I had abused his kindness and his generosity over and over. No wonder Andrea hated me. She was smart enough to know what I was doing.

Unable to calm my mind, I climbed out of bed. I washed my face with a cold cloth. Though my eyes burned, the coolness refreshed me. I wandered into the kitchen. I'd left the light on above the stove, allowing me to pad across the room without turning on the overhead fixture. It was just after eleven. Where was Kevin? He should have been home hours ago. Fear niggled. What if something happened to him? What would I do then?

My heart twisted. If there were a God, surely that wouldn't happen. How on earth would I get through life without Kevin? Even though I didn't deserve him, I needed him. That thought shocked me—I needed Kevin. How come I never realized that before? The answer was simple—because I didn't want to know. I was great at hiding from the truth. I'd done a good job with Bobby Graham—he had used and abused me and I'd permitted him to do it. He was probably laughing at me the whole time. What I didn't understand, though, was why. Why me? What did he get out of it?

Harrumph. I had been so stupid, thinking that by moving into that condo, Bobby would parade me around like a queen. This time, I would not be naïve enough to think those people would be my friends. I would be smarter than when I was married to Ron. I would have no expectations of acceptance. But with Bobby's approval and acknowledgment, my status would be secure. I would be the belle of the ball, the socialite of the development. I dreamed of hosting fabulous parties, and the community would thank Bobby for bringing me into their lives.

The truth was, I would have been a whore, and all those society mavens would ostracize me and treat me as an outcast. I had never wanted to be a fool, but I had been. I had Thelma to thank for saving me from myself. Ha! Thelma would never know she'd done me a favor.

I wandered back down the hall and stood looking into Kevin's room. His bed was made, and everything was neat. I turned to the room across the hall. The door was slightly ajar. I opened it and stepped into Andrea's room. There were a few boxes on the floor;

boxes that hadn't been there when I had stayed in this room before the funeral. These must be her things from Brenda's. Her clothes, her keepsakes, her memories. I reached out to touch a box.

Tears flowed, thinking that she should be the one to open these boxes. I counted. There were seven boxes of varying sizes. Her life totaled seven measly boxes. I compared that to the boxes moved from my apartment—I had seven boxes just for the kitchen. My hand shook as I reached over to touch the top of a stack of three. I ran my hand lovingly over the top and over the edge. My little girl.

For the first time, at least I thought it was the first time, her loss connected with every fiber of my being. Trembling and weak, I moved to sit on her bed as the emotions rolled over and over me like waves lapping the shore. Loss of a loved one is a funny thing. It never seems to come on all at once. It comes in stages. I had little experience with loss. Sure, I had kept myself apart from my family, but they remained in the periphery of my life. Knowing that was a comfort and a threat.

With Andrea, I remembered the shock and the instant pain of her death, followed by my grief. This was different somehow. This emptiness was so deep and complete that nothing would ever fill it. It wasn't like the sands of time would fill in the hole and although it would always be a scar, it would be manageable. It would take more than one lifetime for this to ease.

I couldn't even cry. The lights from Kevin's truck slashed across the window. I scurried from the room down the hall and into my bedroom, carefully pushing the door closed even though I was certain Kevin hadn't yet entered the house. I slipped under the covers, turned away from the door, and tried to slow my breathing. As I lay there, I heard the front door open and close. My ears strained to hear his movements. Kevin paused beside my door, and I held my breath, waiting. I wanted to tell him about my job, but it terrified me he would tell me a few truths I didn't want to hear.

He padded off, and I heard his bedroom door close.
I exhaled as tears pricked my eyes.

CHAPTER FORTY-SEVEN

It took me hours, but eventually I fell into a troubled sleep. Boxes filled my dreams. I opened one after the other to find they were empty. There were so many boxes they threatened to topple over on top of me. My heart pounded as I continued to open one after the other, tossing it away in disappointment. Inside the last one I opened was Andrea's head, her sightless eyes staring up at me. I sat up, my scream dying on my lips as I woke from my nightmare.

Panting, I looked at the clock. It was seven-thirty. Fully expecting Kevin to come in, the house remained quiet. I couldn't smell coffee brewing, as I had every morning since my arrival. I climbed out of bed and padded across to the bathroom. After that, I went into the kitchen. There were clues that Kevin had eaten breakfast and gone to work—the coffee pot was off, there were dishes in the sink and the frying pan on the stove.

Tears welled up as I prepared fresh coffee. I resented Kevin's behavior. Why was he being so difficult? I didn't deserve this, did I? It would end soon or … or what, Barbara? You going to move out?

Maybe you'll threaten to listen to him? What is the enormous threat you might use to change his behavior?

All the arguments left me. Kevin was only looking out for himself. Who was I to make demands? I had no rights, and any expectations I had needed to be set aside. I was only here for another month or two, anyway. Once I started working again, I wouldn't feel so alone. I was just not used to this.

I sat with a cup of coffee, trying not to think about meeting my father. Every time it crossed my mind, my stomach flipped over, and the bridge of my nose tingled. I took a deep breath and reminded myself that the door would be unlocked. I could leave at any time. All I wanted to do was to wish him a bon voyage on his trip to hell.

I took a hot shower, followed by a generous application of body lotion. Before I dressed in jeans and a silk blouse, I fixed my hair and applied my makeup. I loved silk; I loved how it caressed my skin and hung perfectly on my body. Finishing the ensemble, I donned a silver leaf necklace and matching earrings. I looked in the mirror, satisfied that I looked successful. I needed to show the old man that he hadn't won.

Time passed quickly, and before I knew it, I had been driving across the city to my parents' house. After parking out front, I turned off the car and sat there. My heart was pounding, my hands clammy, and I wasn't sure my legs would hold me if I stood. Deciding to leave, I was about to start the engine when my mother rapped on the passenger window. I let out a squeak.

I pulled out the key and exited the car.

"I thought maybe you changed your mind—you sat out here so long," she said.

"I was chickening out," I answered honestly. "I really don't think I'm ready for this."

Mom pulled up beside me, putting an arm around my shoulders. "There is no need to be afraid. He's a sick old man. There's nothing he can do to you now."

More tears. Damn, I was tired of all my tears. "You know, Mom, when we were kids, you taught us that rhyme. Sticks and stones may break your bones, but words will never hurt me. Well, that was wrong. Words can hurt. They can really, really hurt."

She rocked me with her arm, then, still holding tight, she propelled us toward the house. I just put one foot in front of the other and hoped I was doing the right thing.

I hadn't been inside the house for years. It looked the same—the same tatty furniture, with lace doilies on the arms and in the center of the coffee table. The house was also spotless, as usual. It didn't matter how poor we might have been, our home was always clean.

With the door closed behind us, we stood in the entryway as if waiting for permission to enter. The living room was off to the right, and the parlor was to the left. The door to that room was closed.

Mom nodded toward the closed door. "He's in there and he's waiting for you."

I slipped off my coat, folding it over my arm, and stepped forward.

Mom touched my arm. "Be kind, Barbie. He's an old man and he's dying. I know you want to punish him, but please consider that he isn't long for this world."

I looked at my mother, and it was as if I was seeing her for the first time. In her face, I envisioned the young woman who fell in love with the Irish rogue. She never stopped loving him, never wavered in her commitment, and would continue to love him even when he's gone. I think his life was more important to her than her own. It amazed me that a man like my father would illicit such affection and dedication. Maybe I didn't know him at all because the man I knew was without a soul.

I nodded in response to my mother. Knowing what I wanted to do, I was prepared to do it. If I let her know my intentions, she would throw herself across the door and I wouldn't get that chance. I didn't go into the room, guns blazing. I tapped on the door lightly and then pushed it open.

The room wasn't bright, and even though the drapes were open, the sheers filtered out the daylight. A narrow cot sat against the far wall, and a wheelchair rested nearby. In a high-back chair, in the corner opposite the bed, sat my father. He looked small and frightened.

I remembered when he commanded a room just by being in it.

He was no longer that man.

CHAPTER FORTY-EIGHT

"Hello Barbie." His voice was almost a sigh.

"Hello."

He pointed to a kitchen chair, one obviously brought in for this purpose. "Please sit."

I sat in the uncomfortable wooden chair, shifting slightly away from him.

"You look well."

"Thank you."

We sat there in silence. Not wanting to look at him, I stared beyond him. On the wall, there were photos of our childhood. Someone had put them into one frame. I remembered myself at six, smiling brightly into the camera, my front teeth different lengths. I stood and pulled the frame from the wall.

There were pictures of us all together on a camping trip, our tent standing in the background. I longed to return to those carefree, silly days when the world was monster-free.

I stared at my father. I wouldn't say he was smiling, but his face was soft and approachable. He no longer looked like the monster I remember him being.

My heart thawed. There was a tap on the door. My mother bustled in with a teapot and a single mug. I wondered why she wasn't giving me a cup until she moved a TV tray beside my chair and set everything down. "Your father can't have much to drink since his kidneys failed." She answered my unasked question. "Do you want something to eat?"

"Just leave us, Mary. Please."

My mother touched his shoulder and left the room. She looked back once before closing the door.

"I guess we could sit here all day waiting for the other to speak, so I'll start. Before I die, I wanted to see you and apologize to you. You don't have to forgive me, but I hope you will. I don't want to die knowing you hate me. I don't hate you but there is much I regret."

At a loss for words, I said nothing. Everything I wanted to say to him turned to ashes the moment I realized how diminished he had become. I had imagined myself as David to his Goliath until I entered this room. Now, I regarded him in a new light—he was a weary old man, beat down by his choices and left paying a heavy price for them. I steeled myself from letting go completely, though—I didn't want to let him skate off without understanding what he'd done.

"You know, Barbie, drink is a terrible master. It drives you to do things you can't imagine ..."

"I think I can, actually," I interrupted. Crossing my arms, I leaned back in my chair.

He smiled a sad smile and nodded. "Yes, I think you can. I can't forgive myself for some things that happened. It turns my stomach thinking of what I did to you."

Was he apologizing? He was certainly getting close.

"I don't think you have any idea what you did. You stole my innocence." My voice lifted, and I had to take a deep breath to bring it back to a normal tone. I didn't want to shout. That would bring my mother into the room to rescue him.

He nodded. "There hasn't been a day that I haven't relived the horror of that night. At first, I was angry and used that anger to push you away. I was so scared you would tell your mother, and I would lose everything." Tears rolled down his face. "I don't deserve her, you know. She is my angel and my everything, your mother. If it weren't for her, I'd be dead long ago."

"Well, as nice as that is for you, let's get back to what you did to me." Bitterness gurgled in my belly. "I was just a girl, Dad. Just a girl." My voice cracked with emotion and then I burst into tears. Damn it, Barbara, stay strong or he'll take advantage of you again.

"I'm sorry, so sorry, Barbie. Please don't cry. Shush now, Barbie." He leaned forward, reaching out to touch me, to comfort me. I pulled back. He sighed and sat back in his chair. I cleared my throat as I shoved my feelings back into place. Then I stood to replace the photos on the wall. I needed to distract both of us from the emotions that swirled like a dust devil, threatening to erupt into a full-blown tornado.

"Look, Dad, this is new to me. You've been ready to make peace with me for a long time, and I only wanted to keep you as far away from me as possible. I need time to think about what you've said. I don't know if I can forgive you. You don't deserve it." I sat back down. "It isn't just that night either. You changed. We used to have fun, remember?" I pointed to the picture I'd just hung up. "We used to be a family and we lost it all when you drowned yourself in a bottle."

He nodded. "I know, I know. Did you ever wonder why you had no grandparents on my side?"

"Mom told us they were dead."

"Well, they weren't dead. My dad was a boozer. He drank every day and was as mean as a snake when he drank. My mom drank with him. The pair of them would booze it up on the weekends at first, and then it became a couple of times a week, and soon they were boozing every day. They had knockdown and drag-out battles, too. My dad broke my mom's jaw once. She had her jaw wired up, but she still drank, every day. Came a point where us kids, my brothers and I, hardly ever came home. We learned to steal food, bread mostly, but canned goods, too. We lived on bloody canned pork sandwiches in those days."

He caught his breath. I sat there, the mug of tea in my hand growing cold.

"When I left home at fifteen, I vowed I would never, ever be like them. I never went back, and I never went to their funerals either. They died a few months apart, my mom died first and my dad, well he stole the neighbor's truck and drove it into a tree."

Why didn't I know this stuff? Did Patrick and Dennis know our history or was this the first time my dad had ever talked about it?

"It's a sickness you know. I didn't know that. The guys at work used to call me a panty waste for never having a beer after work, always having a cola or something else instead. They spiked my drink one night and had a great laugh when I was falling down and puking. Stupid thing was, that I thought about how I felt before I crossed the line. I had a family to raise, and it was hard, the hardest thing I'd ever done. No one tells you that growing up is shit—sorry, growing up is hard. No one. You're just expected to know how to handle it all. You have mouths to feed and bills to pay and the pressure is on you full stop."

His eyes were unfocused, like he was back there, living those days. "Anyway, in those moments before I went over the edge, I felt happy for the first time in a long time. It was like someone had unscrewed the bolts that held me in the stockade, and I was free to play without worry. I liked that feeling. So, a few weeks later, I ordered my first proper drink. I wanted to feel that again. And then again and again. I lost myself and it cost me more than that in the end. I lost my family, or at least the family I imagined I'd always have."

He stopped talking. His rheumy eyes darting around the room as if looking for relief. He licked his lips, but there was no moisture in his tongue. "Would you get me some ice chips, please. They're in that container by the bed."

I stood and retrieved the plastic bowl on the bedside table. Peeling back the lid, I offered my father the bowl of watery ice cubes. With a shaky hand, he tried to get one from the bowl. He nearly tipped the entire bowl onto his lap before I intervened.

I reached in and scooped out a few chips. In a flash, I envisioned my mother placing those chips on his tongue, feeding him like a baby bird. Unwilling to be that intimate, I put them in his hand. He took them, and with a little difficulty, set them on his tongue. I was miserable. I hated his helplessness. How can you fight someone who is no longer capable of fighting?

CHAPTER FORTY-NINE

A minute passed before he resumed talking. "Well, you know the rest. I couldn't stop drinking after that, and maybe I didn't want to. I used to watch my life, kind of like from the outside looking in and I'd see the person I had become, and I hated myself. I really did." He stared at the wall briefly. "I hated your mother, too—hated her because she loved me when she should have hated me. I would pick fights with her, and she just took it and kept loving me back. In those days, I was punishing myself for being a weak man, but today, I'm grateful she stuck by me."

"You were lucky, Dad. I couldn't do what she did. I *wouldn't* do what she did. That's why I left my second husband. When the drink became more important than anything else, I walked away. All I pictured was you and Mom and I didn't want to live like that."

We sat there staring blankly, neither focusing on the other, just lost in the past. The tea had grown tepid in the pot. I poured some out and swallowed a mouthful. It was bitter, like I felt. My pursuit of justice and restitution was thwarted. I took a deep breath and blew it out loudly. It was my turn to speak.

"I remember thinking that a monster had eaten my daddy. You were here one day and gone the next. That was hard to understand but then …" Blood rushed to my face, and I perspired. The memories were burning. "That night …"

"Don't!" he whispered. "Please don't."

I looked at him, my eyes piercing his soul. "Don't what, Dad? Don't pull that shameful thing into the light so you can see it for what it is?"

"I know what it is."

Speaking in a harsh whisper, I continued. "Do you? Do you really? Do you know it destroyed the person I thought I was? That it has colored every decision, every choice, everything I've done since. Do you know I had nightmares and still do?" Tears flooded down my cheeks. "I don't trust like I should, and I know that I have filtered every choice I made through the shredded remnants of my soul. I …"

Tears flowed down his papery cheeks as I looked at my father. A bolt of guilt zinged my heart as I saw him so vulnerable, and in an instant, it consumed all my rage, as the pot of bitter anger burst into flames. It was over. There would be no restitution, no harsh justice. Instead, I would have to settle for knowing that he was remorseful and that in some perverse way, he was paying for his choices, just as I was paying for mine.

"I need to lie down now. Would you get your mother?"

Before I opened the door, I looked back at him, slumped in his chair. I wanted to feel compassion, but there was only numbness. I stood there, needing to say something, but was unsure what it was. Finally, I shrugged it off and opened the door. Perched on the arm of a chair, my mother focused on the door. She stood and came toward me, her face expectant. "He says he needs to lie down."

She nodded and walked past me into the room.

I stood by the door, watching as she stroked his face and ran her hands lovingly across his shoulders. He looked up at her and smiled, his eyes filled with so much love, I had to look away. Tears welled up, forcing me to leave the room before she helped him into bed. I wandered into the living room, letting the tears flow unabated. I kept moving toward the kitchen. The room was as it always was, just more worn. I ran my hand across the same speckled countertops on which I had rolled pie crust. The color had faded, and the laminate had no color in the places where Mom worked the most.

A fresh coat of paint on the old cabinets didn't elevate the room because they still sported those same tacky brass knobs, the finish worn from overuse. The old table sat in the same place. It was the same dining set we'd sat around all those years ago—the same table where family dinners took place. Patrick sat over there, Dennis was there, I sat there. I pulled out a chair, noticing the duct tape that sealed the cracks of the plastic seat covering. Really? They couldn't afford new chairs or to recover these. My mother had always been frugal, but this was cheap. Were they financially bankrupt? So far removed from their lives, I knew nothing about this.

Waiting for my mother to join me, I sat in the chair. I was tapping my fingers on the table when I thought maybe I should make tea. I was filling the kettle when Mom came into the room carrying the tray she'd brought to Dad's room. Seeing what I was doing, she emptied the teapot, rinsed it and set it aside. Then she sat at the table. Once I plugged the kettle in, I joined her.

"Thank you for seeing him. He is much calmer now, happier in a way." She reached over and patted my hand.

"I did not know, Mom. He's sick."

She nodded. "Yes, I don't expect him to make another year. The doctor tells me to be prepared for him to go anytime. I'd just like to have another Christmas, especially if you're there. One more happy, family Christmas."

I looked at her, aghast. "Are you serious? We're not a happy family and we haven't been one for a long, long time."

"But we could be. You need to let bygones be bygones."

Staring at this older version of the woman who had raised me, I couldn't believe what I was hearing. "You want us to fake it? To fake being happy, to fake being a family for his sake? It's his fault that we aren't a family. I can't believe you're asking me to do this."

"Barbie, he's dying. He's sorry and he deserves to die in peace. Can you not give him that peace?" Her voice was soft, filled with concern and caring. I looked at her, and perhaps for the first time in my life, I realized what my father had seen. Her love for him was unconditional. It knew no bounds and asked no questions. She gave until she was empty and then she gave more.

"Okay, I'll think about it. It might be just what I need anyway. With Andrea gone ..." I choked and cleared my throat.

"Oh, Barbie. I'm so sorry. I've been so consumed with your dad that I totally forgot about you. How are you and Kevin coping?"

"Things are tense between us. I think he wants things to be like they were, and my being there is complicating our friendship. The other night he was talking, and I was trying to be supportive, but he got into my leaving and I mean, geez, we've never talked about it before, and I don't want to talk about it now."

"Why not?"

"Oh god! Not you too?"

The kettle clicked off, and she made tea. She set the teapot, mugs, and a plate of cookies on the table before sitting. I tried to shift the conversation as I poured the weak brew into my cup. "So how are you and Dad getting along financially?"

I moved to pour tea into my mom's cup. She smiled as she placed her hand over her cup. "I want mine a little stronger, thank you." I set the pot down. "We have enough."

"Enough? Look at these chairs. They need to be replaced or recovered."

"No one comes here, Barbie. We don't need to impress anyone, so who cares? I don't care. Things are clean. That's all that is important."

I was beat. I dropped the subject. "So, getting back to you and Kevin, in all the years you've been apart, you've never talked about why you left?"

"What would have been the point? It was done, over, in the past."

"Is it?"

"Yes!" I snapped. "I've moved on, even if Kevin hasn't. He deserves better than me and I get damn tired of his mooning."

Mom reached over and patted my hand. "You need to let Kevin be Kevin. Sometimes, love is too strong. It won't let you go." She removed her hand and lifted the teapot.

Looking at her—taking in her graying hair, her tired face, and I understood. She had tried to quit loving my dad. When? In the early days of his drinking? When I left home? When he fell sick? A love like that was something I would never experience. Love—at least that kind of love—needed a sacrifice of self to exist, and I am too selfish to experience that.

Andrea was different. I still loved her, even though she was gone. My love for her bewitched me, and often, while watching her sleep—my love increased until I thought my heart might burst—it was so full. Picking her up and breathing in her scent, my heart would swell and overflow. It was that love that drove me to leave her behind. I remember seeing my father turn into a monster, and I couldn't do that to her. No child should have to face the demons I lived with. My love for her was deep and selfless—a sweet love, a joyous burden tinted with innocence and naivety.

When I compared that to my mom's love for my dad, I wondered why they were called the same thing. They were very different. I realized that her love for my dad was an all-consuming, burning, spicy mass of passion, desire, and insanity. It was the love that swept you into ecstasy and then smashed you into despair, crushing your soul and squeezing every ounce of selfishness from your bones. Then, it swept you back into heaven, where life was weightless and free.

At least, that's how I viewed her love for my father, and I think Kevin felt that way about me in the early days. I remember feeling ashamed that my love for him was shallow in comparison. Refusing to allow my emotions to fling me hither and yon, I kept them restrained and contained. I was the master, and they would obey me. Taking easy risks that may have made me feel foolish, I never let myself become devastated.

My love for my father came close to destroying me, so I learned to shut down. It was like going into a power plant and pulling the lever, leaving me running on minimum emotions. Except for Andrea, no one had reached my core and forced me to feel more than a twinge of pain, regret, or happiness, depending on where I was in the relationship. Leaving her was the hardest decision but the only one that made sense. I wouldn't have been able to live with myself if she grew up seeing me battle my demons, the demons that were born that night in my bedroom in the dark. The ones who pushed me to seek pleasure in the arms of many men.

Needing to move the conversation away from this uncomfortable topic, I announced my new job.

"Well, Barbara. That's wonderful. When you were a young girl, that was all you talked about. To see you finally there ..." She choked on her words.

I reached over and patted her arm. "It's okay, Mom. I just took the long way, and all those years served a purpose. I learned a lot about customer service, so it's all good."

We chatted about dresses and fashion briefly before my dad called out. "He needs me." She stood.

I stood, too, moving the cups to the sink.

She looked back over her shoulder before she left the room. "Think about Christmas, will you? It will be his last."

·I nodded.

"One more thing?"

"What?"

"Figure out a way to stop running."

Before I answered, she disappeared into the next room. I followed as far as the front door. As I slipped into my coat and boots, I heard her talking nonsense to him, cooing and fussing.

My mom would be free when Dad died. But would she be happy?

I couldn't bear to think about it.

CHAPTER FIFTY

I came home from my visit with my dad feeling less than liberated. Returning to my mother's words, I agreed to be scared, but running was all I knew. She had unknowingly picked at a scab and left me vulnerable. Unable to deal with the implications of her words, I shoved them out of my mind and focused on the meeting with my dad.

I was unsettled about it. Going over and over his words, I looked at him from every direction in my mind, trying to figure out his sincerity. He glossed over how bad things were, and he hadn't taken responsibility for destroying the person I was. I changed from a carefree child the day I'd gone into my parents' room to find him lying there, blind drunk, and stinking in his own excrement and vomit. Who was I really meant to be? What would my life be like if my father had stayed the way he was in the beginning?

But life unfolds one day at a time, and I didn't have any answers, and I certainly didn't know how to help myself or Kevin without opening myself to the pain of my own actions. Just as my father did not know what his actions had done, I was only beginning to understand that my leaving all those years ago did not differ from my finding the monster in my father's body. Both had left deep scars. I naively thought that my leaving would prevent my family from going through what I did. I was wrong.

I examined the slow process of coming to grips with my actions. How much of what happened, including Andrea's death, was my fault? Was Kevin going to tell me? I was too fragile to stand under the weight of his accusations. He was the strong one. He was the one I turned to. If he blamed me ... well, that weight would crush me. Running away was the only way to save myself.

When Kevin came home for supper, I introduced my new job as the dinner topic instead of asking where he was last night. I set the plate down as Kevin came in from washing up, and before I dug into my salad—I said, "I got the job."

He looked at me and smiled. "Atta girl. I knew you could do it. When do you start?"

"Tomorrow. I think she wanted me to start today, but I had that meeting with my dad today."

"Oh shit, I'm sorry. I completely forgot. How did that go?"

"As good as expected, I guess. He's old and frail, so much smaller than I remember. He said he was sorry, but I'm not sure if he knows what he's sorry for."

"How do you mean?"

"Well, he had this speech prepared about how drinking is a sickness, and then he apologized. It was like he was saying he wasn't to blame because he was sick."

"Hmm, I see. Well, it's hard accepting responsibility ..."

I hoped to avoid this, yet somehow, we'd wound up right in the same place in a few quick minutes. Drastic action was required to stop this. "So ... I'm ... I guess I'm a little nervous about starting work tomorrow. I'm excited and happy and scared all at the same time."

Kevin looked over at me. "Before you fell pregnant with Andrea, all you ever talked about was owning a dress shop. You drew pictures of clothes all the time. I'd find sketches in the bread box, in the cutlery drawer, in the bathroom, in our bedroom. You were obsessed with fashion. It always surprised me that you went to work as a server. Instead of doing retail, you were that focused."

I blushed. I knew why I hadn't gone into retail, which had nothing to do with not liking fashion. It was because I wouldn't meet many men in a dress shop. And what I needed was to meet men, to nourish the demon inside me. I kept quiet because those thoughts were private. They were my dirty secret.

"I was in a bad space then but never lost that dream. I thought ..." I let the words die because I couldn't tell him I hoped Bobby Graham would set me up in my own shop. Those words would cut deep.

"Well, I'm proud of you. We should celebrate."

"Root beer floats?"

"Root beer floats!"

While I cleaned up the dishes, Kevin went to the store and bought a brick of vanilla ice cream and a two-liter bottle of root beer. I pulled two steins from the freezer—mugs Kevin sometimes used for beer and filled them with ice cream. Slowly, he poured the root beer over the ice cream. It fizzed and settled, and he poured more. I dug deep into the back of the cutlery drawer for the long spoons we used to have, hoping they were still there. And they were.

"Um, this is so good. I haven't had one of these in ... I can't remember when, but it's been forever."

"Andrea and I had them to celebrate report cards and passing into the next grade. She preferred orange, though."

Another zing. I didn't know that about Andrea. I did not know she preferred orange floats or that she even liked floats. This information took the joy out of the celebration, and I resented Kevin for saying it aloud. Even as that ugly little troll climbed the hill of my consciousness, I understood it was wrong to blame Kevin. It was all my fault. Acknowledging that didn't distill the resentment because he knew all about our girl.

The conversation lagged while we ate our floats. When we finished, Kevin rinsed the glasses and put them into the dishwasher. I sat on the stool, watching him work, his large hands gripping glasses and shifting dishes to make room. I imagined them doing other things. Dammit, Barbara. Get ahold of yourself. Kevin doesn't need your complications unless you're willing to live here permanently.

Would that be so bad? To be loved and supported? No, but what are you giving in return? Girl, you know it would be just sex for you, but more for him.

I took hold of my raging libido and marched to the bathroom. Staring at myself in the mirror, I realized I was in trouble. I had buried my feelings for Kevin under all my failings, and there were a lot of them. Being back in this house, under the same roof, eating meals together was shifting those barriers. It scared me.

I remembered what I'd sensed that afternoon about my parents and their love and how I was the one with all the fear. Mom even said as much. I was afraid of my feelings, especially my feelings for Kevin. I was making excuses for not taking risks and assigning feelings to Kevin because it was easier than asking the hard questions of myself. For all I knew, he was not in love with me, but he was nice and taking advantage of the opportunities presented. He had also likely never stopped loving me, and I couldn't decide which scared me even more.

Chicken! There, I'd said it. I was trying to find excuses to run. I was good at running. Splashing cold water on my face, I lost track of my thoughts. I didn't want to think anymore. I brushed my teeth and my hair and came out of the washroom. The house was nearly dark, save the light over the stove. I heard the dishwasher chugging away down the hall. I wandered into the kitchen, hoping to find Kevin waiting. The room was empty. My heart wrenched, and misery encompassed me. What was going on? It wasn't late.

Tiptoeing down the hall, I saw Kevin's door was closed. Noticing the light burning under the door, I stood staring at that narrow band of warmth. Part of me wanted to storm the fortress, pound the barrier with my fists, and demand an explanation. Another part of me, knowing the pain and sorrow of separation, wanted to crawl under the covers in my room and sob my heart out. Sorrow won out. I whirled around, ran to my bedroom, and slammed the door.

I didn't throw myself onto the bed, though—I paced the floor. Kevin was shutting me out, and I wanted to lash out at him. How dare he. Trying to calm myself, I paced back and forth, wearing a path in the rug. When I talked myself down, I realized I could go out on my own. I didn't need Kevin's permission. But where would I go? Since I had been working nights for so long—I didn't know where the hot spots were.

I scurried out of my room to the front door, shrugged into my coat, slipped on my boots, and left before I changed my mind. It was cold, so I let my car warm up for a minute while keeping my eyes on the house. No new lights. I pulled away from the curb like a teenager sneaking out of the house. I drove across town to the first bar I thought of. Sacred Garden. The parking lot was near capacity. That was a good sign. The place was busy, at least.

I heard the thump of the bass as I climbed out of the car. As I walked across the parking lot, I passed a couple of young people leaning against a car, groping at each other. I remember those days when the lack of privacy was a turn-on.

I walked on. A group of young boys came out, the crotch of their pants hanging at their knees. Why did they think that was a good look? I avoided eye contact but felt their eyes follow me as I pulled open the door and stepped inside.

.It took a minute for my eyes to adjust. I stepped away from the door, but not fully into the dim, sour-smelling room. A band of four stood on a stage, gyrating and hurling grunts and squeals at an apathetic audience. No one was dancing, but I noticed a table of young girls near the front paying close attention to the band. Groupies or girlfriends. The average age was twenty-three, give or take five years. This was not the place for me. Out of touch with the nightlife, I turned to leave.

The next place I stopped, I sat in my car, watching the patrons before determining this place was also for a younger crowd. I tried a few more, and at each stop, I became more and more reticent about getting out of my car. What was I doing? I raised my standards and drove a few more blocks to the Irish Stew. It was a restaurant with a separate lounge. Because there was food served, it seemed less forbidding to enter alone. A perky young girl greeted me and then ushered me into the lounge. It was bustling with a more palpable clientele. People nearer my age, or at least over thirty.

I sat at the bar, looking at the menu. I wasn't hungry, and I didn't drink. What was I doing here? I looked around the room. A man was sitting at the far end of the bar. He was staring into his drink. I assessed him. He had a full head of hair, an enormous nose, and a wedding ring. I ordered a Virgin Caesar and sipped at it while I continued to assess him. Finally, he looked up, and I noticed his lips and shuddered. I couldn't imagine kissing those lips. I ducked my head. After finishing my drink, I dropped a ten-dollar bill on the counter and left.

Back in the car, I sighed with relief. I had escaped something horrible. As I waited for the car to warm up, I realized I wanted sex, but I wanted to have it with Kevin.

I drove back to the house. The outside light was on. I hadn't turned it on, so Kevin must have heard me leave.

Slipping quietly into the house, I tip-toed to the bathroom, where I brushed my teeth and washed my face. Back in my room, I closed the door and turned on the light.

I let out an enormous sigh.

I did not know until that moment that I was holding my breath.

CHAPTER FIFTY-ONE

The alarm startled me out of restless dreams. Today was my first day at Fashion Sense, and butterflies took flight in the pit of my stomach. Fear and excitement mixed into a heady blend that would make eating impossible.

I showered and dressed, taking extra time with my makeup and hair. Kevin was in the kitchen when I walked in. He was pouring hot water into the teapot.

"Good morning," he called over his shoulder. "I wasn't sure whether you wanted coffee or tea, so I made peppermint tea to calm your nerves." He moved the pot to the eating bar and pulled the Tea Cozy over it. "Did I do okay?"

I wanted to kiss him for knowing what I needed, and I wanted to punch him for being so damn caring. Why wasn't he punishing me for going out last night?

"I'll make you some dry toast. If you take a granola bar to eat when your stomach settles, it should keep you until lunch."

"Why are you being so kind to me?"

"Why not?"

I shrugged. Why not? Because I was a mad cow who didn't know what she wanted. Because I didn't deserve any better. A myriad of excuses.

"Thank you." I sighed, as I didn't have the energy to fight with him. "I am so nervous."

"You'll be great—you know your designers. You know fashion, and you have always had good taste. She'll be over the moon with you."

"Yeah, I know a thing or two, but there is so much more that I don't know."

"So, you'll learn. You're a smart girl, Barbara. Just give yourself some credit."

I nodded, uncovered the tea, and poured myself a cup. Kevin set a plate of dry toast in front of me before placing his plate of bacon and eggs down. The thought of greasy eggs made my stomach turn over. I averted my eyes and breathed deeply through my mouth.

"Sorry. Is this bothering you?"

"It's okay. Sometimes my mind goes places my stomach isn't ready for."

He chuckled.

"What?"

"Never change, Barbara. Never change."

I laughed, and at that moment, my soul warmed. "Thanks."

"You're welcome." He took a bite of his breakfast. "I'm not a bad guy as it goes."

"I know," I muttered into my mug, wanting to weep. Then I grazed his arm lightly, and that wave of desire I thought I'd put out of my mind reared up, and my face flushed.

"Are you okay?"

I looked over at Kevin. He was gawking at me with alarm. "Yes, I'm fine." I looked away.

"Well, you went red suddenly."

"I know. It's nerves. It'll calm down in a minute."

He went back to his breakfast, and I shook my head. Get hold of yourself, Barbara. Sheesh!

I finished my tea and one slice of toast. Kevin took the other piece and mopped up his plate. I slipped down the hall to brush my teeth. At eight o'clock, Kevin left. He started my car on his way, so when I stepped out ten minutes later, it was toasty and warm. The roads were busy at this time in the morning, everyone heading to work. I turned into the back alley and parked in the stall Stella had pointed out to me. It was twenty minutes after. I was supposed to start at eight-thirty. Perfect timing.

I walked across the alley and knocked on the door. No one came. I stamped my feet. It was cold out here. Then I noticed the buzzer beside the door. I pushed it, and less than a minute later, the door opened. A large man with a broad nose that looked like it had seen a few fights in its time stood at the door. I gulped.

He grinned, showing off a full set of large, impossibly white teeth. "You must be Barbara."

I nodded, not sure if I could speak. He stepped out of the way, holding the door open with one arm. I had to turn sideways to get past him. I averted my gaze as I brushed past him. The door closed with a slam. I walked ahead of him to the lighted hallway by the dressing rooms. I didn't slow, feeling very uncomfortable with this man behind me.

Stella appeared. She clapped her hands together. "Good morning, Barbara. I'm so glad I didn't scare you off."

"No. No. You didn't." I stood awkwardly, waiting for further information.

"You've met Gino?"

"Well, sort of."

"Gino, this is Barbara. Barbara, this is my husband, Gino. Gino isn't usually here, but my car is in for service, so he drove me this morning." She turned toward the shop floor. "Okay. I will take you through a few things. Of course, you know the floor."

"Darling, I'll be in the office if you need me," Gino said.

Stella smiled in his direction, and he turned and walked back the way we came. We continued into the showroom. The stands of dresses, skirts, blouses, and pants were mere shadowy lumps without the overhead fluorescents burning.

"When we open, this will be your domain. I will show you how to use the equipment a little later." She gestured at the cash register area. "For now, let's focus on the merchandise." She walked between racks. "This rack is for clearance. To move this merchandise, we mark down all the items on this rack by fifty percent." She walked on. "The front three racks are for new arrivals. These are changing constantly as new orders come in. Dresses, of course, are here." She pointed to the wall. "We display coordinating pieces here, there, and over there." This time she indicated the half mannequins on top of several racks, sweeping broadly across the room. "I will allow you to put these together, to come up with looks that will entice the customer to buy an entire outfit, not just the slacks, or the blouse, or the sweater."

My stomach constricted as the burden settled onto my shoulders. Was I capable of doing this? Had I bitten off more than I could chew?

"Now, let's go back into the warehouse. This is the 'behind the scenes' work that you will do every morning." We walked back the way I'd come in.

Stella flipped a couple of switches—the storeroom lights came on. There were boxes stacked neatly in several locations and more racks of clothes. She explained the receiving and storage, how to use the steamer safely, and how and where to apply the garment tags and security devices.

The list of duties overwhelmed me. I followed her around the store, nodding and making appropriate remarks. By the time the store opened, my eyes had glazed over, and I was exhausted. The traffic through the day went in fits and spurts. Most browsed through the racks, some tried on outfits and left empty-handed. Some bought more than one item.

By the time Stella flipped the closed sign over at six, I felt shattered. I had walked three blocks to Jake's Café for lunch, had a bowl of soup and a sandwich, but that seemed like weeks ago.

"So, how do you feel?" she asked as she crossed back across the floor.

"Honestly, I'm overwhelmed. There is a lot to learn."

"Yes, there is a lot of fiddly, behind the scenes stuff, but it's easy. Once you get the routine down, I'm sure you'll do fine. The important thing is that I watched you today with the customers. I listened to your words, and you are natural. That woman who came in for navy slacks and left with navy slacks, a blouse and a sweater, was good sales technique."

I smiled, embarrassed at her comment. Seeing how the blue sweater set off that customer's eyes, I gambled that once she saw it on, she would buy the ensemble. "I took a chance."

"Yes, and that's what this is all about. Not everyone will be as receptive to your suggestions, but getting people to see what they might wear, is something not everyone is comfortable doing." She clapped her hands together as she changed subjects. "Now, here is the time sheet. Fill it out daily. I should have probably given this to you this morning, but sometimes I forget the basics. I'll also give you forms to fill out for our payroll person. Payday is every second Friday, cut off is the Friday before. On this schedule, next Friday is the last day of the pay period, and you'll get your first check on the Friday after that. Do you have questions, or have you had enough for one day?"

"I do. What are my hours? What days will I work?"

"I have a part time girl, Penny, who works Thursday and Friday nights and all-day Saturday. She's been with me for years now. You'll like her. Your hours are nine to six, Tuesday to Saturday. Once I am gone, we will pay you overtime for your lunch break on the days you work alone because you can't leave the store. I highly recommend that on the days that Penny is in, you take advantage of the hour off and get out of here for a while. The break will do you good."

Well, I was working the same days as before, but daytime hours rather than evenings. I was pleased.

As Stella walked me to the back door, she rambled on. "Now of course, I can see that you are going to do well with the customers, selling the goods. Managing the store, even as an assistant for the first while is going to be a learning curve and as you take on more responsibility, we will increase your compensation." She opened the door for me, and I stepped out into the frosty night air. "See you in the morning, Barbara. Today was a good start."

CHAPTER FIFTY-TWO

I drove home, feeling a tickle of excitement at her words. Things were changing for the better and I was looking forward to the future. I couldn't wait to tell Kevin and Andrea. As that thought rattled through my brain, the second car on the train pulled up. Andrea was dead. The emptiness of that thought took the wind out of my sails. I couldn't believe that I had forgotten something so vital. Stirrings of anger surged within me. I was going after my dream, but she wouldn't be there to see me make something of myself.

I steeled myself against the emotions that intensified like a tidal wave, threatening to swamp me on the drive home. My hands shook as I moved the shifter into park. The lights inside Kevin's house glowed behind the curtains and I rushed toward its welcoming warmth. The door opened, and I scrambled inside. Pushing the door closed with my back, I slid down to the floor as the tears started in earnest.

Kevin appeared, wiping his hands on a dish towel. In two steps, he closed the ground between us, wrapping his arms around me. "What happened? Was work that bad?"

I groaned and held him.

"Shh. Shh." He rocked me back and forth. As my hysteria slowed, he pulled back, peering into my face. For one second, I thought he was going to kiss me. I imagined his lips on mine—I really wanted him. The spell ruptured as he spoke. "Are you able to move to the couch?"

Nodding, he helped me to my feet, led me to the couch, and settled me on one end. "I'm just going to check on supper. I'll be right back." He disappeared into the kitchen. The room felt empty without him. I pulled my knees up, wrapped my arms around myself, and laid my head down on my arms. Kevin returned. "Peppermint tea will be ready in a jiff. Do you want to talk about it?"

Staring at his face, I noticed the care and concern in his eyes. "I had a fantastic day." I watched Kevin's brow furrow in confusion. He was so readable, and I loved him for that. "It was exhausting, and I have a lot to learn, but just being there was so exhilarating. This is what I've always wanted to do." Then my face crumpled again, my mouth contorting with the pain of my thoughts. My next words came out in a whisper. "I was driving home, and I wanted to tell you and Andrea all about it, to share my hope for the future, but Andrea is dead. Why? Why did she have to die? I just can't believe it."

Kevin, with tears running down his face, leaned in and kissed me. His lips were wet and salty. His tears and mine mixed as our kiss deepened. My body reacted, and I pressed myself closer. His hands moved down my back, pulling me tight. Passions intensified, and some clothes fell to the floor. The peppermint tea was all but forgotten.

Before we were completely naked, Kevin pulled me to my feet, and we hurried down the hall to his bedroom. With one arm, he swept the covers back, with the other, he held me close. Then he removed my underwear and laid me back on the bed. I watched as he stripped off his clothes, his desire clear as he joined me, pulling the covers up over us. We explored each other with our lips and our hands—I shifted to bring him in. He stared deep into my eyes, leaning down to capture my bottom lip. I closed my eyes and sighed. I was home—I knew it in my heart as I lifted to meet him.

As we uncoupled minutes later, my emotions swelled. Tears rushed down my face. Kevin scooped me close, letting me cry. He kissed my ear and whispered, "Just like to old days, eh?"

I nodded. It was. In the early days of our marriage, I often cried after sex. The emotions of the ritual were too immense to hold inside. We lay there, nestled together. My heart was at peace, and I wasn't sure how to tell him. My stomach rumbled. He rubbed it and smiled. "I think we should feed you."

"What's for supper?" I asked, wondering whether I wanted to get out of bed for it.

"Beef stroganoff."

I turned my face toward him. "Really? You made me beef stroganoff from scratch?"

"Hey, I'm not just another pretty face."

I turned around to face him, looking deep into his eyes. He stared back. I moved in and kissed him tentatively before letting my passion loose. My hands moved over his body. My hunger for him replaced my hunger for food. Our lovemaking was tender and slow, perfect in so many ways. This time, there were no tears. This time, peace settled around me.

We lay in each other's arms a while longer and then I said what I should have said nineteen years ago. I looked into his eyes—I reached up and stroked his face and smiled as he twisted to kiss the palm of my hand. "Thank you, Kevin."

"For what?"

"For being you. I love you—you know."

He looked at me as tears slipped down his cheeks. The sound he made was somewhere between a growl and a howl. He nestled his head into my neck and wept. I stroked the back of his head, allowing my own tears to flow. We held onto one another until it seemed safe enough to look at each other. "I love you, Barbara. I always have and I always will." He kissed me firmly on the lips.

"I have been a fool." I confessed. "Seeing my father yesterday made me realize that I have allowed him to dictate my behavior for too long. I realized then, sitting at the table having tea with my mother, that I was going to have to face up to this soon. She even told me to stop running, but last night I was doing the opposite."

"I know."

Looking into his face, I recognized the pain I'd caused him etched into the lines around his eyes. "I am so sorry. I don't know why you love me and why you've put up with me all these years. I don't deserve you."

"It's not about deserving or being unworthy. I fell in love with you when you spit on my shoe that day in high school. I can't explain it. It broke my heart when you left us ..."

I put my hand over his mouth to stop the words. "Please."

He kissed my hand, and I pulled it away. "We need to talk about this. At some point, we'll have to, you know."

I nodded. "I know. Just not tonight, okay? I just want to be here with you."

He snuggled back down, and we lay there silently for another minute before his stomach rumbled loudly. "Well, I think maybe we should get something to eat. I'm famished."

We climbed out of bed. I walked naked to my room, grabbed my robe, and followed him to the kitchen. He reheated the stew while I set the table. We ate our supper quickly, each of us touching the other from time to time.

"Let's skip the dishes," Kevin said as he mopped up the last of the gravy from his plate.

I looked at him, my eyes wide. "Again?"

"Hell, yeah!"

Letting out a whoop, I leaped off my stool and ran down the hallway toward Kevin's bedroom. Dropping the robe on the floor, I scooted under the covers moments ahead of him. I let out a fake shriek as he took me in his arms and kissed me. We took our time touching, feeling, stroking, and kissing.

As we lay together, Kevin's arms wrapped around me, my back to his chest, I whispered, "We need to talk about Christmas. Mom wants us to come to her place since it will be the last one with him."

Kevin pulled me tighter against him. "I wasn't looking forward to Christmas. I wasn't even sure I wanted to put up a tree or deal with the fuss." He sighed. We were both thinking about Andrea. "Val and Doug wanted me to come out there, but that was before you ..."

Lost in our own thoughts, neither of us spoke for a minute. Then Kevin continued. "But maybe doing something different is what we need to get through it, so if that's what you want, then that's what we'll do."

"Just that easy?"

"Just that easy."

We lay there in the dark, and I listened to his breathing deepen. I thought about how much my life had changed in the weeks since Andrea died. In my wildest dreams, I never imagined I would be back here, and certainly not knowing how right this was. We had a long way to go. There were wounds to heal and fences to mend, but I could finally allow it to happen.

I wiggled against him, loving how wonderful it was to be in his arms.

The rhythm of his breathing lulled me, carrying me off to sleep, complacent and at peace.

CHAPTER FIFTY-THREE

The next week was busy and happy for us. We shopped for presents together—we made love often and shared the housekeeping duties like we'd been doing all our lives. The undercurrent of unresolved issues was there. I was aware of it, but we didn't let it ruin the season. It was the first time in years a tremor of real hopefulness settled between us. Opening that box from the past wasn't on my agenda. It was on Kevin's, though, because on Saturday morning, after breakfast, he suggested we get a tree and decorate it.

We drove to the lot, picked out a perfect little tree, and came home to set things up. Kevin was straightening the tree when Mom called. She and I chatted for several minutes about Christmas Day. Patrick and his wife were buying the turkey. Dennis and his wife had already picked up a tree and decorated it, and she wondered if there were anything I wanted to bring over that would make Christmas perfect for me.

A bottle of Jack Daniels? I didn't say it, but it was my first thought. "I don't know. It's been a very long time since I've celebrated Christmas. I don't even know what you need?"

"Well, I'll have the usual vegetables: Brussels sprouts, turnips, sweet potatoes, and mashed potatoes. So, what about pies or tarts?"

My mind spun. I was not a homemaker. I was a decent cook, but Andrea was a girl the last time I baked anything. But I was nothing if not valiant. "Okay, Mom. I can do that. Any requests?"

"Oh, pies are always good. Mincemeat pie is my favorite, though I haven't had it in years because making mincemeat involved brandy, so I wouldn't make it. But squares are good, too. Nanaimo bars, date squares. I really don't care what you bring, but I wanted you to feel part of this, not an outsider coming in."

"Thanks for that, Mom, and I'll bring something. I'll give it some thought."

"You can always get something from that café we went to for coffee that day. They have an enormous selection of desserts you can buy. I love their carrot cake."

That was a good idea. I enjoyed the cinnamon bun I'd had at Jack's Diner, so I knew the quality of the goods there. Probably better than me trying to bake something from scratch. "Okay, Mom. Leave it with me. I'll bring the desserts, whatever that might be."

"Thank you." She paused. She had more to say, so I waited for her to pick up her thoughts. "How is the new job going?"

I updated her on my work and told her I was learning a lot, which seemed to satisfy her. "Well, it must be going well. You sound happy."

"Do I?" My thoughts flew to Kevin. "Well, I am enjoying this new job. Stella is elated with how well I understand the position, and I am making sales, which, of course, is ultimately the goal."

"I am happy for you. Maybe we could go for coffee one night. It would be wonderful to see you."

"Sure, Mom. I'll call you."

"Okay, dear. I hear your dad calling. I'd better go. Talk soon, okay?"

"Bye, Mom." I hung up, feeling a little disappointed. Part of me wanted to share my newfound happiness with her, to tell her that Kevin and I were back together. Part of me wanted her to sense that things had changed and ask me. But neither had happened, and a niggle of regret ran up my spine.

When I entered the living room, Kevin had the tree in place and several rubber totes on the floor. He was also untangling the lights and checking the bulbs. "How's your mom?"

"She's good. She wants me to bring the desserts for Christmas Day."

"You?" He grinned at me.

I put my hands on my hips in mock anger. "Yes, me! I thought I'd order them from Jack's Diner."

"There's the Barbara I know and love."

I smiled as I walked over and touched his cheek. "I love you, too."

He grabbed my hands, kissed each palm, and then pulled me close to kiss my lips. "I will never tire of hearing those words. Oh God, I love you so much."

We spent the next hour wrapped in each other's arms, enjoying the pleasure of being together. Laying there contented, I turned to Kevin. "Well, I think we should get that tree decorated."

"Yeah, we should." He shifted onto his elbow to look down at me. "But I'm starving. You want a sandwich or something?"

"Something." I ran my hand down his arm.

"God, you're insatiable." He leaned down and kissed me again. Then he slipped into his jeans and walked into the kitchen.

Left alone, the floor felt cold from being naked. I gathered my clothes and wandered down to the bathroom, where I cleaned up and dressed. When I arrived in the kitchen minutes later, Kevin had sandwiches on plates, pickles, and a few vegetables in a bowl. He even had dip alongside. The kettle was rumbling to life, and the teapot was sitting ready beside it.

He'd retrieved his shirt, though he hadn't done up all the buttons. I ran my hand across his chest. "This looks fantastic."

"Dig in," he said. "Tea is almost ready."

We ate in silence. I was thinking about how peculiar life was. How fast things had changed, and how the elephant in the room needed to disappear. I didn't want to face the words that would come—eventually. I was still a coward.

"Mmmm. This is good. You always made a great tuna-fish sandwich." I smiled at Kevin, and he smiled back.

The elephant of the past clawed its way up my spine and sat on my chest. I wanted to run away again—to get out of the house. That itchiness under my skin screamed for attention. It was going to happen, this conversation I had been avoiding for years. Those words that would rip out my heart and tear me asunder. I almost choked on the next bite, so I put my sandwich down and waited.

Kevin grabbed two mugs and poured tea for both of us. I studied his face. He was thinking sad thoughts. I shifted in my chair, the need to run mounting as I worried about myself.

With his hands wrapped around his mug, Kevin sat staring at his plate. I waited, wondering if I should say something to derail what was coming. All I did, though, was hope that he would be kind.

"Well, let's get that tree decorated, shall we?" Kevin rose from his stool and moved toward the living room. The oppressive air lifted, a reprieve from this unwelcome conversation. The elephant followed us into the other room and made himself at home, stealing the air and making it difficult to breathe. Kevin went back to stringing the lights. I opened the first tote and found garland and tinsel inside. I opened the next one. Shiny boxes of ornaments lay one atop the other, along with many homemade bobbles set delicately among them. I recognized a few from past years—Andrea's handiwork. I lifted one and held it up.

Looking over, Kevin said, "She made that one in grade four. There are several of them in there that she made over the years. That's Santa, of course."

I smiled at him, tears brimming. "I missed out on so much."

"Yes, you did." There was no sugar coating. I sucked in a breath to ease the pain of the barb that pricked my heart.

Kevin looked over at me. "You know you didn't have to go, right?"

I stared back at him. "Yes, I did." It came out as a whisper.

"I don't agree. I knew about those men, and I was aware there were demons driving you. Remember, I lived with you, and I loved you."

I nodded. "But I couldn't pretend anymore. It was agonizing to think about Andrea or you seeing me turn into a monster. I hated what I was doing to you both. I tried, but I couldn't stop it."

Kevin was silent for a moment. He clipped lights on the branches and moved around the tree. "I think it's time for honesty, and I know how I felt when you left. I understood those demons. They were already part of you when I met you. I didn't know what, but something bad had happened to you. But I thought, wrongly, of course, that my love would keep them away." He paused. "I still wonder, with a little help, if it should have. But you gave up on me, Barbara. You gave up on us the first time you had sex with another man."

I stood there, stunned at his words. They were cutting right through me. I couldn't breathe properly. The need to run was growing. I wanted to escape this, but somehow, my legs wouldn't move. I just stood there, with that Santa ornament dangling from the ends of my fingers, letting his words cut away the putrid story I'd lived with for years.

Tears streamed down my face. He was right—I was a coward then. Running was easier than trying to fix what was wrong. For the first time, I clearly recognized how wrong taking the easy way out had been. I'd hurt Kevin. I was just beginning to see how much.

"Your leaving shattered me. I had a daughter to raise, a daughter who didn't understand why mommy wasn't coming home. She cried every single night for weeks. What was I meant to tell her, eh? I couldn't tell her that her mother's issues were more important than she was. She was three years old, and nothing made sense to her. She stopped playing, acted out, and had temper tantrums. It took a long time for her to heal, and just when I thought we were getting better, you'd show up. Her birthday, Christmas, Easter, Halloween, and I'd spend the next few weeks picking up the pieces.

"I thought of telling you to stay the hell away, but I kept hoping that seeing us would jog something inside you and make you realize what you were missing. It never did. You filed for divorce and married that first loser and then another. I didn't know what you saw in them and couldn't help comparing them to myself. I thought you could do better. But part of me kept hoping that you'd be happy with one of those guys and I would move on, and part of me hoped, I mean really hoped, that you'd compare the two of us and come home where you belonged."

He took a breath, clipped a few more lights on the tree, and then resumed his story. "Life was hard for me, Barbara. Try as I might, I just couldn't stop loving you. I even thought about drowning my pain in a bottle, but I had a daughter who needed me, so I kept putting one foot in front of the other until it was normal." He snorted. "Normal. I do not know what normal is."

As I continued to stand there, I didn't offer him words of comfort or excuse. I just let him share his pain. My heart burst under the weight of regret and recrimination. Nausea weakened my knees, but I kept heaping it on—kept taking it. I shoved aside my fears for the first time in my life to understand what I had done.

"I tried to date in the early years. It was awkward. I think I went out with four or five women. They were pleasant enough and all that, but they weren't you, so in the end, those relationships went nowhere. Once Andrea was in school, lots of women threw themselves at me—other mothers from Andrea's class, some married, some not. I turned them all away until they stopped finding excuses to stop by on made-up pretexts, hoping I would ask them out or invite them into my bedroom.

"The years melted into one another, and Andrea was my life. She was so curious about everything, and I loved taking her to the library to look up something or other. I learned from her, even as I taught her things. She was forever bringing other kids into the house—the house was alive with noise and life. I wouldn't trade those years for anything unless, of course, it was to live them with you. I often went to bed wishing you'd been here for this or that. Life was good. Well, as good as it can be under the circumstances. Both Andrea and I had scars, but we were okay."

I had scars, too. Deep ones. But now wasn't the time to share. Now was the time to listen. Kevin deserved that much.

"Things changed when she went to college. I wanted her to stay here. It made little sense for her to live on campus. However, she argued that college was supposed to be experienced outside of parental restraints. She wanted to get everything she could from it, which meant having the freedom of not living at home. I told her I'd give her freedom. God, I can still see her rolling her eyes. Freedom at Dad's house wasn't the same as having freedom under your own roof. I stopped arguing, and she moved out a week before college started.

"That's when things fell apart for me. I had too much time on my hands. I was alone, rattling around in this house, and lonely. My purpose was gone now that Andrea was off living her life. You were doing your thing, and I ..." His voice caught, and he stopped talking to clear his throat. "That's when I started missing you again. I didn't want to be alone and hated coming home at night, so I worked longer and longer hours. I lost weight because I wasn't eating properly or at all some days."

Kevin clipped the last light on the tree and moved away from it. He sat on the arm of the chair. I turned toward him, but I didn't move closer. He leaned over, ran his hands through his hair, and let out a deep breath. Then he straightened up and looked at me. The raw emotion etched on his face terrified me.

"Matt stopped by the shop one night." He continued. "It was gone seven, and I was just getting ready to start another project when he walked in. He didn't yell at me but told me he was worried. I blew it off, but he was unyielding. He told me that maybe I needed to talk to someone. A psychiatrist. I grew angry, and he left.

"But his words wouldn't leave me alone, and I sat in the shop thinking. As hard as it was, changes needed to be made. So, I flew to Arizona and spent a week with my folks. Mom and I had a long talk, probably the first time we'd ever discussed some of that stuff. She helped me to see that I had a choice in all this. She told me I would have to learn to let you go or figure out how to get you back. I don't know why we didn't have that conversation years earlier. I guess I wasn't ready."

My insides squirmed because I recognized where he was going. I remembered the day he'd called as if it were yesterday. By then, I was living with Greg, and I thought he was calling about Andrea because that's always the pretense he used whenever he called. But this time, he didn't talk about her. She never even came up in the conversation. I remember hanging up and feeling puzzled, but I never gave that conversation much thought because I had a new man in my life.

"When I arrived home, I called you. I tried to feel you out, and you were so evasive, so exasperatingly evasive. I wanted to crawl through the phone and shake you. In the end, though, I understood. You were still running, and you might never stop. I decided that day to walk away from you—to learn how to let you go. I was going to stop dreaming that one day, you'd figure out I was the best thing for you and the only person who truly loved you, and you'd come home. That Christmas was the first time I didn't call to invite you to dinner."

I remembered. Greg and I had only come to open presents. We arrived about ten in the morning at a house bustling with activity. Matt and Jenny were there with their kids, and Kevin was gracious but not welcoming. At the time, I thought it was because I was with Greg. I didn't realize he was trying to distance himself from me. We left because I'd seen Greg ogling Andrea, and I had never realized until then that there was no invitation. The pain that ripped through me was punching me in the stomach. I wanted to bend over and hug my ankles until the ache subsided.

He paused as if trying to gather his thoughts. "I saw a therapist for a while, trying to figure out how to get past all this. But you ..." He pounded the left side of his chest. "You were right there, stuck in every fiber of my being. I didn't know how to get you out, and after several sessions with the therapist, I realized I didn't really want to. So, I quit that because I couldn't quit you." He looked at me, tears swimming in his eyes. He blinked, and they rushed down his face. I moved to wipe them away, but he caught my hand before it reached his cheek.

"That's why I want to make sure that this isn't a game. It is real to me. I've lost Andrea, and don't know if I can go on ... without ..."

I leaned in and kissed his lips. Then I sat back and looked up into his face. "Ever since I moved back in here, I've been fighting myself to keep away from you. It seemed wrong to be together because of our history, and the only reason I wanted you and you wanted me was because we'd lost something we both loved—and I loved

Andrea."

"I know you did." He kissed the palm of my hand.

"When I went to see my dad that day and watched my mom with him, I realized something about love. My mom loves my dad, even though she hasn't always liked who he was or what he did. She said as much when we had tea later, and it clicked for me then that you felt that way about me."

He nodded, and I continued. "When I got home, I was even more determined to get out, to save you from yourself—to stop you from making the mistake of being with me. I'm damaged goods, and I don't know if I'll ever be whole or if I'll ever be able to love you like you love me."

"I never cared about that." He protested.

I shook my head. "I know, but I do."

He stood and paced the room. "So, what are you saying? That this is just a bit of fun, and you're already preparing to leave?"

Shaking my head, I replied, "Quite the opposite, actually."

Kevin stopped pacing and looked at me. I tried to smile, but my lips quivered. "That first day of work, I realized I was fooling myself. I have been running my whole life—I've been running from love because I didn't believe I deserved it. I did everything I could to prove to myself and the world that I was the tramp my father turned me into. Mom told me the other day to stop running, and believe me, in the past hour, I've wanted to rush out the door to avoid what you had to say. Not because it didn't need to be said but because I am to blame for all of this. Anyway, at that moment, when I realized the only people I wanted to share my joy with were you and Andrea, all the pieces of my broken life fell into place, and I realized that the only place I wanted to be was with you. But I didn't know if you wanted me because you couldn't bear to be without our baby girl or if you truly wanted me for myself."

"Oh my God, Barbara. It's always been you. It will always be you." He took me in his arms and hugged me.

"There is something else I think I need to say," I said against his chest.

"Okay." He kissed the top of my head but didn't loosen his arms. Wiggling a little, he let me go.

I needed to look into his eyes when I said this. "I need … damn, this is hard."

He took my hand and squeezed it.

"Um … okay … I need to, um … wow. I have it in my head, but I can't get the words to come together." I paused and wet my lips. "Okay … I need to ask your forgiveness for … well …" I was thinking about all the men I'd slept with, for all the times I had shut Kevin out because of my fear. "Well, for everything."

"You are forgiven." He pulled me back into his arms, holding me close, and together, we wept away our lost years. I can't explain the intimacy of that moment. It was like we were one—one heart, one mind, one body—tied together with threads of loss, love, hope, and forgiveness.

When we stepped apart, Kevin looked deep into my eyes. "Can we get a bit of counseling in the future? It will help us make sure we've built an excellent base for our new start."

"Sure, if that's what you want. If you think we need it."

"I do. Regardless of what we've just done, I want us to communicate better so we don't get lost again. And we've just had an enormous loss, which, even though we might not want it to, it might get in our way in the future."

We decorated the tree together, carefully placing each handmade piece. Everything that had happened jangled my nerves. I'd committed to working on my relationship with Kevin and was aware of our immense loss. Kevin was right. We needed to get a better footing. Sex was wonderful. It had always been good, but if we wanted this to work, we needed more.

"What are your parents going to say when we tell them?"

"I've already told them."

I looked at him, my eyes wide. "When?"

"When I was making lunch. I called them while you were in the bathroom."

"But you were making lunch!"

"I learned how to multitask when Andrea was little. I had to. Some mornings, it was a zoo. I can't imagine how I would have coped with more than one."

"God, I wish she was here," I said as tears pricked my eyes.

"Yeah, me too. Me too." Kevin leaned over and hugged me from the side.

We delved into our own thoughts again until I remembered he hadn't told me what his parents said. "Hey, you didn't tell me what your folks said."

He laughed. "Well, I wasn't trying to avoid it. They said ... well, my mom said ..." He raised his voice an octave. "Oh, my boy, I'm happy if you are. But for goodness sake, get some counseling this time." He watched me, his eyes twinkling. "And my dad said ..." He dropped his voice an octave. "Take a lesson from this old duck: a woman gets better in every way with age. She'll keep you on your toes, keep you feeling young, and, best of all, keep you warm at night. I'm happy for you, son. I've always liked that girl."

"Your dad said that?"

"Well, I might be paraphrasing, but it's pretty much what he said."

"So, is the counseling your mom's idea?"

"Absolutely not. I was thinking about it all week, but until I spilled my guts ... until I knew you were staying, it didn't seem right to bring it up."

I sighed. It gratified me that Kevin was not a puppet to his mother's wants.

I pulled the last box from the plastic tote—a red star with a circle of white lights—and handed it to Kevin. "The final touch."

He handed it back to me. "Not this year. I was shopping a couple of weeks ago, and I found something better."

He walked to the front closet and pulled a plastic bag off the top shelf. He angled his back to me as he unboxed the surprise. When he turned to me, I gasped. He held the most beautiful angel I'd ever seen. She had dark hair—her gown was gold brocade with tiny white lights along the hem. She held a candle in her hands.

"When I was in the store, I saw this and had to bring it home even though I didn't know if I was going to put up a tree this year. It's Andrea, our angel. She will grace our tree every year from now on."

I reached out to run my fingers lightly over the beautiful fabric of her gown. Her face was serene, and her halo was set perfectly like a crown. She was truly beautiful and so much like Andrea—it was uncanny. Kevin took the gown and placed it easily atop the tree. After a bit of a struggle to find the cord end, he connected it and stepped back. "Okay, are you ready?"

I nodded, not trusting my voice. He reached down and flipped the switch, and the tree lit up. He stepped back beside me, put his arm around my waist, and we stared at the tree. It was stunning. The decorations, the lights, and the beautiful angel looking down from above. Tears welled up but didn't fall. "It's perfect."

Kevin squeezed me a little tighter but said nothing. We stood there, side by side, each lost in our thoughts. I was thinking about all the Christmases I'd missed. I shook my head to lift myself from my reverie.

"Okay, let's get this stuff put away." Kevin gathered up the packaging and boxes and put them inside the totes. I helped, and when we cleared the space, Kevin took them downstairs. While he did that, I went into the guest bedroom and pulled out the packages

I'd wrapped from the closet. I tucked them under the tree.

I stepped back and smiled. It was such a good feeling to be here. We had lost a lot of time together, memories we'd never have because of my choices, but starting now, things were going to be different.

This was a new beginning for us.

I sighed before heading into the kitchen to start supper.

CHAPTER FIFTY-FOUR

Time flew by, and before I knew it, it was Christmas. Kevin and I had spent Christmas Eve hosting a meal for Matt and Jenny. For the first time in years, Kevin wasn't hosting a Christmas dinner, so he invited them to come for supper. Things were a little tense at first. Jenny had always been stiff with me, and that night was no different. But I was no longer a guest. I was the hostess, and I used all my expertise as a hostess with customer service to win her round. As we relaxed, the banter grew warmer, and the evening was a success.

We went to bed late, not bothering to set alarms. When I woke, the outside world was lit up by the reflection of the streetlamps on the snow. I always viewed this light as eerie—the light of the city in winter.

"Merry Christmas," Kevin said, rolling toward me.

"Merry Christmas."

"What time do we have to be at your folks?"

"Mom wants to eat at one, so I guess if we have a quick bite at ten-thirty and then head over, we'll be in time to help. I don't want to spend too much time sitting around. Idle hands, busy tongues …"

"Well, I'm sure your mother has asked the boys to be on their best behavior."

"I suppose. Patrick has been so angry with me, though. I haven't spoken to Dennis in years. My stomach is already in knots just thinking about today. Why did I agree to go? What was I thinking?"

"It'll be okay. If it turns ugly, we'll just leave." He kissed me lightly. "And I'll be right by your side all the way."

"Thank you."

"Now, if you're not too busy fretting …" He cupped my breast.

"Oh! Is this my present?"

"No," he said as he captured my bottom lip with his lips. "It's mine."

~ ~ ~

We spent an hour in bed before getting up for a leisurely breakfast. Pancakes, bacon, and Kevin had a couple of eggs. I had yogurt. Then we moved into the living room. There were gift cards under the tree for my family that we would take with us. I had grilled Mom hard for suggestions. Having spent so many years alienated from them, I did not know what to get. She wasn't much help, so I picked up a variety of cards for stores in the city—grocery stores, the mall, a big box store, and a few restaurants.

I was feeling a little clueless about Kevin's gift, too, until Stella gave me an idea. Taking pictures of Andrea from the photo albums, I scanned them onto a memory card. I bought one of those revolving frames, inserted the card, and the pictures scrolled through on a timer. He could also set it to stop on one picture and leave it stationary. I thought it was a brilliant idea, and when I sat watching it flip through—I bawled like a baby. Kevin would love it as well.

After I had opened my gift, a delicate silver rope necklace with earrings to match, I handed Kevin his gift. He removed the wrapping paper and looked at the box.

"Take it out to see it properly," I whispered.

Shaking, Kevin removed the frame from the box.

"There's a little button on the bottom." I pointed with my finger. "Right there."

He flicked it on, and the screen came to life. Andrea, in grade two, smiled out from the screen. Then, with gradual persistence, it faded, and there was one of her and Kevin and a snowman in the front yard. Pictures of school concerts, holidays, playing with friends, and even a few that I'd taken with me when I left: bringing her home from the hospital, her first Christmas, her second.

Kevin watched the pictures go by, tears streaming down his face. He tried to speak as he squeezed my hand. "This is the best gift …" He choked on his tears.

I just nodded, tears running down my face as well.

I didn't have time to watch the entire series. We had to get ready to leave, so I went to shower, and when I was done, Kevin climbed in. I was clipping on the earrings he'd given me when he stepped up behind me, dressed for the day. He smelled nice. I turned to kiss him.

"We'd better get a move on."

Coats and boots and a car ride, we pulled up across the street from my parents' house. Patrick and Dennis were already there by the vehicles parked out front. My stomach constricted.

Kevin looked at me. "It'll be okay. We can do this together. Remember, we can always leave if things go off the rails."

Mom opened the door and ushered us in. Kevin set the present on the deacon's bench while Mom fussed about our coats. She disappeared with them, leaving us to face the group in the living room. Dad was there, looking paler and thinner than a few weeks ago. He tried to smile, but it appeared like a grimace.

Patrick was sitting close to Dad. He waved a greeting but didn't get up. Dennis was standing by the tree with a cup of eggnog. Crystal and Chelsea were nowhere in sight. They must be in the kitchen. Sure enough, the door swung open, and they came out together. The two had been best friends since childhood. Married to brothers, they remained in each other's lives. Laughter filled the air as they came into the room.

It died when they spotted me and Kevin standing awkwardly in the entryway. Damn, if Mom hadn't taken my coat, I'd be out that door without looking back. Crystal set her mug on the coffee table and moved to where I stood.

"Barbie. Kevin. Merry Christmas." She extended her arms, and I stepped forward for a hug. She wrapped her arms around me and whispered in my ear. "I'm sorry about Andrea. So very sorry."

Then she hugged Kevin and moved back into the room. "Come in and take a seat."

CHAPTER FIFTY-FIVE

We moved together, and Kevin stayed close to me.

Before we sat down, Dennis intercepted. "Merry Christmas, Barbie. Kevin." He extended his hand, but he lowered it since we were carrying the presents.

"Oh, the presents." I looked under the tree. No presents were sitting there. "Should we just pass these out?"

"You brought presents for all of us?" Patrick asked as Mom came back into the room.

"Yes, and for the kids, too. Where are they?"

"The kids are upstairs playing video games," Chelsea said.

We passed the presents out and then sat together on the couch. Chelsea moved over to let us sit together.

"Merry Christmas, Chelsea," I said. "It's good to see you."

"You too. You look good." She split the tape on the tiny box with her long, polished red nails.

"Thank you."

The room was quiet for a few seconds while the gifts were opened. Patrick held up his assortment of gift cards and said, "Hey, this is perfect. I go to all these places. This will come in handy when the January bills start rolling in, and I can no longer afford to eat." He chuckled, and the group laughed with him. I didn't know if he was serious or mocking my gift. I did my best not to let it bother me.

"Thanks, sis, really," Patrick said to me as he moved across the room to hand the cards to Crystal. "I feel bad that we didn't get you anything—I really didn't expect you to show." Shrugging it off, I had all I wanted. The only change I would have made was to have Andrea with us.

Dennis took the gift cards upstairs to the kids. I left Kevin talking to Patrick and went into the kitchen to help Mom. As Chelsea and Crystal worked together, I seemed to be in the way. Sitting at the table, Mom sat across from me. I told her about my job and how I loved it. The other two joined us at some point. Crystal was interested in my job, but Chelsea was less so. We'd never been the best of friends, anyway. I wondered if she was worried about losing Crystal's friendship to me. It would not happen, but people get wound up about those things.

Mom decided we couldn't all fit at the dining room table, which comfortably accommodated only six people. So, the grandkids would sit there because kids are more apt to spill, and the adults would eat in the living room using TV tables. The boys had brought their sets from home, so we would each have one of our own. We set up the buffet on the kitchen table and counter.

Shortly after one, Mom called for the family. She had us gather together. The kids came down the stairs carrying various electronic gadgets. Nathan, Patrick's oldest, had a shaggy mop of brown hair over sharp features. He looked exactly like his father. Madison and Michael were also dark, with a smattering of freckles. All of them had blue eyes. Dennis's two girls, Trisha and Tara, were tiny replicas of their mother. They had Chelsea's blond locks and were carrying a little extra weight.

There must have been earlier discussions because Dennis and Patrick held out their hands, and the kids, with some reluctance and perhaps a bit of annoyance, placed their gadgets in their father's hands.

"Now, before we eat," Mom said, "I need to say something." She took a deep breath and looked around the room. "This may be the last time we will all be together in this room." She reached down and took my father's hand, smiling down into his face. I reached for Kevin's hand.

"Now, family is the most important thing in the world, and we, your father and I, have always been grateful for all of you. We welcomed each of you into our lives and celebrated birthdays and Thanksgivings and Christmases together, even after you flew the nest. Now, there isn't a family alive that hasn't had issues and arguments, but thank you for putting aside your differences and coming here this Christmas. It will ..." She cleared her throat. "It will probably be Michael's last one with us." She burst into tears.

"Oh, Mary, please don't cry, sweetheart," Dad murmured to her. If he had looked around the room as I did, he would have seen tears in everyone's eyes.

"I'm sorry," Mom said. "I don't mean to cry. It's just that I know we're not complete." She looked across the room at me. "Andrea isn't with us."

A few mumbled words of sympathy surrounded me as people acknowledged our loss. My stomach was upside down. I wanted to wail, but I also wanted to hold it together in this room.

Kevin squeezed my hand. I squeezed back.

"Anyway, let's be grateful that we are here, and let's just enjoy the day. Merry Christmas."

Choruses of "Merry Christmas" echoed around the room. Trisha and Tara were leaning against their mother, and Dennis stood with his hand on Chelsea's shoulder. If I were a photographer, this would have been a perfect family picture.

"Okay, let's eat." People dispersed toward the kitchen. My dad sat in his recliner as Dennis and Patrick set up TV tables. Kevin moved over to help them. Nathan came over to me. "I wanted to thank you for the gift card and to tell you I was sorry about Andrea and all that."

"Thank you, Nathan."

"You did a great job with the funeral, too. She would have been happy with the music and all."

"You were there?"

"Yeah. I was sitting with some of her friends near the front. We used to hang out together sometimes. I liked her a lot."

"You and Andrea were friends?"

"Well, yeah. She helped me with stuff, like you know. Girls." He lowered his eyes and blushed.

"Wow, I did not know."

"I know she was mad at you a lot, and she couldn't understand why you left, but she loved you." He looked at me shyly. "She said that's what made the world insane, loving that which you wanted to hate. She had lots of thoughts like that. I miss her."

Tears ran down my face. "Thank you, Nathan. Thank you for sharing that with me." I whispered this to him as I squeezed his upper arm. He nodded, stepped back, and twisted on his toes before heading to the kitchen. Dennis and Patrick had already disappeared, but Kevin was there, hovering. He came over, wrapped his arms around me, and hugged me close. I let the tears flow. I didn't share what Nathan said, only whispering that I was okay and that I'd tell him at home.

"Hey, you two," Mom called from the kitchen door. "Come and dish up."

Looking at her, I couldn't miss seeing my dad sitting in his chair, smiling at me. I understood exactly what Andrea meant at that moment: loving that which you wanted to hate.

I grabbed Kevin's hand and pulled him toward the kitchen.

As we passed my dad, I bent over and whispered, "Merry Christmas, Dad."

Then I walked out of the room.

CHAPTER FIFTY-SIX

The rest of the day passed uneventfully. After our meal, Dad went to bed and didn't make another appearance. I helped with the dishes and then escaped to the fresh air in the living room. Patrick and Dennis disappeared to watch a football game. I told Kevin he should go, too, so he did for a while.

Trisha, Tara, and Madison were playing a board game in the corner. Mom was lying down, and Chelsea and Crystal must have stayed in the kitchen. The kids had taken back their electronics—the stack was gone. Nathan was sitting in the far corner, staring at the small screen in his hand and typing madly with his thumbs.

I sat on the couch and watched the young people. Michael, named after his grandfather, brought his gadget over to me. He called it an iPad. He showed me how it worked.

I must admit that I am technologically challenged. My cell phone is too smart for me, and I never considered using the camera and all the other features I don't touch. I watched Michael play some games, amazed that he knew what to do. He asked if I wanted to try, but I shook my head. So, he went on playing while I sat beside him, watching.

The afternoon faded away. The girls finished their game and disappeared up the stairs. Nathan hadn't moved. He was still watching his screen and typing from time to time. Chelsea and Crystal finally came out of the kitchen. Chelsea made an excuse to check on the girls and headed up the stairs. Crystal took a chair near me but said nothing for a few minutes.

"It's been a good day. I'm glad you came. Your mom was so happy when you agreed."

I just nodded, wondering where this was leading and wishing Kevin would miraculously appear.

"So, what's going on with you and Kevin?" There. That's what she and Chelsea had been scheming in the kitchen. They wanted to know about me and Kevin.

"Well, after Andrea died, I lost my job and my place to live, so I moved into the guest room at Kevin's while I get back on my feet."

"You lost your job? I just assumed you quit. What happened?"

"Well, do you know Thelma Graham?"

"Oh, yes. I know Thelma." She nodded to emphasize that knowledge.

"Well, she told me that if I'd been a better mother, Andrea wouldn't be dead." That old anger rose with the memory of those words. I pushed it back. "Anyway, I just lost it on her. It was childish and immature, and I instantly regretted it, but there is no going back."

"Wow, you kicked old Thelma's ass?"

"Well, I wouldn't put it that way, but the result was I got fired."

"Okay, but why didn't you stay in your apartment and just get another job?"

I wanted to climb under the rug and disappear. "Well, I had arrangements to rent one of those units in that new condo development on the golf course. But guess who owns it?"

"Bobby Graham?"

"Yes, and of course, he was there when I attacked Thelma, so I lost my lease and my job at the same time."

"He can't do that, can he?"

"I didn't investigate the legalities. I mean, I just lost Andrea, and I was already struggling with feeling like a terrible parent—a bad person. There was no fight in me, so I just let it go."

"Oh, wow. Talk about a lot of stuff falling on your head all at once."

"I suppose. I'm just thankful that Kevin was open to letting me stay in the guest room while I pull myself together."

"So, there's nothing else going on? I mean, I saw the hand holding."

"Well, he came today to support me and with Andrea ..." I stopped as my throat closed. "Ahem, it's hard, you know. All these firsts."

"I can't imagine."

"If I wasn't living it ..." I let the thought hang in the air.

We sat in silence for a while longer. Crystal smiled at me. "Well, I guess I should round up the kids. It's getting late."

"Oh, me too." I stood up.

I followed her to the basement rumpus room, where the guys were watching the game. Kevin saw me and stood. "You ready to go?"

"In a few minutes. I'm going to go up and say goodbye to Mom, so you have about twenty minutes, give or take."

"Sure." He kept his eyes on me—but sat back down.

I went back up the stairs. Mom was awake. She was lying on her bed with a blanket across her legs. She rose when I came in the door. "Don't get up. I just came to say goodbye."

She pulled herself back into a sitting position, stuffing some pillows behind her back. Then she patted the other side of the bed. I obeyed and sat facing her.

"Thank you for coming and making today so good for your dad."

"You're welcome, Mom."

We sat and smiled at each other. "I have missed you, Barbara. I'm glad you came today." Her eyes filled with tears.

"I have been so wrapped up in my life, living it my way, without ties or binds, that I forgot how comforting it is to have people on your side. I'm glad I came for me, you, and Dad, too." Rolling my eyes, I continued, "And maybe for the others, too."

"Family ties never truly break. They might get stretched mighty thin, but you can't shake them."

"True."

She looked at me with a goofy smile on her face. "Speaking of family ties, what's going on with you and Kevin?"

I wondered what to tell her. Should I be honest? Or should I keep the story the same for everyone? I decided on the latter. "Kevin and I are living under the same roof. We've lost our daughter—we are sharing the grief of that. So today was about honoring our daughter without being melancholy and morose. It's also about being in a place I haven't wanted to be for a very long time. I don't know if that's making any sense, but life has changed for both of us. We're trying to find our footing."

"Oh, Barbie, I know how hard it is. I thought I lost you all those years, and it was hard knowing you were just across the city and you didn't want any part of us. I couldn't understand it. Really, I still don't. I know your dad, and you were fighting and couldn't get along. But it was still hard. Every Christmas and birthday without a word …" She broke down and sobbed.

"Oh, Mom. Please don't cry. I know I'm screwed up. I've been so selfish and self-centered. After I left Kevin, I really felt so judged. No one understood what I was going through. All they wanted to do was tell me I was a bad person, a terrible mother. I hated I couldn't stay with my girl—it was practically unbearable, but I didn't think I had any other choice at the time."

She calmed down, wiping her tears with the back of her hand. "I never understood that either. Marriages break up all the time these days, but the mother always … well, nearly always takes the kids. I don't think I understood why either."

"And I can't make you understand." It annoyed me she was still sitting in judgment. "All I can tell you is that the decision was difficult, and if I had to do it again, I would."

"I'm sorry. I didn't mean to offend you."

"Well, I wouldn't say you offended me, but I didn't make my decision lightly. I agonized over it for months before I left. Then I cried myself to sleep for a long time, and I still cried whenever I had a day with her and had to leave her with Kevin. I did it for her, and she resented it." Now, it was my turn to cry. As the emotions rose and choked off my words, I squeaked out the agony of my heart. "She died, and we never reconciled this issue. I am devastated to the very core of my being that she never forgave me and died with that in her heart. Devastated!" Tears flowed, and I looked for a tissue. I stood and stomped out of the room, returning with a wad of toilet paper. I wiped angrily at my tears, frustrated that my emotions always overwhelmed me.

As I returned to the bed, Mom took my hand. "I cannot imagine. But I'm glad you and your dad reconciled before he …" She didn't finish.

Squeezing her hand, I said, "I know. I know."

We sat there quietly, holding hands and enjoying the peace of the moment. I realized I had missed so many years of being with her, and it was sadder that my selfishness kept us apart. So many years lost, years that I couldn't get back. I didn't even know how to make up for lost time.

"Okay, I have to go. I'll call you tomorrow." I hugged her

awkwardly. We had never been a very demonstrative family. "Merry Christmas, Mom. I love you."

I left the room, my emotions right on the edge of the cliff. As I made my way down to the main floor, I took several deep breaths to gain control. Kevin was waiting in the living room. He and Nathan were peering into the screen of a small tablet. He looked up, tears in his eyes. "You need to see this."

I walked over and sat on the other side of Nathan, everyone shifting to make room. On the screen was a picture of Andrea. It disappeared, and another one took its place. These were pictures taken at the university, a skating party, and a house party. Andrea was laughing into the camera. "Can you send that to us?" I asked, wondering how to get them into the frame I'd given Kevin.

"Sure, they're on the cloud, but I can put them on a stick."

Cloud? Stick? "Okay? I don't know what either of those things are, but whatever."

Kevin laughed. "You have so much to learn, Barbara. A stick is fine. I will pay you for it, too."

"No need. I work part-time at a computer place. I can get those things cheap. It's okay."

"Thank you, Nathan. You're a good kid."

He blushed, looking up at Kevin with a smile. My heart nearly burst, and I wanted to leave before I broke down and sobbed. I stood, ruffled his hair gently, and then walked to the door. Kevin followed.

In the car, I let my emotions go. The tears were first. "I really missed out on so much, haven't I? I feel like I've come back from the dead and discovered that life has gone on without me. What the hell is wrong with me?"

Kevin started the car and pulled away from the curb. "Nothing that some self-love wouldn't have made better. And hindsight is always twenty-twenty. You might not appreciate what you have if you hadn't walked the barren land. You need to take life as it comes,

Barbara. And stop beating yourself up. You cannot undo anything that's done. It's over. Let's just move forward."

We drove several blocks, and neither of us said anything. I was wiping tears and feeling sorry for myself. "I think this is one thing that a counselor will help us with. How do we live with regrets? Because we can't go back, can we?"

"No, we can't." I sighed. "God, why does life have to be so hard?"

"Because nothing worth having is easy?"

"That's crap. Whoever said that is totally insane."

He laughed, and as his rich chuckle filled the car, I laughed with him. My heart swelled with affection, and I reached over and touched his arm. "I love you, Kevin Pritchard."

"And I love you, too, Barbara. I will always love you."

We drove the rest of the way in silence, each lost in our thoughts. I wasn't sure what the future had in store, but I was surely glad for the place where I found myself at this moment.

CHAPTER FIFTY-SEVEN

Boxing Day was a big day for electronics sales, but clothing never made the list of must-haves. A few customers were looking for evening wear for New Year's Eve. Stella and I discussed the displays, and I sketched out my ideas for the front windows. We would change them early in the new year.

Kevin and I also had our first counseling appointment in the new year. I was looking forward to it and terrified of it simultaneously. I was ready to pick a few scabs, but I wasn't sure I wanted to look underneath. Kevin assured me he would be with me if I wanted and that private sessions were available, too. He agreed to pay the cost so we could have a solid foundation this time around.

I called Mom after supper on Boxing Day. "Hi, Mom, how are you?"

"Oh, Barbie, I'm glad you called. Your dad isn't doing so good. He won't eat and says he's nauseous. I don't know what to do."

"Have you called the doctor?"

"Yes, the doctor wasn't in, so his answering service said they'd have him call me."

"Well then, I'd better get off the phone so he can call. Call me back after you've spoken to him. Okay?"

She agreed, and we hung up.

"What's wrong?" Kevin asked, coming into the living room.

"It's Dad. Mom says he hasn't eaten today, and she's worried."

"Do you want to go over there?"

"I think so. Do you mind?"

"No, of course not. I can handle things here."

"Oh, I was actually hoping you'd come with me."

"Oh. Okay."

"You don't have to."

"Well, if you think I can help, I'll go. But I don't think you need me."

"What if it's bad?"

He thought for a moment, screwing up his face, and anger bubbled up inside. What the hell? I was trying to express a need, and he was blowing it off as unimportant.

"What else are you going to do?" I snapped.

Kevin looked at me, a little shocked at my outburst. "Well, hold on a minute. Why are you mad at me?"

"Because you're being a jerk."

"I'm being a jerk?" He repeated my words.

I vibrated with anger. Why was he being so difficult? He always did what I said. He was the most agreeable person on the planet. I didn't want him to assert his independence when I needed him. "Yes. You're being a jerk."

"Hold on a minute. Why are we fighting about this? You said you were going. I said go, and now I'm the bad one because I didn't read between the lines and understand that you meant we when you said I?"

"Yeah, but then I said we, and you're humming and hawing."

"I am because, in case you forgot, Barry and Agnes are coming over."

The next-door neighbors! I took a deep breath. "I'm sorry. I had forgotten."

"Man, Barbara, that was total rubbish. You can't have a tantrum every time I disagree with you, or we'll never get anywhere."

I cried. "I know, and I'm sorry. It's just wrong, you know. I have spent years hating that man, but the thought of him dying ..."

Kevin stepped forward and wrapped his arms around me. He held me while I cried. I couldn't believe I was so upset. "It's okay," he whispered. "You feel worse about this because you're still raw from Andrea's death. It's just compounding things."

Perhaps he was right. I know I had grieved for Andrea most of my adult life. Her death had made that final.

The phone rang. It was Mom.

"The doctor called. He's sending an ambulance. If you want, would you meet me at the hospital?"

"Sure, Mom. I'll be there."

"Thank you." She hung up.

"He's going to the hospital," I said, turning to Kevin.

"Okay. Let me call Barry and head them off."

"Thank you."

I went to the bathroom, splashed cold water on my face, and brushed my hair while Kevin made his call. He was hanging up as I returned to the living room.

"You ready to go?"

"No. But ..."

"I know."

CHAPTER FIFTY-EIGHT

We headed out, taking Kevin's truck so he could drive. He parked in the hospital parking lot. I paid the excessive fee but grumbled about how unconscionable it was for the hospital to take advantage of families with sick loved ones by charging so much to park nearby. We arrived at the emergency ward as they were bringing Dad in. The nurse directed Mom to the admission desk while the attendants rushed Dad down a hallway to the left.

Mom sat on a chair, tears in her eyes. A nurse came to the desk and took information from her. When the paperwork was complete, she advised us to find seats in the waiting area. Patrick and Dennis arrived a few minutes later. Both looked worried. Patrick stuck close to Dennis, perhaps fearing this would cause him to relapse into the bottle.

An hour later, a nurse appeared to tell us Dad had been admitted to the ICU. We were to go up and wait in the family room outside the unit. Once he was settled, we visited him in groups of three. She said little, but with her expression, I understood it was a matter of days now, not weeks or months.

Mom, the person most affected by this, seemed to cope the best. She was strong, while Dennis was taking it hard. I noticed Patrick was wrestling with the news, too, but he was more concerned about his little brother. Mom asked if Patrick would call Father Flannigan. He nodded and moved away, pulling out his cell phone as he entered the foyer.

None of us moved. A calmness fell over me. He was in excellent hands. Surely, there was something they could do. I didn't have forever, but unlike with Andrea—I had at least a few hours, maybe a few days, to make peace. Even if he was in a coma, I was going to take that chance. I was going to say what I should have told him earlier that month. I was going to lay bare my scars, and even though I wouldn't get what I wanted, I might get what I needed. It would be enough to know that he would know.

When Patrick came back, we took the elevator to the third floor. We followed the signs and found the room the nurse had mentioned. We settled in to wait. About half an hour later, a nurse advised us Dad was in room eight. We agreed that Mom, Patrick, and Dennis would go first. I told Kevin he should go home if he wanted. He said he would stay for a little while. Mom and the boys disappeared through the door.

Kevin sat on the couch. I grabbed a dog-eared magazine off the table and flipped through it absently while I leaned against him. The minutes dragged by. Though it was less than an hour, it seemed like an eternity before Dennis came out, Patrick on his heels.

"Dennis, settle down," Patrick urged.

"No, it's not right, and Dad wouldn't want this." Dennis spun around—his eyes wild.

"I know, but this is Mom's call. All we can do is advise."

"What is going on?"

"They've connected him to some renal machine, and now, at

Mom's insistence, they're intubating the poor bastard," Dennis shouted.

"Okay, okay," Patrick muttered, running his hands over his face. The gesture was reminiscent of Dad, who did the same thing.

"They should just let him go, for God's sake. Hasn't he suffered enough?" Dennis paced some more. "I need some air."

With that announcement, he turned and walked out the door. Patrick looked at me, shrugged, and followed him.

I looked at Kevin. "Go," he said.

I went into the ICU wing. The lighting was dim, the space quiet. I walked past a couple of open doors, around the desk on my left, and then I noticed my mother standing by the door to a room bustling with people in pastel smocks. The doctor was there, too, standing on the far side of the bed.

Mom was crying.

"What's going on?" I whispered.

She clutched my hand. "They are intubating him."

"Let's let the doctor work. Come back to the room. We'll come back in ten minutes. They should be done by then."

I pulled her down the hallway to the waiting room, where she collapsed in a chair. I kneeled before her, doing what I could to soothe her. "Kevin, would you find us some tea? Lots of sugar."

"Yeah, it's right here. He opened a closet door, revealing a counter and cabinets. In the little sink, he filled the kettle and put it on to boil. Then he flipped open the doors, looking for tea bags and cups. When the tea had steeped, he handed Mom a cup.

I looked at him, grateful again for his presence. "Sorry," he said. "There's only Styrofoam cups in here."

"It's okay. It's hot. That's all that matters," I said. "Would you do one more thing?"

"Sure, what do you need?"

"Would you check to see if we can return to Dad's room?"

Kevin nodded and left quietly.

"Drink up, Mom. Kevin's gone to check on Dad."

A few minutes later, Kevin returned. He nodded to me. I said nothing to Mom. She was staring straight ahead, sipping at her hot, sweet tea. When she had drained her cup, I took it and tossed it in the garbage. Looking back at her, I perceived her as a small, scared woman. All my life, she'd been formidable. This situation dwarfed her. A tremor of fear rippled through me. I had heard stories of spouses dying when they lost their partner. Coping with my dad's death seemed manageable. At least, I thought it was, but I wasn't ready to lose her.

"We can go back and see Dad now." I helped her up, and together, we walked back into the unit. It was calmer in his room now. One nurse was taking vital signs on the far side of the bed. Machines were beeping and shushing. Dad lay there under the covers, his eyes closed. He, too, looked smaller than I remember. Mom moved up beside him, taking his hand in hers. He didn't move.

I pulled the lone chair from the back wall to where Mom stood. She sat gratefully, her eyes never leaving my dad. No one spoke. The nurse finished up and left without a word. I moved around the bed and stood on the other side, looking at my father's face. A rush of affection overcame me, causing tears to sting my eyes. I had loved this man, and I had hated this man. Abuse and alcohol and unforgiveness complicated our relationship. I couldn't take back all the years of anger and disappointment, and I wondered who I might be if this hadn't happened to me.

It occurred to me that Kevin and I may have never met had it not been for my rebellion against the things I used to stand for. I wouldn't have been on the school grounds that day. Instead, I would have been studying in the library with my best friend. I wouldn't have spit on Kevin's shoe, and my life would have gone entirely differently.

As I sat there, staring at the face that had given me nightmares, and yet it was so like my own, I thought my heart would explode with all the things unsaid. I didn't want him to die, not knowing that he had once been my hero. He also needed to know how much he had hurt me, but despite that pain, I forgave him. That, too, seemed unfair at this point. He should leave this world unencumbered by my bitterness. He'd have enough to account for if there was any atonement for the stuff you did this side of heaven. I didn't want to bear the responsibility of sending him to hell. He wasn't an evil man. He was a man who had made poor decisions.

The doctor came in and motioned for us to leave the room. "We need to discuss our options. Is the rest of the family here?"

"They were," my mom said.

"Good. There's a private room across from the family room. If you can get everyone together, I'll meet you there in ten minutes."

Another doctor entered Dad's room, and a nurse was close behind him.

Mom and I walked down to the family room. Only Kevin was inside. "The doctor wants to meet with the family in ten minutes," I told him.

"I'll go find the boys. They're probably outside so Dennis can smoke."

"We'll be over there." I pointed to the room across the hall. Kevin nodded and left. Mom and I moved across the hall. This one was very plain and could hold ten people. There were no couches, just straight-back chairs set against the walls. We waited, tense and silent. I don't know what my mother was thinking, but I was wrestling with the end.

Kevin came back with Dennis and Patrick. He turned to leave. "Please stay," I whispered. He nodded and took the chair to my right. Dennis sat three chairs away from Mom, looking determined. Patrick sat between the two of them.

We waited for what seemed an eternity. Dennis was ready to

burst out of his skin. Dr. Collins came in and looked around the room before closing the door. He took a chair from his left and pulled it into the middle of the room. He sat so he could face Mom. "Michael is in awful shape. His liver is bleeding, and things from this point will not be pretty. We intubated him at your request, but this is only temporary. His body is shutting down."

Mom's tears turned to gulps and sobs as he spoke. He moved his chair closer to her and reached for her hands. "Mary, you know what's coming. We've talked about this before. I know it is hard."

Mom looked at him, her eyes wet with tears. She nodded and then broke into another sob. I rubbed her back, but her focus was on the doctor. "There is nothing?"

He shook his head, sorrow in his eyes. "Nothing," he whispered. "He's sedated now, and when we remove the intubation, we'll stop the sedation. You will have a chance to speak to him, but I must warn you ..." He looked around the room at all of us. "Things are going to be ugly. He's going to bleed from his eyes and his nose, and it's going to be nasty. This isn't television. There is no slipping blissfully into the hereafter in this situation. There will be a death rattle as his lungs fill, and he may even convulse. We will do our best to keep him comfortable for as long as it takes. If you need to vomit, leave and do it. Few are strong enough to stomach what is about to happen." He spoke gently despite the harshness of the content, wanting us to know what to expect.

"Do you have questions?"

"How much time?"

"It's hours now, not days. It seems he hung on through Christmas and then gave up." Dr. Collins stood. "Give us a few minutes to remove the equipment. Then I suggest you come—one at a time, say what needs to be said, and let the next have their turn. Then you can all sit with him to the end—should you choose to do that."

"No rule of three?" I asked.

"No rules when we're at this stage." He turned to go. With his hand on the doorknob, he turned back to the room. "I'm sorry there isn't more that we could do."

Patrick stood, catching the doctor before he left. "Thank you," he said, extending his hand. Dr. Collins shook it and then left. Patrick fell onto a nearby chair. "I can't believe we're here."

CHAPTER FIFTY-NINE

No one replied. We sat there in shock, each of us lost in our own thoughts. My mind whirled, trying to focus on my time with my father. I closed my eyes, took a deep breath, and asked for the right words. The clock seemed to have stopped. It was an eternity before a tiny little nurse knocked on the door to advise us we could see him. We looked at one another, each of us fearing to go first and afraid we wouldn't get a chance if we didn't.

"I'll go first," Patrick said.

We nodded as one, and he left. "Should we move back to the other room?" Kevin asked. "I can make tea while we wait."

No one replied. I squeezed his hand, reassuring him that everyone heard and appreciated his offer.

When Patrick came back, he was a wreck. His eyes were red and puffy, and his complexion white. He shook his head, not willing to discuss the experience.

Dennis stood. "Okay if I go now?"

We nodded, and he left quietly. He was gone longer than Patrick, or maybe it seemed that way because I was next. Dennis didn't stay when he was done. He poked his head through the door to let us know he was out and then walked away. I noticed that Dennis's disappearance worried Patrick, but he wanted to stay with Mom. I sat there for a few seconds, gathered my courage, and stood.

"Be gentle with him, eh, Barbie?" Patrick cautioned.

My temper flared. "You are such an asshole, Patrick. Mind your own business."

"See, that's just what I mean. You can't help yourself."

I spun around, marched over, and stood directly in front of him.

"Barbie, please," my mother cautioned.

"No, enough is enough, Mom," I said, not taking my eyes from Patrick's face. "No one told you what to say or do when it was your turn. So, although you're perfect, you don't get to tell me what to do either. You know nothing about me—*nothing*." I hissed, my anger raging. "He's my father, too. I will tell him what needs to be told, regardless of your wishes." I continued, turning toward my mother.

I was ready to burst into tears. Kevin stood and opened the door for me. "Go. Talk to your dad."

I whirled around, ready to tell him off, too, but when I saw his expression, I just walked out the door. Empowered by the fight with Patrick, I marched down the hallway, using all my anger to propel me through the unit and into his room. A nurse stood beside his bed. She held a bloody rag in one hand. She stepped back when she noticed me.

I moved to the bed and stared at my father's waxy complexion. The dry rattle in his chest scared me, and the hair on the back of my neck rose. I shivered and took a deep breath. The nurse left, and I sat in the chair next to the bed.

I don't know where the words came from or how they came out, but in those next few minutes, I emptied the bitterness and rage I had harbored and offered love, acceptance, and forgiveness for all that had transpired between us. I even told him I didn't want him to die, which surprised me because that had often been my wish on my darker days.

When I had said my piece, I sat for a few minutes, expecting something. I think I hoped he would sit up and tell me he loved me, that he was sorry, that he wished he'd made an effort all those years ago to make peace with me. As I noticed the blood flowing from his nose, I looked around, found a box of tissues, and wiped it away.

"Goodbye, Dad," I said, kissing his forehead. Then, I left the room to let my mother say goodbye.

The rest of the night was a blur. Fatigued, I sent Kevin home, telling him I'd call if I needed him. He left reluctantly but with some relief. Being there at the end of his life was a reminder that he didn't get this chance with his daughter.

The staff found chairs for us, and the four of us sat, two on each side, taking turns talking. We told stories of our travels and good times while waiting for something to happen. A foul smell like I'd never experienced before caused me to gag. I jumped up and left the room, gasping for breath. The others followed, except Mom, who sat there stoically. The nurses cleaned him up, changing the linens, and then we went back in.

"He's lost most of his blood." My mother said matter-of-factly. "It won't be long now."

And it wasn't. Father Flanagan arrived, taking a position near the back of the room. Twenty minutes later, my father's breathing changed. His mouth opened and closed twice. Father Flanagan moved forward and performed the last rites. When he breathed his last, it seemed surreal in the mystic of that ritual.

We sat there, watching things, almost willing Dad to take one more breath so we could have one more second with him. Dennis was the first to stand. He shoved his chair back and walked out of the room without a word. I followed him as Patrick helped Mom to her feet. There was a moment of comfort when the old priest took her hand in his, offering his condolences. There were no tears now. We were numb—at least, that's how I felt.

We left the ICU together, following Dennis down the hallway to the elevators. "Are we supposed to tell someone or sign something?" I asked.

No one answered me, so we kept walking. The elevator arrived, and we entered the car, automatically turning to face the doors. The ride down was quick, and soon, we walked across the main lobby, past the closed gift shop, and into the half-lit cafeteria. Out the main doors, the chilly night air slapped at us. We shrugged deeper into our coats and walked toward the parkade.

Patrick helped Mom into the front seat while Dennis and I climbed into the back. On the road, I looked out the window at the winter wonderland. I noted the houses we passed, wondering if the people inside were laughing and enjoying the season. Christmas lights twinkled in many homes and trees. It was a magical time of year but did not bring me joy tonight.

A hand touched mine. I looked over. Dennis sat there, his eyes swimming in tears, and my heart broke anew. I took his hand and squeezed it hard. Then I undid my seat belt and scooted across the car to cuddle up to him. We shared our sorrow until Patrick pulled up in front of Kevin's house. I was reluctant to leave. I wanted so much to take back all the years I had spent with my back to my family.

Dennis and I had been close once upon a time. Now, I didn't even know him, but I loved him. I had spent years trying to forget I had a family, and now I wanted to embrace them, even prickly Patrick.

I leaned up between the seats and kissed Mom on the cheek, and then spontaneously, I kissed Patrick, too. After one last squeeze with Dennis, I slipped out of the car and ran up the steps to the front door.

Kevin opened the door as I arrived. He waved to my family as they backed out of the driveway and ushered me inside.

Closing the door, he wrapped me in his arms and held me as he whispered his sympathies. My emotions welled up, and I sobbed. It wasn't just for Dad, though. I cried because I had been a fool, allowing my fears—and the sorrows of a little girl to dictate my life. In some strange way, I believed I was saving myself from the pain of entanglement and involvement by staying aloof and entering only into superficial relationships that kept me safe. My heart was full of regrets because now I clearly saw that I had spent those years in the wilderness, frightened and alone. Missing out on the love and support of family, the loving that comes from interaction and understanding, was bad enough. But I had missed out on life.

I hadn't even made any friends. Not real friends—not confidants. I had friendly acquaintances and casual strangers. In two short months, I lost two important people. I would never get another chance to know either. And that utterly broke my heart.

A hot bath, followed by a hot cup of tea, and I was ready for bed. I didn't even know what time it was. I had lost all track of the days, even. Kevin pulled the covers up over me, and I took his hand.

"Stay."

He sat on the side of the bed and stroked my forehead. I snuggled under the covers and drifted off.

The room was light when I woke up. I did not know how long I'd been there. Laying there, listening to the sounds, I made out the mechanical tones of a television or radio, but it was far off. There were no other sounds in the house. I would have stayed there cocooned forever, but my bladder demanded relief, so I slipped out of bed.

After brushing my teeth and hair, I wandered down the hall to the kitchen. Kevin was sitting at the dining room table with a stack of papers and a laptop computer. The kitchen radio was providing background noise. "What are you doing?"

"I'm just doing some of the paperwork. My accountant does most of the bookkeeping, but Andrea used to do most of the data entries to keep costs down. I just realized that no one has done anything since October, and maybe some of my suppliers are looking for payments." He chuckled without mirth.

"Maybe I could help," I offered. "The computer is a little foreign to me, but I could learn."

"Thanks, but I think you are handling a lot at the moment. Your mom will need you, and you've just started a new job. I also don't want to lose any momentum between us by having you do paperwork. I can do it while you're with your mom, and then our time will be our time."

I walked over to him and laid my arm across his shoulders. He pushed his chair back from the table, allowing me to sit on his lap. He nuzzled my neck.

"How are you doing?" he whispered in my ear.

"I'd be a lot better if you'd come to bed with me."

"But it's eleven o'clock in the morning." He protested with a laugh.

"Is it really?" I turned toward him—my body alive. He pulled me close, kissing me lightly, then pushing a little deeper.

I pulled away, stood, and sauntered to the doorway. Then I turned back and wiggled my finger, gesturing for him to follow me. When he stood, I shrieked and ran down the hall. He cut me off at the kitchen door, catching me around the waist. I laughed as I pulled away, leading him down to the bedroom. I climbed onto the bed, shedding my nightgown in one swift motion. Kevin sucked in his breath before capturing my lips with a growl.

Later, as I lay snuggled against his chest, I wondered if I had any right to be so happy, considering everything. My mother was devastated. My brothers were struggling, and here I was, feeling something akin to joy, even though I, too, had lost much in the last year.

I sighed, nestled closer, and slept.

CHAPTER SIXTY

The next few days passed in a blur. We gathered at Mom's house, where neighbors and friends popped by with food and condolences. It was surprising to see that though the faces of some neighbors had aged—they were still recognizable.

I also spent time with Dennis. At first, he seemed a little lost, but as the ceremony approached, he appeared to be standing taller. It was like watching a little boy grow up overnight. He told me he was going to quit smoking in the new year. "It's time to man up," he told Kevin.

Patrick was there, helping Mom and taking care of us as usual. I watched him and wondered if he would break or, more importantly, *when* he would break. Was there a real man behind that mask of self-assured confidence? I never saw him falter, though, taking everything in hand and handing out instructions like a drill sergeant.

The funeral took place on the afternoon of New Year's Eve. There were about forty people there, mostly couples Mom and Dad knew from the old days. After the service, Mom spent all her time shaking hands with old neighbors and old friends. By the time the hall was clearing, she looked worn out. Patrick to the rescue. He swooped in on his white horse and took her home to his house. He said he didn't want her to stay by herself.

Kevin and I went home. Life would never be the same, and the uncertainty of what the future held seemed daunting. Kevin chose a beer as I made tea. I needed something hot and soothing. Neither of us spoke for quite a few minutes. I was trying to get my thoughts together, and I hoped Kevin wouldn't turn on the television before I arrived. He didn't. When I looked over, he, too, was lost in thought.

"What are you thinking?"

"I was thinking about how much has changed in the last few months and how I am really missing Andrea." I looked into his teary eyes.

"Oh, Kevin." Putting down my mug, I moved over to him. I sat on his lap and wrapped my arms around him, holding him tight.

"I don't think I would have made it without you, you know."

Leaning back, I stared deeply into his eyes. "I don't think you're giving yourself enough credit. You are much stronger than you realize."

"Actually, Barbara, I'm much weaker than you realize."

"How so?"

"Remember that night I came over to your apartment, and we went for that walk?" I nodded. "Well, I came over because if I had spent one more minute alone, I was going to kill myself."

His words sent shock waves down my spine. "You mean figuratively?"

"No, literally. There was nothing to live for. I was going to end it."

"So, what stopped you? As I remember, I wasn't particularly nice to you. In fact, you walked away from me."

"Yes, I did. That was when I realized I had been living for you and Andrea and that needed to learn to live for myself. I don't know exactly how to say that, but I understood I was as important as you were. Or even Andrea, for that matter. I counted. And when I realized I didn't want to end it all, I wanted to learn how to live."

"I'm sorry you felt that way, and I'm glad you're still here. I don't know if I'd have gotten through all this without you. You have been my strength through it all."

"But that's just it, Barbara. You are strong enough for both of us. You are the strongest person I know."

I thought about his words as they echoed through me. Was I strong? I guess sometimes I had to be. I lived with an alcoholic father, and I survived. But I ran away from the two people I loved most in the world because I was afraid to face my fears. That wasn't strength, that was cowardice. My life choices continued to put me in unkind situations, to say the least.

A husband who drank, another who abused me emotionally, and a boyfriend who was a lecher. And then there was Bobby Graham. What was he? The worst of the lot because he pretended to be more than he was. He accumulated women like some men accumulated cars. He would have been the worst thing I'd ever done, but fates or whatever conspired to take me in a different direction. I found my way home, though I'm not sure I deserved to be here. I was grateful that I was.

I kissed Kevin on the lips. "Thank you for the compliment." I didn't bother to tell him he was wrong. He saw me as he liked, and I would endeavor to live up to his opinion.

He kissed me back, and soon, we were shedding our clothes and forgetting that death had come knocking on our door.

At midnight, he leaned over me as the digital alarm flipped over. "Happy New Year, Barbara. I hope it's the best one yet. We deserve a little happiness."

I showed him just how happy he would be.

CHAPTER SIXTY-ONE

The weather in January turned colder, and the little dress shop was in a lull. Stella continued to train me, and I learned a lot during this time. You would think that a little retail outfit would be simple to run, but the devil was in the details, as Stella loved to remind me. Everything meant something. The displays sold outfits—the store layout drew people in past the new lines to the sale items in the back. It was conceptual and concise. The ordering process was a little harder to understand.

Stella recently pooled her resources with several other independent dress shops to form a consortium, which maximized their buying power. The group demanded a lot of attention in the weeks leading up to the launch of the new season. She disappeared for days on end, leaving me to my own devices.

I arrived home each night dead on my feet. Whether we had a good or slow day, I was exhausted. I figured my emotional rollercoaster had taken its toll, and I was just getting caught up. In mid-January, Kevin suggested we tackle Andrea's possessions. He said leaving her things in boxes was disrespectful and that we should go through them, keeping some things and donating or tossing what was useless to anyone.

I was reluctant to assist, as I didn't think I had the right to make those decisions. But I put on a sweatshirt and jeans and mucked in.

Her clothes were typical—jeans, blouses, T-shirts, undergarments. Kevin pulled out a worn T-shirt and hugged it to his chest. Tears ran down his cheeks. I sat back and waited. With emotions gripping his throat, he turned the shirt around and showed me the emblem: "The Red-Hot Chili Peppers."

"I took Andrea to this concert. She was twelve. It was her first concert." He sucked in a deep, ragged breath. "She was so excited she barely slept the night before. She was so grown up that night like she'd done this a hundred times before. I bought this T-shirt for her, and she insisted I get it two sizes larger than she wore so she would have it for years. She wore it for pajamas. I can still see her standing in the kitchen with the shirt falling off one shoulder because it was too big. She grew into it and eventually stopped wearing it. I thought it had gone to the charity shop years ago." He hugged the shirt to his chest again.

"Then, that one is for the keep pile."

Kevin nodded. "For now."

I found a large journal in one box. I pulled it out and rifled through the pages. It was Andrea's journal, which was relatively new because of the number of empty pages. I turned to the first page. The date was nine days before her death.

"What have you got there?" Kevin asked, reaching for the book.

I handed it to him without a word. He flipped it open and read. Tears filled his eyes, and he closed the cover. He handed the book to me. "I can't read this right now, but I think you should. It's her very private world. It might help us understand where she was."

I nodded and set the book beside me. We continued through the boxes, keeping only those mementos that were precious. Most of the clothes went into a box for the thrift store, and some went into a bag for rags. Kevin explained that T-shirts made the best rags for removing stains, as there was no lint.

The boxes were emptied and repacked, and Kevin moved them to his truck. He would dump the trash into his dumpster behind the shop and take the clothes and other items to the thrift store. I changed and went to pick up Mom. She was back home, having had to tell Patrick she wasn't an invalid. I had helped her to clean out the room where Dad had been. She decided to sell the house and move into a senior's condo. With her eyesight failing, she felt it was best to be where she wouldn't truly be alone. Patrick and Dennis agreed to help her financially if she needed it because those places weren't cheap.

Today, Mom and I were having one of our weekly coffee dates. We usually did them on Friday nights, but last night, she was going to a birthday party for a neighbor, so we opted to go this afternoon. We always went to Jake's because we loved their desserts, though I confess I didn't always indulge my sweet tooth.

That night, as Kevin watched a football game with Matt, I curled up with Andrea's journal. There were only nine entries, the last one being the afternoon before she died. I took a hot cup of tea with me and sat down to listen to what she had on her mind.

October 19th

In the brief span of ten months, my relationship with Caleb has risen, soared, and, little by little, lost its brilliance. Like tarnished fool's gold, green with envy, and it no longer gives me joy. Actually, if I think about it hard enough, the joy was short-lived, but the hope took a little longer to go. I held on even after the signs showed me that Caleb wasn't the man I thought he was because I hoped my love and faith in him would be enough to change him. Brenda would remind me that people don't change and that I should leave all too often, and it threatened at times to destroy our friendship. I was stubborn in my resolve to make this work. Watching my mother go through so many relationships over the years, I vowed not to be like her. I thought she was weak and unwilling to fight for love. Now I see she was much better at looking after her own needs than I will ever be. I need to learn to be more like her, and maybe once things settle down, I will call her and get to know her better. If she wants to, that is. I'll talk to Dad about that because I don't want to get in her way or be a burden to her.

I still don't understand why she left us all those years ago. I needed a mom. I wanted a mom, and I guess that's why I befriended so many of my friends' mothers. And don't forget Mrs. Horowitz. She was old enough to be my grandmother, but she was the best thing that happened to me. I know she loved me, and I loved her. It was hard when she died.

I had a talk with Brenda this morning, and on the 26th, she will borrow her dad's truck, and we'll move me out. I know Dad will be mad because I am not moving home. But moving home would prove that I couldn't leave the nest properly. I'll be just like everyone else, running home to the folks when life gets a little hard. I hope he understands. Brenda says I can stay rent-free with her for a few months until I figure out what I am doing. She is such a great friend, standing beside me through this. I just have to pretend everything is okay. I will write in my other journal now, the one Caleb checks, though he doesn't know I know. It was a real eye-opener when I found out a month ago that he was reading my journals, trying to catch me out. I thought he respected my privacy. I am a total loser.

Setting the journal on my lap, I wiped the tears from my eyes. It was a bittersweet read. She was brave, but I saw she was afraid, though she didn't actually say that. Maybe I was projecting the fear I experienced with Ron, my third husband. The terror of an unstable man, a charmer who, until the day we were married, never put a foot wrong.

CHAPTER SIXTY-TWO

No one realized what I went through in those last days with Ron. He had become increasingly paranoid in the last year of our marriage. I made excuses for his behavior, just as many other women in the same situation do. I couldn't imagine that I had married another monster. My second husband, Lenny, had been charming, too. He was also fun-loving and decent until he hit the bottle hard. Then, he was just like my dad: angry and verbally abusive. I put up with his behavior longer because he didn't drink often, not at first. We were married for four years, and I left him when it became apparent that he was headed down that path. I would not be my mother.

Oh, he begged me to come home, promising me the world and then hurling insults when I refused to budge. He didn't contest the divorce, though, and married again a month after the decree was final. I heard he moved to Calgary, which suited me. I hoped they were happy together.

Ron was much older, and I thought that would give me some stability. He was a big man, tall and broad. He was so much fun in the beginning. Having the money to do things, he thought nothing about booking a weekend away here or there. Oh, he wasn't Bobby-Graham rich, but he always had a pocket full of bills and was generous to a fault. I think that's why I fell in *like* with him. I don't know if I ever loved him. He was fun, and his money took me to places I'd never been—Vancouver, Disneyland, San Francisco, Las Vegas, Palm Beach.

I remember the first time he took me to Vegas. What a weekend that was. I had never seen so many lights, and the energy of that place was addictive. Even at three in the morning, gamblers filled the rooms, each trying his luck somewhere. Slots chimed and whirred non-stop.

The second time we went to Vegas, we married on a lark, which was something different to do. An Elvis impersonator performed the ceremony. It was so surreal that I honestly wasn't sure we were officially married. But we were. I gave up my tiny apartment and moved into his sprawling ranch-style home in the swanky neighborhood called "The Pines." It wasn't a gated community; it wasn't exclusive, but it was posh. The houses were large, and the yards were more substantial than the normal city developments. He made me feel like a queen at first. Ron made sure I had a new vehicle, and everything he did made me feel treasured.

In that first year, we argued about only one thing: he wanted me to quit my job so I could look after him like a proper wife. His rants grew tiresome, but they wore me down. I stopped working to make his meals and do his laundry, and—he took me out dancing or swept me off for weekends away. Life was pretty good. At first. The dancing and the weekends away dwindled to monthly. In no time, we weren't going out at all. Every night, it was supper in front of the television, watching sports. At first, I playfully tried to get Ron to take me out, but he was stubborn, claiming to be too tired.

Life became dreary. I hardly got out of bed. I stopped looking after the house as proficiently as I had been. Dust was on the shelves, and the dishes weren't always done. Laundry piled up. I was so bored. Trying to fit in with the neighborhood women—they didn't make it easy. They never made me feel like I belonged. Ron criticized me. I tried harder for a while, but my heart wasn't in it.

I begged Ron to let me go to work, assuring him I could still care for him. However, he kept insisting that I stay home, claiming that I wasn't doing a great job with only the house to care for. He didn't believe I'd do better by working, too. I tried to tell him I was unhappy and that I needed to interact with people. He wanted to know why he wasn't enough.

In the end, after weeks of arguing about it, I went against his wishes. I accepted a part-time job at the Skyview Lounge. That was the first time Ron beat me. I took my punishment like a trooper, believing I deserved it, though I refused to quit. I bought some long-sleeved dresses to cover my bruises and continued to work. The house grew colder as Ron's anger grew. He would remind me I was no longer trustworthy because I had disobeyed him. He was hot and cold, his behavior shifting erratically from day to day. I loved it when old Ron came home. He would be jovial and talkative, and I could breathe properly.

I never knew which Ron was coming through the door until I saw his face. By then, it was usually too late. I had nowhere to go, no place to hide if he stormed in angry. The last time he beat me, he came into the kitchen with a face like thunder. His eyes were mere slits as he glared at me. He stood by the kitchen island, his fingers drumming on the countertop. My heart exploded in my chest. I was terrified. He stared at me, with his fingers tapping out a message I didn't understand.

I smiled brightly, though my lips quivered in fear. I greeted him with a warm hello, doing my best to pretend I wasn't aware of his mood. He didn't stop drumming those fingers. I panted as fear sat on my chest, restricting my lungs. My heart was jumping, the blood coursing through my veins so quickly that I broke into a sweat. My cheeks bloomed a nice flush like I'd just been outside. I slipped the knife I was using to chop onions for supper into the drawer in front of me. Out of sight, out of mind, I hoped. My hands shook as I moved to the sink to wash them. The drumming continued, louder and a little faster.

I turned around to grab a towel to dry my hands. Ron stepped up behind me, wrapping his arms around me and pinning my hands at my sides. He leaned down and whispered the lie he'd heard in my ear.

"I hear you've been putting yourself about?" His voice was soothing, though his words sounded sharp.

I shook my head. "No, Ron. I haven't. Honest."

"Honest? You don't know the meaning of the word." He laughed, again his tone belying his intentions.

I stood still. I knew better than to make him understand. My pleading only escalated his anger. "Got nothing to say for yourself, do you? I knew you were a whore. I knew it as surely as I know the sun rises. Two-bit trash that climbed out of the gutter to pose as a lady." He squeezed me a little tighter. I could no longer catch my breath. I gulped for air.

"Ron, please," I begged. "Don't do this. I love you."

"Do you? Do you really? Or do you just love my money?"

"I'd love you if you were penniless. You're fun to be with. You make me smile and laugh—you make me happy."

He released me and turned me around so I could face him. "So, you're telling me that when I heard you were having a drink at the Blue Cat Lounge with Monty, that person was lying? Look me in the eyes and tell me they were lying. You don't even drink, so tell me what you were doing there."

I couldn't look him in the eyes. I had been there. That was the place I went to when I was looking for someone to play with. I was bored. I needed somebody to remind me I was a woman. Ron hadn't touched me in weeks. Then Monty Parsons, Ron's second in command, came in, and I realized he would tell Ron, so I abandoned my plan. Ordering one more Virgin Mary, I sat with him and left when my drink was empty.

Tears running freely down my cheeks, I raised my eyes to look at Ron. "I was there, Ron. But nothing happened."

The slap across my face sent me reeling back into the cabinets behind me. I stumbled over my feet and hit the floor. Ron took hold of my hair and hauled me to my feet. I swatted at him, cursing him, but I never made contact. His arms were longer than mine. He pulled me into another hold, one hand still holding my hair. I was once more pinned to his body. He pulled my hair, forcing my head back so I could look into his face.

I don't know why I ever thought he was handsome. His beefy face was mottled in anger, his cheeks had broken capillaries, and his eyes were cruel and barbaric. My stomach contracted, and I gagged.

"Nothing happened, eh? Only because Monty came in. Otherwise, you'd have spread your legs for some bastard without giving me one shred of consideration. You are my wife, but you act like a bitch in heat. You disgust me." He pushed me away from him. I fell against the counter, my shoulders heaving as sobs racked my body.

"I won't stand for this behavior, Barbie. You will do well to remember this warning. Do it again, and I will see you on the street where you belong."

He turned and left. I heard the front door open and slam closed behind him. Sinking to the floor—all my energy gone—I sobbed until there was nothing left. Then, I planned my escape. Staying with Ron was no longer possible. I didn't love him, and I never had. The next time he came home like this, he might kill me. I needed a place to stay and a good job, and in the meantime, I would walk that fine line to keep from being battered.

It turns out that it didn't matter. Ron had a massive heart attack a week later. He might have survived it, but he was driving. A semi-truck broadsided him when he went through a red light. The paramedics pronounced him dead at the scene.

Just like that, I was free, and I suddenly thought about all the money Ron had and how it would be mine. Fate wasn't smiling at me, though. Ron was deeply in debt. His business hadn't been doing well—he'd made some terrible investments. The setback should have slowed his spending, but he continued living like he always had and racked up enormous debt.

He also lapsed on the life insurance policies, failing to pay the premiums. It was a mess. I sold the business to cover the debts and legal fees involved. Then, I sold the house and paid off all the mortgages. I walked away from the experience with a few expensive jewels, a handful of designer dresses, and enough cash for a security deposit on a new apartment. Then, I went to work full-time.

I vowed never to get married again. No man would control me or demand that I be what he wanted me to be. I was going to live my life for myself. I had married for love, fun, and security. All three of them had ended. Lenny turned out to be a drunk, just like my dad. Ron was abusive, and Kevin—well, I still loved Kevin.

Changing my name back to O'Shea was an effort to put that horrible chapter behind me. I didn't want to think of Ron every time I signed my name. I wanted to wipe away his memory, the abuse he meted out, and my complicit allowance of it. Why didn't I leave the first time he hit me? Just like my daughter, I stayed because I thought I could change things. I could make things better.

I stayed, and only fate intervened to protect me from Ron. If he hadn't died, he might very well have done something to me that would have ended my life. I wasn't special; I was lucky. Sitting on that chair in the bedroom, I wept for Andrea, who wasn't as fortunate as I was. She didn't deserve what happened to her any more than I did. She paid the ultimate price for her willingness to believe she was stronger than the anger directed at her.

It was an anger that stemmed from a fear and self-loathing that began the first time these men found themselves in a situation they couldn't control. They used this power to intimidate and control the people in their lives, hoping to make them draw closer. They never understood that it was the worst thing they could do. Fear and anger don't draw people to you; it drives them away. It had the opposite outcome, which sparked anger, fear, and more drastic outbursts intent on changing the situation. A vicious circle that usually ended badly.

Unable to read anymore, I set the journal aside. I stripped off my clothes, took a hot shower, and climbed into bed. I didn't hear Kevin come in but found great comfort in feeling him beside me when I rose to near consciousness during the night. I snuggled closer to him and went back to sleep, thankful that I had come full circle.

CHAPTER SIXTY-THREE

It was several days later before I had the time and the inclination to open Andrea's journal again. This time, Kevin was going to be late coming home. He had to deliver some finished pieces to a customer who lived in Grandville. He rarely delivered, expecting his customers to collect their pieces at the shop, but this was someone special.

Mrs. Murphy was an antique hunter. She had been building a collection of fine pieces for forty years. She was one of Kevin's first customers when he started up, and she continued to use him, bringing at least three or four pieces to him every year since. Some she kept—some she sold to other collectors. She recently lost her husband, and Kevin agreed to deliver this latest piece to her until she could make other arrangements.

I ate quickly and then curled up on the couch to read.

October 20th

I went to see Dad today. What a mistake that was. He was such a jerk. Of course, he was angry that I was still with Caleb, given what was going on, but my promise to leave by the weekend fell on deaf ears. He wanted to go over and clean Caleb's clock and teach him a few home truths about how to treat a woman. Good grief - cave dweller behavior.

Why do men have to act like that? I tried to tell him that how he was acting was just like Caleb acts, but he couldn't see the correlation. He was protecting me. Caleb was abusing me. Idiot! Doesn't he understand that forcing me to do anything against my wishes is abuse? What would locking me in my room achieve? Nothing!! That's what.

* * * *

I've had time to calm down, and I'm not mad at Dad anymore. Brenda and I had a long talk while Caleb was at work. She helped me to see that he's just scared for me. He shouldn't be. I can take care of myself, and I'm treading on eggshells until Caleb goes away on Thursday night on that astronomy course trip. It was a once-in-a-lifetime opportunity to go to the Calgary Observatory to see some comets, but I forgot which one. He wanted me to go with him, but I told him I had to work. He had a meltdown, and if I hadn't promised to stay away from Brenda, he would have bailed. I told him I would redecorate the living room, something we'd been talking about for a while. I even showed him some material swatches for a new slipcover I would sew. He seems content that I would be fine in his absence.

So, four more days, and then after Caleb leaves on the bus ...

I have to write in my other diary now. The one Caleb sees. He doesn't know that I know he reads my diaries. I know I am being dishonest, but I can't trust him with my private thoughts anymore.

Setting the book aside, I pondered her words. These journals allowed me to get to know Andrea a little. She was resourceful and had a plan, so what went wrong? Would the next entries tell me what I needed to know? Would they tell me why she ended up in a vehicle on a country road with the person she was leaving? I went back to the journal.

October 21st

Brenda is certain that Caleb will come looking for me on Friday night. So, we are going to spend the weekend at her parents' place in Grandville. I'm looking forward to it. I like her parents. And her sister Linda is a card. She'll have us laughing in no time, and her brother won't be there, thank God. He's in the States somewhere at a rodeo college.

I think Brenda always harbored a secret yearning that I would marry her brother. I like him, but I'm not sure we're meant for each other. He is rodeo through and through, and I've never even attended one. Brenda thinks we should go to some this year. Deep sigh. So much change.

Brenda has asked her friend Mark and his friend Todd to help on Friday. Todd has a truck, so we can move everything in one trip instead of squeezing everything into Brenda's car. She couldn't get her dad's truck. If Dad hadn't been so insistent on me moving back home, I would have asked him if I could use his truck. I need to call Dad and let him know I'm not mad. Maybe I'll see him next week. I hate it when we are at odds with each other.

October 22nd

I am on pins and needles here. It is much harder playing the game than I thought. Caleb can't suspect anything, so being too happy—or being too sad are both wrong. I need to be normal, but inside, I feel like I've swallowed a bag of jumping beans. There are no settled feelings inside. I can't eat without feeling like I'm going to throw up. God, this week is dragging!!!!!!

Okay, I've told no one at work what my plans are. I'm even scheduled to work because sometimes Caleb calls to check up on me. I don't want anyone to reveal my secret accidentally or gossip about me where Caleb can overhear. They, above all, must be normal, too. Brenda is the only one who knows. Of course, Mark and Todd know, too, but Caleb has never met either of them. They are Brenda's friends from college. I've only met them twice myself.

I wish I could go to college this term. I can't tell Caleb it was not about the money but about needing space. He was constantly checking up on me and getting angry with me if I was talking to anyone he didn't know, and especially angry when there was a guy in the group. I didn't want to deal with that again, so I faked financial difficulties. Of course, since he checks up on everything, he isn't aware that the account with my college fund doesn't have a bank card. I have to go to the bank to withdraw funds. Looking at my bank balance and seeing how meager my savings are, he's content to believe me.

I don't even know if I can go back in January as planned. Brenda and I have talked about this. She thinks Caleb will be a problem if we are in classes together. I'm hoping he'll get over it and leave me alone. My stomach is on Brenda's side, but it could be just nerves. This is an unpleasant situation to be in. I wish I'd been smarter, like how my mom ditched that loser last Christmas. She just walked away at the first sign of trouble. I should have done that when he was playing head games in the beginning. Instead, I fell for his passive/aggressive routine. I got sucked right into his world without knowing I was in danger. How stupid am I????

OK - Brenda would pitch a fit if she read this. She's always telling me I'm too hard on myself and that I don't believe in myself enough. Maybe that's true. She says it's because my mom left. She says I have "abandonment" issues. Brenda is already practicing with me. She's going to be a brilliant psychologist one day. She says I'm an excellent candidate for study. Sometimes that pisses me off - that she's analyzing me all the time. She says she isn't, but I'm sure she is. I guess if it really bothered me, I'd be on Caleb's side, and Brenda would be history and, therefore, no longer a threat to him. Maybe if she wasn't part of my life, Caleb and I would be happy.

Nope, he wouldn't. There'd be somebody else. There would always be somebody else. Someone who talked to me or looked at me or whatever. He's so jealous. Brenda thinks he has family issues. I know he and his dad have a tense relationship, but his mom is lovely. She made me feel right at home when I met his family. And she came to the apartment, too. I really liked her.

Well, time to update my other journal. What should I say today? That I am not looking forward to Caleb being gone? Would that make him stay? I know. I'll add something about how I couldn't ask him to stay, that he would regret this once-in-a-lifetime opportunity if he stayed behind. That should seal it. Until tomorrow.

I set the journal on my lap. I was feeling her fear. She was playing a game with her life. A trickle of fear ran down my spine. I knew the ending of the story—yet reading these pages seemed like maybe she would change the outcome. Not knowing anything about Caleb before these journals, her description of him proved he was a disturbed young man.

"But he had a lovely mother." Andrea's words echoed inside my head. I wondered what she was like and what she endured when she heard the news.

Was she devastated for Kevin and me, or was she just sorry for herself? Was she as lovely as Andrea suggested?

I remember trying to call them right after Andrea had died. There was no voicemail, and no one answered back then. I grabbed the phone book and looked up the city of Freyden and then Joe Bradshaw. Joe and Joan. I dialed that number.

Again, like it had months ago, the phone rang and rang. I hoped this time it would go to voicemail. Everybody had voicemail these days. But they didn't. That was frustrating. How was I going to give this woman a piece of my mind or find out what she thought about the grief her son had caused if I couldn't talk to her? I put the phone book back in the drawer and went back to the journal.

CHAPTER SIXTY-FOUR

October 24th

I think Caleb is suspicious. He's been acting weird. When he came home from school on Tuesday, he started hovering—I hate when he hovers. He thinks he's being protective. It's sickening. He didn't go to school yesterday. It was my day off, and he said that since he was going away, he wanted to spend the day with me. I had so much to do and couldn't do any of it. Instead, I had to play happy family with Caleb. Thankfully, during a brief private moment in the bathroom, I texted Brenda to tell her. Then, I deleted the thread. God, I hate having to do this stuff. I hate that I didn't get to vent here yesterday, but I wrote in my other journal.

Caleb was attentive. Back in the spring, when he was like this, I was beside myself with joy. I thought his attentions were signs of his love and affection. Now, I see them as signs of his control and manipulation. I'm supposed to feel so loved, yet I feel more like a caged bird, unable to take wing and no longer willing to sing. But sing I must, or I shall die.

I think I'll use that when I get back to school. I think that would make a good analogy for a story or whatever. Maybe I should start writing a book. What kind of book would I write? Most of my writing is personal. The classes in journalism don't really allow us to write too much fiction. They want us to write current events or human-interest stories. I like it, but I'm not sure I want to confine myself to the facts. Ha ha. I think I would like to expand or explore other forms of writing. Hey, maybe I should go for an English degree. I'll talk to Dad about that next week and maybe see a counselor at the university. Oooh. Now, I am getting excited. The future is a ripe berry, ready to be picked. I just need to reach out and take it.

I'd better get a move on. I have things to do. Caleb needs clean laundry before I leave. (I know - I know - I can hear Brenda cursing from here!)

October 25th

At eight o'clock, I saw Caleb off. About twenty other guys and girls were heading to Calgary on this trip to the observatory. Crawford had a strong astronomy club, which is one reason they invited the Crawford group to this event. This comet thing is apparently a big deal, and Caleb is very excited about seeing it. I told him to text me photos so I could be part of it with him.

I was very demonstrative at the bus, too, when I said goodbye. Partly, I was acting because I needed him to leave, and part of me is sad that when he gets back, we will no longer be a couple. I feel like a coward for not facing him directly. But I know he'd go ballistic, and I'd rather not end up in the emergency ward, which is where I'll have to go after he beat the shit out of me. He's come close too many times with no provocation. Consider the potential actions he would take if he reached his breaking point.

Frankly, it scares me. This is the only way it could have gone. But I cried when we hugged that last time. He was all concerned, and I just told him—no—you have to go. He seemed a little more assured when I told him I would miss him. I even promised a proper reunion when he returned. Reminding him I couldn't stand in the way of this opportunity for him, regardless of how much I'd miss him. Besides, I told him again—I had planned to make those slipcovers, and he would find it boring to watch. He seemed reassured. I stood on the curb waving until the bus rounded the corner and disappeared from sight. Then, I stood there for five more minutes to make sure.

I drove his car home, half expecting to see him waiting on the doorstep, but he wasn't there, and the band around my chest loosened. I packed. My nerves were on edge. Every sound made me jump. Every time someone came down the hallway, I tensed, expectant. Brenda came after school with Mark and Todd. We loaded everything into Todd's truck. There wasn't much, but there was more than I thought there would be.

When the last box was gone, I set my keys on the

counter. I thought about leaving the fake journal behind with a last entry. I even wrote it, but in the end, I took it with me. Maybe Brenda and I will burn it in the fireplace at her parents' house this weekend.

I am now partly settled in my room at Brenda's. She usually has a couple of renters sharing her townhouse, but this fall, she didn't even advertise for one. I think she hoped I'd need the space. She doesn't need the money, anyway. Her dad bought the place for her when she went to school. Of course, Linda will start using it next year when she starts college. I think I would like that - if I'm still here, that is. It's a year away, and anything can happen.

I rose and stretched my legs, making another cup of tea. While I waited for the kettle to boil, I thought about that day, the day she bade a tearful goodbye to a boy who didn't deserve her. I wondered, not for the first time, what had happened to this person to make him so controlling. He wasn't that old—what—twenty years old? What kind of upbringing did he have? Or was he born a monster? How many other girls had he abused before he found my Andrea? Why had no one seen the signs and done something before it went this far?

Again, I wanted to yell and scream at his parents. I wanted answers. Answers I wasn't sure I would ever get, and even if I did, would I like what I heard? Would they tell me he'd been cruel all his life? That even they were afraid of him. Did he have a police record? I never even bothered to wonder about that before. Did he? What did Kevin know about him? I needed to ask.

With a fresh cup of tea, I returned to the book. Kevin would be another hour. I longed for him to be here, even if he was puttering in the basement workshop. I wanted his forceful presence to warm the house that had grown cold with our daughter's last words.

October 26th

Brenda and I got up early and headed to Grandville. Mrs. Taylor was in her kitchen baking up a storm. She sang gospel songs at the top of her lungs when we entered the kitchen. I don't know if I've ever known anyone so happy - all the time. She praises the Lord nonstop, giving him credit for everything, including us coming for the weekend. If she weren't so completely sincere, I would think she was off her nut. Brenda warned me we would go to church with her on Sunday. It was a concession that Brenda allowed her mom. I don't think Brenda believes in God - at least not like her mother did.

When Linda returned home from school, the three of us went to the basement. We played Mario Kart for a little while, then went upstairs to help Mrs. Taylor put supper on the table. That night, the table was lively, with laughter and joshing.

I watched Mr. Taylor at supper. For a big guy, he's not very intrusive. He is just sort of there, holding his girls together. That's how I see him—the container that keeps his family from spilling out into the world.

We went to the local bar for a while. I think Mrs. Taylor would have been happier if we'd gone to the youth group with Linda, but she didn't press the issue.

A few local boys were sniffing around the table. Brenda put them all in their place, though. She was protective of me, and I hoped it was a short-lived protection because I sure didn't want to have her as a gatekeeper to my heart forever. But for now, it was good that she was running interference.

We didn't stay late. The stress of the week exhausted me. We were home and in bed long before Linda got out of the youth group. As I lay in bed, I thought about Caleb. Had I done the right thing? I don't mean leaving him. That was a straightforward decision, but I had gone off the grid. When we arrived in Grandville, I turned off my phone after blocking Caleb on every social media site. He was going to be angry, and I didn't want to read the ugly things he would say about me. I'd heard them often enough.

Just before midnight, I needed to know. I turned my phone on. One hundred and twenty-seven missed calls and fifty-seven voicemail messages. The text messages numbered two hundred, but that was the limit of allowable messages per conversation on my phone. The messages were less than an hour old. Caleb had gone ballistic. Brenda climbed out of bed and confiscated my phone. I had already read the first couple of messages. They were horrible.

She asked me why I hadn't blocked his number. I shrugged, unable to give her an answer. She then blocked his number, explaining to me it would do no good to read the messages. She didn't delete them, though, stating they would be evidence when we pressed charges for harassment. Reading the messages herself, she grew angry—I demanded she take a deep breath and calm down. She was pacing the floor between our beds, shaking her head—muttering and cursing. If I hadn't been so freaked out, I might have laughed.

I had a bad feeling in the pit of my stomach. This was a dangerous situation, and I had just lit the fuse on a stack of dynamite. This was going to get uglier before it got better. I've put my head down and turned off the light eight times since I checked the phone, but I cannot seem to sleep. Maybe writing this down will help me find the peace I need. Now, I'm going to try again.

I put the book aside. My earlier fear intensified. This entry made every hair on my head stand on end. She knew in her heart-of-hearts that she had started something she wasn't capable of handling. The impression her journal gave was she was in danger. So why did she come back to Crawford? Why didn't she go to the police?

Silly question. I knew why. We never think we're in danger— we think we're overreacting. We cannot fathom that another human being would ever be so dangerous. I cried as I thought about how scared she must have been, how uncertain this place was for her. She should have been home with her family. She should have been safe from this type of tyranny. Every woman should be free of fear. Why the hell did men think they could act this way and get away with it? Because the deterrents weren't stringent enough.

I had been in a few situations that exposed me to the dangerous side of a man's aggression. But I had never felt my life was in danger. Bodily harm, yes, but death, no. I did nothing to prevent it from happening to me again in the future. I tried to pacify my abuser. How insane is it to think that we can control men who cannot control themselves?

I stood and paced the floor. I was angry now, angry that the world wasn't a safe place for everyone. We claim to be a civilized society, yet this troglodyte mentality still exists. What was that saying—evil lives when good men do nothing? Something like that. And that's what we did. Kevin should have shoved Andrea's protests aside and given that young man a good whooping. I shook my head. Yes, and Kevin would have ended up in jail because men like Caleb—regardless of age—would cry foul. The victims suffer repeated victimization.

Civilized society, indeed!

There were two more journal entries. I wanted to read them, to finish the story before Kevin returned. Then I would ask him to read them, knowing he would feel as outraged as I was.

I picked up where I left off.

CHAPTER SIXTY-FIVE

October 27th

Brenda let me sleep in. We had no formal plans for the day, just to be away from Crawford. We will have to go back tomorrow. Brenda has school on Monday, and I need to get back to work. My boss was more than generous in giving me this time off on such short notice, but I also needed the money, so even if I wasn't ready ...

I had begged Brenda not to share the phone messages with anyone, but she struggled with her promise. After breakfast, I told her she could tell her mom if she wanted to. She said she only wanted her mom to pray for us. I rolled my eyes when she turned away. What good was prayer going to do? I needed someone to scrub out the words that kept looping through my brain. Horrible, ugly words that I won't give a second voice to by writing them down here.

The day went slowly. I was edgy and cranky. Finally, Brenda suggested we go for a walk. "Burn off some of this energy," she said. Linda begged off, sensing that something was going on, but she was not sure exactly what or really wanted to get in the middle of it. She was a lot like her mother. She was a spiritual warrior, believing that God could do all things. Silly girl?

The wind was sharp, so we bundled up and walked around the small town. We eventually ended up at the Java Shop. The place was quiet. We ordered coffee and sat in the back at a table next to the window. Watching the cars go past on the street outside, I wished I was in one of them - a car going somewhere far away. I couldn't explain what was going on inside. Brenda would understand, but I didn't. All I knew was the numbness was as scary as dread - both feelings wrapping themselves around my heart so tight I couldn't breathe properly. I was all a-twitter - if that is a word? It was like my insides had turned to jelly—they wiggled and shook for no reason. That is the best way to describe it. Being on edge was too succinct—too clean.

I hoped the weekend would be enough time for Caleb to calm down. Not being a praying person, and having only gone to church a handful of times in my life, I was looking forward to going tomorrow. Mrs. Taylor might think she was forcing me, but if she didn't ask, I would insist we go. I was going to pray that this situation gets resolved. No more fear. Enough!!!

The next entry was the last one, the last words my daughter ever wrote. I was almost afraid to start it, knowing that when I finished, it would be over. I ran my hand lovingly over the page before I took a deep breath and read on.

October 28th

The church was different from what I expected. It wasn't quiet. The music was lively, and yet under all that vibrancy was a feeling of calmness. It was cozy, secure, and filled with peace—kind of like coming home. Tears pricked my eyes, but I didn't want to cry—not here in this place. People were looking, curious to know who I was, this stranger in their midst. They were definitely friendly enough.

The pastor preached a sermon on faith. It was actually inspiring. Made me curious about church and God. At some point, he asked people to come up to receive prayers. I wanted so badly to go, but I didn't move. Standing there, staring straight ahead, I hoped God or whoever was up there saw my heart and knew what I wanted. I didn't even know how to put it into words. My whole life seemed a jumble of thoughts and feelings that were so bent and twisted around each other that it would take a genuine miracle to unravel them.

After church, we had a lovely dinner, and then Brenda and I headed back to the city. Sitting at her place, we were trying to decide what to do with our evening. Brenda had some homework, and I just wanted to get lost in some movie or something requiring little thought. Then Mark called Brenda, wanting to meet up. I didn't think going out was a good idea, but Brenda can be very convincing. So, we're going out. I'm taking a moment because she can't decide what to wear. She likes Mark and wants to look nice for him. (Eye rolls) We're such a silly bunch—us women. God, a man should bust out all the stops for us, not the other way around. Ha ha.

I remember getting all dolled up for Caleb. Where did that get me? Nowhere in the end. I think it will be a long time before I get dolled up for any man. I think maybe I'm going to go to church. That preacher made me think about things, and I'm still a little out of sorts about it all. Brenda sneered when I told her, but her upbringing in the church influenced her reaction. Linda would be happy if I told her what I was thinking. Maybe next year when she's living here, she and I can go together?

But it's only thoughts. I haven't decided, and, like Brenda said—no church is the same as another. The people and the pastor make it what it is. I'll see how I feel next week. First, I have to get my life back together to feel normal again. I'm not sure how I feel about anything anymore. The sermon may have influenced me, or perhaps it's the culmination of everything that has occurred, but I find myself in an introspective state, and life right now feels surreal - like nothing holds meaning anymore.

Tomorrow, I will go back to work, too. I feel weird about that. It's not the right thing for me anymore. Where do I fit now? I wish I had stayed at the Taylors' just a little longer—it seemed safe, so much like home—like "A" home. That reminds me, before or after work tomorrow, I'd better go see Dad and make it up. He may not understand all this—I don't know for sure either, but at least I know he loves me.

Oh - there's Brenda, finally ready to go. I'll write more about this later - about how I am feeling about things. Until then ...

That's where it ended. She sounded so lost and insecure. I wanted to reach out, wrap her in my arms, and tell her that life was unfair. I wanted to tell her it doesn't always go how you want, but you could take it two ways. Do as I did and run from your problems, or turn around and face them head-on, dig for the gold inside, and find the wealth of life that makes every day worth it.

She had no inkling that danger lurked a few hours ahead. Moving in with Brenda made her oblivious to it, thinking she had escaped it but hadn't. She hadn't even understood how much danger she was in when Caleb allegedly confronted her at the bar. Oh, I don't think she believed she was invincible, but I know she was unaware of the depth of depravity that beat in that boy's heart. He was twisted, and how he got there is something we will never know. How had he ever imagined that killing people was the answer to anything?

Again, curiosity about his parents settled in my mind. Were they like him? Were they right out of some backwoods community? Did they support and love their son, or did they fear him? Was he tyrannical? Not according to lots of Andrea's friends. He was aloof and perhaps standoffish, but no one suspected he was capable of this. It was one of life's unsolved mysteries.

I heard Kevin coming in. I set the journal aside and went to meet him. Finding my way back here was the gift that came out of this whole mess. It was a brutal wake-up call. I was certain of only two things now. Kevin and I loved each other and that life would give us no guarantees of happiness. Much of that was our responsibility to ourselves. It meant that we would have to communicate better and allow each other space to breathe should any circumstances dictate that. We needed to be honest and open, which sounded easy on the surface but wasn't always easy in practice. I was, however, up to the challenge.

CHAPTER SIXTY-SIX

I stood in front of the mirror, fussing with my hair. It's a lovely spring day. June 20th, Andrea's birthday. Kevin and I are going to go to the graveyard and place some flowers on her grave. A lot has happened since last fall, and we haven't been to the graveyard since my dad's funeral in December, and that wasn't a true visit. There wasn't time.

Kevin told me he'd been by twice with flowers. It made me feel bad that, once again—I was the parent of neglect. I was fighting hard to get past that belief.

Mom had sold the old house and moved into a senior's only building. She loves her new life—she was always doing something—and the facilitators had them doing crafts, chair exercises, and many other activities. We teased her about basket weaving, but she was actually pretty good at it and had made a couple of nice baskets that she'd donated to charity. She seemed to have blossomed a little in the past months. Her old sparkle was back. I was thrilled for her and visited at least once a week.

In the beginning, Patrick and Dennis offered to help her out financially should the need arise. I was aghast at how expensive those places were. Kevin and I could never afford to live in a place like that unless we won the lottery.

Patrick and I had made our peace. He stopped over at the house one Sunday in February, begging for forgiveness. The sermon at church had hit him hard, and he realized he had been feeling responsible for all the anger in our house. He said it was "elder child syndrome" or something like that. He wanted everybody to get along, and I was always doing things to upset him. So, he tried to use anger to get me in line, and when it failed to work as expected, he grew frustrated and even angrier.

When he left, I realized we'd never be as close as we had once been, but an open door was there. I was quite relieved about it.

Dennis had survived the months after Dad's passing with considerable grace. We were all worried he would fall off the wagon, but he'd been so strong. After that ride from the hospital, I made sure we met for coffee at least once a week. It was hard at first finding things to talk about, but we'd start reminiscing, and the walls between us eventually tumbled down. He is a hilarious man with a great sense of humor, and he had a take on a life that bordered on the edge of reason. I grew to love him more each week.

He quit smoking, too. That was a tremendous relief to all of us. He put on a few pounds; his complexion improved. Life in the wake of Dad's passing was good for all of us. There were days I wished Dad had lived to see his family thriving, but more often, I was grateful for his passing. I asked Kevin if that made me a bad person. He always shook his head, saying it was life. Embrace what it is, he would say, and I would roll my eyes in mock derision and laugh with him.

"Are you ready?" Kevin hollered down the hallway.

I took one more look at myself in the mirror and smiled.

"Coming!" I called back.

We drove in silence to the graveyard, holding hands like teenagers, the bouquet resting on my lap. We parked in the lot and walked across the flat expanse to the mound of dirt where our daughter lay. There was already a bouquet there. I looked at the attached card. They were from the Taylors. I made a note to call them and thank them for remembering. I wondered where Brenda's grave was. Probably in Grandville. I should make a point of finding out and paying my respects. She lost her life protecting my girl. It was the least I could do.

Chastised for not thinking of it earlier, I guessed I still had some selfishness in my heart. I shook off the old voice before it berated me into dust. I was learning to be better about silencing it since Kevin and I began counseling. It was the best thing we did for ourselves and our relationship. We were better communicators and better lovers than we'd ever been. Life was good.

I arranged the new bouquet and the one from the Taylors into the little vase attached to her headstone. Kevin spread out a blanket, and we sat down. Both of us were silent for a few moments, taking in the solemnity of our situation. Andrea had been the best thing to happen to us, and she was taken far too soon. She had lived something that no woman should have to live, and she became a sad statistic when that boy had taken her life.

Earlier this month, I received one of Andrea's journals. I found it in our mailbox at the house, along with a handwritten note from Joan Bradshaw. She expressed her sympathy and sorrow for what her son had caused our family. She included her phone number and said that if I ever wanted to talk, she would meet with me. I hadn't called her. I didn't know what a meeting would achieve. Andrea would still be dead. But I kept the number tucked inside my wallet just the same. Maybe one day.

Kevin took my hand and talked to Andrea as if she were right there. He started by reminding her of previous conversations he'd had when he'd visited her grave. "You remember me telling you that your mom and I are back together. Well, since I was here last time, I must tell you we were married again. Just a small ceremony at the courthouse. Your uncles and your aunt Valerie were there, as were your cousins, of course, and your grandparents. So, I guess it was maybe that small." He chuckled. I squeezed his hand.

"Well, we have a bit more news for you, and I know you'll be happy for us. We're going to have a baby." Tears sprang to his eyes, and he choked a little on the words. "I know it's a little much to take in. I was more than a little astonished myself, but it feels right somehow. We owe you so much, and we'll never have time to give you what you deserve. A proper loving home and a united family. These are things we're determined to give this baby." He broke down then, unable to continue.

I rubbed my thumb across his hand, trying to provide solidarity and togetherness. Then I spoke. "Andrea, you missed out on so much. I failed you, and I failed myself, too. I wish you were still here so you could know how much I always loved you and how precious you were to me. Can you let me know somehow that you're okay with this baby and that you forgive me? I don't know if I'll feel it. Maybe I'll only make believe so I can live with myself."

"Hush, don't talk like that," Kevin whispered.

"But it's true," I cried. "She's not here to hug me and tell me she's okay with it. She's gone forever, and I hate that."

He placed his arm across my shoulders and pulled me tight to him. I wept, and as I allowed the sun's warmth to beat down upon me—I felt it. The deepest sense of peace that I have ever experienced. I realized that from somewhere out there, my girl had read my heart, seen my sorrow, and understood it all. She had forgiven me and offered me her blessings for the future. I don't know if I can ever truly make another understand how it was. It was something not of this world. I wept in gratitude.

Much later, Kevin helped me to my feet, pulled me into a hug, and whispered, "I love you."

Feeling the baby kick, I placed my hand on my belly. Kevin put his hand on mine. The baby kicked again. We smiled at each other, feeling peace for the future. It wasn't what either of us expected at this time in our lives. Kevin would be forty before the baby arrived, so it seemed a little late in our lives to have a baby.

I had given Stella notice that I wouldn't be working after the baby came. She encouraged me to stay part-time, one or two days a week. Kevin agreed with her, and I had to agree that I didn't want to give up on my dream either. However, I insisted that this time around, the baby, boy or girl, would come first.

We took one last look at the headstone, said our goodbyes, and walked away, hand in hand, across the large grassy expanse toward the unknown, toward our future.

AFTERWORD

Dear Reader,

Before I finished writing my first draft of *AFTER … Joan's Story*, my writing group encouraged me to tell the story of Andrea's mother. What happened to her and her family? Did they fall apart like Joan's family did? Or did they ride out the grief and pain growing together?

I had given no thought to this story prior to that. I had already been thinking about another story: a young girl ostracized by her father after becoming pregnant at seventeen. Her journey through that experience and the trauma she endured.

With the group's encouragement, I shifted my focus. Again, all the characters are completely mine. They do not reflect anyone I know. I started by contemplating where Andrea came from. What was her relationship with her parents and her world? I drew from my life experiences.

I have never been married, but I love children. I think of them as tiny miracles, soaking up the world through experiences of life and love. They learn to talk and walk, to run and play. They are simply amazing little creatures.

In my thirties, my church family recognized my love for children. They asked me to provide childcare for twenty kids caught in the aftermath of relationship failures and fractures. The group was for single mothers, and as the women sat upstairs, working through their pain, grief, and sorrow, while I, along with two helpers, spent time with their kids, talking about their feelings and helping them understand what was happening had no reflection on them.

It was difficult to spend time with children who were fearful of having mommy out of their sight because daddy left, and she was all they had. They were anxious and confused. But we played games, made crafts, sang songs, and learned to have fun. It was the most rewarding experience to see them be more willing to come down the stairs, not only assured that mommy would be there when we were done but also that the program was helping them heal and have fun.

I loved every minute of my time in this group. My fondest memory was working with a little boy named John, who could have passed for my child. He was so insecure and terrified in the beginning. I finally got him to sit with me, and we grew very fond of one another. His parents eventually reconciled and moved away.

Months later, I ran into John and his parents. He came right up and said hello. I was so thrilled to see him. I picked him up, swung him around, and put him into a big hug before setting him back down on his feet. He leaned up against the door frame, trying to be as casual as possible, and said, "I'm five now." My heart just about burst. He was such a little man. I never saw him again, but I still think about him and often wonder how he is.

My experience in that group set the tone for this book. Divorce is hard on children and parents. During my time in the group, I read many books on keeping marriages strong, like Gary Chapman's *The Five Languages of Love*. For the children, I followed the *Rainbows for All Children* program. All this experience helped me create characters for this story.

My own life was less fraught. My parents never divorced. Dad worked away from home quite a bit, so I understand the single mom aspect. My mother had to be both parents a lot of the time, and when Dad came home, we were advised to be on our best behavior. He got to play with us. She was the disciplinarian. She didn't want him worrying that she couldn't manage without him as he worked to put food on our table. It wasn't a simple life, but the best world to grow up in. I am grateful for my parents and their love for us and for each other.

The last thing I want to mention is that there are many news stories of men murdering their wives and girlfriends. It's an epidemic. In Canada, an intimate partner perpetrates sixty-six percent of all murders of women. In the United States, that statistic is only thirty-four percent. This information is from 2021 and even if it may have dropped—it's still too high.

As a reader, writer, and total mystery buff, there is nothing like a good murder. Unless it happens in your family. Then, it becomes something else. Thankfully, murder has never happened to me, but it shaped my fear of intimate relationships.

The towns I placed my story in are fictitious. I avoided setting the book in any specific location because intimate partner murders aren't limited to a single city, province, state, or country. It happens all over the world

Thank you for coming along on this journey of Barbara's growth. I appreciate your time, and I hope you enjoyed meeting her. Caleb and Brenda's mothers have their own books. If you liked this novel, *Joan's Story* is available now. Please stay tuned for the release date of the last stand-alone book jumping off from the murder/suicide of Brenda, Andrea, and Caleb.

God bless you all. Stay safe.

Leslie Johnson

leslie.johnson2014@gmail.com

ABOUT THE AUTHOR

Leslie Johnson grew up in the shadow of Chief Mountain near the Alberta / Montana border. She loves to read, spending countless hours inside a good book. Many nights, her mother would find her under her covers with a flashlight reading her latest library find, long after she was supposed to be asleep. She still lives in windy southern Alberta where she moderates a writing group. If she's not writing, reading, or gardening, she's working on a jigsaw puzzle, playing with her cat, Milo or taking a walk in one of the many parks in the area.

AFTER ... Barbara's Story